The Scarlet Harvest

DODGE CITY PUBLIC LIBRARY
1001 N. 2ND AVE
DODGE CITY, KS 67801

DODGE CITY PUBLIC LIBRARY
1001 N. 2ND AVE
DODGE CITY, KS 67801

THE OVATION DUOLOGY
BOOK ONE

The Scarlet Harvest

KATE ASHBROOK

KINCARDIN
PRESS

This is a work of fiction. The characters, events, organizations, and locations in this novel are products of the author's imagination or used fictitiously. Any resemblance to events, past or present, or persons, living or dead, is entirely coincidental.

THE SCARLET HARVEST. Copyright © 2021 by Kate Ashbrook

All rights reserved. Printed in the United States of America. Purchase grants personal use only. No part of this book may be copied, scanned, reproduced, distributed, or uploaded to information storage and retrieval systems without written permission from Kincardin Press,
921 S. Orchard Street G, Boise, ID 83705.
www.kincardinpress.com

Library of Congress Cataloging Data
Library of Congress Control Number (LCCN): 2021904561
The Scarlet Harvest / Kate Ashbrook
Summary: Sixteen-year-old Wren is coming of age in a society that oppresses women. She must unravel government conspiracies to discover her true identity and leverage the secrets hidden in her DNA to protect those she loves before it's too late.

ISBN (paperback): 9781736375709
ISBN (hardcover): 9781736375716
ISBN (ebook): 9781736375723

First Edition, 2021.
Cover Art: Depositphotos / Sofia Zhuravets, Chernetskiy

*For my mom:
Thank you for believing in me
and supporting my dreams.*

Table of Contents

One *1*

Two *19*

Three *26*

Four *36*

Five *40*

Six *49*

Seven *56*

Eight *66*

Nine *75*

Ten *83*

Eleven *90*

Twelve *97*

Thirteen *106*

Fourteen *119*

Fifteen *125*

Sixteen *132*

Seventeen *145*

Eighteen	*153*
Nineteen	*160*
Twenty	*177*
Twenty-one	*182*
Twenty-two	*189*
Twenty-three	*196*
Twenty-four	*208*
Twenty-five	*215*
Twenty-six	*229*
Twenty-seven	*236*
Twenty-eight	*247*
Twenty-nine	*255*
Thirty	*262*
Thirty-one	*276*
Thirty-two	*289*
Thirty-three	*301*
Thirty-four	*316*
Thirty-five	*331*

Thirty-six 344

Thirty-seven 356

Thirty-eight 368

Thirty-nine 372

Forty 379

Forty-one 391

Forty-two 404

Forty-three 417

Forty-four 427

Forty-five 435

Forty-six 444

Forty-seven 449

Forty-eight 459

Forty-nine 464

Thank you xi

Acknowledgments xii

About the Author xiii

One

Genova Island, August 2072

"Mom, do you really think the guards will let me leave Hillcrest tonight?" I lean forward from the backseat, peeling my thighs from the cracked leather, wedging myself between the baby carrier and front seat.

Mom glances up from her transceptor. The screen casts a soft glow on her face as if she were holding the moon in her lap instead of her work tablet. She watches Dad through the windshield of our government-issued 1956 Dodge Coronet.

The headlights slice through the night like spotlights illuminating the guard station. Mist rises from the damp asphalt, creating a shimmery, steamy haze around Dad and the young guard facing him. The guard looks like a stick of gum Dad could easily tear in two, but then again, everyone looks scrawny next to Dad.

After a long silence, Mom says, "Your dad can be very charming when he wants to be."

Dad wears his average-Joe smile, the smile he uses to disarm people and gain their trust. He gestures toward our car and then toward the Valley on the other side of the gate. More words are exchanged. Dad pats the guard's back and returns to the car.

He raps his knuckles against my window. "Step out of the car, Wren. Corporal Simon agreed to update your passport privileges."

I slip on my flip-flops and step outside. Beads of perspiration form on my upper lip. Drops of sweat trickle down my back. It's always humid on the island, but the month of August is unbearable. I tug the collar of my t-shirt and use it to fan myself.

The young guard approaches with a passport scanner.

Dad says, "I appreciate this, Corporal."

The Corporal nods toward the cameras mounted on the guard station. "Let's make this quick. Passport tampering is illegal."

"If anybody gives you a hard time, have them call me. My wife, Jackie, is the highest-ranking Reproduction Enforcer in Hillcrest."

"Yes, sir. I know of Sergeant Weiss." The Corporal raises his hand to acknowledge Mom.

Mom nods from the front seat.

Corporal Simon invades my space.

His freckled face shines with sweat and he's so close, I smell the mint on his breath. "Turn around and lift your hair, please."

I do as told. Corporal Simon presses the passport scanner against my neck. The cold metal feels good on my clammy skin. A tickle travels down my spine and my passport vibrates.

Corporal Simon withdraws the scanner. "You're authorized to enter the Valley for exactly one hour. One hour only. You must return to the border before passport privileges expire. If you are one minute late, you will be terminated. Understand?"

I drop my hair and spin around, running my fingertips across the ridged implant on the back of my neck. "What if we don't make it back in an hour?" I hear myself croak as if fear has a stranglehold on my throat.

How many times have I wondered if the passport would malfunction and kill me in my sleep? How many times has a slight tingle sent me over the edge?

Dad squeezes my shoulder. "Don't worry. The other Enforcers got a head start on the raid. We'll be in and out in less than an hour."

Don't worry? Easy for him to say. He's not the one with a ticking time bomb attached to his neck. Enforcers like my parents are authorized to enter the Valley to enforce the one-child policy.

The rest of us are never permitted to leave our assigned residential cells—and when I say never, I mean *never*.

It's ten fifteen. *Tick-tock, tick-tock.* My heart ticks twice as fast as the secondhand on my watch. I'm not sure if the sweat forming at my temples is from the humidity or my anxiety.

Corporal Simon's eyes dart from Dad to me to the cameras. He clears his throat. "My shift ends at midnight. If something happens and you aren't back on time, I'll tell investigators I didn't see the girl." He stands up straight and tries to sound tough, but he sounds about as tough as my ten-year-old brother.

Dad extends his hand to Corporal Simon. "We'll be back on time. Thanks again, son."

They shake hands. The veins on Dad's forearm are ropy and bulging. He always works out before raids. I take my place in the backseat. Dad walks around to the driver's side.

"That didn't take long," Mom says.

Dad rubs his thumb across his fingers. "Your husband still has the magic touch."

I don't have to see Mom's face to know she's rolling her eyes and shaking her head.

"That was Vic's youngest boy. Good kid. Started working the borders six months ago." Dad drives through the open gate.

I tense up. I've never been close to an electrical barrier. I've never even been out of Hillcrest. I trace the outline of my passport. "Dad?" My voice trembles.

Dad stops the car and faces me. "Why are you holding your neck? Is your passport emitting a warning signal?"

Mom looks in the backseat and studies my face.

I place my hands in my lap and look at the night sky. Charcoal clouds enshroud the full moon, smothering her light. "Never mind. It's nothing."

Mom doesn't look convinced. "Do you feel a burning sensation in your neck or spine?"

I shake my head. The only thing I feel is paranoia.

Dad's shoulders relax. He eases up on the brake and steers the car down the steep hill. "She's fine, Jackie." He meets my eyes in the rearview mirror. "You'll be fine. We would never put you in danger."

I snap the rubber band off my wrist and wrestle my thick hair into a ponytail. "Can you crack the window? It's hot."

Dad rolls down his window. "I've been meaning to get those window cranks in the back fixed. I don't know why the Nuclei didn't update car interiors when they converted engines to clean energy."

I tilt my chin up and let the breeze stir my hair and cool my face. At the bottom of the hill, the smooth asphalt turns to gravel and the breeze turns to dust.

The running trail in Fidelity Forest hugs the edge of the cliff behind us. From up there, the Valley looks dirty, dusty, and drab, as though a giant hand carved a gash between green peaks and tossed a handful of dice-shaped buildings into it.

Mom twists around. "You'll be scheduled to take the Assessment any day now. Have you given any more thought to becoming a Reproduction Enforcer?"

Here we go again. I wish I could get the Assessment over with so they would stop pressuring me to become an Enforcer. "I don't have a choice, do I?"

"That's not true. You'll be assigned to a department and a job category. You'll have plenty of jobs to choose from. If you're placed in Health and Human Services, I can pull strings and get you moved to Reproductive Services."

"What if I get stuck somewhere like the Department of Finance?" I exhale in an exasperated huff.

"No daughter of mine is going to be a bean counter." Dad chuckles, obviously amused by the thought. "See what you think of the raid tonight. There's a lot more to being an Enforcer than home visits and pregnancy tests. It's one of the most prestigious jobs in Hillcrest."

I shift in my seat. "Can we talk about it later? I don't even have a test date yet."

"You're almost sixteen. It's time to start thinking about your future." Mom sounds frustrated.

I think about my future all the time, but I can't tell my parents what I really want. I can't tell them I want to go to medical school in Clairemont.

They would take it personally. They would say I'm being selfish, that I'm abandoning them, abandoning my brother and sister: Abe and Addie. But they would be wrong.

Few careers include inter-cell travel privileges. The Nuclei allows Clairemont doctors to travel for medical emergencies. If

I were assigned to Clairemont, I could visit my parents and the twins. I don't want to leave them behind. I just want a better life and more opportunities than Hillcrest has to offer.

I check my watch. Ten twenty-eight.

Our car veers left at a fork and the outskirts of the Valley come into view. On the left, hundreds of barren acres sprawl to the cliff. On the right, buildings rise: midnight shadows blotting the moonlit sky.

A toppled cross sits atop rubble on a corner lot. Before World War III, people congregated in churches to share superstitions about life after death. Back then, people believed broken mirrors and black cats could bring bad luck. In the New World, we don't believe in luck or superstition; we believe in science and truth.

We pass a half-dozen dark, empty streets. Light spills across the road from a side street. Voices swell and fade. Dad slows the car as we draw near the lit street.

Mom grabs her badge from the dashboard and clips it to her uniform. "Don't stop here. They need our help on Centriole Street."

Dad rotates the wheel to the right. "We'll go the long way. I want Wren to get the full experience."

The busy street teems with Security Forces, Enforcers, and Valley dwellers. Floodlights, high and bright, bleach the entire scene in blinding light. I shield my eyes and take in the multi-level gray apartments and the clotheslines stretching between them like gallows from which threadbare uniforms hang. There are no trees or shrubs or flowers or grass: just dirt and dust, gravel and cement.

Security Forces stand at intervals in full riot gear: helmets, face shields, body shields, batons. The sound of walkie-talkies clicking and beeping, fists banging, doors slamming, people screaming sends a sense of unease spiraling through me.

Dad motions toward the action. "This is what we call the war zone. Valley dwellers in this section are non-compliant. Illegals hide out here. The key to a successful raid is scheduling them infrequently so residents relax and let their guards down, so they—"

"Stop the illegal!" A man's voice booms.

Dad hits the brakes and leans over to look out the passenger side window.

A Security Forces officer and his German Shepherd chase a barefoot boy down the sidewalk straight toward us. The skinny kid cuts a path through the horde of people, dodging onlookers, elbowing Enforcers, jumping over obstacles.

The dog is snarling, growling, gaining on the kid.

Dad yells, "Get the little bastard!"

I shrink into the backseat willing my heartbeat to slow. Using the hem of my shirt, I dab the sweat on my forehead. Valley dwellers pour into the streets from alleys and open doors and start coming together like oil in water, coalescing into one unit.

Security Forces build a wall of body shields in the boy's path. Eyes wide, arms and legs pumping, the boy looks terrified as he runs past. I swivel to watch him through the back window. Right before he collides with the wall of Security Forces, the boy bolts toward a side alley.

That's when it happens.

That's when the dog—jaw swinging, black snout snapping, teeth gnashing—rears back and lunges forward. Time hiccups and seconds start unfolding in slow motion, as if the Valley is submerged underwater.

The dog stays suspended in midair for seconds that feel like minutes. I want to close my eyes, to look away, but all I can do is stare and silently scream: *Run, Run, Run!*

The hairy, sharp-toothed projectile slams into the boy like a bullet. The impact sends the child flying, limbs flailing, mouth wailing.

While he's tumbling, plunging, falling, a roaring white noise fills my ears. Everything is muffled, muddled, garbled. I grip the edge of the baby carrier so tightly, the plastic cuts into my palm.

The boy's skull smashes into the concrete with a resounding crack I feel deep in my bones. I gasp. My ears pop as though a drain was pulled and sound surrounds me: crisp and clear, I hear the yelling and screaming, the feet and fists beating.

The boy lies motionless. From his head, blood blooms: a crimson ribbon unfurling across the pavement in a slow, steady stream. The officer praises the dog, drags the unconscious boy into the alley, and handcuffs him.

Valley dwellers surge forward, fists in the air. Security Forces rush toward them, heads down, shields out, batons raised. The smell of body odor, blood, and sweat seeps into the car as the clashing sides advance toward one another, growing larger, louder, closer. A swath of black uniforms, combat boots, and superiority complexes blurs by my window.

"Can we go now?" I ask, turning my back to the window.

Dad reluctantly tears his eyes away from the scene and guides the car to the end of the street. Mom's head remains bowed over her work.

I catch Dad's eye in the rearview mirror. "Why did they hurt that little boy?"

"If Valley dwellers would obey the law, nobody would get hurt. How many illegal pregnancies have been recorded in Hillcrest in the past decade?"

"Zero," I answer.

"That's right. How is it that everyone in Hillcrest can adhere to the two-child policy, but Valley dwellers can't follow their own Family Planning laws? I don't know if they're lazy or just stupid."

I want to understand things from his perspective, but I don't understand how he justifies hurting people. "What will happen to that boy?"

"Same thing that happens to all illegals," Mom says in a casual tone as if this is just an average Friday night. "Illegals don't have passports so they'll take him to the station, collect a DNA sample, and run it through the database. Once they locate the parents, they'll start an investigation."

"Then what happens?" I hug the front seat, pressing my face into the wind flowing through Dad's window.

"That's up to the Nuclei." The indifference in Mom's voice disturbs me.

Dad pulls onto Centriole Street and parallel parks behind a white van. Compared to the last street, Centriole Street is sleepy and subdued.

Male residents lean against the apartments, talking and smoking. Enforcers scan children's passports and conduct hormone tests on female residents.

I'm struck by the sameness of the Enforcers. The men are clean-shaven with buzz cuts. The women wear the same chin-length bob with blunt-cut bangs. Mom says female trainees chop off their hair in Enforcer Basic Training as a symbol of solidarity.

Dad cuts off the engine. "Stay put. We won't be long."

He and Mom exit the car and join a group of Enforcers interrogating a handcuffed couple.

Ten forty-five. Thirty more minutes.

I'm burning up. I thrust my hand under the front seat until my fingers brush against cool metal. I align the window crank to the peg on the door. One crank. Two cranks. The window jerks open but offers little relief from the heat.

Out of nowhere, a woman crashes into the passenger side of the car. The steel window crank falls to the floor, crushing my pinky toe. I swallow the cry that climbs my throat.

"How many months?" I recognize Dad's no-nonsense tone. He holds the woman's shoulders, pinning her to the front passenger door.

The woman clears her throat and opens her mouth, but no words come out.

"Craig, get over here," Dad shouts over his shoulder.

A junior Enforcer materializes at Dad's side. Tobacco juice lines his gums and stains his teeth. He spits tobacco at the woman's feet.

"How far along, boss?" The junior Enforcer takes a wide stance, grips his belt with both hands, and rocks heel-to-toe while leering at the woman.

"That's what I need you to find out." Dad releases the woman and steps back.

Craig unbuckles the holster at his side and withdraws a slender silver tool used to detect illegal pregnancies. "You Valley people think you can do whatever you want. But tonight, I'm here to tell you, you're gonna answer for your infidelity to the Nuclei."

The cloying sweetness of his snuff wafts through the window and makes me want to gag.

"Get on with it." Dad's words are punctuated with impatience.

Craig leans intimately close to the woman and shoves the hormone reader into her forearm. She cowers and cradles her stomach. After a minute, the tool beeps.

Craig tilts the monitor toward my dad. "Ninety thousand hCGs."

"Escort her to the extraction line," Dad says before walking away.

Brandishing a smile soaked in self-righteousness, Craig digs his fingers into the soft flesh of the woman's upper arm and pulls her toward the sidewalk.

The woman collapses, scraping her knees against the gravel. Sweat and tears run down her face. "Please. I'm begging you." She sobs, rocking back and forth, hugging herself.

A middle-aged man steps out of the shadows. Tattered clothes hang from his wiry frame. "Listen here," he says through decaying teeth.

"We're good people. My wife and I work long hours for the Nuclei. We ain't even took a single day off work in years. Y'all don't have to kill our baby."

Craig ignores the Valley man.

"This is downright murder." The Valley man raises his voice and points an accusing finger at them.

"We can do this the hard way or the easy way, ma'am. That's up to you." Craig's face has grown slack with boredom. He spits, wipes the back of his hand across his mouth, and hauls the crying woman to her feet.

She lifts her head and locks eyes with me. Her silent plea roars through my veins. Heat slithers up my spine, coils around my neck, and scorches my cheeks. I want to help, but I feel helpless, powerless.

I scan the crowd. Where did Dad go? Where's Mom? Straight ahead, a line of Valley women forms near a parked ambulance. Medics pull the women into the ambulance one by one.

The man's words take root in my mind: *this is downright murder.* He accused the Enforcers of murder. My parents? Murderers? I rest my hand on the door handle, trying to work up the nerve to open the door, to intervene somehow.

A gurney being pushed by two men races down the dirt road, bouncing over rocks and careening dangerously through the crowd. The gurney skids and stops next to the crying woman. The two men lift the woman and throw her onto the stretcher. She kicks and fights and spits. They strap down her arms and legs.

"Now woman, I told you, we didn't have to do this the hard way, but you wouldn't listen." The junior Enforcer gives a curt nod to the men handling the stretcher.

One of them presses something against the woman's protruding stomach. Her body spasms. Her lips twitch. Her eyes close. Her husband moves to her side and takes her hand.

Mom emerges from a stairwell holding an infant. I've never felt such relief at the sight of someone. She ducks inside the backseat and straps the child in the baby carrier.

I point at the woman on the stretcher. "I think something bad happened to that lady."

Mom's eyes flit to the unconscious woman. "Standard procedure. Now, keep an eye on this baby while we wrap things up."

"How much longer?" I ask, chewing on my lower lip.

"Five minutes, give or take. Tonight was a success. We identified several families in violation of the law. The Nuclei is going to be very pleased."

Gravel crunches under Mom's retreating combat boots. She moves methodically from Enforcer to Enforcer gathering information for the report she will submit to the Nuclei.

The Nuclei promoted Mom to Lead Sergeant when I was in elementary school. The Lead Sergeant oversees the monitoring of fertile women and compiles reproductive data into monthly reports.

The gurgling baby kicks her stubby legs and breaks into a gummy smile.

I enclose her hand in mine. "Hi, happy baby."

Engines crank to life. Patrol cars head back to Hillcrest. Curtains are drawn. Doors are closed. No residents linger in the streets. Enforcers load orange containers marked TOXIC into the back of a van.

The car rocks as my parents slide into the front seat.

"Well, what do you think, kiddo?" Dad's question is heavy with expectation.

I know what he wants me to say, but if I wasn't certain before, I'm certain now that I don't want to be an Enforcer.

"It was okay." I'm glad my voice comes out smooth, despite my churning insides. I don't want to deflate my parents' dreams. Not yet.

"Raids can be intimidating, but you get used to it. Soon, you'll be the one riding along with your mom while I kick back and relax at home with the twins." He winks and eases the car into the street.

The baby squeezes my fingers. I sweep my thumb over her tiny knuckles. So soft and delicate. "Can we keep the baby?"

Mom shoots a disgusted look at the baby. "These Valley dwellers keep breeding low IQ, worthless criminals. That baby may be all sugar and spice now, but she'll grow up to be just like the rest of them. The one-child policy for the Valley is generous. If it were up to me, they would all be sterilized at birth."

As the baby's eyes grow heavy, I feel the urge to protect her from Mom's harsh words. A pink neon sign on the left advertises Charlie's Bar. Under the sign, three men stand bathed in the garish neon light. The tallest man elbows the man next to him and nods toward our approaching car. One man hides something behind his back. Another drops a cigarette and crushes it under his worn shoe.

Dad lowers his window and directs an icy stare at the group. The window crank bounces around my feet, making the floorboard vibrate. I kick it away.

"Joe, not tonight." Mom looks up from her notes.

Dad decelerates and crawls past the bar as if he's taunting the men to get a reaction. Something strikes the rear windshield and clatters over the hood. I flinch and my pulse quickens.

"Enforcer assholes, y'all think you're better than everyone!"

Dad punches the brake pedal and jerks the gearshift into reverse. The tires grind to a spinning stop, slamming me forward, throwing dust everywhere. The air smells like rubber and tastes like dust. I sneeze into my hand. In the side-view mirror, I watch the jeering men hastily retreat into the bar. Dad, one hand on the car door, reaches for his stun gun.

Mom grabs his arm. "Not tonight," she repeats in a firmer tone. "We still have to deliver the baby and get the kids to bed."

"Dad, please. It's eleven o'clock." I'm embarrassed by the whine that creeps into my voice, but I swear the skin surrounding my passport is getting hotter every minute.

The vein on the side of Dad's neck is thick and throbbing. Without saying a word, he shifts the car into drive and pulls away from the bar. I exhale and lean against the headrest, trying to ignore the pain in my toe, the pounding in my chest, the heat emanating from my neck.

I'll close my eyes until we reach the guard station. Otherwise, I'll torture myself by staring at the face of my watch as its hands shave off precious minutes. The car is silent other than the *click-click-click* of Mom's stylus.

The car starts climbing uphill, and the gravel gives way to smooth pavement. We're almost home. I open my eyes. Eleven ten. We're going to make it. The little girl has fallen asleep: head resting on her shoulder, fingers clinging to mine.

At the Hillcrest guard station, Corporal Simon recognizes Dad and waves us through. As we turn into the neighborhood, rows of white houses with manicured lawns become visible in the golden glow of streetlamps.

All houses in Hillcrest are the same: fifteen-hundred square feet, rooftop solar panels, three bedrooms, one bathroom, white siding, black shutters.

A government flag hangs from each porch. The four overlapping circles on the flag represent the genetic traits measured during the Assessment: intelligence, health, symmetry, strength.

Our car takes a series of familiar turns: left on Patriot Drive, right on Loyalty Lane, right on Honor Street. The scent of freshly cut grass is a welcome contrast to the dust I choked on in the Valley.

Dad pulls up to the curb at the intersection of Honor Street and Acacia Lane. He looks like he belongs here. His hair is trimmed as tightly as the lawns. His face is free of stubble. Mom leans over and kisses his cheek.

I follow her into the house as the taillights fade into the night. "Where is he taking the baby?"

"Somewhere safe."

Two

The smell of cafe con leche wakes me. I throw off the sheets and scoot to the edge of the bed, raising my foot to examine my injured pinky toe.

Swollen with a purple-tinged toenail, it reminds me of an unripe grape. I wiggle my toes. Slight pain, but not bad. I limp down the narrow hallway past the kitchen and sit at the dining room table.

Dad sets before me a mug of cafe con leche, a bowl of fruit, and toast.

"Thanks."

"No problem, kiddo." He squeezes my shoulder on his way to the kitchen. I watch him handwash dishes through the cut-out between the dining room and kitchen.

Mom sits at the head of the table reviewing records from last night's raid. She moves the stylus over the transceptor screen, pausing occasionally to chew on the stylus.

On the wall across from me hangs the painting that all Enforcers receive upon completion of Basic Training. It depicts a lush garden overrun with weeds. An attached silver plaque reads: *Enforcers, Class of 2045. Cultivating the Garden of Life: Replacing Weeds with Harmonious Seeds.*

Next to the painting is an old photograph that hangs in every house and classroom. Ten scientists pose at the foot of a NASA rocket on a sunny launch day just months before atomic bombs exploded over Earth. Their Mission to Mars saved their lives.

After the war, surviving scientists established the Nuclei government on Genova island, formerly known as Cuba, and segregated survivors based on a test we now call the Assessment. Today, only six Nuclei members are still living: three women and three men. Dr. Hahn is their leader and our President.

"Mom, why don't they have houses like ours in the Valley?" I take a bite of mango.

Mom keeps her eyes on her work. "They have smaller families, so they need less space."

Popping a grape into my mouth, I try not to think of my toe as the grape skin tears and juice splatters against the inside of my cheeks.

Dad rounds the corner. "Which Enforcer was assigned to 306?"

"Adkins." Mom powers down her transceptor and slides the stylus behind her ear.

"Hmm." Dad moves his head from side to side, massaging his chin.

Are they talking about the woman from last night? I normally tune out their work discussions, but today I'm curious. I sip my espresso, pull my toast into bite-sized pieces, and pretend to be uninterested.

Mom stands and grabs the car keys. "Adkins logged three visits to 306 in the past six months. He administered a hormone test during one of those visits. Nothing unusual in the reports."

"Either Adkins is slacking or 306 lied about her pregnancy," Dad says.

"Sit up straight, Wren." Mom constantly nags about my posture. I straighten my spine, clear my dishes, and eavesdrop from the kitchen.

"I'm meeting Adkins in a half hour at the office. Do you want to join?" Even on Saturday Mom wears the heavily starched Enforcer uniform, ready to get back to work.

Dad shakes his head. "I'm going to stay here. Work out. Mow the yard. Spend time with the kids."

After Mom leaves, Dad joins me in the kitchen. "What did you think about the raid? Can you see yourself as an Enforcer?"

I pull loose threads from the kitchen towel I'm holding. "What happened to the lady on the stretcher? Did she die?"

He rearranges dishes in the sink. "No, she didn't die. We are in the business of helping people, not hurting people."

"What happened to her?" I push.

"She broke the law. Family Planning laws serve a purpose. Before the war, people overpopulated and lived off government assistance instead of getting jobs to support their families.

"The Nuclei created laws to ensure our society never deteriorates to that point again. The genetically inferior will remain in the Valley and work for a living in exchange for housing and food. No more handouts."

I place the towel near the sink and meet his eyes. "Don't you think there are good people in the Valley?"

"I admire your idealism, but I've been working in the Valley for over twenty years. Those people aren't like us. They lie and steal. Their hobbies include drinking, gambling, fighting. I agree with your mom. They shouldn't be allowed to reproduce at all."

"Why doesn't the Nuclei grant waivers to families in the Valley who have more than one child? You and Mom were allowed to keep the twins even though it violated Hillcrest's two-child policy."

Dad rinses his mug and makes himself a second cafe con leche. "Some families in the Valley also get waivers for twins."

"That lady, 306, looked nice to me." I search Dad's face for a sign of compassion.

"As an Enforcer, sympathy is your worst enemy." He says it with conviction, as if it's the Enforcer mantra.

Abe appears in the kitchen doorway. "Can we play outside?"

"Stay in the yard and don't bother the neighbor's cat," Dad replies and then turns to me. "You'll be an adult soon. You need to figure out what you want to do with your life."

"I know what I want." I hesitate before adding, "I want to be a doctor."

"A doctor?" Dad jerks his mug away from his lips. Hot liquid sloshes on the counter. I hand him the kitchen towel.

Frowning, he sops up the spill. "People in Hillcrest don't become doctors."

"I know. But if I do well on the Assessment, I could get assigned to Clairemont. I could go to medical school. I could visit you and Mom in Hillcrest." The words splutter from my mouth in a rapid-fire pile-up.

"If you're assigned to Clairemont, you may never see us again. Is that what you want?" Dad rubs the back of his neck and stares at the sink.

I knew I shouldn't have told him. "It's not fair that all the colleges are in Clairemont. What if people in the Valley and Hillcrest want to go to college?"

"Valley dwellers aren't cut out for college and people in Hillcrest are happy to graduate high school at sixteen and start job training."

Dad leaves the kitchen. The worn recliner in the living room sighs from his weight. "I can't remember anyone from Hillcrest being assigned to Clairemont in at least ten years."

I sit on the couch and refrain from correcting him. Five

people were assigned to Clairemont from Hillcrest in the past decade. They're considered legends at school.

Celeste is the only one from my class who received an assignment outside of Hillcrest. She was declassed and transported to the Valley months ago. I've asked my parents to deliver letters to Celeste during their visits to the Valley, but they refuse to associate with Valley dwellers any more than they have to.

Dad nods toward a framed picture on the end table. In the photo, he and Mom are teenagers. Dad has wrinkles around his eyes now and his hair has grayed, but overall, he looks the same. Mom, on the other hand, is unrecognizable. Her head is thrown back in laughter, loose curls spring down her shoulders. A floral skirt hides her knees. I can't remember the last time I saw her out of uniform.

"That picture was taken the day before your mom took the Assessment." A nostalgic smile warms Dad's face. "In school, I was the jock who set records for bench pressing and deadlifts. Jackie was the smart one who graduated as valedictorian."

He sips his half-spilled drink. "Your mom wanted to be a professor in Clairemont."

"Mom wanted to be a professor?" My voice carries a note of incredulity. Mom had never shared this with me.

"She studied for the Assessment while the rest of us goofed off that summer. None of us have control over the genetic hand we're dealt, so she focused on what she could control."

"What happened?" I ask.

He shakes his head and stares into his empty cup. "A gene mutation reduced her score and disqualified her from Clairemont."

I can't imagine my dreams going up in smoke over a single gene mutation. "Could I have inherited the bad gene from Mom?"

"Fortunately, you and the twins inherited the healthy version. After Jackie received her Assessment results, she locked herself in her room and cried for days. Two weeks later, before we entered Basic Training, I asked her to marry me."

I feel stunned that I never knew about Mom's dreams or disappointments. I've never even seen Mom cry. She taught me to never let anyone see me cry: to cry is to show weakness. Dad's eyes shift to the picture hanging over the couch.

I don't have to look to know what he sees: himself in a tan suit on the beach, beaming at the camera; Mom in a flowing dress wearing a slight smile and a pink hibiscus in her hair.

"Don't get your hopes up. I don't want you to experience the heartbreak your mother did. And, please, don't share your Clairemont aspirations with her. If being a doctor interests you, you might consider going to Basic Training to become an Extractor."

Dad sets his mug on the table and goes outside. The lawn mower starts humming. I head to my room to listen to music. From the hallway, I glance at my parent's wedding picture. For the first time, I notice the sadness in my mom's eyes.

Three

At dinner, Mom turns to me. "Have you given any more thought to becoming an Enforcer?"

"I was thinking of going to Extractor Basic Training." I push food around my plate, building a french fry fortress between the corn and beans.

"I don't see you as an Extractor." Mom sounds surprised. "They deal with blood and guts and emotions."

"Stop taking my food," Addie shrieks.

Abe shoves a handful of french fries from Addie's plate into his mouth. Broken french fries protrude from hollow areas where his crooked adult teeth are still coming in. He grins at me and I smile back. Addie threatens to stab his hand with her fork if he tries it again.

While Mom reprimands them, I inhale my food and plan my escape. If I stick around much longer, Mom will put the spotlight back on me.

"Wren is interested in a medical career where she can help people," Dad says. "You never filled me in on how 306 reached the fourth month of pregnancy undetected."

I look up from my empty plate. Dad winks at me. I excuse myself as Mom recounts her conversation with Adkins.

"Wren?" Dad calls from the dining room.

"Yes?" I pause in the hallway.

"The weekly Nuclei broadcast will air in ten minutes. Dr. Hahn will be speaking tonight."

"I'm going to study for the Assessment." If you've heard one Nuclei broadcast, you've heard them all.

In my bedroom, I open the Assessment booklet to the beauty section that shows symmetry calculations. When my best friend, Opal, and I were younger, we took turns measuring each other in search of the mysterious golden ratio. We found none.

Standing in front of the mirror, I detach the paper ruler and hold it lengthwise and then widthwise over my face. No changes since I last measured.

I don't see any trace of my parents in my reflection. My face shape differs greatly from Mom's square face. Where Dad's face has sharp angles and a prominent jaw, my face is soft and full. Everyone in my family has brown eyes. How did I end up with blue?

Mom and the twins have golden-brown hair, the color of fresh-brewed coffee as it streams into the first cup of the day. My hair resembles the last cup of coffee poured from the same pot after it sits on the burner for hours: stronger, thicker, darker, not quite black, but almost.

Grasping my hair at the base of my neck, I push it forward to see what I would look like with a chin-length bob. I hate it. I can't imagine becoming an Enforcer.

Sometimes, I wonder if I could have been adopted or switched with another baby at birth. What if my real parents are in Clairemont?

Not much is known about Clairemont, but it's enough to know that those assigned to Clairemont are the best and brightest. I imagine Clairemont as a sophisticated city—superior to Hillcrest in every way—where academics spend their days discussing books and theories and solutions.

A knock on my door interrupts my daydream.

"Come in."

Addie runs, jumps, and belly-flops onto my bed. "I know you sneak out at night." A smirk slides across the cute little face I normally want to cover in big sister kisses.

I put a finger over my mouth to shush her. "Do not."

"Do too!" She squeals. "Where do you go?"

"Can you keep a secret?"

She nods.

I lower my voice, as if I'm about to make a serious confession. "Every night, teenagers meet up to make roasted marshmallow chocolate sandwiches over the biggest bonfire you've ever seen. The chocolate gets ooey-gooey-melty. It's the most delicious dessert in the whole wide world."

"Are you going tonight? Can I go?" She clasps her hands together, begging.

"Got 'cha." I tickle her ribs until she begs for mercy. "I just run at night, Addie-bee."

"For the strength test? Can you run an eight-minute mile?"

She knows a lot about the Assessment. Many kids aren't interested. Others, like me, spend their entire childhood training to beat it.

"Five-minute mile," I respond.

Addie's face grows serious. "Do you think I could run a five-minute mile like you when I grow up?"

I smooth her messy curls. "You can do anything if you work hard."

As I tiptoe down the hallway, light spills across my running shoes from the night-light in Abe and Addie's room. I scrunch through the front door and cling to the shadows outside. My parents would kill me if they knew I ran alone at night. The fear of getting caught sends a shot of adrenaline coursing through my body.

I cross the street quickly and quietly, ponytail flying behind me. I steer clear of the pools of yellow light puddled under streetlamps and turn my face away from cameras mounted to the light posts. The only way to escape the feeling of being watched is to go where there are no cameras: the woods offer an escape from Nuclei eyes and ears. As soon as I step into Fidelity Forest, nervous laughter erupts from my lips.

Tonight will be a leisurely run since my pinky toe is tender. For the first half mile, I focus on my breathing. After warming up, my breath and feet settle into a synchronized rhythm. I inhale the earthy smell of the forest and listen to the chirruping cicadas and trilling crickets.

At the halfway point, the brush clears on my left to reveal the cliff overlooking the Valley. Twinkling lights glitter across the Valley as if it's draped in a starry canopy. Wrapped in a cloak of darkness, the Valley actually looks pretty.

The Valley is no longer a place defined by my parents and other people. I saw it with my own eyes. I had always been told Valley dwellers were criminals, but they didn't look like criminals. They looked poor and scared.

I follow the trail as it curves sharply to the right. The warm breeze cools the sweat on my brow. My shoe slides over a rotten mango. The smashed fruit smells sweet and putrid. I rake my shoe across a tree root to dislodge the fruit and then find a broken limb to dig out the remaining pulp.

A scraping sound to my immediate right startles me. I tighten my grip on the tree limb and scan the area. A blue blur smudges my peripheral vision. It's gone as quickly as it appeared.

My heart jams a distress signal through my arteries; my pulse hammers out a rapid-fire SOS. I shouldn't have come this close to the border. Branches crackle. Goose bumps crest on my neck and crash down my arms. I spin on my heels and start running, adrenaline flooding.

The forest comes alive with menacing shadows pulsing, something malevolent lurking. Knobby fingers of gnarly branches tear at my hair. Jagged leaves scratch at my face. Weeds wrap around my legs. I stumble over a tree root and catch myself.

Something hooks my rib cage, knocking the air from my lungs. My feet fly out from under me. I try to scream, but my vocal cords freeze. A hand covers my mouth—calloused fingertips dig into my cheeks. I'm being pulled away from the trail, deeper and deeper into the bowels of the forest. Terror rips through me.

I raise my arm and slam my elbow into the gut of my attacker. The grip constricts, crushing my ribs. I continue to kick and struggle. After a short eternity, I'm released like a plastic toy in one of those stupid vending machines at the market. Tumbling to the ground, I land on my butt behind a row of scraggly bushes.

A boy my age stands over me. He crouches and places a finger over his mouth. With his other hand, he points into the distance. A hazy blue mist rises behind tree silhouettes. The voices of approaching figures become audible, but I can't make out their words.

Three boys from the Valley stop on the path in front of our hiding place and peer down the cliff with their backs to us. I could throw something at the closest one and land it squarely on the back of his head.

How did they cross the electrical barrier?

"You go first," one says to another.

A third boy stands behind them. "Why don't you both go first?" He shoves them.

They disappear over the ledge. I gasp. The remaining boy turns and looks right in my direction. I crouch lower. He backflips off the cliff. Seconds later, I hear a splash and laughter.

My attacker doesn't seem as threatening. He pulled me off the path so the Valley boys wouldn't see me.

He breaks the silence. "You can see in the dark?"

I frown. "No. Why do you ask?" I stand, brush off my pants, and pull twigs out of my hair.

"You saw the boys when they were hundreds of yards away." He raises an arm over his head. "It's so dark, you shouldn't have been able to see the movement I just made, but you did."

He's testing me. I tear my eyes away from his arm and busy myself with tightening my ponytail. He pulls something from his pocket. A bright light hits me in the face.

"What are you doing? Trying to blind me?" I feel a flash of anger and instinctively knock the flashlight from his hand.

It thumps against the ground and rolls away. He retrieves it and aims the beam at his face. A reflective layer beneath his retina glows gold when the light catches it. A tiny scar runs through his left eyebrow.

"I can see in the dark, too," he says.

"I don't know what you're talking about," I snap.

His admission makes me uneasy. I've never met anyone like me. By elementary school, I knew I was different. Neighborhood kids used to play hide and seek after nightfall. Even on moonless, starless nights, I could easily see them hiding in bushes, under cars, behind basketball hoops. When I figured out other kids couldn't see in the dark, I pretended I couldn't either.

At night, the landscape becomes muted shades of gray and blue. The glow that emanates from people and animals is so intense, it nearly blinds me. Now, I focus on the ground to avoid looking directly at the boy.

He pockets the flashlight. "Do you live in Hillcrest? I've never seen you in the Valley."

"Yes," I answer, stealing a glance at him. I can't believe his eyes are like mine.

"Why are you alone in the woods this late? It isn't safe." He sounds concerned.

"Training for the Assessment. It's too hot to run during the day." I slide my eyes toward him once more. "So, you live in the Valley?"

"I live there, but I don't belong there," he replies.

"Have you taken the Assessment yet?" I ask.

Girls take the Assessment two weeks after they start their periods. No matter their age, if they are assigned to a different residential cell, they move immediately. Boys are tested on their sixteenth birthdays; they always finish school in their home cell.

"I'll be sixteen in two weeks. What about you?" He cocks his head.

My face flushes. He might as well have asked if I've started my period. At fifteen, I'm considered a late bloomer. Most of my classmates have already received their Assessment results. Some have even completed job training.

"Not yet," I stammer, embarrassed.

"What's your name?" he asks.

I cross my arms over my chest and continue to look away. "Wren."

"I'm Fritz. It's short for Friedrich. I mean, it should be short for Friedrich…"

People say parents in the Valley are too stupid to know a birth certificate should include a formal name. In the Valley, the twins would remain Abe and Addie as adults, instead of having more grown up options like those on their Hillcrest birth certificates: Abner and Adelaide.

"You have debris on your shoulder." Fritz takes a step toward me and removes the debris.

I draw back and feel an overwhelming urge to run away.

"It's late. I better go." I turn and sprint down the dirt path that leads home.

"Wait," he calls after me, but I keep running.

All of my life, I thought I was the only one. I thought I was a freak. I thought I would be ostracized if anyone found out I could see in the dark.

The boy from the Valley can see in the dark, too; I'm not the only one. There are others like me. Others like us. A smile buoyed by hope and wonder lifts the corners of my lips.

Four

*N*o matter how tightly I close my bedroom curtains, the morning sun persists until it finds a vulnerable opening in the fabric. Normally, I would yank the curtains together to block the sun's advance and go back to bed. Today, I flip my feather pillow to the colder side and bury my face in defeat. The encroaching day is the least of my concerns. My lower back aches from being thrown to the ground last night.

I should force myself out of bed, shower, and study. Yawning, I slog down the hallway and peek in the twins' room. They hunch over a microscope taking turns looking through the eyepiece.

As water cascades down my face in the shower, so many questions swim in my head. What was the Valley boy doing in Fidelity Forest when there must be running trails closer to his home? The electrical barrier is supposed to keep people within their assigned cell.

Did one of our passports malfunction or does the electrical barrier have blind spots?

I rinse my hair and turn off the faucet. Pink water swirls around my feet. Is my toe bleeding? Bracing an arm against the shower wall, I stand on one leg and lift my foot. My toe is fine. The blood can only mean one thing. My stomach twists.

I toss my towel in the hamper, get dressed, and rush to my bedroom. How am I going to tell my parents I started my period? And when? I'm not ready.

Combat boots thump down the hall. Mom knocks on my door and enters. "How are things going?"

"Fine." I sit cross-legged on my bed, leaning against the headboard.

"Do you have something to tell me?" she asks in a conversational tone, as if that question when asked by a parent or teacher doesn't cause a kid's nerve endings to crash and collide and misfire.

I squirm and avoid her gaze. Did Dad tell her I'm interested in attending medical school in Clairemont? Did Addie tell her I sneak out at night? Does she know I started my period? I decide to refrain from blurting out all my secrets at once.

"What do you mean?" I nonchalantly pluck lint from my bedspread and pretend my nerves aren't going haywire and my heart isn't racing.

Mom sits on my bed, stills my lint-plucking hand, and clasps a black band around my wrist.

"Wear the tracker at all times. Your assigned Enforcer will monitor your menstrual cycles and pregnancies throughout your reproductive years."

So that's what this is about. My periods and pregnancies are nobody's business. Resentment builds in me like steam in a teapot. I bite my lower lip to keep my thoughts from pouring out. Mom would not be sympathetic to my feelings. Reproduction Enforcers value adherence to Family Planning laws above all else.

Most girls my age are proud to wear this symbol of adulthood. Not me. I run my thumb over the four overlapping circles etched into the glass face and try to hide my contempt. Mom taps the disk twice. The screen displays a calendar.

"Mark every day of your period. Entries are transferred to the data warehouse. You'll take the Assessment in two weeks. After you are officially assigned to Hillcrest, your Enforcer will schedule a consultation to discuss your obligations as a fertile member of Hillcrest."

"What do they do with data submitted on the tracker?" I shoot a distrustful look at the band on my wrist. Being forced to share private information about my body makes me feel exposed and subhuman. I might as well have a stamp on my forehead that reads: GOVERNMENT PROPERTY.

"The Nuclei monitors the data to make sure everyone obeys Family Planning laws. You must never lie. Illegal pregnancies carry grave consequences. You could be fined, forced to terminate the pregnancy, sterilized, or Galileo forbid if you were to carry the child to term, the Nuclei could confiscate it."

"If I were assigned to Clairemont, I could have as many kids as I wanted." I can't hold back my frustration. Why can't I decide where I live, what I do for a living, how many kids I have?

Mom stands and walks to my bedroom door. "If women were allowed to choose how many kids to have, we might end up right back where we were before the war. Women can't be trusted to make their own reproductive decisions."

I start to object. "But, Mom—"

"Have you ever been hungry? Thirsty? Have you ever gone without?" She dips her chin and raises her eyebrows.

"No," I mumble, looking away.

"Be grateful for everything the Nuclei provides," she says, stepping into the hall.

Five

After five days spent with a heating pad under my back to ease cramps, I feel more like myself tonight. I've been cooped up all week itching to get out of the house, itching to see Fritz. I can't stop thinking about our conversation. What if there are hundreds or even thousands of people like us?

I used to dissect the faces of Hillcrest residents hoping to find a single person with eyes like mine. My searches always came up empty-handed. My hope is that someday, I'll be able to look people in the eye without caring about being different.

Different is not something you want to be in Hillcrest. I think of white-haired Hazel Hanover, aka ghost girl, eating alone in the school cafeteria. I think of the sideways glances, the whispers, the withheld invitations. Students steered clear of Hazel as if albinism were contagious. A twinge of guilt worms through me. I was never mean to Hazel, but I could have done more to make her feel included.

I change into running gear and hit the trail. At the location where the Valley boys jumped off the cliff, I pause to stretch my calves and hamstrings. The headlights of a lone car heading out of the Valley toward the guard station pierce the darkness below.

The night is eerily quiet. No sign of Fritz. Disappointment gnaws at me. I pick up a rock and chunk it over the cliff. Seconds later, a soft splash breaks the surface of water.

Stepping away from the cliff's edge, my eyes are drawn to a soft blue glow extending halfway up a tree. My body stiffens and my pulse quickens. I take cover behind a nearby tree, pressing my back against its trunk, flattening my palms against rough bark.

"Wren?"

I whirl around and see Fritz approaching with a lantern.

"Did you have to creep up on me like that?" I gasp, clutching my chest.

"Well, if you weren't hiding, I wouldn't have to creep up on you. I had to make sure you weren't part of a night patrol."

"Give me a break." I roll my eyes. "I've never seen a night patrol on this trail." Everyone knows night patrols are concentrated in the Valley. The monthly *Nuclei Newsletter* has an entire "Crime & Punishment" section with ludicrous crimes that set tongues wagging.

Last month, a Valley resident was arrested for stealing a government backhoe and crashing it into a leather factory after hours. He was found passed out at the wheel, naked and under the influence.

"Can't be too careful." Fritz stops a couple of feet from me and holds the lantern high. The bright flame wraps us in golden light, thawing my night vision, allowing me to see his face for the first time.

The boys and men in Hillcrest look as if they were made from the same factory mold: average height, average build, clean-shaven with buzz cuts. Fritz is the exact opposite: tall, muscular, tan. Brown hair falls in loose curls, framing his scruffy face.

"You're on a running trail in the middle of the night, but you aren't wearing running shoes," I say, staring pointedly at his flip-flops.

Fritz looks past me and dims the lantern. "I came here looking for you. Let's talk somewhere more private."

I glance in the direction he was looking. "What's wrong with talking here?"

"Teenagers from the Valley hang out here sometimes."

"Where else is there to go?" I ask.

"There's a creek that way." He gestures toward the woods behind me.

Curiosity blooms beneath my aloof exterior. I hesitate and dig the toe of my shoe into the trail. Everyone says people from the Valley are dangerous, but he doesn't seem dangerous; he seems like a normal boy, except for the whole seeing-in-the-dark thing we have in common.

"What's wrong?" he asks, wrinkling his forehead.

I should go home, but I want to find out what he knows about our vision, and I want to know if there are people like us in the Valley. "I'll go with you, but I can't stay long."

Fritz smiles and tips his head to the right. "This way."

I follow him off the beaten path into a brambly thicket and shoulder my way through the dense foliage. Spindly limbs stab my arms, scrape my face, tangle my hair. I imagine nocturnal creepy-crawlies—beetles, centipedes, millipedes—weaving in and out of the scrub, their scaly legs skittering over my skin. Wherever he is taking me, it better be worth it.

"A few more feet," Fritz faces me and parts the foliage like a curtain for me to step through. My shoes sink into mud on a trail overgrown with waist-high weeds.

The trail snakes through a copse of walnut trees. As I wrench my feet free of mud, Fritz ducks under a bowed tree branch and disappears. I stoop and join him at the edge of a rocky creek glazed in moonlight. Fireflies spark in the dark like flakes of falling stardust. An astral crown sits atop the circular clearing, glittery and glimmering. It's breathtaking.

"We're going over there." Fritz lifts the lantern, shining it on a rust-colored boulder jutting over the water on the opposite bank. "The creek is slippery but shallow." He freezes and looks at the sky. "Wait. Don't move. Do you hear that?"

"Hear what?" Fear creeps up my spine.

Fritz extinguishes the lantern, grips my elbow, and drags me into the brush. I suddenly feel vulnerable being alone with him.

After a couple of minutes, the ground begins to vibrate. At first, I mistake the low vibration for the accelerated beating of my heart, but as it grows stronger, Fritz points to the sky. Two helicopters fly by, low and slow. Their rotor blades chop up the air, producing violent winds that smash the undergrowth flat. Nearby trees twist and turn in a tone-deaf tango.

My ponytail is sucked skyward. I brush my hair out of my eyes, cover my ears, and take another step away from the clearing. Fritz moves with me. His chest heaves against my back and rumbles with words I can't hear. His breath tickles my neck. The closeness makes me uneasy. We remain motionless until the helicopters disappear.

"Night patrol," he says, stepping in front of me.

"How did you know they were coming?" I study his moonlit features.

He looks away and rubs the back of his head. "I heard them."

"You heard them?" I arch an eyebrow. "Minutes before they appeared?"

"Let's cross the creek. I'll explain." He turns, lights the lantern, and hops across the wet rocks. The lantern casts an amber glow over the water.

Looking back, he says, "Don't be scared. Step on the wide ones."

"I'm not scared." I raise my chin defiantly and kick my sneaker against a diamond-shaped stone.

I feel Fritz's eyes on me. I don't want him to think I'm a chicken. Starting with the closest stone, I dart across the rolling riverbed. Icy water floods my shoes and makes my socks squishy. My shoes make sloppy, sloshing sounds. Water and sediment swim between my toes.

Fritz climbs the boulder and sits on top, tucking one leg and propping an arm across his raised knee. I sit across from him and all I can think about is my muddy shoes, snagged clothing, and rumpled hair.

"You said you were looking for me tonight?" I remove my socks and shoes, wring the water out of my socks, and lay them flat to dry. My toes are like ice cubes. I flatten my feet against the boulder and soak up the warmth emanating from its surface.

"I've been looking for you every night. Where have you been?"

"I..." My hand flits to the band on my wrist.

He glances at my tracker. "Does this mean you have a test date?"

"Next weekend. You?" I twist my ponytail around my hand, pulling my heavy hair away from my neck where it traps heat.

"Monday," he says.

"Do you think you'll be assigned to the Valley?" I ask, trying to sound normal and nonchalant when there is absolutely nothing normal about being alone with a Valley dweller, or any guy for that matter. I scan the woods for movement.

He shakes his head. "I don't plan to spend the rest of my life in the Valley, that's for sure."

Focusing on the trickle of water flowing downstream, I attempt to suppress my paranoia about being somewhere I'm not supposed to be, with someone I'm not supposed to be with.

"But, how did you prepare for the Assessment? I thought kids in the Valley started working full-time after middle school?"

A half-grin crosses his face. "There's this thing called the library." His words are sarcastic, but his voice is playful.

"Oh." My cheeks grow warm. It never occurred to me that Valley dwellers would spend time in a library. I hate it when my dad and others assume I won't test out of Hillcrest, but I just made the same assumption about Fritz.

"I was thinking it might be cool to get assigned to Hillcrest." The flame from the lantern warms his complexion and dances in his eyes—eyes he hasn't taken off me since we sat. "Do you like it there?"

I picture the cookie-cutter houses and monotonous routines. "Hillcrest is okay." I shrug. "How did you know the night patrol was approaching?"

He hesitates and looks into the distance. "I can make out sounds inaudible to most people like the rumble of distant storms and the calls of bats and rodents. Sometimes I can tune out the noise, but other times it gives me headaches or keeps me awake." Turning his attention back to me, he asks, "Do you have any heightened senses other than your vision?"

"I don't think so." I tilt my head and chew on a broken fingernail. "Are there more people like us in the Valley?"

"I haven't seen anyone else with eyeshine and you're the only person I've told. If there are others, they probably don't advertise it either."

"True," I say, thinking of my sunglass collection.

The longer we sit with no sign of patrols, the more I relax and let my guard down. Leaning back, I watch fireflies pulse through the night like tiny beating hearts and wonder why I never explored the woods beyond the running path. There could be many hidden areas like this to discover.

Fritz leans closer. "Can you meet me tomorrow morning? There's something I want to show you." His tone is half-serious, half-hopeful.

"It *is* tomorrow morning." I point toward the brightening eastern sky where twilight blossoms, blowing out the stars. I stand and brush off.

"There's a facility on a remote part of the island, far from the residential cells. Something weird is going on there. I think it may be related to our heightened senses."

I frown. "But there's nothing outside of cell limits." Hasn't he seen videos of the barren wasteland that surrounds the cells? Only a fraction of the island was inhabitable after the war.

Fritz turns off the lantern, rises, and stretches. The sleeves of his t-shirt hug his biceps. He catches me staring at his muscles. I blush and avert my eyes.

"We need at least seven hours to get there and back." He stifles a yawn.

"How am I supposed to get away for that long?" I protest, but deep down I want him to talk me into going. I want to know what else is out there and why we're different.

"Won't your parents be at work?" He raises an eyebrow, knowing full well that everybody works or goes to school during the week.

"I should go before they realize I'm gone." I shove my sockless feet into my shoes, grab my wet socks, and jump from the boulder. I carefully cross the creek, push through the brush, and head back the way we came.

"Hey, wait up." He catches up, grabs my arm, and pulls me around to face him.

I snatch my arm out of his grip.

"Eight o'clock at the cliff," he says softly. The intensity in his eyes awakens something deep inside me, unearthing questions I thought I had long ago buried.

I look away and contemplate how angry my parents would be if they knew I was hanging out with a Valley dweller. Opal always says what parents don't know won't hurt them; maybe she's right. "I'll go if you promise we'll be home for dinner," I say in a stern tone, fixing my eyes on his face.

"Promise." He grins, as if relishing a win.

Six

The buzzing of my alarm jolts me from sleep. I jump out of bed and hurry down the hall. Dirty dishes clutter the sink, and the kitchen still smells like scrambled eggs. Relieved to find nobody home, I grab a mug and set up the espresso maker to brew while I get ready.

Standing in front of my bedroom mirror, I wrangle my hair into two thick braids, slather on sunscreen, and slip into denim shorts and a t-shirt. I tug a floppy straw hat over my head, adjust the chin strap, and drop a tube of lip balm in my pocket.

In the kitchen, I chug espresso before heading outside. As I skip down the porch steps, a former classmate exits her house and moseys to her mailbox with a bored look on her face.

"Hey, Wren. Where are you going?" She asks, reaching into the mailbox.

"For a hike," I say in an overly-friendly tone, trying not to look or sound like someone who's about to meet up with a Valley dweller to potentially break the law. You never know who could be an informant. Science-deniers, idol worshippers, and those harboring illegals are at risk of being reported.

Her eyes track me. I speed-walk, cross the next block, cut into the woods, and hightail it down the trail to the cliff. From there, I watch the hustle and bustle of trains carrying workers to fields where they cultivate coffee, sugar, and tobacco.

Engines hum and horns blow as conductors announce their arrival and departure. Even at this distance, the faint smell of exhaust pollutes the air.

"Hey stranger." The sound of Fritz's voice behind me makes it real. We're really going to do this. I take a deep breath and turn to face him.

Fritz wears cargo shorts and a t-shirt that looks brighter than white against his tan skin. A black backpack hangs from one shoulder. He's much cuter than I remembered, but then again, this is the first time we've seen each other in daylight.

Shy and self-conscious, I force a smile. "Hey."

"I'm glad you're here. I was worried you might change your mind," he says.

"I still might change my mind." I twiddle my braids and look at the Valley. "Are we going through the Valley?"

"We're going *around* the Valley."

I angle my head so I can make eye contact from under the brim of my hat. "But I don't have authorization to leave Hillcrest."

"You do today," he says confidently.

"How?" Doubt edges into my voice.

"Trust me. I'll show you when we get there." Fritz veers off the path into the woods.

"Trust you? I barely know you." I look toward Hillcrest, fighting off the wave of uncertainty rising in my chest. Bad things happen to people who break the law. I've heard about entire families disappearing, as if the dark mouth of night slipped into their houses while they slept and swallowed them whole.

Fritz circles back, quickly closing the distance between us. "You want answers, don't you?" His eyes dart back and forth, searching my face. "We can't hike along the cliff. It offers no cover. If patrols catch us trespassing, the Nuclei could make an example of us."

"If they catch us trespassing, they could execute us or lock us away in the Caves." I picture the Caves: prisoners trapped in eternal darkness and dampness, the sound of bat wings flapping and water drip-drip-dripping, the smell of earth and sulfur and decay. The Caves of bedtime stories in Hillcrest. The Caves where criminals are sent to rot away.

Fritz steps closer and rests his hand on my shoulder. The flecks in his eyes glint gold in the sunlight. "I've never been caught and we won't be caught today."

His touch sends a current of electricity coiling through me. The air between us feels charged with something—excitement?

Fear? I twist my shoulder away. "You have to tell me *exactly* where we are going. I'm not giving up my dream of becoming a doctor to follow some cute guy to who knows where."

"Cute?" A she-thinks-I'm-cute smile teases the corner of his lips. He tilts his head and cocks an eyebrow.

A blush warms my cheeks and spreads to my chest.

His grin widens as if he's amused by my embarrassment. "I'll tell you more, but first, let's step off the main trail."

I follow him into the cool shade of pine trees. Out of the sun, I push my hat back, letting it fall between my shoulder blades. Fritz drops his backpack and picks up a tree limb. He clears fallen pine needles and uses the limb to draw a plantain-shaped map in the dirt.

"We are here." He points to the center of the plantain. "And this," he draws a line from the center to the bottom of the plantain, "is where we are going. It's the southernmost tip of Genova Island."

"You've been there?" I examine the rudimentary map and decide he definitely isn't an artist. I wonder what kind of work he does in the Valley.

"I came across a facility there months ago. It's everything you would imagine a top-secret facility to be. Guards, guns, soldiers everywhere. A barbed-wire fence runs around the periphery. I haven't been able to stop thinking about it, but I haven't had a chance to go back." He pauses and scratches his head. "I swear the last time I was there, I heard babies crying."

"Babies?" I dramatically drawl out the word and put my hands on my hips. "So, you're taking me to a heavily guarded daycare, hundreds of miles away, that requires us to risk our lives to get there. Sounds reasonable." My words are loaded with sarcasm.

I'm not sure why I'm being so difficult. I want to go with him, but I've never broken the law. I've never even been in trouble. Besides sneaking out, the worst thing I ever did was help Opal dye her neighbor's poodle pink as a prank; we were never caught. I guess I'm scared of being caught. Scared of wasting away in the notorious Caves.

Fritz tosses the tree limb aside and rubs his shoe across the loose dirt, erasing the map. "I know it sounds crazy, but I have a hunch the Nuclei is hiding something important there. If they have nothing to hide, why is it illegal for residents to travel outside of assigned cells?"

I recognize the hunger in his eyes. I see it every time I look in the mirror. I stopped searching for the truth years ago when I realized nobody in Hillcrest had the answers, but the questions still haunt me: How can I see in the dark? Are there others like me? Why does the Nuclei segregate people based on Assessment results? Why do I have to provide information about my body to the Nuclei?

I realize I'm toying with the tracker on my wrist and move my hand away from it. "Do you really know how to get past the electrical barriers?" I ask, eyeing him up and down, trying to figure out how a boy from the Valley could be smart enough to get around the barriers when nobody else can.

"Why don't you spend the day with me and find out?" Fritz challenges me, raising his eyebrows. His brown eyes shine with confidence, as if he already knows my answer.

Most people never leave Hillcrest. In Hillcrest they are born, and in Hillcrest they will die. If I go with him, I may regret it, but if I don't go, I'll definitely regret it.

"Fine. You win." I raise my hands signaling surrender and mentally prepare a list of excuses for being home late, just in case.

"The sooner we leave, the sooner we get back." Fritz picks up his backpack. "People in the Valley dislike the Nuclei because of its treatment of our people, but I distrust the Nuclei."

Carefully stepping over sprouting fiddleheads and scaly pine cones, we weave around skinny palm trees and tall pines, their limbs draped in a tangle of vines that dangle like sleeves swaying in the humid breeze. Fritz pushes aside the hanging tendrils as we wade into thick, unrelenting foliage.

He pulls a chalk-like thing from his pocket and draws a dash on a tree as we pass. The dash gradually fades to a soft glow. "Can you see where I marked the tree?"

I nod.

"Good. If we get split up, the markings will help you find your way back."

I point to the marker. "How does it work? What's it made of?"

Fritz flashes his perfectly straight teeth. "You don't want to know."

"Tell me," I insist.

"Wax and animal urine."

"Eww." I wrinkle my nose.

"The urine throws off ultraviolet rays that help predators track their prey. I'll tag the trees at eye-level so you can distinguish my tags from natural markings."

"Why not use paint or flags to mark the path?" I ask.

"I don't want to leave any clues that may arouse suspicion. Humans can't see in the ultraviolet spectrum."

"Makes sense," I say, withholding my other thoughts: If humans can't see the markings, how can we see them? Aren't we human?

As we continue the journey, Fritz diligently marks trees along the path. Hopefully, we won't get separated. It would take only one bad storm to wash away the marks. Daily thunderstorms are the norm during the wet season.

A tingling sensation sweeps across the nape of my neck. I fan my neck to shoo away mosquitoes. The sensation grows stronger. I stop in my tracks. The pin and needles radiating from my neck aren't being caused by a mosquito proboscis. The implant is sending a warning signal.

Seven

"Fritz?" I call, one hand wrapped around the back of my neck.

Fritz rushes toward me with a concerned expression. "We're near the border. Step back." He unzips his backpack, withdraws a black box, and adjusts the attached antenna. "Can you hear that?"

"What am I listening for?" The sound of my racing heart is all I hear. I imagine myself lying on the forest floor taking my last breath after the passport fries my brain. Speaking of brains, there are rumors that people in the Old World ate fried monkey brains. Gross.

"Listen for a repetitive pattern." He looks at me expectantly.

I shake my head. He sighs and looks disappointed. Maybe he was hoping enhanced hearing would be something else we would have in common.

Fritz holds up the black tool. "This records the sound waves from the barrier and allows me to transmit the correct code to the passport."

He stands behind me, lifts my hat over my head, and hands it to me. "Hold this." His fingertips skim the sensitive skin around my passport, sending goosebumps scurrying up my scalp. I feel light pressure against my neck and then a vibration.

"Done," he says. "Let's test it. Walk forward."

I walk beyond the point where the passport had been triggered.

"Good?" he asks.

"I think so." I massage the back of my neck. "Do you think the passport could have secret functions? Could the Nuclei use it to eavesdrop or track our location?"

"It's possible, but there's no evidence. I took one apart and found no tracking devices." He walks in the direction we were going when my neck started tingling.

"Wait." I catch up and block his path. "Did you say you took apart a passport? How did you remove a passport from someone's neck?" I narrow my eyes and cross my arms. How well do I really know him? I glance to the left and right. It's only the two of us in the wilderness.

Surprise flickers across his features and then his face hardens. "I didn't kill anyone, if that's what you're asking." His voice and eyes go cold.

I drop my arms and look away. A rush of heat sears my

cheeks. "Sorry," I mutter. "I'm being paranoid. I've never met anyone from the Valley."

He reaches for my hand and squeezes it. "You can trust me, okay?"

This time I don't recoil from his touch. I sense his sincerity. I wouldn't be here if I didn't trust him. "All of my life, I've been taught that Valley dwellers are dangerous criminals."

Fritz cringes at the words: *Valley dwellers.*

I wish I could rephrase it, but I push on. "My parents, my teachers, my friends. They all talk about the Valley like it's a cesspool of debauchery."

Fritz looks at me as if he's weighing how to respond. Instead, he doesn't say anything. He starts walking and marking trees.

Finally, he says, "There are good and bad people everywhere. Have your parents, teachers, or friends ever met anyone from the Valley?"

I kick a pine cone out of my path. "My parents work in the Valley. They're Enforcers."

Fritz stops and looks surprised. "Your parents are Enforcers?"

"Yeah, so?" My tone dares him to say more on the topic of my parents.

I take off ahead of him. I've always been proud of my parents. In Hillcrest, Enforcers are revered. I flashback to the night of the raid, and I'm not sure whether to be proud or embarrassed.

From behind me, Fritz says, "Where I come from, Enforcers are the criminals."

His words slice through me like a knife, dicing my worldview into a heap of half-truths and lies. I wish I could douse the heap in kerosene, set it on fire, and watch it burn until nothing is left but the truth. I remain silent until the sting of his words fades.

Swatting at a swarm of gnats, I ask, "Don't you need to program your passport, too?"

"I already have the codes programmed in my passport."

"Where did you get the—"

"Decoder?"

"Yes."

"The fence behind my school was aligned to an electrical barrier. My classmates and I dared each other to get close to it. At the fence, the prickle in my neck was accompanied by sounds nobody else could hear.

"Every day after class, we worked in the fields. When the train transported us home, I watched the sun set over coffee plantations and cattle pastures and daydreamed about leaving the Valley. It took a year of experimenting to create the decoder."

"You never went to Hillcrest?"

"No. I spent most of my time at beaches and waterfalls tucked into quiet alcoves away from populated areas."

"Wow," I reply, "that's risky."

"No risk, no reward."

Since breaching the Valley boundary an hour ago, we have been hiking uphill. I dab at the sweat around my hairline and stretch my arms over my head to let the breeze flow through my shirt sleeves.

Birds chatter and chirp and chase each other from tree to tree. Other forest inhabitants like the mongoose scavenge for insects. Hutias scamper through the treetops feasting on leaves with their beaver-like teeth. They peer at us with no fear in their beady eyes. I envy their ability to travel freely across the island. Being bound to Hillcrest makes me feel like a passenger on a train with no control over the itinerary or destination. Mastering the Assessment is the only way to gain control over my life.

"Fritz, look." I point to a furry creature perched on a tree branch. "See the hutia? Isn't it cute?"

He looks at the hutia and smiles. "Do they eat hutias in Hillcrest?"

"Who would eat those furry rodents?" I scrunch up my face.

His eyes shine with mischief and his lips form an impish grin. "We cook them with fruit and nuts in the Valley."

I widen my eyes and drop my jaw in exaggerated disbelief. "You're kidding?"

"Nope. Totally serious. I can roast one for us later if you like. Or maybe you would prefer hutia stew?" He teases.

I laugh out loud at the image of him cooking hutia stew. He looks pleased with himself for amusing me.

Fern fronds, knee-high weeds, and wispy grasses brush against my legs. I rub my hands up and down my shins to alleviate the itching. A wall of haphazardly stacked boulders obstructs the view ahead. The sound of rushing water makes me aware of how dry my mouth is. It was foolish to forget to pack food and water.

Fritz points to the boulders. "After we climb over the wall, we'll take a short break."

"You expect me to climb *that*?" The wall rises above the treetops. My knees feel shaky just thinking about climbing it.

"I'll go first. Just follow my lead." Fritz centers his backpack, wedges his foot into a space between two boulders, and begins climbing. He makes it look easy.

Hanging from one arm, he looks over his shoulder and points to a boulder that's mammoth wide and as tall as I am. "Start over there and don't look down."

Had I known we were going to be climbing a sky-high wall with no equipment, no helmets, I would have stayed home. I trudge toward the boulder, place my hands on top, and swing my legs to the side as if climbing onto a saddle. My knees scrape the rough surface.

I stand and assess the treacherous path above. The steep wall offers cracks big enough for fingertips and toes but nothing more.

"You've got this." Fritz coaches me from the top.

I reach high above my head and dig my fingers into a sandy crevice. Something dry and rubbery brushes across my hand. A lizard shoots out and scurries between two boulders. I snatch my hand back. Gritting my teeth, I pull myself up, scraping my sandals against the wall, feeling for a foothold. I wedge my toes into a shallow nook. Pebbles dislodge and clatter to the ground.

Clinging to the wall with my left hand, I raise my right hand to find my next hold. I draw a deep breath and hold it, willing my heart to stop knocking so loudly, filling me with anxiety. I clamber farther and farther up the wall.

The smell of sweat and dirt fills my nostrils. My biceps bulge and tremble. My shoulder muscles coil into tight pretzels. Sweat rolls down the knots on my back. I want to wipe the sweat away from my eyes, but I don't dare loosen my grip. A blackbird swishes by my face. I stiffen ramrod straight. I need a break. I rest my cheek against the warm stone while the hot sun beats down on me, draining my energy.

"Keep going," Fritz says.

I'm too out of breath to respond. I try to breathe deeply, but my breath sticks to my ribs like bubblegum to a shoe. I suck in shallow breaths.

Inhale. Exhale. Keep climbing.

Don't look down. Don't look down.

I look down.

Palm trees sway in the breeze, their waxy green fronds feathering and rippling. My stomach rolls and drops. The world starts spinning; swirling blues, greens, and browns blur my vision. I dig my fingers deeper into the gritty wall. Sand burrows into my fingertips and falls in my face. My knuckles turn white and tight and feel like they're going to pop right out of my skin. My fingernails bend back and snap. I wince from the blood stinging my nailbeds.

My right foot slips, and for a second, everything goes black and silent and still. I desperately kick the wall. *Please don't let me fall.* Seconds and minutes become thick and distorted; time moves in slow motion like mud in an hourglass.

Finally, my toes lock into a cranny. I exhale and try to push higher, but my arms and legs remain glued in place. I can't keep holding on. Blood roars in my ears. Adrenaline crashes through my veins like a high-speed train.

I see myself falling, bouncing against boulders, splatting on the ground like a bug on a windshield. Just when I think I'm going to black out, something grips my upper arms and lifts me over the top of the wall. My feet hit solid surface; my breath bursts from my lips.

Fritz places his hands on my shoulders. "Are you okay?"

I jerk away, turn my back to him, and catch my breath facing a gigantic waterfall to the left of the craggy peak we're standing on. Rolling sheets of water cascade down a cliff into a basin surrounded by lush vegetation and moss-covered rocks.

Wildflowers sprawl over the hillside. I push my hat off my forehead and blot my sweaty face on my shirt. I tear off two broken fingernails and flick them away.

Chest heaving, shallow breathing, I glare at Fritz over my shoulder. "You should have told me we would be rock-climbing today."

He lifts his shoulders. "You should have told me you were scared of heights."

I ignore his comment and turn back to the waterfall. The cold mist feels good on my face. I clean the dirt from under my fingernails, dust off my hands and clothes, and suck on my bleeding fingers.

Fritz says, "It will be easier on the way back. I tied a rope to a tree over there. We'll use it to rappel down the wall."

I continue to ignore him and roll my shoulders to release tension. The rhythm of the falling water soothes my anger. I inhale the cool, damp air. It smells like things old and new: churned earth, splintered wood, a hint of honeysuckle.

Fritz steps close to me. "I'm sorry. I didn't mean to upset you." His tone is apologetic.

I chew on my jagged fingernail and look at him from the corner of my eye. He looks timid, like he's waiting for me to tell him to go to hell. I drop my hand from my mouth.

"I don't do things like this." I wave my hands around. "I don't take risks. I don't break laws."

"But now that you're here, don't you think it's worth it?"

I take in the landscape. It feels like I'm in a fairytale complete with enchanted forest, flowing waterfall, and handsome sidekick. I feel cheated that such beauty exists near Hillcrest. "So much for a barren wasteland."

If the Nuclei lied to us about that, what else did they lie about?

Eight

*F*ritz sits facing the waterfall and runs a hand through his hair, pushing curls off his forehead. He rifles through his backpack, removes two oranges, and launches one at me. *Whoosh*! I lunge for it and feel surprised when it smacks my palm.

"Good catch." He smiles.

"Thanks." I return his smile and sit next to him.

He passes me a canteen. I'm glad one of us packed something more useful than lip balm. I greedily gulp the cool water and let it soothe my sandpaper throat. I could drink all of it, but I force the canteen away from my lips and pass it back to Fritz; he drinks from it without cleaning the mouthpiece: yuck.

Chunks of orange peel fall around our feet. I tear my orange in half; the juice burns the broken skin under my fingernails, but I don't care. I'm starving. I pop an entire orange slice into my mouth, sink my teeth into its juicy flesh, and savor the citric refreshment.

"It's so peaceful," I say, biting into another slice. "Are there more places like this?"

"There are waterfalls all over the island, including a couple in the Valley." Fritz concentrates on separating two orange slices. "I used to clean up the bottles, beer cans, and cigarette butts at the Valley falls, but eventually I gave up."

I sneak a glance at his profile. The guys at home only talk about sports, girls, and cars. Fritz is more mature, rugged, adventurous. Tucking fly-away wisps of hair behind my ears, I stare into the water, letting its mesmerizing rhythm and babbling burble relax me.

"What's that?" I point to a cable stretching into the forest from a nearby tree.

"*That* is how we are traveling." Fritz stands, scoops up the orange peels, and tosses them into the woods. "It's an old zipline. I'm guessing locals and tourists used it before the war, before passports were invented to keep people locked up like dogs behind fences."

I stand and stare wide-eyed at the cable. It's not like ziplines are completely foreign to me. I've seen them strung up during carnivals and fertility festivals, but I'm always the one on the ground, taking pictures of others who flirt with Death.

"Ziplining is something else you failed to mention." I feel annoyed at the discovery of yet another glaring omission.

"Before we go any farther, it would be nice to know if I'm going to have to jump from a moving train or skydive or walk through fire to get where we're going."

Fritz laughs, the kind of closed-mouth laugh that tickles the throat. His eyes glitter in a good-natured way. "I promise, no more surprises."

He bends down and dumps out the contents of his backpack. "If you can rock-climb, you can zipline. It's easy."

"Maybe we should skip the zipline and keep hiking." I hate that my voice sounds weak and jittery.

Fritz shakes his head. "If we hike, we won't get there until nightfall. If we zipline, we can reach speeds of up to one hundred miles per hour."

"Wow." I raise my eyebrows. "That's twice as fast as traveling by car."

Fritz hands me a belt with a tangle of big loops, little loops, ropes, and fasteners. "Put this harness on. We have to get going."

I hold it up and turn it over. "How do you put it on?"

"Step through the leg holes like this." He twists a larger harness up his muscular legs as if he were stepping into jeans. "Then, put your arms through the straps."

I mirror his movements, lifting the harness until the small loops hug my thighs and the straps hang over my shoulders. Fritz finishes securing his harness and steps closer. He fumbles with the fasteners on my harness and cinches the belt around my waist.

"Is that okay? Not too tight?" His hands rest above my hips. He smells good, like toasted coconut and tobacco leaves. My eyes move from his muscular chest, up his broad neck, to his cleft chin, full lips, and dark eyes framed by even darker lashes. His soft skin contrasts his hard body.

"It's fine," I say. My voice comes out thick and husky and all wrong. I clear my throat.

His eyes lock on mine and then drift down my face, lingering a second too long on my lips. A warm blush heats my cheeks. He kneels and adjusts the bands around my legs. His fingers graze my thighs. My cheeks redden for the second time and an uncomfortable pressure builds inside me.

"Good?" he asks, looking up at me.

I nod. When he steps away, I feel relief, like air was let out of a balloon that was about to burst in my chest.

"Come over here." Fritz tugs on the zipline and adjusts the pulley.

I join him next to the cable. He latches the thick rope dangling from my harness to a metal claw attached to the cable. "Hold on to the rope and lift your legs off the ground."

I do as he says and the harness transforms into a seat. The seat starts to bob and spin. My heart bobs and spins with it. Fritz grabs the rope and steadies the seat.

"Ready?" he asks.

The word that pops into my head is: *no*, but I keep it to myself.

Fritz leads me closer to the cliff's edge and guides my shaky hands to the rope over my head. "At the end of the cable, you'll see a platform encircling a tree. Wait for me there. I'll be right behind you." His voice is gentle and encouraging.

Fritz pulls me back until my body tilts forward and I feel totally, utterly, insanely out of control. Without warning, he launches me into wide open space like a rock from a slingshot.

Terrified, I rocket down the cable, screaming, bouncing, swaying, gripping the rope like it's the only thing between me and Death.

My scream echoes through the forest, bouncing from tree to tree, until eventually my voice locks up and fades to a raspy wheeze. The waterfall sprays my face as I hurtle past.

The wind seizes my braids, as if they were reins and whips my hair up and down against my back: *tha-thunk, tha-thunk.* The sunlit water beneath me becomes the murky underbelly of the forest, a blur of deep shadows, blinking eyes, hungry mouths. I wait for the ground to open up and devour me, but after a few minutes, the zipline becomes smoother, steadier, more stable.

I loosen my grip on the rope and let the blood rush back to my burning fingers. Something bubbles up in my throat. I throw back my head, letting loose a wild burst of laughter that reverberates through the forest; birds stir and trees blur by. Abe and Addie would love this.

Just when I think I'm going to collide with a tree straight ahead, the line slopes up, slows down, and I glide to the cable's end, landing softly on a creaky wooden platform. Clinging to the tree, I feel like I'm still moving. My heart races, not from fear or exertion, but from exhilaration. I can't stop smiling at the thought of doing it again and again.

I kick dried leaves off the edge of the platform and watch them float twenty feet, forty feet, sixty feet down. My stomach rises in my throat. Fritz barrels down the zipline looking totally relaxed, arms resting at his sides. I move out of the way as he lands.

"Not bad, huh?" He beams at me, the kind of smile that's so bright, it could melt metal.

My hands drift to my windblown hair. I rarely think about my appearance, but when I'm with Fritz, I see myself through his eyes. Fritz disconnects both of our harnesses. We walk around the platform, and he reaches for the carabiner on my harness.

"I'll do it." I take the carabiner from him and attach it to the next cable.

"Go for it." Amusement dimples his scruffy cheeks. He steps back to allow me to go first.

I look down the cable, lean back on my heels, and throw myself forward. Jostling along the line, I yell over my shoulder, "Race you!"

I see the flash of a smile before I lose sight of him.

This time, I release the rope and relax my arms. Tilting my head back, I enjoy the wind whipping through my hair and imagine myself as a bird, wings extended, gliding through the tropical jungle. No boundaries. No rules. No Assessment. I savor the temporary gift of freedom Fritz has given me.

My sandals hit the next platform: the impact rocks me from my feet to my knees. I steady myself against the tree. Fritz is nowhere to be seen. I disconnect my harness from the line, walk around the tree, and reattach it to the next cable. I leap off for another ride. And another.

At the fifth stop, I wait for Fritz. I pull my mango lip balm out of my pocket, slick it across my lips, and roll my lips together. What is taking him so long? The grind of metal on metal tickles my eardrums. Within seconds, Fritz shoots down the zipline. He jumps onto the platform, steps around me, and zips down the next line.

"Woohoo!" He lets out a cry of victory and takes the lead.

"Cheater!" I hurl myself off the platform and whiz down the line after him.

Just as he jumps onto the next platform, I crash into him, accidentally squeezing his bicep.

"Oops, sorry." I gain my balance and quickly release his arm.

He grins and winks, as if he thinks I squeezed his muscles on purpose. "You have quite the competitive streak. Let's take a break."

We sit on the platform, legs dangling over the edge. Around us, leaves drift to the ground like swirling ribbons of green confetti. Fritz reaches into his backpack and hands me the canteen.

I take a drink and pass it back.

He turns it up and finishes it.

"Mango?" He smacks his lips together.

I blush and look away. "Do your parents know where you are? Do you have a curfew?"

Fritz scoots back against the tree and pulls a knee to his chest. "The woman who raised me allows me to come and go as I please."

"You were adopted?" My voice rises in surprise. Adoptions are unheard of in Hillcrest.

"Ms. Klein, the school nurse, was living alone in an old apartment on the east side. One rainy November day, she found a covered basket on her doorstep. She thought it might be a gift of fruit or homemade bread from a neighbor. When she pulled the cover back, she was startled to find—"

"You?"

Fritz nods. "I was a few months old. The basket included a card with a name and birthdate."

I pick up a leaf, twirl the petiole between my fingers, and watch the blades spin. "Do you ever wonder about your biological parents?"

"When I was younger, I looked for faces that resembled mine, but I never found what I was looking for." His voice is flat.

I think of how little I resemble my parents. Could I have been left on their doorstep? No. Impossible. They are my parents. They have to be.

Fritz interrupts my thoughts. "Earlier, you said you dream of becoming a doctor?"

I think back to this morning when I let it slip that I thought he was cute and feel embarrassed all over again. I kick my legs and watch birds chittering overhead. Streaks of color—green and yellow feathers, orange beaks and gnarled feet—swoop and swirl, high then low, skating over and under webbed tree branches.

My dad's words sting my ears: *People in Hillcrest don't become doctors.* "I've always wanted to be a doctor, but I never tell anybody."

"Why don't you tell anybody?" Fritz looks at me curiously.

I shrug and meet his gaze. "People think it's impossible to test out of Hillcrest."

"So, prove them wrong." Something in his tone makes me feel like he believes in me. A warm glow spreads through me, like the feeling of sitting by a crackling fire with a hot drink after coming in drenched from a storm.

He stands and offers his hand. "Let's keep moving. We're an hour away."

We detach, reattach, and zoom through the forest for the next hour.

Nine

"Almost there," Fritz says in a serious tone. "At the final platform, be extremely quiet." He clips onto the last cable and disappears beyond a clump of evergreens.

The sound of running engines and the grind of tires on gravel spoils the serenity of the forest. As I speed toward the last platform, I worry the screak of the zipline will give us away. Dread settles in my stomach like a heavy stone.

When I land, Fritz has a pair of binoculars cupped to his eyes. His harness lies in a jumble on the platform. I free myself from my harness and toss it on top of his. I massage my legs where the harness left an imprint.

Through a patchwork of quivering leaves, I make out a chain-link fence topped with skin-slicing barbed-wire. The humid air smells of manmade things like asphalt and rubber and gas. The wind carries the sound of distant voices, marching feet, hammering tools.

Fritz hands me the binoculars. I scan the sprawling compound. The magnified barbed-wire seems so close I could prick my fingers on it. Inside the fence, dark green utility vehicles are parked in neat rows around a half-dozen white buildings.

Men in gray camouflage enter and exit the squat structures. Soldiers? We learned that militaries breed aggression, aggression breeds war, and war begets death.

If the Nuclei is anti-military and anti-war, why are soldiers here? And not just any soldiers: giant, muscle-bulging, Big-Bad-Wolf-looking soldiers.

In an empty grassless lot to the left, hundreds of soldiers march in formation. To the right along the bay, cargo barges dock near stacks of colorful shipping containers. In the far distance behind the compound, empty roads lead to abandoned houses and businesses. No pedestrians cross streets. No cars carry workers to their offices. No trains deliver supplies. Mountains and trees surround the deserted town on one side while the ocean wraps around the other side.

I bring the binoculars back to the busy compound and zoom in on a stone watchtower. At the top, a gray-garbed guard leans back in a chair with his legs outstretched, combat boots perched on the open window ledge. He slices an apple with a pocketknife. A rifle is propped against a table cluttered with random equipment.

I lower the binoculars and whisper to Fritz, "Why do they have guns?"

Fritz lifts his hands in the air, gesturing *I don't know*.

Guns are illegal in Hillcrest. Before the war, people had easy access to guns and it was common for innocent people to lose their lives to gun violence.

Next to a glass-enclosed guard station, a wide gate screeches open to permit entry to an eighteen-wheeler. The truck rumbles through the gate coughing up a plume of exhaust. It heaves forward, then rolls backward, carefully parking near one of the buildings. The driver, a man in a baseball cap and jeans, jumps out of the cab, walks around the back, and unlatches the trailer doors. Sun glints off the doors as they swing open.

Two soldiers climb into the trailer and reappear carrying an orange container marked TOXIC: the same type of container Enforcers loaded into a van the night of the raid. The soldiers unload the trailer, carrying containers into the building the way pallbearers carry caskets, one soldier on each side. I hand the binoculars back to Fritz.

"See the radio tower over there?" He points in the opposite direction of the busy compound. Over my shoulder, deep in the woods, a metal structure punches through the treetops.

Fritz continues, "If we get separated, climb the ladder on the radio tower until you see the return zipline. Take it to the waterfall and hike home from there."

My stomach drops at the thought of climbing the radio tower. Fritz sets the binoculars next to our harnesses. He pulls a rope from his bag, secures one end around the tree, and lowers the other end over the platform. He drops over the ledge, quickly descends the rope, and from the ground motions for me to join him.

Wrapping my hands around the rope, I cautiously lower one leg and summon the courage that got me through hours of ziplining. Tightening my grip, I push off the platform.

The rope bounces and sways, as if it were a guitar string plucked by an invisible hand. The shaky movement strikes a chord of terror within me. The rope twists in circles, around and around it goes. If it doesn't stop spinning soon, I'm going to retch.

Fritz jerks on the rope and stabilizes it. A wave of motion sickness breaks over me. I swallow the mucus building in my throat and wish I had a glass of water. Visualizing Fritz descending, I relax my knees and maneuver down the way he did.

When my feet touch the ground, Fritz puts one finger over his mouth and advances toward the fence. I shake out my swollen, rope-burned fingers and follow. He continues marking trees with the wax.

Pretending to navigate landmines, I tiptoe around fallen branches and dry leaves as we creep toward the back of the closest building.

Fritz pauses near the fence. I look at the tower to see if the guard has moved; the soles of his combat boots remain propped on the window. A faded sign hangs from the chain-link fence. I move my lips in an attempt to pronounce it. *Gua? Guant?*

"Guantanamo," Fritz says. "It's a Taino word meaning land between rivers. Spanish colonialists wiped out the Taino, but statues the Taino carved to honor their ancestors still stand near caves in the Valley. They believed the souls of their dead ancestors returned at night to hunt the living."

"How do you know about the Taino? I've never heard of them."

"The Nuclei sterilized indigenous survivors on the island but didn't kill them so their stories live on."

I frown. "Why did they sterilize survivors?"

"Children of people exposed to nuclear energy might have undesirable gene mutations."

"Oh, that makes sense." A clean gene pool is a healthy gene pool.

We crouch at the fence. A butter-yellow butterfly flutters by. The nearest building is at least a hundred yards away across an open lawn. Shadowy figures move past the windows. A playground at the far corner contains a swing set, slide, and sandbox filled with toy trucks. No guards patrol the back of the property.

"Do you hear that?" Fritz sounds alarmed.

I hear the murmur of faraway conversations, the crunch of gravel, wind thrashing, waves crashing, the low grumble of thunder. Nothing unusual.

"What do you hear?" My anxiety is coming back full force.

Fritz hesitates, as if I won't believe him. "Crying babies."

I recall the baby girl my parents confiscated from the Valley. Could she be here? I cock my head and listen. After a few minutes, I perk up.

"I hear the babies," I whisper, eyes wide. "We have to find a way inside."

"Told you," Fritz says, removing the backpack from his shoulder.

Fritz unzips his backpack and withdraws wire cutters. He bends down and starts clipping fence links. *Clip. Clip. Clip.* The sound rattles my nerves. A sheet of fencing lands at my feet. The missing piece creates a hole big enough for us to squeeze through but small enough to be inconspicuous from a distance.

I glance at the reassuring glow on the trees. It's mid-afternoon, but the forest looks dark and ominous under the roiling gray clouds. Fritz shoves his backpack under the fence. I wait for gunfire to rain down from the sky obliterating the backpack, but it just sits there, unscathed.

I touch my passport.

Fritz notices. "Don't worry. I don't hear an electrical barrier." He reaches through the fence and moves his backpack aside.

I'm suddenly filled with apprehension. "Wait, aren't you scared?"

Fritz pushes windblown hair out of his eyes. "I'm a little nervous, but we came this far for answers, and security seems lax. They aren't expecting people to break in."

I glance at the front gate, the watchtower, the building ahead. Fritz is right. The soldiers are going about their daily routines. The watchtower guard isn't watching anything. The barbed-wire and guards may be in place to prevent people from escaping.

I give in. "Okay, but at the first sign of trouble, we run."

"Deal." Fritz lies on his stomach and squirms through the narrow opening. He squats on the other side, the front of his shirt smeared with dirt.

I remove my hat, pass it to Fritz, and worm under the fence. The earth gives way beneath me, cold against my abdomen. I jerk forward, straining to squeeze my hips through the tight space. The fence clanks and claws at me. My shirt rips. My muscles tense. I pull myself through and crouch next to Fritz. He returns my hat. A thin line of blood rises to the surface of a scrape on his forearm. He follows my gaze.

"It's fine." He points to the middle of the building where black awning juts over a walkway. "If we run to the corner closest to us, we can duck under the windows and make our way to that door."

The cry of a baby sends a shiver down my spine despite the ninety-degree heat.

"Ready?" Fritz asks.

"Ready as I'll ever be." My mouth says yes, but my body screams *NO*.

"On the count of three. One... two..."

I take off before he reaches three, pumping my legs as if the soul-eating dead Taino ancestors were nipping at my heels. Fritz's footsteps beat against the ground behind me.

Halfway there, the wind rips my hat from my fingers. I freeze and watch in horror as the hat twirls through the air in slow motion like a graceful ballerina being swept high and low by the wind within view of the windows. Fear squeezes my mind in its unrelenting grip. Should I go back for it?

"Wren!" Fritz growls under his breath as he runs by me.

His voice jerks me back to reality. I run as fast as I can. When I catch up to Fritz, I feel like I've soaked in a bathtub of coffee and absorbed gallons of caffeine right through my skin. My heart reacts by pounding against the prison bars of my ribs, threatening to break out and zipline home without me, but it's too late to turn back now.

Ten

A keypad attached to the doorknob may require a code on most days, but today a piece of wood is wedged between the door and frame. Fritz opens the door wide enough for the two of us to slip inside. Before entering, I look back and see my hat pressed against the fence.

Hallways branch off to the left and right from the main corridor. Fluorescent lights buzz overhead and coat the tile floors and concrete walls in jaundice yellow. The smell of pine-scented disinfectant singes my nose. I hesitate to walk across the polished floor with my dirt-caked shoes. This place is more like a hospital than a prison.

"This way?" Fritz tilts his head toward the first hall on the left.

We inch down the hallway together. At the first door on the left, I peek through the vertical glass pane. It looks like a classroom, but instead of neat rows of desks and chairs, furniture is randomly scattered around the room. Bookshelves are filled with strange objects like spoons, knives, candles, blindfolds.

In the next room, a man and woman in white lab coats stand on each side of a seated boy who stares blankly ahead. On a table near the child, a row of ten blades glitter silver against a red velvet cloth. The knives vary in size from steak knives to large hunting knives.

The woman places the handle of the smallest knife in the child's right hand. Seconds later, the boy hurls the knife in a straight line toward—I gasp—a child strapped to a spinning wheel.

The knife strikes the wheel within millimeters of the child's ear. The boy strapped to the wheel doesn't move. Fritz and I exchange bewildered looks, and he gently pulls me away from the window.

I'm shaken and unsure if I want to see what lies behind the next door. Two women in black robes pace and bounce babies in a room full of bassinets. A man with an empty syringe poised in the air hovers over a sleeping baby. He lowers the syringe and the child lets out a howl. One woman exchanges the bundle in her arms for the screaming baby. I look for the little girl my parents confiscated, but I don't see her.

The last room contains only medical equipment. On the other side of the hall, science labs are filled with microscopes, Petri dishes, and organ models. Mice scurry back and forth in glass cages.

Before we step into the main corridor, Fritz furrows his brow and inclines his head. I recognize his expression as the one he makes when listening intently. After he signals thumbs up, we turn left into the corridor.

The right side of the hallway has large windows that look into individual rooms. Each room has a bed and desk. The doors have numbered keypads. I glance into each bedroom as we continue down the corridor. Empty... empty... empty. Not empty.

A young boy smashes his face against the window of his room. His eyes are fixed on the fluorescent lights in the hall. I approach the window and kneel facing him. He doesn't acknowledge me. The fluorescent lights flicker faster, more erratically. Purple and gold sparks fly from the light above us. It pops and hisses and bursts to black. The other lights continue to flicker, casting weird shadows down the hall.

I whisper, "What is this place? A hospital? A mental asylum? A prison?"

Fritz shifts from foot to foot while monitoring the exit. "I don't know. Let's check out the other hallways."

The sound of a slamming door sends adrenaline rushing through me. Voices drift down the corridor. I grab Fritz's arm. We sprint for the door marked STAIRS. The footsteps are getting closer. I dart into a hallway on the right. Fritz keeps running.

"What do you think you're doing?" A man's voice roars down the hallway.

Fritz's shoes squeal across the tile floor as he takes cover in a hallway across from me. Footsteps charge down the corridor. Terror grips me by the throat. I have to hide.

Red doors. Blue doors. Silver swinging doors. Which door leads to the least terrifying room? Flashing red lights erupt from the ceiling and ricochet off the walls.

I rip off my shoes and make a barefoot run for the double swinging doors at the end of the hallway. Heart tottering, I slide between the doors. A screaming alarm threatens to rupture my ear drums. I crouch in the corner behind the doors and cup my hands over my ears.

The room is full of occupied hospital beds. Bags of clear liquid hang next to each bed. The closest heart monitor reads forty-five beats per minute—a sleeping heart rate.

How are they sleeping through the screech of the alarm? Even with my hands over my ears, the shrill blare tickles my spinal cord.

I rise from my crouching position to look for a better hiding place. Is there a closet or bathroom? I haven't used a bathroom in hours. My bladder feels like a balloon ready to pop.

Staying low, I slink past the swinging doors and weave around the hospital beds. The cold floor is slick beneath my feet.

At the unoccupied bed farthest from the entrance, I uncover my ears, pick up a folded hospital gown, and shake it out with fumbling fingers that feel like noodles. Can't tie the gown. Screaming alarm. Can't think straight. I slide my shoes on, climb under the sheets, and grit my ringing teeth.

I plug my ears and look at the patient on the bed next to me. Oily brown hair matted against her shiny forehead and cheeks conceals most of her features. The only sign of life is her rising and falling chest. A swell rises under the sheet revealing her pregnancy. The girl's pale complexion looks waxy like the dolls I played with as a child. Would her skin feel warm and pliable like my own if I poked her cheek, or would it be stiff, artificial, doll-like?

At least fifty girls and women lie here in various stages of pregnancy. A pungent odor fills the room, but it's overpowered by the smell of fresh linen. It's like when I layer on deodorant instead of taking a shower. I shudder at the thought of being trapped here, pregnant and attached to machines.

The alarm stops. I unplug my buzzing ears. The absence of sound is more terrifying than the screaming alarm. Does the silence mean they found Fritz?

Men's voices surge down the hall. "You take that room. I'll take this one."

I grab a pillow from an uninhabited bed, arrange it over my stomach, and pull the sheet up to my chin. The swinging doors burst open, flapping back and forth like the clapping hands of an audience eager to find out what happens next. I flinch and close my eyes. Heavy footsteps enter the room. I slide my trembling hands under my hips.

Sweat rises on my brow. They didn't see me. They won't be looking for me. Every time the heel of a combat boot thuds, I have to refrain from jumping and running.

When the boots stop near me, the fear of the unknown is more than I can handle. I have to open my eyes. *Don't do it. Don't do it.*

I peek through my eyelashes. A soldier stands at the foot of my bed, looking right at my fake stomach. Every muscle in my body petrifies. One touch is all it would take for me to crumble to dust.

I recall lessons on meditation. Focus on breathing. Visualize a calming place. I'm lying on a moonlit beach. I exhale each time a wave crashes against the shore. I inhale as the water recedes and flows back to the full moon hanging low on the horizon, an iridescent pearl, in a sky full of diamonds.

The smell of aftershave vaporizes my visualization of a peaceful ocean. The soldier must be standing right over me. Why me? Rough hands scrape my neck and lift the sheet.

It takes all my effort not to cringe. My heart kicks into overdrive. My legs twitch. Did he see me move? *Stop freaking out! You can outrun him! But I can't outrun his bullets.*

As I argue with myself, a voice outside my head yells from the hallway. "I found something!"

Sweaty skin brushes my arm. The sheet falls against my chin. The soldier zigzags around the beds and bulldozes through the swinging doors, banging them against the wall.

I crack one eye open and blow out a breath. I'm alone: not counting the unconscious people. If I wake the others, it might distract the guards while Fritz and I escape. I slide off the bed, throw off the hospital gown, and squeeze the shoulder of the girl closest to me.

"Wake up." I shake her.

Her arm falls and dangles over the side of the bed. I recognize the black onyx overlaid with the initial *C* on her ring finger. A chill runs down my spine. The ring was a gift from her parents before they died in a car accident.

"Celeste?"

Her eyes remain closed. Celeste was always a little heavy, but this girl looks gaunt. How did Celeste end up here when she was assigned to the Valley?

I feel like I'm straddling a doorway between two worlds. One foot is stuck firmly in reality, while the other is in this strange place where girls are kept in a state of unconscious pregnancy.

A bruise spreads under the IV needle taped to Celeste's arm. Could the IV liquid be causing their deep sleep? I push her hair off her forehead and rest my palm on her stomach. The life inside her moves under my hand.

"I'll come back for you, Celeste. I promise."

I move toward the swinging doors. Warning lights are still flashing, but the hall is empty. I tighten the straps on my sandals and get ready to run.

Eleven

I hurry toward the main corridor, feeling as vulnerable as a deer in an open field. The red light pulsing through the veins of the building irritates my retinas. I try to blink away the dots blotting my vision.

The smell of disinfectant isn't that unpleasant after being stuck in a room reeking of body odor. How did Celeste end up here? I should have tried harder to wake her. I should have taken her with me. Guilt batters my conscience.

Comatose pregnant girls. Crying babies. Catatonic kids. What else are they hiding here? A susurrous hum comes from the main corridor: a whisper of male voices, a swish of starched pants.

I should keep moving down the hall in search of an exit, but curiosity draws me toward a red door the way a magnet draws a box of nails. I can't resist. I inch across the hall and look in the window.

Young boys and girls lounge in recliners with their heads back and eyes closed. Blood-sucking needles feast on their forearms, directing blood upward to translucent bags. A glass case contains labeled bags of liquid in rich shades of gold and crimson. I shudder and back away.

I poke my head into the main corridor. Three armed guards assemble near the door Fritz and I entered. One of them holds my crumpled sunhat. My heart quakes. They know Fritz isn't alone.

In school, they taught us to take the stairs in the event of a fire or other emergency. Stairwells always have exits. The door is only fifty feet away. I could reach it in seconds. Sweat swells on my neck and rolls down my back. I have to make a run for it.

I swallow the fear rising in my throat, take a deep breath, and sprint into the corridor, streaking toward the stairs, staying on my toes: *go, go, go.* Adrenaline charges through my veins. I look where I last saw Fritz. He isn't there.

The flashing red lights bounce off the walls and floor, as if the building has a hyperactive pulse: manic, frenetic, apoplectic. The pulse in my neck hammers as erratically as the flashing lights.

Twenty feet.

Ten feet.

If I can just make it to the stairs.

Five feet.

I stretch out my arm, reaching for the door. My sandals screech. The high-pitched squeal screams through the halls. My heart stops. One hand on the door, I dare to look over my shoulder.

Eyes and mouths stretched wide with shock, the guards stare at me.

"Freeze!" The big bald one barks in a voice that could scare the enamel off teeth.

He reaches for his gun and fear fills my belly like a paperweight pinning me to the floor. I shove open the door. It crashes against the inner wall with a deafening bang. Blood-red metal stairs lead in only one direction: straight down.

I race down the stairs like my shoes are on fire. Combat boots charge down the hall, slamming against the floor, moving toward the stairwell door. I cling to the railing, keeping my eyes fixed on my feet. The air is becoming cold and damp and cutting.

The stairs vibrate from the weight of the men pursuing me. My heart thrashes against my chest like a June bug trapped in a bottle. My feet are moving so fast, I imagine myself missing a step, somersaulting down the remaining flights, and looking up to find gun barrels aimed at my face.

A putrid smell rises from the bowels of the building like it's infected with gut rot. With each flight of stairs, the stench of manure and rotting food gets worse. When my feet finally strike dirt, I feel a pinch of relief and look around to get my bearings.

I'm in a dark, cavernous tunnel that goes on forever. Maybe an old subway. The malodor is overwhelming. I squeeze my nose and cover my mouth to suppress my gag reflex.

"Faster!" a brusque voice bellows as footsteps thunder down the stairs.

I rush into the tunnel, scurrying along the right side, skimming my fingertips over the bone-cold surface of the wall in search of an exit or hiding place.

My eyes adjust. The tunnel brightens. Fear of the unknown fades. I speed up and stay in the shadows. Hair-raising noises echo off the walls. Beastly snorts punch through the hollow blackness. A rustle, a scratch, a grunt, a groan. It's probably mice. My heart stutters like it isn't convinced.

Flashlight beams hack through the murky tunnel, chopping shadows into pieces, blanching the cracked walls and dirt floor. A rivulet of hope flows through me. The flashlights mean my pursuers can't see in the dark.

The wall under my fingertips gives way. I peer into the alcove. Hundreds of eyes stare back at me. I stumble, startled. Cages stacked from floor to ceiling in neat rows contain dozens and dozens of cats. The cats start yowling, begging me to free them. I wish I could.

"Over there!"

Flashlights arc over my face and body. The guards are closing in. I dig my heels into the soft earth and fly deeper into the tunnel. Inhaling the dank air, I try to ignore the foul stench that makes me want to vomit. I pass more gated rooms on my right.

"Stop and put your hands up!" The enamel-melting voice yells.

A gust of air pushes my hair forward. Something whizzes by my ear and disappears into the tunnel ahead of me. A bullet? A tranquilizer dart? What would they do if they captured me? I would rather die than be imprisoned in this freak factory.

I run by another gated room and slam my hand upward against the steel latch. The gate staggers open. If I can put something, anything between me and my pursuers, I have a better chance of escaping.

I shove open the next gate. And the next one. Hundreds of shuffling feet. Dogs? Cats? Blood-sucking cannibals? That would explain the bags of blood stored upstairs. I imagine half-human creatures ripping me apart. I suck in a deep breath and beg my legs to keep up the breakneck pace.

I'm fatigued. I need to rest soon. The chaos behind me is undeniable. Animals squeal, snort, and snarl. Confused men bark orders at each other. I can't make out their words over the stampede.

A sliver of light in the shape of a crescent moon illuminates the ceiling ahead. Horseshoe-shaped rungs climb the arched wall, providing a footpath to the light. I imagine the ladder as a finish line and give myself a final push. I'm moving so fast and breathing so hard, I feel like my heart is going to explode.

I launch toward the ladder, grab the first rung, and pull myself halfway up before looking back. Pigs and sheep scramble through the tunnel, a surging wave of hooves and snouts and fluff. The stampede knocks down a guard and tramples him. A gun fires and the herd scatters.

A sharp pain shoots up my left leg. I cry out. A guard holds the ladder with one hand and crushes my ankle with the other.

"Who are you?" he growls in a thick accent.

The light from above bounces off his shaved head. Horn-shaped shadows circle his skull. His teeth, framed by a goatee, glow yellow in the dark. Bulging eyes demand answers. The grip on my ankle tightens. He yanks hard. My lower body swings away from the ladder.

I dangle, gripping the iron rungs between my sweaty palms. I clench my abdominal muscles to stabilize myself. My stomach heaves. Orange juice burns my esophagus from the orange I ate hours ago. I swallow hard and take a deep breath that smells like blood, guts, toenails, manure. Pressure builds in my esophagus. My stomach contracts. Waves of nausea rack my body.

As the man reaches for my other leg, orange projectile puke explodes from my mouth and splatters all over his face. He grunts and loosens his grip.

With all my strength, I kick my free leg outward and upward, aiming my heel at the man's puke-covered face. I was never a good aim in sports. When I was up to bat during baseball games, it was always *three strikes, you're out!*

Imagine my surprise when my foot crashes into his face, landing squarely between his eyes. The impact rocks my body. I grip the rungs tighter. Rust chips cut into my palms.

The man releases my leg, stumbles backward, and falls flat on his back. Air ejects from his lungs and splooshes from his lips. He lies motionless like an overturned beetle, bug eyes wide open.

Did he expect me to allow him to pull me back into the smelly tunnel without a fight? The small victory renews my energy. Tilting my head back, I inhale the fresh air coming from above. My nostrils still burn from vomiting.

I shove my fingers through the crescent-shaped crack. It's a manhole cover. Bracing my knees against the wall, I push the cover until my arms quiver. Metal grinds against asphalt.

The narrow opening smashes me as I squeeze through. It spits me into the middle of the deserted town miles from the compound. The dazzling daylight reflecting off the cream-colored buildings is blinding. In the tunnel, animals swell around the bald man. He's kicking and kneeing and cursing.

I imagine him emerging from the tunnel, grabbing my ankles, and pulling me back into the suffocating darkness. My heel still throbs where it made contact with his forehead. I push away thoughts of getting caught and run for my life.

Twelve

I bolt down an adjacent street between rows of abandoned office buildings. *Faster. Harder. Go, go, go!* Heart slamming, I dart into an alley. Long and narrow. Too clean. Nowhere to hide. Bursting from the alley like a bullet from a barrel, I cut left. Right. Left again.

Black storm clouds gather overhead. The baritone rumble of thunder fills the air seconds before sheets of rain join the ominous melody. Raindrops mercilessly drum my skin and obstruct my view of potential hiding spots. Disjointed voices cut through the downpour. I cup my hands over my eyes and squint into the distance.

Within a quarter mile, the cross-topped steeple of a dingy white chapel pierces the heavy sky. Near the chapel is a rundown grocery store. The closest building has a red roof with golden arches looming over it. A sign that reads *McDonald's I'm Lovin' It* throws a long shadow across a colorful playground.

Maybe it's a former preschool. I speed toward the golden arches. As I approach the back door of McDonald's, dread settles over me like the black clouds above me. If anything is inside, it can't be worse than the men pursuing me. I shiver and it's not from the wet clothes clinging to my skin.

I twist the doorknob. Locked. I pound my shoulder into the door and throw my body weight against it. Voices are getting closer. I push wet hair out of my eyes, rear back, and land another blow.

The door submits and swings open. Tripping over the threshold, I grip the door for balance and then spin, slam the door, and slide the deadbolt.

Standing as still as death, I listen for movement. Water drips from my rain-soaked hair and splatters on the orange tile floor. Otherwise, it's quiet.

I'm facing a grimy kitchen reeking of decades-old grease. Vats of used cooking oil line the left wall. A gross, lumpy film stretches across the oil's surface. On a smell-scale from stinky cheese to decaying fish, this place falls somewhere in the middle near rotten eggs.

Beyond the kitchen is a dining room with dust-covered tables, wooden chairs, and boarded windows. Sunlight burrows through cracks in the plywood, providing dim lighting throughout the abandoned restaurant.

Squares of paper litter the kitchen floor. I reach for one near my feet. It reads:

2 Cheeseburgers

2 Large Fries

1 Happy Meal

2 Cokes

Whatever a happy meal is, it sounds like something I could use right now. My stomach growls at the thought of food, but even if a table was spread with all my favorites, I would be too anxious to eat.

I still have to pee. There must be a restroom somewhere. I poke my head through a door on the left. Bingo! I tiptoe across the hall to the ladies' room. As I'm emptying my swollen bladder, a blast startles me. Where the toilet paper should be, my fingers brush against an empty cardboard roll. Just my luck. No paper towels near the sink either. I pull on my shorts and crack the door.

In the dining room, shattered pieces of glass glitter in broken sunlight. Another blast sends the remaining shards from the fractured window crashing to the floor. My pulse patters wildly against my neck.

Should I make a run for the grocery store or chapel? They could have the McDonald's surrounded. I have to stay here and hide. I sneak into the kitchen, crouch below the counter, and look for a hiding place.

Two doors break up a row of stoves. The metal door is probably a freezer. I dash across the greasy floor toward the other door. My feet slip and my left elbow and hip slam against the floor. Pinpricks radiate from my elbow, as if a match was struck against my funny bone. Flaming neurons race to my fingertips.

A groan escapes my lips. I cradle my arm against my side and peel my damp shorts from the sticky floor. The entire place is covered in grease and dust; now I am, too. I shake out my arm and waddle to the door.

"I'll sweep this place. You keep moving. She couldn't have made it far." The guttural voice belongs to the guard I kicked in the face.

I squeeze into the mystery room. It's a storage pantry. Massaging my elbow, I look for a place to hide. Crackling bug carcasses—beetles and cockroaches—crunch under my sandals. Could this day get any worse?

I move toward a wooden barrel in the back corner, carefully stepping over rotting food and dented cans. I pull the barrel forward and wedge myself behind it. Bringing my knees to my chest, I wrap my arms around my legs, and shrink into myself.

The door bangs open. My body quivers like a slug bathed in salt. A flashlight sweeps the room, darting in and out of corners. I feel the weight of something in my hair. Fear threatens to break my silence. I hold my breath. The flashlight pauses near the barrel. Combat boots approach my hiding place.

A tap on my head causes me to recoil. I look up expecting to see the bald man with a heel-battered face glaring down at me, but instead, maggots slither over a pile of rotting food on a shelf overhead. A maggot slides down my hair and lands with a plop on the front of my shirt. The sticky, white lump convulses near my collar. My eyes stretch open in horror.

Tap. Tap. Tap. More maggots land in my hair. My throat constricts. My stomach threatens to pitch another curve ball up my esophagus. I clasp both hands over my mouth and swallow hard.

Something sticky writhes against my chest. One of the legless larvae fell down my shirt! I can hardly refrain from screaming and jumping up to shake the slime balls out of my hair. I close my eyes and count to ten, but all I can think about is the maggot infestation. I shudder at the thought of maggot eggs hatching in my hair.

The man's footsteps retreat. A rat scurries across the floor. He halts and turns back.

"Just a rat," he mutters and leaves the room.

Tables and chairs clatter. Glass pops. A door slams. The restaurant becomes silent. I inch the barrel forward. He could still be out there, trying to lure me out of hiding with his silence. I stand and shake off my shirt. As the minutes tick by, my heart rate slows.

Suppressing my disgust, I pull sticky maggots from my hair and throw them to the ground. They hit the floor with a loud snap.

After I remove the final muciform glob from my hair, I wipe my hands on the front of my shorts. Just when I thought the day couldn't get worse, I was proven wrong.

I exit the pantry and peek into the kitchen. The restaurant looks empty. This is one of those times Fritz's hearing would come in handy. Speaking of Fritz. Is he hiding somewhere or is he on his way home or did they catch him?

I work up the nerve to cross the glass-strewn dining room to look out the busted window. Slivers of glass burrow into the outsoles of my hiking sandals and scrape against the floor. I flatten my back against the wall and peer out the window.

The town looks as deserted as it did from the zipline platform. The sun is low, but there are several hours of daylight left. My legs are weak and my stomach is queasy, but I can't rest. Not yet.

I cut through the kitchen to the back door, unlatch the lock, and poke my head outside. The formerly brooding sky is now serene with no trace of the downpour that soaked my clothes earlier. I can reach the forest within fifteen minutes if I run at full speed.

I flex my calves, reach for my toes, and stretch for as long as I dare. I release the stretch and take a deep breath before bursting out the door toward the woods. The wind in my hair, the smell of the ocean, the familiarity of running calms me. My confidence soars.

My heart pumps in sync with my racing feet. My chest heaves. I cross the periphery of the forest and lean over, gulping mouthfuls of fresh air: the crisp, clean smell of things growing—green and wild and new—is restorative.

After I catch my breath, I move along the edge of the forest to the perimeter of the compound. I feel an itchy-pinch on my arms and legs and realize mosquitos are feasting on me. I brush off the bloodsuckers, step away from a stagnant puddle of water, and watch soldiers pile into trucks forming a search team. They would never guess I'm standing within a rock's throw of the gate.

The wind rushes through my hair and cools my skin as I hotfoot it to the zipline platform to retrieve my harness. I see the rope dangling and feel a rush of relief, like being thrown a lifeboat after falling overboard. I run to the rope and start pulling myself up, hand over hand. Please let there be only one harness at the top.

I hoist myself over the edge. Both harnesses lie exactly where we left them. Disappointed, I pick up the binoculars and pan over the compound. No sign of Fritz. Utility vehicles painstakingly comb the streets of the abandoned town. The choppy drone of a helicopter snaps me into motion.

I buckle the harness around my waist and grab the rope. The helicopter hovers dangerously close. Two people in the helicopter's body wear the uniform I know so well: black combat boots, black fatigues.

Why are Enforcers here? Do my parents know about this place? Could they be involved? I throw myself over the platform, dash down the rope, and run for the radio tower where the zipline will take me home.

From behind the trees, I observe Honor Street and Patriot Drive. Government flags hang limply in the breezeless night. Outdoor sirens wail. The Nuclei blares them to warn of natural disasters. Neighbors huddle together as Security Forces conduct door-to-door interrogations. My parents are far away with their backs to me.

I skulk across the periphery of the woods, sprint across the street, and crouch in the bushes next to the porch. I can make out fragments of conversations: "fugitives… male and female… reward…"

The amplified sound of my heartbeat drowns out the sirens. If I wasn't familiar with anatomy, I would swear my heart was jumping up and down on my ear drums. Sweat trickles down my face. I wipe my brow. The humid night is suffocating.

I build up the courage to climb the porch and enter the house. In the bathroom, I hardly recognize the tangled-hair, wild-eyed girl staring at me from the mirror. I strip off my filthy clothes and take a speed shower, scrubbing the dirt from under my fingernails and wincing as soapy water runs down my skinned knees.

I jump out of the shower, towel-wrap my torso, grab my clothes, and head down the hallway. Abe calls out and sits up in his bed while Addie sleeps nearby.

"The sirens are scary. When will they stop?" He rubs his eyes.

I sit on the edge of Abe's bed. "It's just a hurricane drill. The sirens will stop soon."

I want to believe what I'm telling him, but I suspect Security Forces are looking for me and Fritz. I rearrange the blankets on Abe's bed. He yawns and nestles his head into the pillow. I dash to my bedroom, throw on my pajamas, and hide my dirty clothes under my mattress.

My pillowcase smells faintly of butterfly jasmine—the mariposa flower grows in wild clusters in the backyard around the clothesline. I've never been so happy to be home.

As I drift to sleep, the creak of the front door jerks me awake. My eyes fly open and my ears stand at attention. Footsteps in the hallway pause near the twins' room. Next, my door opens. The thud of combat boots hitting my bedroom floor reverberates through my core. I feign sleep until the footsteps retreat.

Thirteen

The day I have been waiting for has finally arrived: Assessment Day. This day always seemed so far away, so out of reach. Dad hasn't said a word during the drive to the Community Center. He stares out the windshield and occasionally lifts a hand to wave at neighbors browsing the Farmer's Market.

A week has passed since I last saw Fritz. I looked for him every night this week, but he wasn't in the woods. If he made it home safely, wouldn't he have found a way to let me know? He took the Assessment last week. Maybe he received a job assignment in a different cell. I would rather believe that than any of the nightmare scenarios that wreak havoc on my mind and keep me awake at night.

The car rolls to a stop at the Community Center.

"I'll pick you up in four hours and prepare your favorite meal for dinner. Sound like a plan?" Dad smiles, but his eyes look somber.

One arm draped over the steering wheel, he turns to face me. "No matter what happens tomorrow, you will always have my love and support."

It's not like Dad to be sentimental. "Are you okay, Dad?"

Dad lets out a long sigh. "I don't tell you often enough how much I love you."

I lean over for a quick hug. He holds me like he doesn't want to let go. Why does it feel like he's telling me goodbye? Just two weeks ago, he was telling me how unlikely a Clairemont assignment would be.

"I know you love me. I love you, too." I squeeze his arm and hop out of the car. I'm not good with lovey-dovey, touchy-feely conversations.

Empty chairs line the walls of the blue-themed waiting room. A receptionist sits behind a tall counter.

The receptionist pushes her glasses up and focuses on me. "How may I help you?"

My stomach dips. This is it. I force myself to approach the desk. "I have a noon appointment for the Assessment."

She confirms my identity and drops a key in my palm. "The locker room is over there. Change into the athletic gear provided in locker number twenty-seven."

Inside the locker, I find a pair of tennis shoes, black athletic pants, and a matching top with the government logo—all in my size. I change clothes, slide the key in my pocket, and head back to the reception area.

The receptionist's manicured nails peck the keyboard. I sit by a table stacked with the *Nuclei Newsletter*. It features articles about scientific breakthroughs and interviews with residents who praise the Nuclei for its generosity and ingenuity.

"Wren Weiss?" A tall woman with dark brown skin and short black hair with sideswept bangs enters the room carrying a transceptor. She wears a white lab coat over a red suit.

I stand. "I'm Wren."

"I'm Dr. Charlotte Sorrell. I will administer the Assessment today." I follow her into a brightly lit hallway where she motions for me to enter a room on the right. "Have a seat on the medical exam table. I'm going to ask a few questions. Then, I'll measure your height, weight, and blood pressure. First, I need to confirm your identity."

The tissue paper on the exam table crinkles and shifts as I sit and pull my ponytail away from my neck.

Dr. Sorrell adjusts the height of her stool before scanning my passport. "Birthdate?"

"November thirtieth, 2056."

"Date of your first period?"

My cheeks redden, my lips furrow. "Two Sundays ago."

"Sunday, August fourteenth." Dr. Sorrell moves her stylus over the transceptor in a series of dashes, dots, and swirls. She then records my weight and height.

"I'm going to take an updated blood sample." Dr. Sorrell cleans the crook of my arm with a damp cotton ball. "Make a fist."

I hold my breath and look away, wincing as the needle pierces my skin. A poster on my right displays the four overlapping circles that represent Assessment categories. People who score above average in each category are considered exceptional. Those people don't live in Hillcrest; they live in Clairemont.

"All done." Dr. Sorrell applies a bandage to my arm. "Which three positions would you like me to document as job preferences?"

"I want to be a doctor." I study Dr. Sorrell's face and wait for her to discourage me or guide me toward other career choices, but she doesn't react.

"What else?" She lifts the lid of a machine on the counter and inserts the blood sample.

"Nothing else."

She closes the lid and focuses on me. "Your job preferences will be taken into consideration *if* you provide them. If you do not, assessors will rely solely on aptitude and Nuclei needs."

"I understand," I say, unwilling to provide a list of jobs I don't want.

"Follow me." Dr. Sorrell leaves the room.

As we walk down the hall, cameras mounted to the ceiling watch us. Who monitors the camera footage? What if Dr. Hahn himself is watching?

Dr. Sorrell pushes open swinging doors. Images of comatose pregnant girls behind silver swinging doors flood my mind. What if there are rooms like that here? Goosebumps rise on my arms.

Dr. Sorrell pokes her head into the hall. "Move along."

I push away the terrifying memories and walk through the swinging doors. The room holds a tall cylinder that looks like a chrome rocket. I extend my hand toward its smooth surface.

"Please don't touch the equipment."

My hand falls limply to my side. I view my warped reflection in the mirrored surface.

Dr. Sorrell motions to the rocket. "Step into the symmetry scanner. Be still while it performs calculations. The scan will be complete within two minutes."

After I board the rocket, Dr. Sorrell adjusts my shoulders. "Shoulders back, eyes straight ahead." She pulls my arms away from my body and steps back. A whiff of cinnamon-clove perfume triggers a faint memory of Mom sitting on the couch, sipping cinnamon hot tea and reading a book before the twins were born, before she became a workaholic.

"I'm going to close the door. You may hear a slight hum and feel a vibration." Dr. Sorrell presses a button on the exterior of the cylinder. A panel moves across the entrance until not the slightest needle of light penetrates it.

I hate being in enclosed spaces. My heart rate increases and my hands become clammy. The machine hums through the sole of my shoes like the rocket is about to blast off. Tiny green dots appear all around me. I imagine being in outer space looking out on a night sky lit by emerald constellations. The green dots lengthen into narrow lines crisscrossing my face and body.

After a minute, the lasers disappear. The vibration under my feet quiets. The door slides open. Bright light fills the interior of the cylinder.

"Please, step out."

I exit the rocket and study Dr. Sorrell's expression. "Did I score okay?"

"You will receive your test results tomorrow." Her face remains neutral, unreadable.

I didn't expect a direct answer, but I hoped to at least have an inkling about my results today. I follow Dr. Sorrell into a room with glass-enclosed desks along the back wall. Some desks are occupied by other students.

"Sensory input chamber number three." Dr. Sorrell walks to one of the glass-enclosed desks and opens the door.

"Have a seat. This cap will monitor your brain waves while you complete the next tasks." She attaches to my head a thingamajig with cascading wires. "You will be shown a series of short video clips for the emotional intelligence test. The next test will assess your reading, science, and math skills. Use the stylus to select the best answer from the choices on screen." Dr. Sorrell steps back and closes the door.

The screen above the desk lights up. WELCOME, WREN WEISS. THE TEST WILL COMMENCE IN 3-2-1. The screen displays a video of sleeping kittens. Fuzzy cat hair tickles my fingertips. One of the kittens wakes and climbs over its siblings. I smile. The image fades.

A musty odor fills the chamber. Cockroaches scurry across the screen. They crawl up my arms, their antennae scratch my skin, their hungry mouths salivate across my neck, their sticky legs run up my nose and out my ears. My mouth expands as it fills with crispy cockroach bodies. I run my tongue across the back of my teeth relieved to find no bug legs stuck between them. I make a fist and feel cockroach exoskeletons pop in my palm.

I recall stepping on cockroaches in McDonald's right before maggots fell in my hair. My heart rate spikes. *Calm down. It's not real.*

The odor disappears. A baby swaddled in pink coos at me. The chamber fills with a scent that reminds me of lazy days on the beach. The sun warms my hair. Sand presses into my skin and waves crash at my feet.

A blazing building appears. Flames erupt from the door and windows. Smoke fills the chamber. My skin scorches. I start coughing and reach for the door. The sensation passes. The screen goes black. A start button appears.

I pick up the stylus and start solving equations and analyzing reading passages. When the test is over, I exhale and roll my shoulders. I aced this test, but I'm not so confident about the symmetry scan or the genetic screening.

Dr. Sorrell opens the chamber door. "Remove the cap and follow me, please."

I toss the cap on the desk, spring to my feet, and take

long strides to catch up with Dr. Sorrell. Other doctors shuffle students past us, doors open and close in adjacent halls, and a murmur of voices float down the corridor. The students we pass avoid eye contact. It's a nerve-wracking day—the doctors hold our futures in their hands.

"Is the strength test next?" I ask, trailing behind Dr. Sorrell.

"The hearing and vision tests are next."

Dr. Sorrell stops abruptly and waves her hand over a microchip scanner. The internal mechanics of the nearby door grind, hiss, pop. I don't know anyone in Hillcrest who has a microchip implanted. An eye chart with letters and numbers hangs on one wall of the small, windowless room.

"Enter and raise your right hand each time you hear a sound. After you finish the hearing test, the vision test will begin. Any questions?"

I shake my head. I have questions, but I no longer expect her to provide answers. The door slams. Spinning in a circle while staring at the black dome overhead, I try to picture the viewers behind the camera, but I conjure up faceless blobs.

After the hearing test, the speaker crackles and Dr. Sorrell instructs me to read the eye chart. When I finish reading the bottom row, the door opens.

"Good job, Wren. I ran preliminary tests on your blood sample. Based on the results, I would like you to complete one more test. Then, we will move on to the strength assessment."

Dr. Sorrell leads me into a room with tables covered in game pieces and approaches a table. "This set of dominoes includes twenty-eight pieces. You have one minute to memorize their placement. After one minute, I will mix them up and you will put them back in the order you see here."

A memory test. I'm totally going to fail.

"One-minute timer begins now." Dr. Sorrell punches a stopwatch.

I prop my arms on each side of the table, lean over the dominoes, and pick out memorable patterns. Six dots next to none. Three dots above six. Four dominoes in a row with two dots on the left.

"Time's up." Dr. Sorrell sweeps the dominoes into a box, shakes it up, and pours the dominoes back onto the table. They clack and clatter across the surface. "Take as much time as you need," she says.

I flatten the pieces, turn them upright, and slide them around. Four dominoes in a row with two dots on the left. I try to ignore the ticking of the stopwatch and the clicking of Dr. Sorrell's high heels as she paces behind me. I flip a domino through my fingers. Where was this one? Somewhere on the bottom. Done. I look at Dr. Sorrell. She walks to the table, reviews the results, and makes a note in her transceptor.

"Did I get it right?" I ask.

"You will receive your test results tomorrow."

I roll my eyes at her back, pretend to walk on high heels, and mimic her: *You will receive your test results tomorrow.*

The next hour is spent doing pull-ups, push-ups, sit-ups, and running. I return to the locker room sweaty and weak. My whole body trembles. I shower, change clothes, and wait for Dad to pick me up. Tomorrow I'll learn my fate.

I expect Dad to interrogate me on the way home, but he's silent. Is he thinking about how disappointed Mom was when she received her test results? It must have bothered him that, if given a choice, she would have chosen a life in Clairemont over a life with him.

A thread of guilt needles me because, if given a choice, I would choose Clairemont, too. Mentally and physically drained, I lean against the headrest and zone out on the short drive home.

Dad pulls into the driveway, and we exit the car. Climbing the porch steps, my shoes feel as heavy as bricks. Nervous energy crackles behind the front door. The moment I step inside, the smell of coconut sauce greets me. My stomach celebrates.

Addie launches herself at me, wrapping her arms around my waist. She breathlessly babbles, "I have been waiting for you all day. Was it hard? Will you be an Enforcer like Mom and Dad? Will you cut your hair like Mom's? Cody told my class his brother had to eat chocolate covered lizards to pass the Assessment. Is that true?"

I smile and affectionately cup her cheek. "Next time you see Cody, tell him it's chocolate covered grasshoppers you must eat.

Rubbery lizards would take too long to chew." It's tradition for older siblings to provide material for the rumor mill at school.

"Ew." Addie scrunches up her face.

"How did it go?" Mom places utensils on the table.

I'm reminded of Dr. Sorrell's instructions to refrain from discussing the Assessment. "Easier than expected."

I join Dad in the kitchen. "How can I help?"

He hands me a platter overflowing with steamed rice. "Take this to the table. I'll be right behind you with the shrimp and plantains."

"Abe, Addie, time to eat." Mom raises her voice.

I pile my plate high with rice and liberally spoon coconut sauce over it until the rice swells from over-saturation.

"Will we ever see you again?" Abe asks.

I put my fork down. "What do you mean?"

"What if you get taken away?" Abe's face is etched with concern.

"Don't be stupid, Abner." Addie rolls her eyes at Abe. "Wren is going to be an Enforcer like Mom and Dad."

"Apologize to your brother. We don't call people stupid," Dad says.

Addie looks at her plate. "Sorry."

I reach across the table and rest my hand on Abe's. "Don't worry, Abe. Even if I were placed outside of Hillcrest, I would find a way to stay in touch, okay?" I make the promise without knowing if I can keep it.

Mom says, "The Nuclei requires everyone to pack a bag prior to receiving test results. I packed some things in your Grandmother Eliza's old suitcase."

"Thanks, Mom." Does Mom believe there's a chance I could be placed in Clairemont?

After dinner, I help clean up and then head to my bedroom. I approach the suitcase on my bed and trace its worn leather edges with my fingertips. Suitcases are relics from the past when people traveled around the world. I've never thought about leaving Genova Island. Why would I? Nothing but sea surrounds us.

"Come in," I respond to the knock on my bedroom door.

Abe enters. "I wanted to give you this." He places a photo in my hand. Mom, Dad, the twins, and I smile into the camera from the front porch.

"Thanks, Abe. That's sweet of you." I wrap his hand in mine. He studies my face. Then, he leans close and places his head against my chest. I cradle his head for a minute before he pulls away.

As he backs toward the door, he says in a quiet voice, "You're not like us. They're going to take you away."

After Abe leaves, I frown at the closed door. What has gotten into him? Turning back to the suitcase, I note that Mom packed clothes and toiletries. Should I pack anything else? I doubt anything will change tomorrow, but shouldn't I be prepared?

I'm excited about the possibility of becoming a doctor in Clairemont. I'll be devastated if I receive a career assignment outside of Hillcrest that doesn't include travel privileges. But then again, I won't be exactly happy if I have to spend the rest of my life in Hillcrest either.

While the neighborhood sleeps, I meander through the woods. A gentle breeze stirs the leaves and feathers my hair. Most summer nights the air is thick and humid, but tonight it's clean and crisp. I fill my lungs with the scent of the forest: pine, moss, earth.

At the cliff, I listen for voices. Concerns about Fritz plague me. I need to see him. I need to know he's okay. The night offers only silence. Frustrated, I kick a piece of shriveled fruit. I locate the place where we hid from the Valley boys, brush twigs out of the way, and sit.

Near my feet, paper edges poke out from under a stone. I dislodge the paper, shake off the dirt and debris, and find one word handwritten in the ultraviolet spectrum: *Wren*.

My stomach flips as I unfold the paper and read the handwriting glowing brightly before me: *Until we meet again, keep your eyes down and trust nobody.*

I reread the letter until the words are imprinted on my brain. What did he learn that makes him think we can't trust anybody? Fritz's words reverberate through my head on the walk home. Are we in danger? I need answers. But how will I get answers if I can't find Fritz?

Fourteen

*N*oise, commotion, voices. I check the clock on my nightstand. It's 8:00 a.m. Addie is asleep next to me. She must have snuck in overnight. I slide out of bed, tiptoe to my door, and crack it open.

"There must be a mistake." Mom's voice is high-pitched.

"No mistake, ma'am," a man responds.

"How long do we have?" Dad asks.

"Transportation leaves in fifteen minutes."

I step into the hallway. A flashing blue light penetrates the front windows and boomerangs around the living room. Two men stand near the door with my parents. The tall one wears a formal white uniform. The silver stars on his shoulders match his hair.

The other man wears the gray Security Forces uniform. Syringes and other questionable items hang from his belt. His face is scarred from acne and leathered by the sun.

"Commander," he says, without taking his eyes off me.

I wish I wasn't wearing flamingo pajamas. Government officials at our house on a Sunday morning could only mean one thing: they know I breached the Hillcrest boundary. I open my mouth to defend myself, but the words and sentences pile up in my throat like a log jam choking me.

"Wren…" Mom starts to say more but stops and stares at the floor. This is the first time I've seen Mom speechless. Dad stands next to her with his brow furrowed, arms folded.

The silver-haired one referred to as Commander says, "Wren Weiss?"

I place a hand on my bedroom door frame to steady myself. "Yes." The whisper wheezes out my windpipe. I wait for the Commander to approach with handcuffs.

"I'm Commander Cossington and this is Sergeant Lewis. It is our responsibility to ensure your safe journey to Clairemont."

I grip the door frame tighter.

Dad puts an arm around Mom's shoulders. "Wren, you have been assigned to Clairemont. Say goodbye to Abe and Addie and get your things."

Conflicting emotions yank me back and forth, as if I'm the rope in a game of emotional tug-of-war. On one side, fear and anxiety pull with crippling force. On the other, excitement and disbelief grip me.

My mouth goes dry, my legs go weak. Fear and anxiety take the lead. Isn't this what I wanted? Shouldn't I be happy?

Faced with losing my family and leaving Hillcrest, I don't know what I want.

"I heard voices." Addie sits up and rubs the sleep from her eyes.

I take Addie's hand. Years of preparation, of hard work, studying and late-night running, didn't prepare me for the moment I would be forced to say goodbye to my family. Goodbye to the only life I've ever known, to the only place I've called home.

A dull ache starts in the center of my chest and branches out farther and farther, deeper and deeper, growing stronger and stronger until my heart and lungs and stomach feel tied-up, twisted, tangled in a ball of regret. Regret that I spent my time studying when I could have spent more time with the twins. Regret that I didn't appreciate my parents' desire to keep our family together in Hillcrest. And regret that my decisions have affected not only me but my entire family.

I lick my lips and clear my throat. "I have to go away for a little while."

"Please don't go." Addie scoots closer and presses her face into my shoulder.

"I was assigned to Clairemont."

"Will you come back to see us?" Her voice wobbles as if she's holding back tears.

"Of course." I force a smile despite my uncertainty and pull her into a big sister hug.

I grab Fritz's letter from under the pillow, hurriedly change into jeans and a t-shirt, throw on my favorite flannel, and slide Fritz's letter into my back pocket.

Turning back to Addie, I say, "Study hard for the Assessment and maybe you can join me in Clairemont someday. I love you, Addie Bee."

"I love you, too." Her bleak tone and cheerless eyes break my heart.

I pick up the suitcase and join Mom, Dad, and Abe in the living room. The smell of coffee makes me wish I could sit at the table and dine with my family, if only one more time. They all wrap their arms around me.

Footsteps pitter-patter down the hall. Addie throws herself against me. Ten arms intertwined, five sniffling noses. I imagine my tonsils as a dam, holding back the tears building in my chest.

I don't want them to see me cry.

The front door opens. "Two minutes!"

"I'm proud of you." Mom's voice cracks and her lips tremble. "We love you more than you'll ever know."

Mom is usually so brisk and business-like. Seeing her struggle to hold back her emotions makes it harder for me to do the same.

"I love you, too." I give Mom, Dad, Abe, and Addie a final squeeze and ruffle Abe's hair.

Outside, flashing blue lights mounted to the roof of the

Security Forces vehicle have attracted a crowd. The car parked in front of it is silver and futuristic-looking. A digital timer on the car door appears to be counting down.

"One minute!" Sergeant Lewis loads my suitcase into the trunk and returns to my side. "I need to update your passport."

I pull my hair to the side and feel a slight vibration on my neck. As I marvel at the miniature car, the passenger door slides up.

Commander Cossington says, "Take a seat in the Helix and make yourself comfortable. The center console contains water and snacks."

After I lower myself into the car, a seatbelt automatically locks over me and the door closes.

A voice inside the car starts counting down. "Ten... nine... eight..."

My heart starts racing. Where are the door handles? The steering wheel? I search the interior for a hidden latch or button, but there's no way out. I need fresh air. I need out of here. I beat on the interior of the passenger door.

On the porch, Dad holds Addie while Abe leans on Mom, wrapping his arms around her waist. Their eyes are fixed on me. *Relax.* I don't want them to see me panicking.

"Three... two... one..."

Houses and faces whiz by the windows, but it doesn't feel like the car is moving. It feels like I'm in the quiet eye of a hurricane as it rips everything from me that I've ever known or loved.

I rest my forehead against the window until my house and family are out of sight. A familiar face runs toward my house. It's Opal. I press my hand to the window. She stops, puts her hand in the air, and maintains eye contact until we can no longer see each other.

Warm tears blur my vision. The last time I cried was during a race in middle school when a fellow runner tripped me moments before I would have crossed the finish line in first place. I hear Mom's voice: *Never let them see you cry. Never show weakness.* I take a deep breath, dry my eyes, and stare out the window as the car carries me away.

Fifteen

The Helix glides down the tree-lined road. Sunlight strikes the windshield through the shadows of passing trees. Light and darkness, like love and loss, cannot exist without the other.

I picture my family sitting around the kitchen table without me: five dining chairs, one now empty. How long will they feel my absence? With every minute that passes and every mile between us, my sense of loss grows deeper.

"Now entering Clairemont. Population 8,211."

Where did that voice come from? I probe the interior for speakers and direct my voice into the vertical strip above the windshield. "Hello?"

No answer.

"You said the population of Clairemont is 8,000?"

"That is incorrect, Wren. The population of Clairemont is 8,211." The voice is fluid like water washing over river rock: timeless, soothing, melodious.

"Who are you and how do you know my name?" I'm proud my voice doesn't betray my nervousness.

"Your identity was determined by scanning your passport upon Helix entry. Wren Weiss of Hillcrest, born November thirtieth, 2056 to Reproduction Enforcers Joseph and Jacqueline Weiss. Passport privileges updated today, August twenty-eighth, 2072."

"Who are you?" I repeat louder, feeling the weight of unknown eyes.

"I am Golgi, your artificial intelligence companion."

"Golgi? Like Golgi apparatus?" I learned about the Golgi apparatus in my Cellular Biology class.

"Yes. Like the Golgi apparatus in eukaryotic cells, efficient transport is one of my responsibilities."

It's just AI. Nobody is watching me. I sink into the seat and try to relax. The Helix slows as the road widens. Palm trees rise from the center median in a long line like graceful ballerinas stretching skyward. Their green fronds sway in the breeze under blue skies.

Heavy vegetation on my left thins to reveal a bay of turquoise water caressing white sand beaches. Beyond the bay, mountains meet the horizon like protective arms encircling the city.

We pass a sign that reads, *Welcome to Clairemont*. At first glance, Clairemont is charming, tropical, inviting. The sky seems more saturated, the grass greener. Colorful buildings stretch for miles in bright bursts of orange, yellow, and teal.

When the Helix enters a crowded street, neoclassical buildings with wrought-iron balconies, Ionic columns, and grand arches obstruct the ocean view. The architecture looks centuries old and well-preserved. There must have been minimal damage in Clairemont during World War III, whereas Hillcrest was destroyed and rebuilt with homogenous homes and businesses.

I press my forehead against the side window as the Helix cruises through town. In contrast to the century-old Fords and Buicks we have in Hillcrest, passing cars are modern, sleek, and sexy. The Helix sways as they pass in close proximity.

Little girls in bright dresses and polished shoes skip around a fountain in a square teeming with people. Peals of carefree laughter intermingle with the murmur of adult voices and the hum of traffic.

The men exude confidence in perfectly tailored suits that hug their masculine frames. The women wear cardigans and skirts in tropical colors. Opulent jewelry dangles from earlobes, necks, and fingers. Instead of combat boots, their feet are balanced on dainty high heels. I wiggle my toes, thankful for my comfy tennis shoes.

The Helix makes a series of turns. On each street, a similar scene unfolds. Women sashay down the sidewalk arm in arm, hips swaying, stilettos teeter-tottering. Men inhale cigars and blow smoke that swirls and curls around the brims of their fedora hats. Little girls chase each other through the streets.

Clairemont isn't far from Hillcrest, but it buzzes with a different type of energy. Everyone seems so happy. People in Hillcrest strive for duty and honor, not the frivolous pursuit of happiness.

I chew on the corner of my mouth and consider the differences between the place I grew up and the place I will spend the rest of my life.

Will I fit in if I don't smear my face with makeup and adorn myself with colorful dresses and extravagant jewelry? Should I tell people I'm from Hillcrest or will they judge me? Will I marry a man who wears fedoras and smokes cigars? I picture Fritz in a fedora mingling with the crowds in Clairemont.

The excitement of arriving in Clairemont temporarily dulled the sadness of leaving home. I peel my forehead away from the window and lean back. My shoulders sag under the weight of my sadness. I close my eyes and try to block out melancholic thoughts.

My hand spasms and my chin dips. I jerk open my eyes and look around. The road has narrowed and become surrounded by scrappy vegetation. Downtown Clairemont shrinks on the horizon, miles and miles behind us. I face forward and squint to read the road sign we're approaching: *Leaving Clairemont. Authorized Access Only Beyond This Point.*

Leaving Clairemont? My muscles tighten. Does my passport have the proper authorization?

"Golgi, why are we leaving Clairemont?" My voice shakes.

"I am transporting you to your final destination."

"Clairemont *is* my final destination."

"That is incorrect, Wren. Final destination coordinates are 23.1354° North, 82.3590° West."

"I don't understand coordinates. Tell me *exactly* where you are taking me."

"Please relax and enjoy a snack in the center console," Golgi says.

"How do you know I'm not relaxed?"

"Your vital signs indicate anxiety."

Great. Not only is the Nuclei monitoring my period, but this stupid robot car also has access to my heart rate and blood pressure.

"Golgi, in what direction are we going?"

"We are traveling north."

North. I'm not being transported to the facility. My passport didn't react when we crossed the Clairemont border; I have authorization to travel beyond Clairemont, but what in the world is beyond Clairemont? How will my family ever know where I am?

My stomach gurgles. I take Golgi's advice, pry open the center console, and remove a bottle of water and an apple.

"Golgi, how much longer until we arrive at the final destination?"

"We will arrive in two hours, eleven minutes, thirty-one seconds."

I take the last bite of apple and toss it in a compost bin near my feet. I'm consumed by thoughts of my family and my hopes and fears about the future.

Farmland rolls by the window. Coffee crops sag with clumps of red and green coffee cherries; fruit orchards—apples, lemons, and mangos—stretch endlessly in a mosaic of edible color.

Silver machines sparkle in the midday sun and move seamlessly between manicured rows of coffee trees. Metal arms pluck ripe cherries and deposit them in a glass tumbler where they soak up the sun and dry out.

I'm glad I never had to work in the fields. Every year would be the same: coffee, sugar, rice, coffee, sugar, rice. Life would be so boring. Maybe someday machines will be capable of doing all agricultural work. Then, people in the Valley could enjoy more leisure time like residents in other cells.

The Helix makes a sharp right onto a gravel road. Puffs of dust envelop the vehicle as it approaches an enclosed cylinder running parallel to the main road. The Helix climbs a ramp and rolls to a stop when its front-end touches a circular door made up of two interlocking panels.

"Entry to the Hypertran is granted." A robotic voice penetrates the Helix cabin.

The panels slide open and the Helix jerks left to right as it enters the narrow cylinder. It's much cooler now that the sun isn't beating down on me. Shivering, I button my flannel shirt.

My seat starts reclining, forcing me into a supine position. I try to sit up, but the seatbelt is too tight. Staring at the ceiling of the Helix makes me feel like I'm buried alive in a coffin. I want to dig my nails into the ceiling and claw my way out.

The Helix rocks and drops. A whirring purr fills the interior.

"Wheels retracted. Propeller initiated. Prepare for takeoff." Golgi's voice is barely audible over the racket coming from the front-end.

The Helix hurtles forward as if launched from a rocket pad. An invisible weight crushes my chest and pins me to the seat. I dig my fingers into the seat's edge. Narrow bands of white light whiz by the windows.

I desperately want to sit up, but the invisible force holds me down. I push my feet into the floorboard wishing I could apply brakes. A wave of nausea threatens to make the ride even more unpleasant. My saliva thickens and I feel feverish.

After what seems like forever, the pressure on my chest abates. I can breathe. I release my grip on the seat. The noise in the cabin quiets to a hum. It feels like I have cotton stuffed in my ears. I stretch my jaw to make my ears pop. As the Helix speeds through the tunnel, it seems more like a rocket or a train, instead of a car.

Exhausted from prolonged emotional highs and lows, I relax my arms and legs, shift to my side, and curl up as much as possible while being restrained by the seatbelt. I close my eyes and as I drift to sleep, I wonder where we will be when I wake.

Sixteen

I crack open my eyes as the seat moves to an upright position. We're no longer in the Hypertran tunnel. Shielding my face from the sun, I reach for my sunglasses.

The Helix climbs a hill. I lean forward, but I can't see what's on the other side. My impatience grows like kudzu, invading every inch of my body.

As the vehicle crests the summit, glistening glass mansions rise from oceanside cliffs. The square structures look like ice cubes floating in a blue-sky beverage. I imagine them melting under the brutally hot sun and washing down the hill.

The Helix parks at the curb. "Please exit and await further instruction."

The seatbelt disengages and the passenger door opens. Fresh air smelling of salt, sand, and sea foam rushes into the cabin. I swivel and swing my stiff legs outside the Helix, stretching my calves before standing.

The pop of the trunk startles me. After I remove my suitcase and set it on the curb, the Helix disappears down a narrow cobblestone street. I feel stranded, abandoned, alone.

A tall figure stands in the doorway of the closest mansion. Shadows obscure my view of the person's face. A second figure emerges and descends the long, winding path from the mansion to the road. The approaching brunette wears a light blue collared dress with a stiff white apron, white tights, white shoes, and a paper hat.

I wait for her to make eye contact, but her eyes remain focused on the path. I cross my arms over my flannel shirt and tuck my trembling hands.

I should have stayed in Hillcrest. I should have been satisfied with my life there. Maybe it's human nature to never be satisfied, to always want more. Or maybe it's just a personal defect, maybe something's wrong with me.

The woman crosses the sidewalk. Her unsmiling eyes assess me from head to toe. "You're Wren?"

"Yes." I smooth my hair and straighten my shirt. I extend my hand for a handshake, but she ignores me.

"We were notified last month to expect you. I'll take your bag." She picks up my suitcase and turns toward the mansion. No smile. No introduction.

"You were notified last month?" I ask, following her up the steep steps to the house.

"That's right," she says.

How were they notified last month? I took the Assessment yesterday. Maybe she has me mixed up with someone else. The closer we get to the mansion, the more intimidating it is. The double doors slide open and the woman takes my suitcase inside.

"Well, don't just stand there. Come in," an authoritative voice commands.

My feet grow heavy with trepidation. I drag them across the threshold. A statuesque woman stands under a modern light fixture in the foyer, her dark skin radiant against a sleeveless purple gown. A sheer cape attached to a jewel-encrusted choker billows behind her as she moves toward me. Thin, gold bands separate her bulging deltoids and biceps.

Her hair is darker than mine, but instead of hanging limply down her back, it boldly reaches skyward. The number 1001 is tattooed in white ink across her upper chest. I try not to stare, but I can't help it.

She dismisses the woman carrying my suitcase. "Take the suitcase to Wren's room and return to your duties."

"Yes, Saphronia."

"Golgi, have Prisha report to the foyer."

A familiar voice answers, "As you wish."

The woman directs her attention at me. "I understand you were raised by Enforcers in Hillcrest?"

"Yes, that's right." I feel like a shrimp on a grill being seared by her intense gaze. I shove my shaky hands into my jean pockets and focus on a vase of fresh flowers on the nearby console table.

"I'm Saphronia, the Zenith of this house." Her gold sandals click on the hardwood floor.

Channeling my mother's confidence, I square my shoulders, straighten my spine, and meet her eyes as she stands uncomfortably close. To say I feel underdressed in my jeans and flannel is an understatement. I feel like a peasant in the presence of royalty.

"You called for me?" A girl my age steps into the foyer. Thick black hair flows from her ponytail. She wears a zip-front black jumpsuit with her name embroidered in white on one side of her chest and the government logo on the other side.

"Prisha, please give Wren a tour and go over the daily schedule. I expect to see both of you at dinner," Saphronia says.

"Of course." Prisha gives me a welcoming smile, extends her arm, and offers a handshake. "Prisha Patel. Welcome to Ovation, Wren."

"Thanks." My smile is as weak as her handshake.

Prisha leads me into a bright kitchen. Seamless glass walls provide an unobstructed view of the ocean. Gentle waves lap at the cliffs. Sunlight dances across blue-green water as seagulls circle above.

"Wow," I say under my breath.

"Beautiful, right?" Prisha says. "I arrived months ago and I'm still not numb to the view."

The kitchen and dining room are bigger than my entire house in Hillcrest. There are seven chairs at the dining room table. Saphronia probably sits in the ornate chair at the head of the table.

"All materials in Supernova houses are derived from nature. The table was made from acacia trees. The counters are stone from a local quarry. You won't find plastics here. The chemicals in man-made substances are not healthy for Supernovas." Prisha points to the refrigerator. "Drinks are served in glass instead of plastic."

The transparent refrigerator stretches to the ceiling. The top two rows contain bottles filled with green and orange liquid. Below the drinks, fruits and vegetables are coordinated by color.

"What type of drink is that?" I point to the green concoction.

"The green one has folic acid and other important vitamins. The dark orange one includes beta carotenes and antioxidants. We drink one bottle with each meal. In addition to the vitamin drinks, we must drink two quarts of water each day. The water pitcher on the nightstand next to your bed must be empty before lights out at 10:00 p.m."

"Why are there so many rules about what we drink?"

"You get used to the rules." Prisha adjusts her ponytail.

"Where are you from?" It's an innocent question, but her body language changes as soon as the question leaves my mouth.

Her eyes narrow and she crosses her arms over her chest. "The Valley."

"Oh." I try to hide my surprise. How did she end up here? Everyone knows Valley dwellers never test out of the Valley. She must be really smart. Could Fritz have been assigned here, too? I want to ask more, but the change in her demeanor tells me the topic is off limits.

"We have scheduled mealtimes. Breakfast at 8:00 a.m., lunch at noon, dinner at six o'clock. Saphronia joins us only for dinner."

I can't refrain from asking the question I really want to know. "When will I be given a job assignment?"

"Well, you're here, aren't you?" She says in a matter-of-fact tone as if I should already know my job assignment. "I'll show you around. Then, you'll watch a video that explains what's expected of you in your new role."

Impatient to find out about my new career, I follow Prisha down a wide hallway. She steps into a library on the right where long tables are sandwiched between bookshelves holding thousands of identical brown leather books with gold-embossed lettering.

"Every day after lunch, we spend study hour in the library. Make sure it's a productive hour." Prisha nods toward the camera mounted on the ceiling. My arms break out in goosebumps and the hair on the back of my neck stands up.

Prisha continues down the hallway. "Next is the gym. We

exercise for an hour a day. The laundry room is on this floor, but you won't need to worry about laundry. Drop your uniform in the laundry chute in your bathroom. The Nadirs will take care of it. The ocean view room on the left is for meditation and yoga. The last two ocean view rooms are Nadir quarters. Supernova quarters are on the second floor. Zenith quarters on the third floor are off limits."

It's like Prisha is speaking another language. Nadirs? Supernovas? Zeniths? She presses a button next to an elevator in the center of the hallway. A few seconds later, the elevator doors open revealing two giggling girls dressed in black jumpsuits like the one Prisha wears. We step back to allow them to exit.

"Nice flannel, newb." The tall blonde elbows the shorter girl and sneers. My cheeks flush. I want to respond with something clever, but I can never think of something smart on the spot. The short girl has interesting hair—jet black with bubblegum pink tips.

"Leave her alone, Everly," Prisha says. "Her name is Wren."

"Oh, isn't that cute. Meek little lamb Prisha is going to teach the new baby bird to fly," Everly says as the two girls walk away.

Prisha steps into the elevator. Trying to fit two people into the tiniest elevator I've ever seen would be like trying to cram an apple into a walnut shell. My heart rate accelerates.

"That was Everly and Maris. Everly is a bully with a big mouth. Maris isn't bad when they aren't together." The elevator doors start to close. Prisha puts her foot between them. "Are you getting in or what?"

"Are there stairs?" I ask, looking toward the end of the hall.

Prisha steps out of the elevator. "Are you claustrophobic or something?"

"I, um, no. I was cramped in the Helix for hours and need to stretch my legs."

She looks at me skeptically as we continue down the hall. The doors to Nadir quarters are closed. The stairwell is awash in sun from a skylight. We climb the stairs.

Prisha holds the door open to the second-floor hallway. "Your room is the last one on the right. Including us, six Supernovas live on this floor. You saw Everly and Maris downstairs. You'll meet Clover and Blaise at dinner."

Prisha enters the only door on the left. "This is the recreational room. During leisure time, we socialize here."

"The view is breathtaking." I walk around the couches and game tables and stop at the glass wall overlooking the city. "What's that massive building with the white dome over there?"

Prisha moves next to me. "That's the old Capitol building. They renovated it and use it for special occasions now. I heard the floors are made of marble imported from Germany and Italy before the war."

"The tall building over there?" I point to a mirrored skyscraper that looks out of place.

"Academy of Science and Technology," she says.

A gate with three sky-high arches marks the entrance of a massive cemetery. Religious figures sit atop the entrance. Aboveground tombs decorated with crosses and angels sprawl for miles. It looks like a divine entity barfed religious symbols all over the cemetery.

I nod toward the cemetery. "I can't believe people used to bury the dead and think they would be resurrected someday. It seems so silly."

Prisha shrugs. "Selling eternal life was a billion-dollar business back then. It made a lot of people rich."

"I thought the Nuclei destroyed all religious symbols and churches," I say.

She tugs free a strand of hair tangled around her earring and looks toward the cemetery. "They preserved the original structures on this part of the island."

I picture the crude apartments in the Valley and cookie-cutter houses in Hillcrest. My parents think they lead a privileged life. If only they could see this place where people live in oceanfront mansions.

Prisha signals for me to follow her to a media room tucked into the back corner. "Have a seat. When the video ends, head to your bedroom, change into the Supernova uniform in your closet, and I'll see you at dinner. If you need anything, my room is next door to yours."

I sink into the plush recliner. In the bedroom closet, will I find a jumpsuit like Prisha wears or the ugly dress and apron the other girl wore?

Prisha backs out of the room. "Golgi, play the orientation video."

The lights dim and the seat reclines. Cheesy music plays as images of the solar system move across the walls and ceiling. Constellations twinkle around me. I extend my arms and watch the stars sparkle on my fingertips. A warm baritone voice fills the room.

"For thousands of years, Christians, Jews, and Muslims tortured, stoned to death, and beheaded those who didn't worship their chosen god. Although they called their god by different names, all predicted a return of dead prophets after a final battle between good and evil. Extremists took it upon themselves to pave the way for the Second Coming.

"In the years leading up to World War III, religious groups invaded oil-rich lands and sold the oil for profit. They amassed billions of dollars, which they used to achieve their goal: acquiring nuclear weapons to bring about the end of the world.

"And bring about the end of the world, they did.

"In 2022, NASA launched manned spacecraft, *Orion* and *Artemis*, to Mars from the Kennedy Space Center in Florida. Months later, astronauts watched helplessly from space as nuclear bombs mushroomed over Earth.

"The resulting electromagnetic pulse knocked out power grids from Shanghai to London to San Francisco. The astronauts used solar-powered lasers to warn NASA that Earth was under a coordinated attack minutes before the first nuclear bomb struck America. A handful of NASA employees escaped to underground bunkers.

"When *Orion* and *Artemis* crash landed off the coast of Florida in 2024, the astronauts joined surviving colleagues on a nearby inhabitable island. The survivors agreed that eradicating religion was the only way to prevent future generations from experiencing the devastation of war. They formed a new government, the Nuclei, and elected a new leader, Dr. Hahn.

"The Nuclei embarked on a journey to establish a society built on the foundation of science. A society where truth conquers superstition and where all inhabitants live in peace, harmony, and good health."

I yawn and squirm in the recliner. Is the video going to tell me something I don't know? When is it going to get to the part about my job assignment? I yank the recliner handle, kick my feet up, and drum my fingers on the leather armrest.

"The journey toward a more perfect world leads to you. And from you. Your superior genes have earned you the prestigious position of Supernova. Less than one percent of the population serves as Supernovas, yet from you, the New World will be born.

"During your fertile years, you will take part in quarterly egg harvests. To ensure maximum production of viable eggs, you will adhere to a healthy diet and daily exercise routine.

The thermostat in your personal quarters will automatically adjust based on your individual body temperature to provide an optimal environment for egg production.

"Your comfort at Ovation is a top priority. Supernova accommodations include modern oceanfront rooms with comfortable beds to ensure quality sleep.

"On your thirty-sixth birthday, you will retire and assume the highly respected position of Zenith. You will be moved from the Supernova hall to private quarters. You will manage a Supernova household and provide Supernovas with the tools they need to succeed. As a Zenith and trusted leader in Ovation, you will be treated with utmost deference.

"Welcome to Ovation, where the contribution of your genes is your greatest gift to humanity."

The voice fades and the lights come on. I remain seated, staring at the blank walls. My future falls to pieces around me like someone jabbed a needle into each of my childhood dreams, deflating them all.

Move to Clairemont.

Pop!

Become a doctor.

Pop!

Stay in touch with my family.

Pop!

So, let me get this straight. For the next twenty years, my job assignment is *egg production*? What am I? A hen?

Anger burns like a hot coal in the pit of my stomach: glowing, growing, ready to combust. I stand and head toward the door, but first, I draw back my arm and punch the recliner. I punch it again and again. My knuckles sting. My eyes burn.

Golgi's voice interrupts, "Wren, your vital signs are exhibiting signs of stress. Please report to your room and enjoy a cool glass of water."

I drop my arm to my side. I will not cry. "Golgi, the conversations you have, are they monitored?"

"Communication transcripts are sent to the Nuclei mainframe once a day."

Great. I can't even trust Golgi. Who can I trust? I open the door, relieved to see the rec room empty. The pitter-patter of raindrops pelting the window draws my eyes to the cityscape. I can't tell if the view is blurred from water running down the windows or from tears forming in my eyes.

Seventeen

Of all the doors in the hallway, my bedroom door is the only one ajar. I push concerns related to the video out of my mind, dry my eyes, and move down the hall.

The mean girl from the elevator is rummaging through my suitcase on the bed. I can't see her face from the doorway, but I recognize the dark blonde hair tumbling down the back of her jumpsuit. What makes her think she can go through my things?

"What are you doing?" My voice creaks, as if my airway was punctured along with my dreams.

The girl holds up a pair of my underwear and spins them on her index finger. "Nice granny panties, newb."

Blood rushes to my face. I charge over to the bed and try to rip them out of her hand. She raises her arm so I can't reach. Smirking, she drops the panties on the bed. Then, she withdraws my family photo from the interior pocket of the suitcase.

"Is this your family, baby bird?" She examines the photo. "Too bad you'll never see them again." She arches an eyebrow, crumples the photo in her palm, and slowly brings her hand to her mouth.

Is she going to do what I think she is?

She maintains eye contact, puts the photo in her mouth, and starts chewing. She backs toward the door and dramatically spits out the ruined picture. "It's best not to be sentimental here. Consider this your first lesson." She exits the room and closes the door behind her.

I slam shut the suitcase and choke back tears. I'll never give her the satisfaction of knowing she rattled me. I suppress my emotions, pick up the crumpled picture, and pull opposite corners to straighten it, but it remains wet and wrinkled.

I approach the glass wall that faces the ocean and place the photo in a patch of sunlight. Pressing my forehead and palms against the cool glass, I take a deep breath and focus on the ocean.

It's no longer raining. The setting sun paints the horizon in a pastel palette of peaches and pinks. Under the evening sky, the ocean glimmers and glistens. The rhythm of the rolling water washes away the rage and helplessness I felt moments earlier. I'll adjust to life here. I'll make new friends. It's going to be okay. *I'm* going to be okay.

I turn away from the view to survey my new room. Two ivory chairs separated by an end table sit near the window. The giant bed has a mattress nestled between four thick tree trunks that meet in a canopy of tangled branches.

A fluffy white comforter and four large pillows cover the bed—it looks like a sleeping place for a forest nymph, not a simple girl like me.

Inside the closet, seven black jumpsuits and a plush white robe hang. My name is embroidered on each jumpsuit. Built-in drawers store socks, underwear, and pajamas. I retrieve my suitcase from the bed and dump its contents into an empty drawer.

After changing into a jumpsuit, I lie down and adjust the pillows until they comfortably cradle my head. I move my eyes across the curves of intertwining branches overhead. Is Golgi in my bedroom or restricted to common areas?

"Golgi?"

"Yes, Wren?"

"What time is it?"

"The time is 5:55 p.m."

Dinner is in five minutes, but I have no appetite. My stomach is full of dread and anxiety about meeting the other girls. Will they like me or will they all be hateful like Everly? I jump out of bed and head downstairs.

Voices fill the first floor. I turn the corner to the dining room. Everyone else is already seated.

Saphronia notices me in the entryway and rises. "Take your seat, please."

Sliding into the empty seat facing the ocean, I feel self-conscious.

Saphronia gestures toward me and says, "Supernovas, Wren is our new arrival from Hillcrest. Please welcome her and introduce yourselves."

Five voices murmur welcomes followed by names: Everly, Prisha, Clover, Maris, and Blaise. I study the names embroidered on the uniforms across from me: Everly, Prisha, and Clover, in that order. I feel Everly's eyes on me and ignore her.

Each table setting includes an empty plate, silverware, and a bottle of the orange beta carotene juice. Two girls enter the dining room carrying trays of food. I recognize the one who carried my suitcase from the Helix. The other one wears the same blue dress and apron. They serve food from opposite ends of the table.

A pile of green leafy goop is deposited on my plate. It looks disgusting. I glance around to see if anyone else is grimacing at their food. Everyone is eating, except Clover. She pushes food around her plate.

When I look back at my own plate, meat and vegetables have been added. I poke the green stuff with my fork and bring a bite to my mouth. A burst of vinegar coats my tongue. I gulp the orange drink. It tastes like carrots, dirt, and mint. It isn't disgusting, but it isn't good, either.

"Clover, stop playing with your food," Saphronia says. "Remember, it is your responsibility to maintain a nutritious diet to fulfill your role in Ovation."

Clover cuts a piece of meat and puts it in her mouth. Within seconds, she gags and covers her mouth with both hands. The other girls stop eating and stare.

Clover starts heaving, shoves back her chair, and jumps up from the table. She runs to the kitchen sink, holds her white blond hair away from her face, and pukes. My stomach turns at the sound.

"Not again." Everly rolls her eyes.

Prisha looks sympathetic.

Saphronia says, "Golgi, have Berkeley report to the dining room."

The girl who carried my suitcase enters the room. "You called?"

"Prepare a lemon water for Clover and escort her to her room."

"Yes, Saphronia." The girl leaves.

Clover clings to the sink and wipes her mouth with a towel.

Saphronia stands, facing Clover. "You will cease fertility medication for one week."

Clover's eyes fill with tears and her lower lip trembles. "Saphronia. Please! The Fall Egg Harvest is in a few weeks. I can't stand the thought of being demoted."

"You will respect my decision. I want what's best for you girls. You'll see the physician tomorrow. Until then, get some rest." Saphronia takes her seat.

Berkeley re-enters with a glass of lemon water. She takes Clover by the arm and escorts her out of the room.

"What's wrong with her?" I whisper to the redhead next to me.

"OHS," she whispers back.

What on earth is OHS? Is it contagious? I hope not since I was sitting right across from Clover. We continue eating as if nothing happened. There must be an unspoken rule that every bite must be eaten, because everyone cleans their plates.

Saphronia is first to stand. "Supernovas, you may be excused."

The two girls who served dinner clear dishes. In the hallway, the other girls congregate at the elevator speaking in hushed voices. I head for the stairwell. Soft footsteps follow. The red-headed girl's shoulder-length curls bounce as she springs up the stairs behind me.

I wait for her. "What was your name again?"

"Blaise. Well, my real name is Isabel but my moms started calling me Blaise when I was a kid. They said Blaise was more fitting because of my red hair. It's an anagram of Isabel. If you scramble Isabel, you get Blaise."

"That's creative. You said Clover has OHS?"

"This is her second time. The rest of the girls have been lucky so far."

"What is OHS? Is it contagious?" I can't hide my anxiety.

Blaise stops in the middle of the stairs. Her hazel eyes widen and she raises her eyebrows. "You're kidding, right?"

I shake my head.

She throws back her head and hearty laughter reverberates off the walls of the stairwell. "Sorry, I couldn't keep from laughing," she says, wiping tears from her eyes.

"Nobody has ever asked that. It isn't contagious. Fertility treatments sometimes cause Ovarian Hyperstimulation Syndrome."

"How will I know if I have it?" Knowing it isn't contagious doesn't exactly put my mind at ease since I'll soon be following the same regimen as Clover.

"Trust me, you will know." She continues up the stairs. "Your stomach will swell and you may experience vomiting, diarrhea, or fever. We're to report symptoms to Saphronia immediately, but Clover was trying to endure until the Fall Egg Harvest."

"You knew she was sick?" I sweep my eyes across the scattering of freckles on Blaise's cheeks. "Why didn't you tell someone so she could get help sooner?"

Blaise shrugs and opens the door to the second floor. "It's not my place to report her. I'm not a tattletale, unlike some here."

The sound of vomiting comes from the room closest to the stairs.

"Should we check on her?" I ask.

"No, it's best to leave her alone." She pauses at a door next to the elevator. "This is my room. Knock if you need anything."

I pass the rec room and see Everly and Maris playing pool. I close my bedroom door and retrieve my navy flannel from the closet. It smells like home. I change into my flannel and climb into bed. The sheets feel luxurious against my bare legs. I curl up and face the moonlit window. It's weird to be sleeping somewhere other than home.

Eighteen

The next morning, the sound of wind chimes lures me from sleep. I raise up and look around the sun-drenched room. Reality hits me like a splash of ice-cold water across the face. I sink back into the bed and stare at the canopy.

One word buzzes through my mind: coffee. A pinprick of joy dissolves my concerns. I imagine sitting downstairs sipping from a warm mug of cafe con leche while watching the tide roll in.

I slide out of bed, get ready for breakfast, and step into the hallway.

Golgi's voice pulls me back. "Please remember to take your vitamins."

For the first time, I notice the water pitcher, glass, and a saucer with three pills on the bedside table. I walk over and roll the pills across my palm.

"Golgi, what kind of vitamins are these?"

"The vitamins keep Supernovas healthy."

How would anybody know if I didn't take them? I don't see any cameras, but that doesn't mean I'm not being monitored. I pour a glass of water and swallow the pills.

Downstairs, unfamiliar smells greet me. It definitely doesn't smell like breakfast at home. Saphronia and Clover are absent from the dining room. The other girls are having a lively conversation.

Everly says, "During the Summer Harvest, she produced six eggs. I heard only two were viable. She's going to lose her position as Supernova if she doesn't produce more at the Fall Harvest."

She must be talking about Clover.

"Better her than us," Maris says.

"Cheers to that." Everly and Maris clink together their glasses of green juice. Light catches on the golden layer behind Everly's brown eyes. It catches me off guard and I can't stop staring. Do all Supernovas have night vision like me?

"What are you staring at?" Everly snarls, narrowing her eyes.

I quickly look away and bring the glass of vitamin juice to my mouth.

Blaise says. "Why do you have to be such a virus, Everly?"

"When you're the top egg producer in the house, you can criticize Everly, but until then, show some respect," Maris says in a snippy tone directed at Blaise.

"What happens if you lose your position as Supernova?"

"You get demoted to Nadir," Prisha responds.

"What's a Nadir?" I ask, searching Prisha's eyes for a sign that she can see in the dark too, but her eyes look normal.

Berkeley enters the room and serves big bowls of mush with berries. The girls fall silent. Prisha nods toward Berkeley. Is Berkeley a Nadir?

After Berkeley exits, Prisha responds to my question. "Supernovas who can't meet egg quotas are demoted to Nadir. Nadirs cook, clean, do our laundry, and complete other chores the Zenith assigns. Berkeley and Harlowe are the Nadirs under Saphronia's supervision."

Everly pipes in, "In other words, Nadirs are losers and if you don't want to be a loser, follow the rules."

"It's not that easy, Everly," Blaise interjects, pointing her spoon at Everly. "Everyone responds differently to fertility treatments. Clover followed the rules, but her body struggles to produce quality eggs."

"Whatever." Everly brings a spoon of mush to her mouth.

I force myself to try a bite. Warm, firm, and starchy like mashed yuca. The berries make it barely tolerable.

Everly dips her spoon into Prisha's bowl, scoops up her remaining berries, and puts them in her own bowl. "Mm, delicious. Wouldn't you agree, Prisha?"

Nobody challenges Everly. Prisha finishes her drink and stomps out of the dining room. Berkeley enters and clears Prisha's dishes.

"Where can I get a cup of cafe con leche?" I ask Berkeley.

She fixes her gray eyes on mine. "You still have a lot to learn, don't you?"

Everly and Maris snicker.

"You missed a dish," Everly says in a snide tone.

Berkeley directs a cold stare at Everly. If she could shoot daggers from her eyes, I'm sure she would aim them straight for Everly's heart.

Everly and Maris leave the room together.

Blaise leans over and says, "No caffeine, no sugar, no processed foods. All have negative effects on fertility."

"No coffee? For twenty years?" I gape at her. "What about the Zeniths? Can they have coffee?"

"You would have to ask Saphronia." Blaise gets up.

"So, what happens after breakfast?" I ask, following her.

"Everyone reports to the gym for weight-training and cardio, followed by fertility yoga. Then, we shower and get ready for lunch."

"Is it the same schedule every day?"

"Yep." Blaise enters the gym. Everyone but Clover is already seated on stationary bikes.

"Do we need to change into workout clothes?" I ask.

"The jumpsuits were designed to be comfortable during all of our activities. Drop your jumpsuit in the laundry chute in your bathroom and change into a clean one before lunch."

Blaise points at a shelf. "The water bottles are over there.

Drink from the one labeled with your name. It counts toward the mandatory amount we have to drink each day."

After exercising, my arms and legs feel rubbery. Heat rises from my chest and back. Sticky and eager to shower, I unzip the jumpsuit a little and fan it away from my chest.

My temples throb with a dull headache. Probably from skipping coffee this morning. For a coffee addict, there aren't many things worse than caffeine withdrawal. I guzzle water and join the others in the yoga studio.

Maris points at me and snaps her fingers. "Socks and shoes off, newb."

The floor squishes under my feet. Shades of blue, violet, and pink mix together to form an image of outer space. I sit on the Vega star in the parallelogram-shaped Lyra constellation at the back of the room.

Golgi guides us through breathing techniques and deep stretches. We move from downward dog to warrior pose, from butterfly pose to seated forward fold.

At the end of the session, Golgi says, "Namaste."

The girls rise and collect their footwear.

In the hallway, I catch up to Blaise. "What's next?"

"Shower, change clothes, and report to the dining room. After lunch, we spend study hour in the library and then we walk to the spa. We aren't allowed to be alone outside the Supernova neighborhood, so make sure you stay with the group. After the spa, we meditate, and then we have free time before dinner."

After lunch, voices spill into the hallway from the foyer. Saphronia and a well-dressed man speak quietly near the front door. He makes brief eye contact with me as I pass. I brush my teeth and then make my way to the library.

From Nadir quarters, the voices of Harlowe and Berkeley rise and fall in a heated argument. Berkeley sees me walking by and slams the door. Geez. It's not like I was eavesdropping.

In the library, Blaise and Prisha peruse books. Maris works in sudoku workbooks. Clover solves calculus equations. Everly stares out the window at the city. I admire the rich leather spines on the bookshelf closest to the door, choose a book, and take it to a table near the window.

I flip open my book, *The Greatest Scientific Breakthroughs of All Time,* to a random chapter: "DNA Data Storage."

> In 2012, scientists discovered they could store millions of gigabytes of data in only one gram of DNA by converting the data into binary code that corresponds to nitrogenous bases. Once the data is encoded, computers decode it using DNA sequencing technology. DNA as a data storage medium opens the door to infinite possibilities due to the quantity of data that can be stored, the low error rate, and the indestructible quality of DNA.

I stifle a yawn and skim the diagrams related to decoding data stored in living cells. There must have been a bazillion gigabytes of data before the war when billions of people inhabited Earth. DNA as a storage medium seems irrelevant today. A loud beep pierces my thoughts.

"Five-minute bathroom break before we leave for the spa," Everly says.

Nineteen

I follow the other Supernovas single file down the steps in front of House of Saphronia. The balmy breeze whips through my hair. Being outside with the wind blowing my hair and the sun warming my face brings me comfort in this strange place.

We pause on the sidewalk and watch a Helix pull up to a mansion down the street. A girl climbs out of the Helix, her jeans and t-shirt wrinkled, hair disheveled. Even from this distance, I sense her bewilderment.

A twinge of sympathy flits through me. A Nadir who looks as friendly as Berkeley greets her without a smile and takes her suitcase.

"Another newb arrives in Ovation," Everly announces.

"Where do you think she's from?" Blaise asks.

"Not Hillcrest," I say.

"I didn't see her face," Prisha says.

Everly scoffs. "The only way people from the Valley end up

in Ovation is by mistake. I still don't know how you ended up here, Prisha."

"The Nuclei doesn't make mistakes," Blaise says confidently as if she's a Nuclei devotee.

At the end of the street, a wrought-iron gate blocks entry to town. Or maybe, it blocks access to the Supernova neighborhood. Everly approaches the gate, lifts her hair off her neck, and stands in front of the passport scanner.

The gate yawns open revealing a quaint cobblestone street dotted with various businesses: a florist, a bakery, an art gallery, a store called Gadgets Galore.

The storefronts gleam. Everything is so pristine, so clean. No fingerprints on the glass. No shoe marks on the tile. A billboard cradled by blue sky and nestled between wispy clouds displays a silhouette of a pregnant woman's profile. A red X stretches over the woman.

I nudge Prisha and point at the billboard. "What does that mean?"

"Pregnancies are illegal in Ovation," Prisha says.

I frown. "Illegal? In Hillcrest, pregnancies are celebrated with parties and gifts."

Everly says, "In Clairemont, we have homecoming parties when babies are placed in their new homes. At the Spring Harvest, I was talking to Leo with Security Forces and he said natural pregnancies might be illegal everywhere someday. He works at Headquarters so he hears things."

Maris shoots a quick eyebrow flash and knowing glance at Everly. "You were doing a lot more than *talking* to Leo." She brings the back of her hand to her mouth and starts kissing it. "Oh, Leo."

Everly laughs and shoves her. "Kissing isn't illegal. We can smooch all we want."

Prisha says, "Right after I moved to Ovation, a Supernova at House of Rosalind got pregnant. They did a DNA test to find the father's identity. Then, both were taken into custody."

Blaise says, "You're talking about boy-crazy Geneva. Rules are rules. She knew what she was getting herself into."

"What happened to them?" I ask.

Prisha shrugs. "Nobody ever saw them again. Maybe they were banished to the Caves."

Maris snorts. "Yeah, right. The Nuclei would never allow Geneva's eggs to be flushed down the toilet. They probably have her locked up right under our noses."

A grocery store across the street advertises genetically engineered fruit and vegetables. Nadirs congregate near the entrance. They look at us the way men in the Valley looked at my dad the night we drove by Charlie's bar.

"Why do they hate us?" I ask.

"Because they can't be us," Everly says flippantly as she admires her reflection in each window we pass.

Something furry with long floppy ears darts by, brushing against my foot as it scuttles into a narrow alley near the grocery store. I jump back and bump into Maris. From across the street, the creature watches us with beady red eyes. I stare at it until it turns and vanishes.

"What was that?" I suck in a breath of heavy, humid air.

"You should have seen your face!" Everly doubles over laughing. "Oh my Galileo, that was priceless."

The other girls join in the laughter. Prisha covers her mouth, keeping her laughter bottled up so tightly her body shakes and her eyes water. If I poked her in the stomach, laughter would probably explode from her mouth, nose, and ears.

Boisterous laughter bursts from Blaise's lips, loud and robust, pinballing down alleys, bouncing off surfaces, surrounding us in merriment.

Clover must not be the laugh-out-loud type, but her twinkling eyes and upturned lips reflect her amusement. I smile, relieved to see everyone getting along.

"It was just a harmless cabbit," says Maris between laughs. "It's a hybrid cross between a cat and a rabbit. That's why it looks like a cat with a cotton tail and rabbit ears. They may hiss and growl, but they don't bite."

Blaise says, "Wait until you see the cogs and flurtles."

"Cogs and flurtles?" I thought I had already learned all the weird lingo here.

"Cogs are cat-dog hybrids," Blaise says. "They're cute but aggressive so don't approach them or feed them. Unlike cabbits, they will bite and they have razor-sharp teeth."

Clover says, "Flurtles are bioluminescent turtles. Fluorescent proteins derived from Aequorea victoria are inserted into the genome of the turtle via transgenesis. If done correctly during germ-line editing, the gene is passed to offspring."

Maris moves her hands as if she's using sign language. "Clover is trying to say that jellyfish protein inserted into turtle DNA makes turtles glow. Frogs and flowers also luminesce under certain light conditions. It's pretty cool. Check out the ocean from your bedroom window at night."

"Clover was always the teacher's pet," Everly says with a hint of jealousy in her voice.

Maris playfully tugs on Clover's ponytail. "Remember that time in middle school when you hijacked Ms. Griffin's transceptor and gave everyone in the class higher grades?"

A mischievous smile plays at Clover's lips.

"If I would have done that," Everly says, "Ms. Griffin would have locked me in detention and thrown away the key."

"You all went to school together in Clairemont?" I ask.

"Yeah," Everly says. "Clover was the overachiever, but that isn't working out so well for her here."

If they are from Clairemont and Prisha is from the Valley, where is Blaise from?

We make a right turn and Greenberry Spa comes into view. The sun reflects off the white stucco building, nearly blinding me with its brilliance. A bundle of berries—plump and green and glossy—make up the logo.

"We're here." Prisha swings open the glass door.

A blast of icy air hits my face. It smells cozy and crisp, like lavender and eucalyptus. I admire the posh interior. High ceilings. Marble floors. Black-and-white wallpaper in a seamless loop of damask.

A redhead wearing a black dress and layers of jewelry greets us. "Welcome back, ladies. I see House of Saphronia has a newcomer." Her mellifluous voice floats over the lobby.

"Wren arrived over the weekend," Blaise says.

"From Hillcrest," Everly adds in a snarky tone that makes me want to shove her.

A flick of curiosity crosses the woman's face. "Hillcrest? Interesting. We don't get many of you here."

What's that supposed to mean? I feel a blush sweep over my cheeks. My face is probably as red as her lipstick.

"I'm Lucinda. Welcome to Greenberry Spa." She approaches and vigorously pumps my hand. Then, she moves to the front of the group. "Ladies, you know the drill. I will escort you to the locker room. You will change into robes and take your places for the fertility massage." Spinning on her stilettos, she leads us out of the foyer.

I trail behind the other girls, taking everything in. We don't have spas in Hillcrest. A woman who looks identical to Lucinda passes us. On the right, Zeniths sit in lounge chairs with attendants massaging their feet, shoulders, and temples. All Zeniths wear the same purple gown and have numbers tattooed across their chests.

Saphronia nods to acknowledge us as we walk by. Another version of Lucinda kneels before Saphronia rubbing her feet. Every time I blink, there's another Lucinda. Twins, triplets, quadruplets, quintuplets. Fiery red hair frames the same face.

An attendant inserts a needle into Saphronia's arm. A long tube runs from the needle to a bag filled with blood. I come to a dead stop and stare. Memories lash at me. Crying babies, armed guards, comatose girls. Teenagers, their blood sucked dry. Is that their blood?

Maris grips my arm. "What are you staring at?"

"I… I…" I try to speak, but I can't form words.

"It's just blood plasma transfusions. Rejuvenation treatments. All old people get them."

"Why do Zeniths have numbers on their chests?" I ask.

"It's the total number of eggs they produced as Supernovas."

"Saphronia produced a thousand?" My jaw nearly hits the floor.

"One thousand and one." Maris corrects me.

My mind is jumbled with concerns and questions. Ovation and Guantanamo are connected somehow. We round a corner and enter the locker room.

I open a locker next to Clover and pull out a white robe and slippers. "Did you guys notice all the attendants look identical?"

Everly cocks an eyebrow. "You aren't in Kansas anymore, Dorothy. Ovation is the Nuclei's playground."

"Who's Dorothy?" I ask. Nobody answers.

"I heard redheads were genetically modified to happily serve others. They don't have a lot going on up here though." Maris taps her head and whistles.

"Don't be a moron," says Blaise. "I'm a redhead and I'm smarter than all of you."

Everly and Clover chuckle.

"Where are you from, Blaise?" I ask as I fold my clothes and stack them in a locker.

She starts to respond, but Everly cuts her off. "Blaise was raised in Ovation by Milkmaids."

"Really?" As soon as the word leaves my mouth, I feel stupid for being so gullible.

"True story. Now, let's go." Blaise slams her locker door and leads everyone into the hallway.

We enter a dimly lit room with six massage tables. The other girls disrobe and climb onto the massage tables. I slide under the sheet on the remaining table and shimmy out of my robe.

Six Lucindas enter the room simultaneously.

The one hovering over me speaks in a hushed tone. "My name is Dulce. I will be your masseuse today and every day hereafter. Please lie on your back and relax during the fertility massage.

"Visualize happy, healthy ovaries frolicking in a golden meadow on the eve of the Harvest. Supple ovaries from which the entire world will be born."

She waves her hand over me, as if holding a magic wand. "Deep breathing, relaxation, and visualization are key to a successful Harvest."

I stifle a giggle. Happy, healthy, frolicking ovaries? Dulce places a warm cloth over my eyes. I struggle to relax and visualize happy ovaries. What do ovaries look like? Slimy eggs? Spongy globs? This has to be the stupidest thing I've ever been asked to do.

Dulce rubs warm oil into my arms. The heavy amber scent reminds me of home. A waterfall feature on the back wall creates soothing white noise. I ignore my discomfort as Dulce kneads my arms and shoulders.

When she folds back the sheet, I'm glad I kept on my sports bra and underwear. Her hands move down my ribs and pulse over my lower stomach. It tickles. My stomach muscles tense. I grip the sheets in my fists.

A bubble of laughter expands in my throat. I swallow hard but it floats higher, growing bigger and bigger until a high-pitched giggle spills from my lips. I kick my feet and squirm away from Dulce's hands. The other girls laugh until someone shushes us.

"You are ticklish," Dulce says. "I will change the technique. Now relax, inhale the pure oxygen, and practice your visualization as I massage the ovaries."

I take a deep breath and try to think of anything other than ovaries. I listen to the gushing water and visualize eating oranges at the waterfall with Fritz. I picture the sun in his hair. The way he looked at me. The way he made me feel. Like I mattered. Like I was no longer alone.

As Dulce's palms sweep over my calves, her hands draw the tension from my muscles. Life could be worse than getting a mandatory massage every day. I relax and let a quiet calm settle over me. The cloth covering my eyes is slowly peeled away.

Dulce stands over me and offers a bottle of water. "It's important to stay hydrated after the massage."

"Will it count toward my daily water intake?" If it doesn't count, I'm not drinking it.

"Yes, the amount you drink at the spa is logged into the system."

I take a long drink from the bottle and pass it back to her.

"You may return to the locker room and get dressed." She holds out the robe.

I tie the belt, slide on the slippers, and step into the hall.

"Was that you laughing?" Clover smiles.

"I couldn't help it. I've never had a massage before. I didn't know it would tickle."

Clover laughs and rakes her hair away from her forehead. "I still flinch when they touch my ribs."

In the locker room, Clover points to a basket of rolled towels. "We have twenty minutes to shower." She removes her robe, baring her swollen stomach.

"How are you feeling?" I ask.

Her green eyes settle on mine. I use the opportunity to look for the telltale glow beneath her irises. I don't see it, but her eye color is unnatural: the green is too bright, too brilliant.

"I feel a little better, but I expect the symptoms to return as soon as we start the cycle of shots in two weeks." She drapes a towel around her shoulders.

"Shots?" This is the first time I've heard any mention of shots.

"Two weeks before Harvest, a daily injection is administered for ten days. The shots kick the ovaries into overdrive, causing them to produce eggs as if they were an egg factory. On the tenth day, we receive a trigger shot. Then, we have three days to rest before the Harvest."

"I hate needles. Is there any way to get out of the shots?"

"Nope. Mandatory. Let's shower and get out of here." Clover heads to the shower stalls.

I grab a towel and follow. My bare feet smack the wet floor. Humming water pipes and the voices of showering Supernovas waft over the stalls. I step into the shower, roll my ponytail into a bun, and soap off the greasy oil Dulce applied.

After everyone is showered and dressed, we retrace our steps through the spa. The chairs that held the Zeniths are now empty.

"See you later, Lucinda," Everly calls.

"Have a good day, ladies."

My pupils shrink in the sun. The heat sucks up every ounce of moisture from my skin. On the main street, six girls in green jumpsuits walk toward us.

"Why are their clothes green?" I ask.

Prisha says, "House of Lillith wears green. House of Khadija wears yellow. House of Juliette, red."

Clover says, "House of Lillith outperformed everybody at the Spring and Summer Harvests. Cambria is the only one in Ovation who produces more eggs than Everly. She's the brunette in front."

"Look who it is. House of Saphronia." The girl called Cambria grins at us. Her perfectly symmetrical face could have been the model used in the Assessment packet section on beauty. Oval face, high cheekbones, flawless skin the color of apricots. Thick hair, smooth and shiny, despite the humidity.

"Who's the newbie?" A tall girl with mahogany skin and a head full of braids tilts her head at me. Long eyelashes frame curious eyes.

"She just got here from Hillcrest." Everly looks Cambria up and down, sizing up her competition.

"I'm Wren." I skim the faces of the other girls—all so perfect, so pretty. I smooth the frizzy fly-aways falling out of my bun.

Maris leans into the group and lowers her voice. "Got any smokes on you, Maven?"

"Five ovals." A brunette with frosty lilac lipstick and violet eyeliner arches an overplucked eyebrow and steps closer to Maris.

"Five ovals? For one cigarette? That's robbery. I'll give you three." Maris whines like a child begging for candy.

"Fine." Maven discreetly pulls a cigarette from her pocket. Her purple fingernails flash in the sunlight. Pretending to shake each other's hands, Maven and Maris complete the exchange.

Prisha chews on a fingernail. Her eyes dart down side streets and linger on nearby windows. "Maris, if Saphronia catches you with contraband, you'll get all of us in trouble."

"Saphronia will never know as long as you keep your mouth shut," Maris says.

The girls from House of Lillith say their see-ya-laters and resume their walk to the spa.

"Better luck at the Fall Harvest, Everly." Cambria spins around and winks at Everly.

Everly clenches her fists and narrows her eyes as she watches the other Supernovas walk away. If anyone is a sociopath in this group, it's Everly.

"Maris, what were the things you gave that girl?" I ask.

"Ovals are the currency here. You get one oval for each egg you produce at Harvest. I got fourteen at the last Harvest and still have five left."

"What can you buy with them?"

"I bought moisturizer and a journal this year. There's a black market for sugar, caffeine, and smokes. You just have to know who to ask. You can always count on Maven for smokes."

"Why do you think she sells cigarettes to the other houses, Maris?" Blaise asks. "She doesn't even smoke. She wants House of Lillith to keep winning the Harvest competition. Keep buying smokes from her and you'll end up demoted to Nadir."

"Oh, please. I always produce as many eggs as everyone else despite indulging in a little pleasure occasionally. If you ask me, you could use a smoke yourself, Blaise."

"Yeah, but you affect all of us when you do things known to reduce egg count," Prisha says, kicking a stone out of her path.

"If anybody is affecting all of us with low egg count, it's Clover," Maris retorts. "If you want to complain about somebody holding us back, why don't you talk to her."

"I thought you were my friend, Maris." Clover shoves her hands in her pockets and stares at the ground.

"I am, but you know I'm right," Maris says in an unapologetic tone.

"Can I see the ovals?" I hold out my hand.

Maris fishes ovals out of her pocket and drops them in my palm. The sun glints off the opalescent egg-shaped surface. I flip one between my fingers. It feels fragile, like it could easily snap in two. I pass the ovals back to Maris. She drops them in her pocket as the neighborhood gate swings open.

Maris says to Everly, "Don't let Cambria get to you like that."

Everly responds, "I swear to Galileo if she taunts me again, I will cut out her ovaries, fry them in a skillet, and eat them for dinner. We'll see how many eggs she produces then."

Blaise and I exchange shocked looks. She points to the side

of her head and makes circles while mouthing *cuckoo*. As we climb the steps to the house, she says, "Next we meditate. Then, we have an hour of free time before dinner."

During meditation, I sit in the same spot I chose for yoga. I move to a cross-legged position like the other girls and stare at the ocean waves crashing against the cliffs while listening to a meditation soundtrack featuring bamboo chimes and falling water.

Concentrating on the music and rhythm of the tide, I try to block out Everly's fidgeting. Her legs jounce up and down and she keeps adjusting her position while everyone else sits motionless. When the beep sounds, Everly rushes to the back, puts on her shoes, and leaves the room ahead of everyone.

I tie my shoelaces next to Clover. "What's her problem?"

"Who? Everly? I've learned to avoid her when she's in one of her moods. I suggest you do the same." Clover leaves the room.

Blaise remains seated, stretching. "You can't fix a cracked egg."

I chuckle as I walk down the hallway. Describing Everly as a *cracked egg* is right on.

A loud repetitive thud fills the hall. I glance inside the gym. Everly runs at breakneck speed on a treadmill. I wonder if she can run faster than me. In the stairwell, curiosity overcomes me. I climb the steps to the third floor. The door has ZENITH QUARTERS stenciled across it.

On the fourth floor there's an unmarked door. I feel like I'm somewhere I shouldn't be, like I'll get in trouble if anyone catches me. I push open the door with little effort. Steps lead to a red door with a sign that says ROOFTOP ACCESS. I want to check out the roof, but what if the doors lock behind me? I'll return later with something to wedge between the door and frame.

The Supernova floor is quiet. I close my bedroom door, sit on the floor near the closet, and pull out the crumpled photograph of my family. Despite Everly's teeth marks, I can make out the outlines of Mom, Dad, Abe, and Addie. I kiss my fingertips, place them on the faded image, and try to telepathically send them my love.

Next, I take out the letter from Fritz. I reread the faded message: *Until we meet again, keep your eyes down and trust nobody.* I slide the letter under my pillow and curl up facing the ocean. The sun looms above the horizon like a soft-boiled egg split open, its yolk oozing shimmering shades of copper and amber and gold. Seagulls salt and pepper the egg-white sky.

What would Fritz think of this view? He would probably rappel down the cliffs to explore what lies below. What would he think if he knew that instead of attending medical school and becoming a doctor, I'm just a hen held captive at a hatchery? Instead of getting married and having children and growing old with a partner, I'm destined to be alone.

Forever and always, alone.

My smile unrolls into a frown. I hope Fritz never finds out. I would be utterly embarrassed, completely humiliated if he could see me in this weird world of egg-cubating and fertility rituals. I roll over on my back, let out a sigh, and stare at the tangled branch canopy.

Why does the thought of being alone bother me? So what, if I never get married or have children. It's not like I ever dreamed of meeting my soulmate or planning my wedding or having kids of my own, but now that it's impossible, unattainable, forbidden, I want it more than ever. I want to wake up next to someone who loves me the way Dad loves Mom.

A heavy weight settles on my chest. A lump rises in my throat. I blink back tears. This is my life now. I have to accept it. I have to find happiness here. But how can I find happiness when the path chosen for me is not a path I would have chosen for myself?

Twenty

I sneak up to the rooftop after everyone goes to bed. The roof is as I imagined: wide, flat, and sprawling. The moon provides enough ambient light to prevent my night vision from kicking in. On cloudless, moonlit nights like this, every little star in the sky is visible.

I walk to the side of the roof that overlooks the city. Darkness engulfs neighboring houses while lights burn brightly from the windows of faraway buildings.

I wander to the other side where the ocean and cliffs crash together in nature's endless dance. Bracing myself against the wind, I close my eyes and listen to the timeless chorus.

"Pretty gutsy for you to be up here alone, newb."

I jerk open my eyes.

Maris approaches with a blanket thrown over one arm. She spreads the blanket and takes a seat facing the ocean. "Glorious, isn't it?"

She strikes a match against the roof and lights the cigarette she acquired from Maven. Her pink hair is luminous in the moonlight. She pats the blanket.

I sit next to her. "How do you make your hair pink?"

"I mix crushed flowers with cleaning agents and soak my hair in the mixture."

"I'm surprised they let you do that here."

Maris takes another drag on the cigarette. "They don't care what you do as long as you keep laying golden eggs." She releases a cloud of smoke from the side of her mouth. "What do you think of this place?"

"It's…" I consider the bland food and daily regimen, "nice."

Maris laughs. "Nice? It's nice if your aspirations include laying eggs and never being loved." She holds the cigarette out.

I hesitate.

Maris reads my mind. "There are no cameras up here."

The sweet smell of tobacco takes me back to evenings at home when neighbors sat on porches smoking cigars, watching the day fade.

I take the cigarette, bring it to my lips, and inhale deeply. Smoke fills my throat and chars my lungs. I swear my bronchial tubes are withering, my alveoli shriveling. I start coughing, eyes watering, smoke spilling from every hole on my face.

Maris chuckles. "You might think it's nice, but I'm not staying here."

"But we don't have a choice." I cough the words out of my dry throat and hand the cigarette back to Maris.

"I would rather leap off this rooftop than be a caged chicken for the rest of my life. I'm going to find a way back to Clairemont." She sounds determined.

Picturing the streets of Clairemont filled with men and women flirting in fancy clothes and children laughing and playing, I can't imagine growing up in such a decadent place.

She stands and flicks her ashes. "Look over there. See the flurtles?"

I rise and look in the direction she points. Glowing green and blue dots streak across the shore. Farther out, pockets of water ripple and roll as though bioluminescent mermaid tails writhe beneath the surface.

"Why do you want to go back to Clairemont?" I ask.

The crescent moon reflects in Maris' brown eyes. She looks at me as if trying to determine if I'm trustworthy.

I reassure her. "I won't tell anybody."

"My boyfriend is in Clairemont. We're going to build a boat and sail away together." She stretches her arms toward the water.

On the world maps we studied in school, oceans covered the entire globe with the exception of one thumb-sized land mass: Genova Island. Sailing away from the island would be suicide.

Waves crest and crash and roll in from the dark horizon. Staring at the vast void, I wonder if she's lost her mind.

"What if there's nothing out there?"

"What if there is?" Maris responds.

I lower my eyebrows and chew on my lip, contemplating the possibility that other land masses exist. "How will you get back to Clairemont?"

"Easy. I'll sneak on the train that delivers food and supplies from other parts of the island. It arrives and departs at the same time every Monday and Wednesday."

"How do you know it travels through Clairemont? What about your passport?"

"Think about it. Ovation is on the north coast. Most of the food supply is grown on the south coast near the Valley. The train has to go through Clairemont and Hillcrest. I'm not worried about my passport. We gained additional travel privileges when we were assigned to Ovation."

"Why don't you and your boyfriend just stay in Clairemont?"

"We can't stay in Clairemont." She takes another drag on the cigarette, sits on the blanket, and grinds the cigarette stub on the roof, snuffing out the last spark. Wisps of smoke billow from her mouth and nose. "He's married."

I inhale sharply and stare at her. "But divorce is illegal."

"Exactly," she says. "That's why we're leaving."

I sit. "Why didn't you date someone who wasn't married?"

Maris cuts her eyes at me. "I see the disapproval on your face. Don't judge. All men in Clairemont are married."

"That's impossible." I study her face for a sign that she's joking. "What about the boys at your school?"

"Pfft." She blows air between her lips. "As if there are guys our age in Clairemont. The youngest men in Clairemont are like ten years older than us. You knew guys our age in Hillcrest?"

"I have a younger brother and went to school with a ton of boys." I can't believe how different our lives could be when we lived only hours from each other.

"You have a boyfriend?" Her expression is full of curiosity.

An image of Fritz pops into my mind. I shake my head and change the subject. "Didn't it seem strange that there were only girls at Clairemont schools?"

"Why would it seem strange? It's all I ever knew." Maris yawns and stands. "It's getting late."

I scoop up the blanket and hand it to her. At the door, she bends down, grabs my shoe, and passes it to me. I collect the other shoe I used to prop open the door and we move as silently as ghosts through the house.

Twenty-one

The blanket presses against my sore abdomen. I grimace and toss the covers off. Tiny bumps dot my lower stomach where fertility shots were administered.

We received the final trigger shot three days ago. I feel slightly bloated but not too bad, considering I've been stabbed in the abdomen every day for the past two weeks.

Today is the big day: October first, the date of the Fall Harvest. I still haven't figured out why they refer to the Harvests as Spring, Summer, Fall, and Winter when the island has only a wet and dry season.

I get up, swallow the vitamins, and get ready for breakfast. As I walk down the hallway, Everly emerges from Clover's bedroom. She looks surprised to see me. She quickly closes Clover's door and hits the elevator button.

"What were you doing in Clover's room?" Her hands are empty. She didn't take anything.

Everly ignores me and steps into the elevator.

I knock on Clover's door. "Clover?" No answer. I open the door and step inside. Nothing looks out of place.

On the first floor, voices I don't recognize travel down the hall from the foyer.

"…found this morning," says a male voice.

I glance in the foyer and see Saphronia standing with two Security Force officers. In the dining room, each plate has a single hard-boiled egg centered on it. Instead of juice, there's a glass of water.

I sit and poke at the egg. "Is this a joke?"

I hate eggs. Especially slimy boiled eggs.

"We aren't allowed to eat anything the morning of Harvest except for a single egg for luck," Blaise says.

I raise my eyebrows at her. "Luck? I thought we were supposed to abstain from superstitions, yet they expect us to eat an egg for luck?"

Everly taps her egg with a spoon until the shell fractures. She digs her fingernails into the cracks and peels away the shell. I imagine stinky egg white stuck under her fingernails. Once the egg white is exposed, she holds it in the air.

"To luck." She sinks her teeth into the egg as if it were a delicious apple.

"Supernovas, may I have your attention, please." Saphronia enters with Berkeley, Harlowe, and the men from Security Forces.

"Captain Norcross and Lieutenant Kellum are here to deliver disturbing news," Saphronia says. "The body of a Supernova from House of Lillith was found this morning near the cliffs."

I picture the girls we pass sometimes on the walk back from the spa. Which one was it? Cambria? Maven? The tall brunette? One of the others?

Captain Norcross walks closer to the table. "We suspect foul play. We will know more about the cause of death when the coroner completes her analysis."

"There was one curious detail," Lieutenant Kellum says.

Berkeley and Harlowe raise their eyebrows at each other. Berkeley taps her foot, bites her nails, and fidgets. What are they worried about? A Supernova was killed, not a Nadir.

"The eyes were removed before the body was disposed of," Lieutenant Kellum says.

Prisha inhales sharply.

I glance at Everly. Was the killer targeting people with eyes like ours? Why would the eyes be removed when a Supernova's value is tied to her ovaries? It doesn't make sense. Who would want to kill us and why? A chill settles over the room and sends shivers down my spine.

Captain Norcross says, "Keep your eyes and ears alert at the Harvest today. If you have any information that might be helpful to our investigation, report to your Zenith. Supernovas are one of the most valuable resources in Ovation. Rest assured, we will catch the person responsible."

"Thank you, Captain and Lieutenant. Harlowe, please see the men out so they may notify the other houses." The men thank Saphronia and follow Harlowe.

Saphronia turns to us and says, "Do any of you have anything to share with me?"

We all shake our heads. Clover's eyes are red and puffy.

"If you hear anything suspicious, you will report to me immediately. Despite the disturbing incident, the show must go on. After breakfast, you will find custom-made Harvest dresses in your rooms. Be dressed and in the foyer at ten o'clock sharp." Saphronia leaves and the room is quiet until the sound of her footsteps fade.

Everly breaks the silence. "I hope it's Cambria."

"Everly!" Maris scolds in an indignant tone.

"What?" Everly says. "If she isn't at Harvest, I'll have no competition." She leaves the room with a pep in her step.

The realization that Everly would do anything to win makes me uneasy. Would she kill? An uncomfortable silence expands between me, Clover, Blaise, Maris, and Prisha. I'm certain we're all thinking the same thing, but nobody says it out loud. I get up from the table, leaving the egg untouched. My stomach growls in protest.

In my bedroom, I find a white dress with a black satin sash splayed out across the bed. Shiny black heels stand upright on the floor. I've never worn such a fancy dress or heels. I unzip the jumpsuit, letting it fall to the floor.

Pulling the dress over my head, I gingerly push my arms through the delicate lace sleeves and twist it over my torso. The fluffy layers of the skirt fall slightly past my knees. I tie the sash around my waist and slide my feet into the heels.

I walk to the bathroom mirror to assess my appearance. The lace bodice is lovely. The lace ends where the sash begins. I move my hips and watch the chiffon skirt whirl and twirl.

Taking the hairbrush from the vanity, I pull the bristles through my hair until it shines. I look more like a bride than a Supernova. For the first time, I feel pretty.

Downstairs in the foyer, Prisha, Blaise, and Clover apply sunscreen. Blaise finishes and hands the bottle to me. "We'll be in the sun for hours."

I rub sunscreen into my face, neck, and legs.

Saphronia enters the foyer and says, "Line up single file and face me."

Everly rushes in late and takes her place at the front of the line. Saphronia inspects each of us. She straightens my sash and adjusts Prisha's hem. Then, she hands Everly a compact mirror and a gold tube.

Everly uncaps the tube, holds the mirror up, and applies scarlet lipstick. She rolls her lips together and passes the mirror and lipstick to Maris. Maris applies lipstick and passes it to Clover. When it's my turn, I wish I wasn't last to use it. After I smudge the color across my lips, I smile at the rosy-lipped girl in my reflection.

Saphronia collects the lipstick and compact. "Supernovas, today is your opportunity to give back to the community. Through your contribution, a more perfect world will be born. Never underestimate the importance of your role. I wish you all a successful Harvest."

Carefully descending the outdoor steps, I extend my arms for balance and keep my eyes fixed on my wobbling high heels. It's a beautiful sunny day. Parade floats line the normally empty streets. The House of Saphronia float has an elevated purple throne at the back. A smaller throne is centered under a gold, egg-shaped frame.

Supernovas file out of neighboring mansions and take their places on the floats. They all wear the same white dress with a sash and shoes in the color of their House.

On the sidewalk, an armed guard helps Saphronia onto the float. She takes her place on the largest throne. Next, Everly sits in the center throne.

Five pedestals squat at Everly's feet. Great. I guess that's where the rest of us will be sitting. I squint at the House of Lillith float, but I can't tell which Supernova is missing.

"Step up." The guard offers me his hand. I climb the steps and sit on the last pedestal next to Prisha.

"Bow to your Queen, peasants." Everly smirks from her throne.

Blaise and I exchange eye rolls.

"Security Forces aren't playing around today," Maris says, looking at the armed officers posted around the neighborhood.

"Do you think they found the killer yet?" Prisha asks.

Maris extends her legs and adjusts her dress. "Suicide makes more sense than murder."

"But they said her eyes were missing. Why would you pluck out your own eyeballs before committing suicide?" Prisha's voice is full of doubt.

"Did you see the body, Prisha?" Maris' voice has a sharp edge. Without allowing Prisha to respond, she adds, "Neither did I. Neither did any of us."

Blaise says, "Did any of you see who was missing from House of Lillith?"

Clover shakes her head. "I couldn't make out faces, but I counted only five Supernovas on the House of Lillith float."

"I saw Cambria." Everly's face puckers as if she bit into a lemon.

The first float moves toward the cobblestone street leading to the spa. The other floats follow at a sluggish pace. My mind keeps replaying images of ocean waves tossing an eyeless Supernova against the cliffs.

What happened to her eyes? Is their absence symbolic? Was the killer trying to send a message? Since arriving in Ovation a month ago, I never questioned my safety. Until now.

Twenty-two

*P*ast the iron gate, a cheering crowd greets the floats. Brightly colored threads strung overhead pop yellow and blue and pink against the cloudless sky.

Flower petals rain down on us from open windows and rooftops. I pull a yellow petal from my hair and bring it to my nose. Definitely a rose.

A rotund woman bumps against the float. She thrusts a transceptor and stylus in my face. "Can I have your autograph?" she asks eagerly.

A member of Security Forces steps between us before I can respond.

"Why would she want your autograph? I'm the one sitting on the House of Saphronia throne," Everly says with a haughty look on her face.

"Who are all of these people?" I ask.

Maris says, "Hundreds of people live in Ovation. You

haven't seen them because our neighborhood requires special credentials."

Blaise looks into the distance with a nostalgic smile. "When I was a little girl, my moms would walk me to the neighborhood gate to show me where I would live someday. I couldn't wait to grow up and become a Supernova."

The floats crawl toward a town square filled with people perusing booths set up along the perimeter. An imposing cathedral flanked by asymmetrical bell towers stretches across one side of the plaza.

The float parks near the square. Saphronia is first to disembark. The wind plays hide and seek in her purple cape. "Supernovas, when the bells toll noon, you will take your seats in the cathedral. Until then, enjoy the outdoor festivities." She walks away and joins a group of Zeniths.

"Move it, plebeians." Everly stands.

The smell of fried funnel cakes, buttery popcorn, and chocolate wafts through the air.

"C'mon, let's check out the guys." Everly grabs Maris and they make a beeline for the square teeming with Security Force members who look out of place next to the brightly-colored vendor booths, balloons, and decorations.

Giant eggs painted with tranquil landscapes—cherry blossoms, snow-capped mountains—are placed throughout the square.

Prisha wanders into the plaza and admires a bronze sculpture of a nude female torso. A clock melts down the neck of the statue. An ant crawls across the abdomen next to a giant golden egg.

"Look at that crazy statue." I point.

Blaise stops in the middle of the street and gawks at me. "You've never heard of Dali's Space Venus?"

I shake my head. "We studied Dali, but I don't remember that."

Blaise says, "Supernovas touch the golden egg for luck during Harvests. Dali was obsessed with eggs. In his work, eggs represent birth and renewal, ants represent death and decay, and the melting clock means different things to different people."

Clover says, "I think the clock reminds us that youth and beauty and life are all fleeting. The Space Venus in its entirety represents the cycle of life."

Blaise leads us toward the vendor booths. "Let's see what the vendors are selling."

"How many times have you guys participated in Harvests?"

"This is my fourth Harvest," Blaise says.

"My eighth one," Clover says.

"Does it hurt?" I ask.

"They give you a pill that knocks you out for a few minutes so you won't feel anything." Clover kicks pebbles with the pointy toes of her shoes. After eight harvests, she's probably used to walking in heels. I'm still trying to avoid twisting my ankles on the cobblestones.

A woman dressed in pink steps into our path. "Get your eggs right here! I have scrambled eggs, deviled eggs, raw eggs!

Take your pick, only two ovals each, ladies. I have pickled eggs, egg salad sandwiches!"

She holds out pastel colored eggs on sticks and says, "Who doesn't love hard-boiled egg lollipops? Two lollipops for one oval!"

Blaise hands the woman an oval. "I'll take two lollipops."

"Choose any two you like." The woman motions to a booth where oodles of lollipops are on display.

Blaise reaches for an egg lollipop painted sky blue with clouds. She hands it to me. "Hold this for a second." She stands over the display. "Should I get this one or that one?"

"I hate eggs. Get whichever one you want," I say.

"Get that one." Clover points to an egg painted green with a four-leaf clover.

"Blaise!" A woman in a black robe, white bib, and veil hurries toward us.

"Mother Rose!" Blaise embraces her.

"Isabel!" Another identically dressed woman throws her arms around Blaise.

"Mother Ivy, I've missed you so much." Blaise's voice bubbles over with enthusiasm.

"Look at you. All grown up in your Harvest dress." The one called Mother Rose brushes Blaise's curls out of her eyes.

Blaise beams at the women. "Mothers, these are my friends, Clover and Wren. We live together at House of Saphronia. This is Wren's first Harvest."

The women acknowledge us and continue to fuss over Blaise. Two little girls peek out from behind their skirts.

"Can I give them lollipops?" Blaise asks.

"Of course, dear," Mother Ivy says.

Blaise offers egg lollipops to the girls.

"What do you say, girls?" Mother Rose prompts.

"Thank you," they say in unison.

"Good luck today, girls," Mother Ivy says.

"Blessed is the fruit," Mother Rose says as they walk away.

The Mothers disappear inside the cathedral. I look away but something draws my eyes back.

Is that? Could it be?

My heart leaps into my throat.

"What's wrong, Wren?" Blaise asks.

"I'll be right back," I say.

I rush across the square, weaving in and out of a swarm of swanky summer dresses, fancy hats, bowties, and gloves. Butterflies multiply in my chest; hundreds of fluttering wings carry me forward on a wave of hope and excitement.

Someone bumps into me and nearly knocks me over. "Sorry, Miss."

I keep moving, smiling, and don't take my eyes off him. I run up the cathedral steps, rush to his side, reach for his forearm, and squeeze. I have to keep myself from hugging him. The last time I saw him, his face was scruffy, but today he is clean-shaven and wears a formal uniform.

"Fritz!" I blurt out, breathless, heart racing.

He frowns. "Do I know you?"

"It's me." I frown back. "Wren."

Fritz pulls his arm away. "I suggest you join the other Supernovas. It's almost noon."

His words feel like a butterfly net thrust into my chest—twisting, ripping, tearing the wings off my hope and excitement. How can he not remember me? Maybe he needs evidence to prove it's really me.

"I found your letter in the woods."

"Listen," he says sharply, "I've never seen you before in my life. I don't know what you're trying to do, but I suggest you stop before I report you." He looks over my head.

Why would he pretend not to recognize me? Is he being watched? Was he captured and brainwashed? I notice cameras mounted above the cathedral doors. Is he scared to talk here?

"If you change your mind, I live at House of Saphronia." My voice carries a sliver of hope.

He ignores me. The butterflies in my chest fall and form a pit in my stomach. As I back away, I notice he doesn't have a scar through his eyebrow or callouses on his hands. If he isn't Fritz, who is he? I picture the Lucindas at the spa. Could Fritz have an unknown twin?

Confused and rejected, I sulk on the way back to Blaise and Clover. I dodge little girls running through the square carrying egg-filled baskets and join Blaise and Clover at a booth where they admire eggshell jewelry. Below the vendor's rainbow painted face and gap-toothed grin hangs a necklace of dyed eggs.

"Find anything good?" I attempt to sound upbeat to hide my hurt feelings.

"I was going to ask you the same thing," Blaise says. "Did you know him?"

I shake my head. "I thought it was somebody from home, but it wasn't."

Two bells stacked within the wider bell tower begin tolling. A wave of people pushes forward toward the cathedral. My stomach tightens into a knot. It's time.

Twenty-three

We join Prisha, Everly, and Maris on the cathedral steps.

"It was Freya," Everly announces, twisting from side to side, causing her dress to swish and swirl.

"What was Freya?" Blaise asks, climbing the last two steps to stand next to Everly.

"Freya is the one missing from House of Lillith." Everly tosses her hair over her shoulder and nods toward the House of Lillith girls lining up at the door. Her red lips stretch into a satisfied smile. "This is one harvest they won't win."

"Which one was Freya?" I ask, bringing my hand to my brow to block the sun.

Maris smacks on gum and blows a bubble. "Tall brunette, kind of quiet."

"Wren?" Fritz's voice penetrates the crowd.

My heart skips. Is it the *real* Fritz? Scared to get my hopes up, I turn in the direction of his voice. A figure dressed in white lifts me and spins me. The crowd blurs into a whirl of color orbiting us. I look down and recognize the tiny scar running through Fritz's eyebrow, the cleft in his chin, the big grin.

It *is* Fritz!

He looks so happy to see me. A flutter of revived butterflies rises in my chest. My lips curve into a hopeful smile.

He gently sets me on my feet. "Where are you staying?"

What does he think of my dress and makeup? Self-conscious, I roll my lips together. The waxy lipstick feels heavy and unnatural. "House of Saphronia."

"When can I see you again?" His smile burns brighter and brighter as he awaits my answer.

My spirit soars at the prospect of spending time together. "Tonight? After the Harvest?"

He reaches for my hands and holds them between us. "Not tonight. Security is amped up after what happened to the Supernova at House of Lillith. After the Science Gala next weekend?"

I feel the other girls watching us. I stand on my toes and whisper in his ear. "House of Saphronia rooftop after the Gala."

"I was scared I would never see you again," he says softly, looking into my eyes and then glancing at my lips as if he wants to kiss me. For the first time, I can tell that he likes me, the way I like him.

"I was worried about you, too," I say.

"Our first date didn't really go as planned." He smiles playfully. "I'll make it up to you."

"You better," I say in a flirtatious tone.

A loud female voice says, "Supernovas, line up and take your places."

I look toward the voice. Fritz's hands slip out of mine and when I look back, the crowd has swallowed him.

"Thought you said you didn't have a boyfriend," Maris cocks her head and narrows her eyes.

"I don't." My words deny her suspicion, but my smile confirms her hunch.

"Mm-hmm," she says, as if she knows I secretly wish I did have a boyfriend. And I wish it was Fritz.

Knowing he's alive dissolves the worry I've been carrying for months. I feel lighter. The line moves forward. Ovation residents cluster on the cathedral steps.

"Five ovals on House of Lillith," says a woman in a green dress.

A man wearing a red bow tie with matching suspenders responds, "House of Lillith is down one. They don't have a chance. Ten ovals on House of Juliette."

Are they betting on which House will produce the most eggs? That's sick. I look around and realize people are dressed in the colors of the Supernova Houses as if egg harvesting is a sport and they're wearing the colors of the team they support.

The man catches me staring and mutters, "What are you staring at?"

I break eye contact and follow the others into the church. The pews overflow with people. Everly leads us to pews on the left, second row from the back. I slide into the wooden pew between Blaise and Maris.

Zeniths take their places in seats surrounding the altar. People in white uniforms like the one Fritz wore sit in a balcony on the upper right. It's hard to see their faces from here. The sun pours through skylights above the altar illuminating a statue of a woman encircled by angels.

"Who is the woman above the altar?" I ask Blaise.

"We're in the Cathedral of the Virgin Mary. That's Mary."

"Virgin Mary?" I prompt for more details.

"The story of Mary is about a virgin who gives birth to a holy son."

"How did she give birth if she was a virgin? That doesn't make sense."

"Exactly," Blaise says. "In the Old World, religions set standards women couldn't possibly meet to cast women as impure and inferior to men."

"How do you know so much about the Old World?"

Blaise smooths wrinkles from her skirt. "Some Mothers had Catholic ancestors."

"Shh!" A blond Supernova gives us a dirty look. Maris sticks her tongue out at her.

A woman standing at the altar introduces herself as Dr. Jensen. She wears a white robe with red material draped around her neck. "Thank you for joining us for the Fall Egg Harvest. We are gathered here today to…"

"I hope we aren't first," I whisper to Maris.

"The Houses seated in pews ahead of us will go first."

Dr. Jensen continues, "Please welcome Victoria from House of Khadija."

Supernovas in the front rows stir. A petite brunette moves into the aisle. The yellow sash around her waist represents House of Khadija. I crane to see over the tall people blocking my view. She approaches the front of the church and climbs the steps to the sanctuary.

Dr. Jensen faces her, takes her hands, and says, "Blessed art thou amongst women, and blessed is the fruit of thy womb from which the New World will be born."

The audience responds, "So be it."

Dr. Jensen places a pill in Victoria's mouth and leads her to the altar. The Supernova lies down on her back, crosses her arms over her stomach, and closes her eyes.

The ceremony is supposed to be about birth, but her motionless body displayed on an altar the size of a coffin makes me think of death.

Dr. Jensen stands over the blacked-out Supernova and adjusts the girl's legs so her knees are raised and touching. She tugs the dress down to cover her, then sits on a stool at the foot of the altar, puts on a headlamp, and aims the light between the Supernova's legs.

A sucking sound cuts through the silence for a moment before the notes of a piano drown it out.

I whisper to Blaise, "What is the doctor doing?"

"The tool she uses is like a vacuum cleaner that sucks eggs out of ovary follicles and deposits them in a machine that counts the eggs and displays the totals over there." She points to flat screens hanging above each side of the room. Both screens display the number three.

"That means three eggs?" I ask.

Blaise nods. "You need at least ten per Harvest to maintain your status. Look, Victoria is already up to nine."

The numbers on the display climb higher: ten… twelve… fifteen… eighteen… twenty-one. The music rises in a dramatic crescendo as the number holds steady at twenty-one. People shift in their seats eagerly awaiting the final tally.

Maris says, "Twenty-one is going to be hard to beat."

Dr. Jensen stands and faces the audience. She pulls the headlamp off and says, "Twenty-two for House of Khadija."

The crowd claps and cheers. Supernovas from House of Khadija stand and hug one another.

The flat screens flash to a bar graph with the name of each House across the bottom. The vertical axis is labeled with numbers from zero to one hundred and fifty. A yellow bar rises above *House of Khadija* and stops at twenty-two.

Victoria cries out and sits up. She looks confused. A woman dressed like Mother Rose and Mother Ivy rises from the first pew. She helps Victoria down from the altar and leads her to an adjoining hall.

I lean into Blaise. "Everly called your mothers Milkmaids?"

"Yes, they nourish babies and raise children in Ovation."

"Please welcome Grace from House of Khadija," Dr. Jensen says.

A short, stocky girl marches toward the sanctuary with her chin up and shoulders back. She takes Dr. Jensen's outstretched hands and smiles proudly. The same ritual unfolds.

I move my lips with the audience, "So be it."

There are at least ten rows of Supernovas. This is going to take forever. My stomach grumbles. I should have eaten that stinky egg this morning.

The colored bars on the graph rise during each egg retrieval procedure. Now, I understand why people were placing bets before the ceremony. This could get boring if there were no stakes for the audience. House of Juliette is in the lead with a total of ninety-nine eggs. Ninety-one eggs were harvested from House of Khadija.

Now, the last member of House of Lillith is undergoing the procedure. Cambria of Lillith produced twenty-four eggs, but House of Lillith can't compete with five Supernovas when every other house has six Supernovas. After the last egg is retrieved from House of Lillith, the green bar on the screen climbs to seventy-four.

"Everly of House of Saphronia."

Everly steps on my foot as she moves into the aisle. She probably did it on purpose. I should have tripped her. She sashays down the aisle as if a prize awaits her. She ascends the sanctuary stairs, pivots to face the audience, and grins as if she has already won.

Dr. Jensen takes Everly's hands. "Blessed art thou amongst women, and blessed is the fruit of thy womb from which the New World will be born."

"So be it."

Everly swallows the pill, hops on the altar, and assumes the position. I keep my eyes glued to the egg count and hope it falls short. Three. Five. Ten. Fourteen.

"Nineteen for House of Saphronia," Dr. Jensen announces.

Everly bolts upright and stumbles off the altar. A Milkmaid hastens to assist her. Everly turns back to check the number on the screen. Her face falls when she sees her egg count. She sulks and slinks into the hall.

"Maris of House of Saphronia," Dr. Jensen says.

"Watch this," Maris whispers.

"Bock-bock-bock." Maris waddles down the aisle flapping her arms and clucking like a chicken. She juts her head and clucks all the way to the sanctuary.

I put my hand over my mouth to stifle a giggle. What begins as a smatter of snickers becomes roaring laughter. Dr. Jensen looks on in dismay. Saphronia's usually neutral features tighten in disapproval.

"That's enough," Dr. Jensen says. "Supernovas shall conduct themselves with dignity." She grasps Maris' hands, repeats the creed, places the pill on her tongue, and escorts her to the altar. Seventeen eggs are extracted.

Both Prisha and Blaise produce sixteen eggs. That's a total of sixty-eight eggs from our House. When Clover's name is called, I squeeze her hand and wish her luck.

As the machine sucks up Clover's eggs, I stare at the number on the flat screen. It sticks at three for too long. *Please, don't stop at three.*

The number on the screen flips to four.

Dr. Jensen stands with a somber look on her face. "Four eggs for House of Saphronia."

The crowd gasps and murmurs.

"The Nadir Ceremony will take place after eggs have been retrieved from all Houses."

What is a Nadir Ceremony?

"Wren of House of Saphronia."

My ovaries cower. Onlookers turn to ogle the next egg donor. The long aisle stretches before me like a death sentence. I take a deep breath and prepare to relinquish my bodily autonomy. I feel the injustice Marie-Louise Giraud must have felt as she approached the steps of the guillotine. She believed women should have the right to make decisions about their lives and bodies without government interference. The French government disagreed. They chopped off her head.

"Join me at the front, please." Dr. Jensen beckons.

I put one high heel in front of the other and plod toward Dr. Jensen. People whisper and stare. Are they talking about me? My face reddens. I focus on the flat screen where the number has been reset to zero.

Dr. Jensen takes my hands. Her mouth moves, but her words blur. She presents a shiny red pill. I open my mouth and obediently swallow the capsule. My legs become cinder blocks, my tongue tingles, a haze engulfs me. I lose my balance. Dr. Jensen steadies me and guides me to the altar.

I lie back and study the images of angels and flowers painted on the ceiling. The music flows through my ears and tickles my brain. Winged cherubs lift my knees into the fluffy clouds, such soft, beautiful clouds. Now I'm a cloud, light and fluffy, floating high above the altar. As if she were a lit candle, Virgin Mary's face melts into tears and puddles at her feet. Why is she crying? The flowers bloom and close, bloom and close. The light fades.

An anchor attached to my ankle pulls me under. Water rushes into my lungs. I can't breathe. My enlarged lungs become nutcrackers, squeezing my heart like a pecan. My heart makes for a hasty escape, jumping on my diaphragm, launching up my esophagus, using my tongue as a springboard to forward dive out of my submerged body. My mouth stretches wide as my aorta bursts from my lips. I kick and struggle. My head breaks the water's surface. I take a deep breath, sucking my heart to the back of my throat, swallowing the apple-sized lump whole. Fresh air flushes water out of my lungs. I open my eyes.

A Milkmaid hovers over me. "Very impressive for your first Harvest, dear." She helps me stand. My vision is foggy. My head is muddled. Black robes. Bassinets. Babies crying. My brain tries to put the pieces together.

The Milkmaid leads me off stage. "Have a seat in the chapel with the other Supernovas until the ceremony ends."

Supernovas huddle and talk in hushed voices. Blaise and another girl sit in a secluded corner, their fingers intertwined. I sit next to Maris.

"When did you last see her?" Maris leans into Maven.

"She was at dinner last night," Maven says.

"Who found the body?" asks a Supernova from House of Khadija.

Gretchen of Lillith responds, "When I was getting ready for breakfast, I saw something crumpled against the rocks from my window. I went to Maven's room to show her."

"I told Gretchen it looked like a body, but she didn't believe me." Maven raises her hands, flashing purple fingernails.

Gretchen says, "We went straight to Lillith. A half hour later, investigators showed up."

"How long before you knew it was Freya?" a wide-eyed girl asks.

Maven answers, "Freya never missed a meal. When she didn't show up for breakfast, we knew something was wrong."

A groggy Supernova from House of Rosalind joins us.

"What was your total, Ada?" Everly asks the girl.

"Fifteen," she says, her voice thick and slurred.

"Did anyone see my total?" I forgot to look.

Everly ignores me and chews on her fingernails.

"Twenty-one." Ada rearranges her pink sash.

"Twenty-one? Are you sure?" That's more eggs than Everly produced.

"Yep."

Wow. That's a total of ninety-three for House of Saphronia. We're in second place behind House of Juliette.

I turn to Maris. "Where is Clover?"

"We won't see her again until the Nadir Ceremony," Maris says.

"What's a Nadir ceremony?" I ask.

The Supernovas squirm and look uncomfortable. One of them responds, "You'll see."

A Milkmaid enters with the last Supernova from House of Rosalind. The girl sits with Ada and others from her House.

"Mother Holly!" A girl from House of Juliette calls out to the Milkmaid.

Mother Holly smiles. "Isabel, Gretchen, Quinn, Eugenia. I'm so proud of you girls." She walks toward the side door. "Now that the Harvest has concluded, I need all Supernovas to gather in the cathedral square for the Nadir Ceremony."

Twenty-four

A gossamer veil of cirrus clouds glides across the bright blue sky. As I exit the cathedral, a weight taps against my thigh. From my pocket, I pull out a handful of ovals. The Milkmaid who helped me off the altar must have deposited them. I spot Maris descending the cathedral steps with Maven. I'll ask them where to buy coffee later.

Throngs of people spill from the main doors. Little girls in white dresses with egg-filled baskets form a line facing the cathedral. A row of Milkmaids, their veils flapping in the wind, stand directly behind the children. Nadirs face the crowd from elevated porches flanking the cathedral stairs.

Dr. Jensen stands at the top of the stairs between the Nadirs. Her voice projects from nearby speakers. "First, I would like to congratulate House of Juliette for coming in first place with ninety-nine total ova. House of Juliette Supernovas will indulge in the Forbidden Feast as honored guests of the Nuclei. The

Nuclei's personal chefs will provide mouthwatering delicacies and rich desserts. Please give a round of applause to House of Juliette."

The crowd cheers and whistles and claps. Ovals exchange hands as people settle their bets. Ada and another Supernova from House of Juliette jump up and down hugging each other.

Blaise wraps her arm around the girl she was sitting with in the chapel and says, "Eugenia, sneak me some chocolate."

"Anything for you." Eugenia grins at Blaise, cups her face, and pulls her into a kiss. I quickly look away.

Dr. Jensen quiets the crowd. "It is with regret and a heavy heart that I announce the demotion of Clover Kirkpatrick from Supernova to Nadir. Clover, please join me."

Keeping her eyes down, Clover emerges from the double doors of the church with the color drained from her face and pink splotches around her eyes.

"Ladies and gentlemen, please make room for the Nadir Ceremony," Dr. Jensen says.

Berkeley and Harlowe unfurl red fabric down the cathedral steps and into the crowd, dividing the square in half. When they reach the end of the roll, they barge back up the church steps, lock arms with Clover, and lead her down the red carpet.

Once they deposit Clover in the middle of the square, they rejoin the other Nadirs at the top of the cathedral steps.

Mother Rose guides the little girls into a circle around Clover. Baskets hang from their arms. I recognize the girls Blaise gifted lollipops.

Mother Rose says, "Ready, girls? On the count of three. One... two... three."

Hand in hand, the girls skip around Clover while singing a rhyme.

"*Ring around the Nova,*
Pocketful of ova,
Ashes, ashes,
We all fall down!"

The giggling girls launch a barrage of eggs from their baskets. Raw eggs crack against Clover's white dress. She flinches as the eggs batter her body. Gooey glops stick to her lace bodice while yellow slime drips down her skirt and splats on her shoes. The eggs sizzle and stink in the steamy heat, sunny-side up on the cobblestone.

Blaise leans into me and whispers, "This was my favorite part of Harvest when I was a little girl."

Her comment disgusts me. I realize I don't know Blaise as well as I thought I did. "Humiliating people was your favorite part?" My tone is harsh and judgmental.

"Oh, lighten up. It's just for fun and it motivates the little Novas to follow the rules so they can become productive Supernovas like us one day." Blaise smiles at the girls pelting eggs at Clover.

When the baskets are empty, all eggs gone, Berkeley and Harlowe fetch Clover. I try to catch Clover's eye as she passes by, but she stares at the ground. Her head hangs and her shoulders slump. Tears zag down her face.

Someone in the crowd throws an egg that pops and explodes against Clover's head. She reels and staggers and loses her balance. Berkeley and Harlowe yank her upright. Sticky egg guts ooze down her hair and face.

The crowd pushes forward like an angry mob, closing the gap created by the fabric runner. Clover hesitates at the bottom of the stairs. Berkeley slams her palm against Clover's spine, shoving her forward, forcing her to climb.

Reduced to a soggy heap of goop, Clover silently cries next to Dr. Jensen.

Dr. Jensen says, "Let the transformation begin."

Twenty Nadirs rush at Clover. Two hundred fingers claw at her dress and shred it to pieces. I'm reminded of the cockroach simulation. Clover sways back and forth with her head down. Spectators lean forward with slight smiles, transfixed by the transformation unfolding before their eyes.

The Nadirs tear off Clover's dress, displaying her underwear for everyone to see. Clover crosses her arms over her chest and squishes her legs together, trying to cover herself.

Rage warms my cheeks. I'm reminded of the helplessness I felt the night of the Valley raid. I want to march up the steps and pull Clover to safety.

Nadirs back away from Clover to make room for two men carrying large buckets. They rear the buckets back and launch heavy sheets of water at Clover. Water slaps her in the face with a lightning-crack smack.

She recoils and inhales sharply. Eggy water washes down her frame. She hunches over, hugs herself, and shivers. Berkeley laughs out loud and high-fives Harlowe. I feel an overwhelming urge to punch both of them.

The Nadirs rush in again and surround Clover. Some Nadirs bend near Clover's feet, others push and pull on her torso. Finally, they back away to reveal Clover dressed in a Nadir uniform complete with apron and ugly paper hat.

My heart sinks. Clover doesn't deserve this humiliation. After the transformation is complete, Clover stands alone on display. Egg remnants trickle down the steps.

Dr. Jensen steps forward and says, "Thank you all for attending the Fall Egg Harvest. I look forward to seeing you again at the Winter Harvest. Until then, I bid you well."

Electricity surges through the dispersing crowd. Laughter and idle chatter ring in my ears. Maris, Everly, and I plow through the crowd and head toward the floats. Blaise hangs back and chitchats with Eugenia.

Maris says, "That was really messed up. Clover was the top egg producer in the House before Everly and I moved in last year. I don't understand how she could lose her status so quickly."

Everly says, "They better send a replacement soon or we have no chance of winning the Winter Harvest."

"Is winning all you care about?" Maris snaps at Everly.

I nod toward Blaise and Eugenia. "I didn't know Blaise had a girlfriend. Is that normal here?"

Maris gives me a funny look. "Is *anything* normal here? You act like having a girlfriend is weird. It's common in Clairemont. Are people in Hillcrest homophobic or something?"

I hesitate, thinking of the rumors that swirled around two male teachers suspected of being in a relationship. "People in Hillcrest value conformity and can be judgmental of those who buck norms. They don't talk about alternatives to traditional relationships, but I'm pretty sure they wouldn't approve or be accepting."

Everly says, "It's not like the Nuclei wants Valley dwellers and Hillcrest peeps to breed anyway. The only reason governments cram heteronormativity down people's throats is to get them to produce children."

Maris raises an eyebrow. "That's a big word for you, Evs."

"Shut it," Everly says.

I spot Prisha. She throws back her head and laughs while resting her hand on a boy's arm. I've never seen Prisha so animated. She is definitely flirting. My eyes travel from his arm to his face. Prisha leans into him and Fritz grins at her the way he grins at me. Jealousy rips a black, bottomless hole through my core.

A man standing amid a group of Zeniths calls out, "Nice job today, Wren."

He knows my name? Everly glares at me.

"Who's that?" I ask.

"Nuclei member. Gregor Hahn. Dr. Hahn's son," Maris says. "He's the cutest member of the Nuclei if you ask me. All the others are old."

"I wouldn't turn down Dr. Toussaint if he came knocking with his bronze skin and amber eyes," Everly says, making obnoxious kissy faces.

Maris laughs.

"Should we get Prisha and Blaise?" I ask.

Maris cups her mouth and yells across the square, "Hey, Prisha and Blaise, the party is leaving without you!"

Passersby scowl at Maris. I recall Dr. Jensen's words: *Supernovas shall conduct themselves with dignity.*

Maris' rebellious nature amuses me.

I watch Prisha hug Fritz and pretend it doesn't bother me. She bounds toward the group, giddy and grinning, like she's intentionally trying to annoy me. Later, I'll ask how she knows Fritz. We head back to the Supernova neighborhood. I'm relieved to have my first Harvest behind me.

Twenty-five

"Thank you all for joining us for the twenty-fifth Annual Black Tie Science Gala. It is an honor to be your host.

"Many of you know me, but for those who do not, allow me to introduce myself. I am Dr. Mary Hart, and although I am known for my merry heart, it is Mary as in m-a-r-y and Hart as in h-a-r-t."

Soft chuckles penetrate the black velvet curtain that keeps us hidden backstage. I glance at the other Supernovas in their sequin gowns and fake eyelashes. I'm dying to find out why we spent hours with a glam squad getting our hair and makeup done. The stylists fawned over us, but I think we look ridiculous. At least they chose a tasteful silver dress for me instead of that garish red one Everly is wearing.

"Tonight, we honor the scientists who have dedicated their lives to supporting the goals of the Nuclei. When those goals are achieved, future generations will live long, healthy lives in peace and harmony. Our children will never know the devastation of war. Our mothers will not die in childbirth. Our world will be free of death, disease, and suffering.

"In recent decades, we have made great progress toward attaining these goals through elimination of religion, fair allocation of resources, and gene modification. We have modified genes and enzymes responsible for regulating aggression, depression, and antisocial behavior. We are moving toward a less aggressive, more empathetic society."

The audience claps.

"In the Old World, pregnancy and childbirth killed millions of women, yet governments continued to rely on natural childbirth to replenish the population.

"Through the dedication of the most brilliant minds in Ovation, we have relieved women of the dangerous burden of pregnancy. No longer will women put their lives at risk to bring children into the world. We are now able to develop embryos into viable fetuses and grow them to maturity in artificial wombs.

"In addition to alleviating the suffering of women, we are now able to alleviate the suffering of our aging population. We have eradicated age-related diseases like Alzheimer's and Parkinson's.

"Aging minds will retain all they have learned in their lifetime. Never again will a grandfather forget his own identity. Never again will a grandmother forget a loved one.

"Aging bodies will no longer deteriorate and betray us. Instead of growing feeble with age, our bodies and minds will grow stronger.

"We have many means to achieve this reversal in aging. Over fifty years ago, researchers sutured together an old mouse and a young mouse. After the parabiotic pairing, the mice shared a blood circulatory system.

"Within days, the old mouse showed reduced signs of aging. In the hippocampus region, neural connections were strengthened, resulting in improved learning and memory performance. Delta-Notch signaling increased and restored the ability to regenerate muscle more efficiently.

"The talented Dr. Diallo led experiments that provided us with confidence to apply these anti-aging techniques to humans. Our aging population regularly receives blood plasma transfusions from young donors. Anti-aging therapies also include the use of stem cell technology and telomere protection strategies.

"Age reversal is a marked improvement, but who among us would prefer to eradicate death as we have eradicated other diseases?"

Boisterous applause breaks out on the other side of the heavy curtain.

"We are developing technology that will allow humans to live forever via memory transfer. Dr. Sun's team has proven episodic and semantic memories can be transferred successfully to cloned brain tissue.

"Imagine a future where every eighty years, you wake up a younger version of yourself.

"Since the beginning of time, people have longed for immortality. In the Old World, religion preyed upon this universal desire. Religion could not fulfill the promise of eternal life, but science can.

"Supernovas play a key role in our vision of the future. Tonight, I will introduce you to the latest additions to our Supernova community and to the scientists who created them. Through their contributions, the New World will be born.

"After the awards ceremony, feel free to mingle in the labs adjacent to the ballroom. We have stations set up where you may examine the DNA of each specimen introduced tonight.

"Please welcome to the stage Prototype 1290, Specimen 33, developed by Dr. Shiko Akimoto's team in 2053."

"Wren, that's you." Someone nudges me.

I part the curtain and hobble on stage in sky-high heels. How were women in Clairemont able to stroll the streets so effortlessly with their feet jammed into these tiny, toe-torturing devices? A spotlight hits my face. My pupils shrink and try to take cover under my eyelids.

"Please step onto the platform." A tall, thin woman with silver hair pulled into a tight twist stands behind a glass podium. She wears a long black gown with a dramatic collar that frames her sharp jaw and prominent chin. She stares at me over the red rims of cat-eye spectacles.

Scintillating chandeliers drip raindrops of light onto the black suits, bow ties, and glistening gowns of audience members seated around tables with extravagant floral centerpieces. Hundreds of beady, blinking eyes bore into me. My cheeks flush from the weight of so many unknown eyes.

On the stage to my left, a circular platform rises parallel to the podium. I take a baby step toward the platform. As if the heels weren't bad enough, the long dress feels like a straitjacket restricting my leg movement. *Click-clack, click-clack.* The sound of stilettos crossing the stage stops when Dr. Hart reaches my side.

She grasps my arm and guides me to the platform. I lift the hem of my gown and step up. Dr. Hart resumes her position behind the podium. I straighten my posture and face the audience.

Audience members gasp out loud. Within seconds, the entire room is on their feet. A chorus of applause reverberates around me.

"Thank you for the warm welcome of Specimen 33. Those of you who remember our beloved Delilah Hahn understand why Specimen 33 is so special to Dr. Hahn and the Ovation community."

The applause continues.

"Please take your seats." Dr. Hart smiles at the crowd. "After several unsuccessful trials, Specimen 33 was born November thirtieth, 2056 at the Northeast Coastal Research Center.

"When initial tests yielded no concerns, Specimen 33 was placed with a Golden Ova family in Hillcrest and given the name Wren Weiss.

"Since the inception of Project Aphrodite, Specimen 33 is one of only ten specimens placed in Hillcrest to allow the scientific community to analyze the effects of environment on the development of genetically-modified humans.

"Despite the disadvantage of being raised in Hillcrest, Specimen 33 exhibits no major deficiencies. In fact, during the Assessment, Specimen 33 outperformed similar subjects raised in Clairemont..."

Prototypes? Specimen? Genetically-modified humans? Did she say I was born in a research center? The corners of my vision begin to go black. I raise my arms to catch myself from falling. I breathe deeply until the urge to faint passes.

The platform jerks and begins to spin. The unexpected movement nearly topples me. I fight to stay balanced in the painful high heels.

"Specimen 33 joined the community of Supernovas in Ovation two months ago. During the October Egg Harvest, she yielded twenty-one viable eggs."

Applause ripples through the room.

As the platform spins and my silver dress sparkles, I feel like a cross between a disco ball and a circus attraction. I squint against the spotlight and inspect the faces of Security Forces stationed around the room.

I don't see Fritz. Last weekend at the Fall Harvest, we agreed to meet up after tonight's Gala. I hope he remembers.

"Yes, yes, twenty-one is quite egg-cellent for a first time Harvest. We may need to promote this one from Supern-ova to Supreme-ova." The audience laughs at the speaker's play on words. Dr. Hart takes a mock bow, beaming at her own cleverness.

"The intelligence of Specimen 33 is beyond genius level. She also has a photographic memory. We haven't witnessed such bilateral symmetry since Dr. Diallo introduced Specimen 89 over a decade ago."

More applause.

"There are no mutated carrier genes that could be detrimental to progeny." Dr. Hart sweeps an arm toward me in an exaggerated flourish. "And furthermore, the immune system is resistant to all major viruses."

Audience members gasp. The excitement in the room is palpable, bouncing off every surface, lighting up every face.

"Yes, yes, I know. Quite egg-citing, indeed," Dr. Hart says in a playful tone.

I roll my eyes at her intentional mispronunciation.

"But, wait, there's more." Dr. Hart dramatically waves her hand—fist closed, index finger raised—as if she holds a secret in her palm.

A hush falls over the room. Guests lean forward in anticipation.

"In addition to superior intelligence, symmetry, and health, Dr. Akimoto partnered with our brilliant team of ophthalmologists at the Wyatt Center to bestow an extraordinary gift upon Specimen 33.

"Not only is Specimen 33 a tetrachromat with the ability to see ten million colors, as opposed to the limited one million colors visible to the average human eye, but Specimen 33 is also able to see ultraviolet and infrared wavelengths."

Dr. Hart pauses to allow the audience to absorb her words. She makes eye contact with people around the room. "That's right. During the embryonic stage, specialists inserted the gene responsible for the tapetum lucidum.

"Directly beneath the retina of Specimen 33 is the same light-reflecting membrane that enables animals to see in the dark. This enhancement is hereditary and will be passed to future generations.

"Please join me in a round of applause for Dr. Akimoto and the scientists who contributed to the Prototype that will be used as the exemplary model for future generations." Dr. Hart lifts her hands in a dramatic slow clap.

A petite woman in a gold gown makes her way to the stage. Center-parted black hair drapes her face, camouflaging the roundness of her cheeks.

Dr. Hart lifts a gleaming trophy with an intricate double helix rising from its base. "Dr. Akimoto, please accept this award on behalf of the scientific community and the Nuclei."

Dr. Akimoto accepts the trophy. "Thank you. What an honor it is to be here. I would like to accept this award on behalf of all the talented scientists who trusted my vision for Prototype 1290. My vision would have never come to fruition without the help of genetic specialists whose depth of knowledge…"

Why do they keep calling me Prototype 1290? My name is Wren! Is this going to be my life? Egg harvests, blood plasma transfusions, and mad scientists poking and prodding me? I try to quell the anger building inside me.

"…where both X chromosomes were modified to enhance the subject's vision…"

If I had known acing the Assessment was going to land me in this bizzar-o place, I would have at least tried to manipulate the results to stay in Hillcrest. Would they have allowed me to stay in Hillcrest or was this the plan all along? Berkeley said House of Saphronia was notified of my arrival before I even took the Assessment.

Were my parents complicit? Maybe their loyalty to the Nuclei eclipses their love for me. My burgeoning anger is doused by the sting of sadness.

The jazz band begins playing an upbeat tune. The platform stops spinning. Dr. Akimoto crosses the stage toward me with the trophy tucked under one arm. I wish I had been given the ability to disappear instead of lame ultraviolet vision.

"Step down, please." She takes my hand and helps me off the platform. My equilibrium feels off.

Gala guests resume their dinner and conversations. Dr. Hart studies her notes behind the podium. Dr. Akimoto circles me. I stand as still as prey being stalked by a predator. Dr. Akimoto and Maris have similar features. Could the scientists have used their own DNA in their experiments? I picture Dr. Akimoto with pink hair.

"Open your mouth." She shines a light in my mouth. "Look up." She shines the light in my eyes. "Look to the left. Now, look to the right." Satisfied, she clicks off the light.

"Did you know my biological parents? What is Project Aphrodite?" I ask.

Dr. Akimoto's irises are so dark, I can't tell where her irises end and her pupils begin. She nods at someone over my shoulder. A young woman in a gray dress and lab coat approaches.

"Please escort Specimen 33 to the lab," she instructs the young woman.

The woman takes my elbow and escorts me off stage.

Dr. Hart speaks into the microphone, "Our next specimen comes to us from Dr. Diallo's team. Please welcome Prototype 1179, Specimen 19."

A loud thump draws my attention to the stage. Prisha stumbles and falls through the curtain, landing on her knees, ripping her turquoise dress. I yank my arm free, kick off my high heels, and rush back up the stairs.

Dr. Hart says, "We obviously haven't identified the genes responsible for gracefulness."

The audience erupts in laughter at Prisha's expense. I kneel next to Prisha. The curtain cracks open. Everly looks down at Prisha crumpled on the stage. A satisfied smirk stretches across her face.

"Someone pushed me," Prisha whispers.

I help Prisha to her feet. Then, I step backstage and confront Everly.

"What's your problem?" I demand, poking her shoulder.

The attendants backstage stare at us.

Everly nonchalantly examines her fingernails. "I don't know what you're talking about."

"You know exactly what I'm talking about. I know you shoved Prisha."

"You know nothing." Everly yawns and looks past me.

The woman responsible for escorting me off stage grabs my wrist. "Come with me, Specimen 33."

"My name is not Specimen 33. It's Wren." I scowl at her. "This isn't over," I say to Everly and reluctantly follow the woman.

From backstage, Dr. Hart's voice sounds muffled. "Specimen 19 was raised in the Valley by one of our Golden Ova families…"

The girl digging her fingers into my arm says, "My name is Esperanza, but people call me Espie. I'll escort you to the lab where you will remain until the Gala is over."

She leads me into the ornate hallway. My bare feet strike

the cold marble floor. Audience members, their minds alight with fantasies of the perfect world, clog the hall holding flutes of champagne and glasses of wine.

We enter a room set up to resemble a science lab divided into quadrants. Each quadrant includes a long table covered with equipment used to analyze DNA. I recognize some equipment from the genetics lab at school: microscopes, thermal cyclers, polymerase chain reaction systems.

I come to a standstill when I notice in the back right quadrant a life-size hologram of myself inside a glass cylinder labeled, *Prototype 1290, Specimen 33*.

Holograms resembling Prisha, Maris and Everly stand in the other quadrants. It doesn't surprise me that even the hologram version of Everly wears a menacing smile. Blaise is lucky she didn't have to participate this year.

As we approach my station, I marvel at the hologram dressed in the athletic clothing I wore the day of the Assessment. It looks so real. They must have used the symmetry scan to create the hologram.

Espie opens the glass cylinder. "Step inside. Your weight will trigger the sensor to turn off the hologram. You will remain on display for an hour. When the event is over, your Zenith will release you and escort you home."

The word *home* conjures images of Abe and Addie chasing each other around the living room. I see Dad preparing dinner while Mom sits at the table engrossed in work. Do they miss me?

After I step inside the glass contraption, the hologram folds down and disappears. My breath fogs up the glass. I twist the tracker on my wrist to hide its face from random strangers. The cylinder's open ceiling allows air to circulate but my skin still feels warm and clammy.

The crowd has grown larger, more raucous. Staff flits around the room refilling empty wine glasses. Words like *ethics* and *robots* and *clones* swirl around me. Some guests take turns peering into microscopes. Others point and stare from a distance.

The other girls have taken their places in their respective quadrants. Everly blows kisses to men surrounding her. I roll my eyes. While she revels in the attention, I feel like a fish in an aquarium.

The hour passes slowly through the hands of the giant clock hanging over the doorway. I consider everything I learned tonight. My whole life has been a lie. I've been nothing but a lab rat trapped in a labyrinth where scientists have been manipulating stimuli and observing my responses. I ball my hands into fists, close my eyes, and resist the urge to punch through the glass.

Rocking back and forth, I wiggle my toes and stretch my hands over my head. Sequins chafe the sensitive skin under my arms. I feel the weight of someone's eyes on me.

A gray-haired man stands near the entrance wearing a black tuxedo with three ribbons on his chest. Bronze medals dangle from the ribbons.

Why do I recognize him? I rummage through my memories of teachers, neighbors, Enforcers, but I can't place him.

He begins walking toward me. The people in his path greet him, step out of his way, and watch him approach my station. His brown eyes burn into mine, causing a flush to spread from my cheeks to my ears.

Who is he? I study his tan face and dark eyes, but I'm drawing a blank. I'm relieved when he breaks eye contact and steps to my right. I watch the second hand of the clock rotate while he stares at my profile.

When I no longer feel his eyes on me, I look around. The space he occupied a few minutes ago is empty. I glance to the left where my DNA sample is on display, but the gray-haired man isn't there either.

Saphronia appears in the doorway. After she frees Everly, Prisha, and Maris from their glass tombs, their holograms are resurrected. She frees me and all I can think about is hurrying to the rooftop to meet Fritz.

Twenty-six

From the roof's oceanside edge, I peer down the fire escape hoping to see Fritz. Will he remember our plan to meet? The moment I got home from the Gala, I changed into my jeans, t-shirt, and flannel and hurried to the rooftop.

I pace, snugging my flannel shirt around my waist. Strong gusts of wind sweep the roof, setting my fake eyelashes aflutter. I can't wait to rip off the lashes and scrub my face free of makeup.

Facing the city, I squat and listen to the ocean waves swell and crash behind me. It sounds as though the moon is slurping the ocean to the horizon and then blowing it back to shore in a hypnotic meter.

I prop my elbows on my knees and rest my chin on my hands, turning my face toward the wind to keep my ponytail from whipping my eyes.

Something tugs at my ponytail.

"Hey, stranger." Fritz, as handsome as ever, smiles down at me. He wears black cargo pants, a black t-shirt, and combat boots. His hair is shorter; his face is stubble-free.

"Hi." My smile is shy and my voice is uncertain. It has been almost two months since we last spent time together. I have so many questions: How did he escape the facility? How did he end up in Ovation? What is his job assignment and where does he live?

"You looked beautiful on stage tonight." He sits beside me.

"You were there?" The compliment sets my face aglow. I feel the warmth in my cheeks.

"I was in the balcony," he says.

"You heard what Dr. Hart said about me?" I ask.

Fritz nods and studies my face.

I playback Dr. Hart's words: *Specimen 33 was placed with a Golden Ova family in Hillcrest and given the name Wren Weiss.* Maybe it isn't true. A flicker of hope burns within me. "Do you think it's true?"

Fritz reaches for my hand and gently squeezes. "I'm sorry, Wren."

Fritz's response extinguishes my hope and confirms what I already knew. I swallow the lump of disappointment forming in my throat. How could my parents lie to me my entire life? Did they even love me?

I turn my face away from Fritz so he can't see the tears stinging my eyes. I study the outline of the Capitol's dome.

Fritz wraps an arm around my shoulder. "It's nice to meet you, Specimen 33. I'm Specimen 27."

Shocked, I twist and stare wide-eyed at Fritz. "Wait, you… you're not… are you just saying that to make me feel better?"

He shakes his head and looks into the distance. "When I moved to Ovation, I learned that I was born in a lab. Where we were born doesn't really matter, does it?" He fixes his eyes back on mine.

"I guess not," I say, although it does matter to me. I want to know the truth. I want to know who I am and who my biological parents are. I take a deep breath of the humid, sea-salt air and lift my ponytail to allow the breeze to cool my neck.

"Did you find my letter?" Fritz asks.

Thankful for the change of subject, I nod. "What did you mean when you said not to trust anybody?"

"I saw Enforcers like your parents at Guantanamo." His voice sounds remorseful, as if he doesn't want to implicate my parents.

I don't want to talk about my parent's betrayal or consider their involvement at the creepy facility. As I watch the distant city lights flicker off and on, I'm reminded of catching fireflies at dusk with Addie—twirling on bare toes, glass jars held high, scooping up fireflies—spinning, grinning, jars glittering as though overflowing with swirling bursts of starry sky. I can't believe there was ever a time when life was as simple as catching fireflies and making mud pies.

I suppress memories of Addie and face Fritz. "How did you get away? I worried for days until I found your note."

Fritz blows a puff of air and runs his hand back and forth across the top of his head, leaving his wavy hair rumpled and silver-tipped in the moonlight. "I hid in a supply closet and unscrewed the lightbulb. One guard popped his head in, flipped the light switch, and left. About ten minutes later, a second guard entered with a flash light. As soon as the light hit my face, I knocked him out with a microscope."

"Wait, what? You hit him upside the head with a microscope?" Laughter builds in my throat and spills from my mouth.

Fritz shoots me a sheepish grin. "It wasn't funny at the time. I was scared to death."

I can't stop laughing. I cover my mouth, but swells of laughter continue to bubble up my throat and slip through my fingers. "What happened next?"

"I changed into his uniform and walked right out."

"You're kidding!" My mouth and eyes pop open at his audacity.

"I looked for you, but I couldn't find you. I snuck out and saw a search party forming at the gate. I hurried to the zipline platform and was relieved to find your harness missing. I couldn't have left without you. How did you get away?"

I see the soldier standing over my bed. The bald man in the tunnel yanking my leg. Maggots falling down my shirt. My laughter withers and dries up. "I don't want to talk about it. I'm glad we both got away."

"I'm glad we both ended up in Ovation," he says.

"I saw you talking to Prisha at the Harvest." I immediately wish I could take the words back.

His lips tilt into a half-smile and he raises an eyebrow. "Jealous?"

"No." I lie and narrow my eyes at him as if I'm offended.

"We went to school together." He lies back, stretches his arms behind his head, and looks at the sky.

I twirl my fingers through my ponytail and let my eyes travel from his flat stomach to his broad chest to his face. "How long have you been in Ovation?"

"I was transported here the day after I took the Assessment."

"Where do you live?" I scan the lights of the city and hope he lives nearby.

He sits up and points. "See that building over there with the dome?"

I look in the direction he's pointing. "The Capitol?"

"To the left of the Capitol. Nuclei Headquarters has the cupola surrounded by windows instead of columns."

"Nuclei Headquarters?" I suddenly feel unsettled. "What's your job assignment?"

Fritz reaches for my hand and holds it tightly, as if what he says next might scare me away. "They made me a junior member of the Nuclei."

Feeling the power shift between us, I withdraw my hand and look away, so he can't see the suspicion in my eyes. "You're a Nuclei member." My tone is smooth and unemotional, as if my throat isn't clogged with doubts and my mind isn't raising a million red flags.

Faking a yawn, I stand and back away. "I should go to bed and I'm sure you need to return to Headquarters."

I hasten toward the roof door. Fritz steps into my path and pulls me to him. I wedge my arms between us, resting my hands over his heart. He wraps his arms around my waist and rests his forehead against mine.

"Please don't pull away. You're the only one I trust." His breath warms my face and his words melt my heart.

He caresses my cheek, tilts my head back, and presses his soft lips against mine. My first kiss. My heart leaps against his chest. My eyelashes quiver against his cheeks. Sparks skitter and skate over my skin.

It feels like Earth is spinning so fast, it could spin right off its axis and hurl us into the nebulous cosmos. Unsealing our lips, I'm left feeling dazed and disoriented like when I stepped off the spinning platform at the Gala.

"You have lipstick on your face." I hesitantly run my thumb over his mouth.

He captures my hand, pulls it to his lips, and kisses my palm. "Do you trust me?"

I feel breathless. I can't speak so I nod.

"I'll come back to see you again soon. Okay?"

"I would like that." I look into his moonlit eyes and wish we could stay locked in this moment forever.

He kisses the apple of my cheek before moving toward the roof's edge. I remain on the rooftop until I can no longer hear his footsteps.

My lips still feel the weight of his kiss, my chest feels the warm glow of a thousand shooting stars, and my veins flow with liquid sunshine. I touch my lips and smile. I wish I could tell Opal all about Fritz and our first kiss.

Sneaking downstairs, I feel like I'm floating on a stairway of clouds. A man's voice coming from Saphronia's quarters jolts me out of my dreamscape. I definitely don't want to be caught eavesdropping on Saphronia. Why would she have a visitor after midnight? I blush when I think of my own rendezvous.

As I pass Clover's empty room, guilt gnaws at me. I hope she's okay. I haven't seen her since the Nadir ceremony. In my room, I lie down without bothering to change clothes.

Drifting to sleep, my mind cycles through all the things I forgot to ask Fritz. I'll ask about the other Fritz next time.

Twenty-seven

A sharp pain between my ribs bolts me from sleep. I'm lying on my stomach with my face buried in the pillow. A heavy weight presses against my lower back, trapping me against the mattress.

"Do as you're told or I'll drive this knife between your ribs." Someone grabs my hair and yanks my head back.

My neck pops. Fabric is forced between my teeth, pinning down my tongue. My heart races. Adrenaline sets my veins on fire. I shift and twist and kick. The knife cuts into my skin. Warm blood trickles down my side. I stop struggling. Blackness engulfs my face, blinding and suffocating me. Rope burns my wrists.

"Cover her eyes!"

"Done. Did you bind her wrists?"

"Yes, let's go. The other one is tied up in the hallway with Hamlet."

The attackers grip my arms and rip me out of bed. I crash to the floor and let my body go limp. They sandwich me between their vise-like grips.

"Get to your feet," a female voice hisses close to my ear.

As they drag me toward the bedroom door, images of Freya's ocean-battered eyeless body rush through my mind. I can't let them force me out of my room. I can't let them force me out of the house. I have to fight or I'm going to die.

My hands are bound behind my back, but my legs are free. I step back and lunge forward, forcing the attackers to stagger and loosen their grip. I ram my knee into the girl on my right. She curses and falls.

Breaking away, I blindly stumble for the door. If I could just make it to the hall, I could bang on walls and doors, I could wake up the other Supernovas.

A cast-iron fist smashes into my left temple, sending my head reeling, my knees buckling. My teeth snap together and the taste of blood shocks me. Red and white stars attack my eyes. I try to scream, to call for Golgi, but the scratchy fabric over my face traps my voice; the gag silences me. Panic claws up my insides like a rabid animal.

The cast-iron hands drag me across the floor, lug me to my feet, and shove me toward the hall. "The next time I punch you, I won't be so nice!"

My head throbs. My cheek aches. The laceration on my tongue burns and bleeds. If I could just free my hands. I struggle to pull my wrists apart but they are bound so tightly, the rope tears my skin. My heart pounds against my flannel shirt.

Whispers fill the hallway. "The elevator will be quieter than the stairs. Hamlet, take your Supernova in the elevator first. We'll be right behind you."

Feet shuffle toward the elevator. A muffled voice is silenced by a soft whack. They have another Supernova. Who is it? My brain swells and presses against my skull. I strain to come up with a plan, but my swelling brain leaves no room for coherent thoughts.

Ding. The attackers thrust me into the tiny death box, pressing against me, triggering my claustrophobia. The knife remains against my lower back as the elevator descends to the first floor. My heart thumps and bumps and thrashes, if it pumps any faster, it's going to explode. I try to catch my breath but every time I inhale, fabric goes up my nose. My face perspires under the cloth covering.

The elevator doors open and I'm pushed into the first-floor hallway. Are we passing the gym now? The library? Discomfort in the dark is foreign to me.

Someone shoves me through a door. The wind rips at the cloth covering my face. With every blink, my fake eyelashes catch on fabric. My shoe rolls and my ankle twists over jagged rocks. I try to lift my arms to stay balanced, but I'm quickly reminded of the rope digging into my wrists. Thankfully, I fell asleep with my shoes on.

"Keep moving." The tip of a knife jabs me in the side.

If they were going to kill us, wouldn't they have done it by now? Why didn't they drive the knife into my back and spill my blood all over the sheets while I slept? How did they gain access to the house? Security measures prevent people from entering or exiting Supernova residences after lights out.

Who would be crazy enough to kidnap Supernovas? Could Everly have orchestrated this to get back at me for outperforming her at Harvest? Did she kill Freya? No, if she had killed someone from House of Lillith, it would have been Cambria.

The ocean roars over the voices of the attackers, drowning out their words. They march us in the opposite direction of the spa and central square, away from populated areas.

Fear pours from my pores like steam from a steam engine. And the way steam propels an engine forward, I know at the right time, fear will force me to fight back. For now, I will let them think they have subdued me.

The strong winds that had been whipping against us for the past fifteen minutes become still and the rocky terrain becomes smooth asphalt.

I'm pulled sharply to the right. I trip over a threshold and the girls on each side of me squeeze my arms tighter to keep me upright.

We're in a long hallway. We turn right and then right again. I memorize every turn. The attackers have become quiet. Left turn. Approaching a bright area. The acrid smell of blood and smoke hangs in the air. A fire crackles. I'm pushed into a warm, smoky room.

A new female voice says, "Where are the others?"

After a moment of silence, the girl digging her fingers into my left arm says, "The lights were still on at House of Juliette."

"Porkchop, how many times did I tell you that if you couldn't get them all tonight to postpone Operation Pig?"

"I know Bacon, but we got split up from the group fetching the transgenics at House of Juliette. We didn't know they failed until we had already removed these two deviants from House of Saphronia."

"I should have known I couldn't trust the three of you to follow simple instructions. I should have done it myself. Porkchop, Hamlet, and Chitlins, hurry up and put on your ceremonial robes. Then, remove their face coverings."

Someone snatches the humid fabric from my head. Strands of my hair are ripped away with it. I wince. Ten to twelve girls wearing pig masks and brown robes gather around a bonfire. The masks cover their eyes and noses, but their sneers are visible under their snouts. They look like pig-faced monks.

Massive hooks with rusty tips hang from the high ceiling of the abandoned slaughterhouse. I shudder at the thought of livestock dangling from those hooks. Through the gag, I take a deep breath of the smoke-filled air and cough. Everly cowers in her pajamas with bare, bloody feet. Why us?

Everly makes brief eye contact before quickly looking away.

"Which of you would like to go first?" I recognize the voice as the one referred to as Bacon. Bacon circles me and Everly. "Will it be you?" She grabs my face and turns my eyes toward the fire.

I clench my jaw and pull my chin out of her hand. The movement exacerbates the pain on the left side of my head. I stare at Bacon with defiance I don't feel.

She throws back her snout and laughs. "My, my, my, aren't you feisty."

"What about you?" Bacon lifts Everly's chin.

Everly keeps her eyes down.

"I saw this one prancing around at Harvest like she was better than everyone." She clicks her tongue disapprovingly. "We'll give Prancer here the honor of going first." She snaps her fingers and points to a group of pigs; they rush to Everly's side.

As the horror unfolds before me, I feel like this can't be real. This can't be my life. This has to be a nightmare.

Bacon saunters to a small platform near the fire. "Remove their gags. Nothing pleases me more than the sweet melody of transgenic screams."

The gag is torn from my mouth. I lick my dry, cracked lips. My tongue feels bruised. Two pig-faced girls grab Everly, walk her to Bacon, and force her to step onto the platform. They stand at her sides, each holding one of her elbows while her hands remain tied behind her back. One of the pigs keeps a tight hold on me.

Everly's chest heaves. She rubs her cheek against her shoulder, pushing tangled hair off her face. Her eyes dart around the room like she's looking for a way out. Even from a distance, I can see that she's shaking. I have a sinking feeling when I realize she's not going to put up a fight.

Bacon raises a hand and motions to Everly. "Behold this perversion of nature, this woman mixed with beast. This half-breed transgenic has the audacity to walk among us, to flaunt her perversion in our faces. Do we deserve to live with these transgenic abominations?"

A chorus of pigs scream, "No!"

"What do we do to transgenics?"

The pigs squeal, "Kill!"

"I can't hear you." Bacon prompts in a singsong tone.

"Kill transgenics! Kill transgenics! Kill transgenics!" The pigs chant while beating wooden canes on the concrete floor.

The ground vibrates under my feet and sends shock waves up my spine. Chill bumps rise on my arms.

"Now," Bacon says to the pigs standing next to Everly.

They pull Everly off the platform and shove her to her knees. One pig grabs her by the hair and yanks her head backward over the platform. The back of her head strikes the wooden surface. The sounds makes me flinch. Everly struggles to sit up, but they keep her locked in place.

Bacon stands between Everly and the fire. She nods at a petite girl. The girl pulls a roll of tape from her pocket, tears off two squares, and pries Everly's eyes open. Everly squirms and jerks like a fish on a hook as the pig tapes her eyelids to her brow bone.

I watch in horror. The ball of dread in my stomach grows so large, I swear I can feel it expanding against my lungs, crushing the air out of me.

Bacon waves her fingers in the air showing off extra-long fingernails filed into sharp daggers that sparkle silver in the firelight. She reaches for Everly's face. Everly shakes her head and flinches away.

"Now, let's see if this one is a soprano or an alto." She rakes the tips of her fingernails across Everly's cheekbone in a mocking caress before lifting her hand in the air and plunging her razor-sharp fingernails into Everly's right eye socket.

A blood-curdling scream rips through the room. I inhale sharply and hold my breath.

Bacon spins with the eyeball held high for all to see. The fire glints against the shiny eye impaled on her fingernail. She smiles and shows off her trophy. "Behold, the mark of the beast."

The pigs beat their canes on the floor in a feverish frenzy. Bacon tosses Everly's eyeball into the fire. It sizzles and shrieks like a lobster boiled alive. Blue sparks burst and pop in the air.

Everly screams and sobs. Blood trickles down her face in a squiggly line from the empty eye socket. Both eyes are still taped open. I struggle to free my wrists.

Bacon cups one hand around her own ear and waves her other hand as if she's a composer. "Ladies, we have ourselves a soprano. Keep singing little piggy."

Everly howls.

"Shall we pluck out her other eye or shall we allow her screams to provide background music for our next guest of honor? Hmm, decisions, decisions."

Bacon taps her bloody fingernail against the cheek of her pig mask. *Tap, tap, tap.* She spins and faces me. "Let's move on to the other transgenic. We'll come back to this one."

The pigs yank Everly away from the platform and drop her in a heap on the floor where she slumps forward sobbing and choking and slobbering. I feel disgusted that she didn't fight back—she should have done something, *anything.*

Bacon gestures to the pig next to me. My legs weaken. My heart frantically bangs on my ribs. I glance through the heavy smoke at the doorway behind me. The pig at my side grabs the ropes binding my arms and pushes me toward the platform.

"Please don't do this," I beg, dragging my feet.

I can't see her taunting eyes behind the mask, but her lips turn up in a tight smile. She will enjoy this, just like the others. She slides something into the back pocket of my jeans.

She whispers, "Hide your eyes."

I gasp in surprise. I know that voice.

How did she end up here? Why would she let them do this to us? The pig guides me to the platform. I step up. Wedged between two pigs with Bacon standing between me and the fire, I turn my brain upside-down looking for escape options.

Bacon continues her composer charade, waving her hands over Everly. It infuriates Everly. She wails louder, her mouth and single eye wide-open, screaming, staring. I clamp down on my jaw determined not to let them see me cry, no matter how much it hurts.

The pigs excitedly gather around me as if I'm a trough they're preparing to feast their gluttonous mouths on. They beat their canes against the floor and chant, "Kill! Kill! Kill!"

The heat from the fire penetrates my jeans, scorching my legs. The smoke burns my eyes. I imagine the robed assailants placing an apple in my mouth and roasting me like a pig over the fire. I won't let them. A spark of determination runs up my spine.

Everly's screams light up my nerves. I want to cover my ears. I wiggle my arms and the rope loosens. Clover untied me! My freed hands boost my hope for an escape. Bacon gives the signal to the girls to hold me down and tape my eyelids.

Clover releases my arm. The petite girl tries to push me to my knees. I lock my legs, grab a fistful of her hair, and shove her hard toward Bacon. Like a domino, she knocks into Bacon and they both fall into the hungry fire. Flames melt their skin and singe their hair. They squeal and flail and struggle to escape the flames. The other pigs gape and freeze. The fire sputters and pops, releasing the smell of burning flesh.

I sprint for the hallway. Pausing to look back, I see Everly crumpled and crying. I recall my helplessness when 306 was being harassed by Enforcers and when Clover was being pelted by eggs. I can't ignore my conscience this time. I rush toward Everly, carefully dodging the roasting pigs rolling across the floor.

I squeeze Everly's arm. Her single eye stares at me, but she whimpers and doesn't move. She's in a daze. I haul her to her feet, wrap my arm around her waist, and lead her across the room. The pigs are so focused on extinguishing the flames engulfing their leader that they don't even try to stop us. Right turn, left turn, left turn.

Bursting through the exit, I pull Everly around the corner and loosen the ropes binding her wrists. I can't look at her face. The image of her blood-stained cheek and eyelids taped wide open is already seared into my brain and will probably haunt me forever.

Once her hands are free, she tears the tape off her eyes. The sound of her eyelashes being ripped out makes me cringe. She looks pathetic with her Picasso face and dirty feet.

She puts a hand over her empty eye socket and wails. "They took my eye! I can't see!"

"Be quiet! We have to hide." The arched entrance to the cemetery glows brightly against the night sky. "Over there." I grab her arm. We run toward the cemetery, as if the home of the dead will offer us protection from death itself.

Twenty-eight

We turn off the main road and race through the cemetery gate. My chest heaves. I lean over to catch my breath. The smell of burning flesh clings to my nasal cavity. I gulp fresh air and look for a place to hide. Above-ground tombs dot the landscape, providing plenty of options.

"Split up and hide!" I blast off through the cemetery.

Running past row after row of graves, I look back for Everly; she's gone. Flashlights illuminate the cemetery entrance. I crouch and take cover behind a statue of Mary. I can't just sit here. I have to keep moving.

Two flashlights create light trails near me. Where did they come from? I squat and lean against a mausoleum. The cool limestone feels good against my sticky back. I wipe sweat from my hairline and massage the knot on my temple.

Where should I go? I could make a run for it, but they know the terrain better and there are more of them. Voices grow nearer. I shiver at the thought of hiding in a cramped space with dead people, but at least dead people can't hurt me.

I creep up the steps of a mausoleum and push open the heavy wooden door. A dusty coffin is displayed on a pedestal in the center of the small space. I quietly close the door and rest against it.

Something in my back pocket digs into my flesh. What did Clover give me? I pull out the hunk of plastic. It's a contact case. I unscrew one side. A blue disk floats in clear liquid. Clover has been wearing contacts to hide her tapeta all along. She's transgenic like me and Everly.

"Did you hear that?" A voice drifts through the iron bars of the mausoleum's decorative windows.

I close the contact case and return it to my pocket. Strands of stringy spider webs stick to my eyelashes and hair. I rake my fingernails over my face. The more I pull at the spider-silk, the stickier it gets. I strip off the fake eyelashes and throw them in the corner where a web glows with evidence of its owner's prowess.

"You check inside the mausoleums on this row and I'll check the next one. We can alternate rows until we find them."

"That's crazy! We can't check them all. There are a million graves."

"I know, but Bacon will be pissed if we don't bring her the dark-haired transgenic. We have to keep looking."

They're talking about me. Who are they? How is Clover involved?

Doors slam to my left and right. Too close. A wave of anxiety rolls over me when I realize what I have to do. I reach for the coffin, wedge my palms under the lid, and heave upward. It barely budges. My arms shake as the lid creaks open. I won't look inside. I quickly crawl into the death bed, lie on my back, and let the lid fall.

Bones crack and crumble beneath me. A decaying skeleton jabs its bony tentacles into my ribs, reminding me of my own mortality.

My nose nearly touches the casket ceiling. Dust particles float around me like glitter in a snow globe. I panic at the thought of getting trapped and dying a slow death.

Hairy spider legs saunter across the top of my right hand. I keep my eyes closed and try not to freak out. Something circles my ankle and crawls up the leg of my jeans. Spiders? Ants? I take a deep breath and fight off an oncoming panic attack.

The door to the mausoleum slams open. Footsteps shuffle across the floor.

"I think I found something."

A second set of footsteps enters the cramped tomb. "What is it?"

"Look in the corner. Corpses don't wear fake eyelashes but transgenics do."

"Did you check inside the coffin?"

My breath comes in short bursts. My heart hammers my ears. How could I be so careless? Dust prickles my nose hair. A sneeze lodges in my sinuses. I clamp a hand over my mouth and try to suppress the sneeze welling up inside me.

"Ah-ah…" *Don't do it.* I cover my nose. "Achoo!"

My fingers vibrate from the force. Eyes wide in horror, I wipe my hands on my jeans. After the longest minute of my life, the coffin lid creaks open in slow motion. Golden light from the sunrise momentarily blinds me.

Two wide-eyed, open-mouthed girls stare at me. "It's her!"

I shoot out of the coffin like a toy from a jack-in-the-box and land on my feet near the door. The girls gasp and shrink back. Even without their masks, I don't recognize them. I spring through the door and run for the back of the cemetery.

"Don't let her get away!"

I weave around a maze of tombstones and mausoleums. My shoes slip and slide across grass damp with morning dew. Fog rises from graves like ghosts of the dead swallowing their tombstones whole.

The thick mist makes it impossible to see beyond a few feet. The rising sun will burn off the fog soon, but for now, I welcome the reduced visibility. I don't hear anyone trailing me and they probably couldn't see me if they tried.

I breathe in the humid morning air, brush corpse dust off my shirt, and shake out my smoke-filled hair. Statues of angels, saints, Jesus, and Mary pray over graves.

This place gives me the creeps. I speed toward a fence shrouded in sunlit mist and without slowing down, I grab the fence, hoist myself over, and land on my feet. I run toward the Supernova neighborhood without looking back.

Cutting into the neighborhood, I spin around expecting to see pigs chasing me, but the streets are empty. I exhale and slow down. My legs shake. My head hurts. My heart pounds.

Despite feeling rundown, the desire for vengeance takes root and buds beneath my weariness. Someday, the pigs will wish they had never crossed me. Someday, they will pay.

Flashing blue lights illuminate the street in front of House of Saphronia. Security Forces vehicles hug the curb. Everly must have made it home. I drag my feet up the front steps. Are the girls who abducted me and Everly the same ones who killed Freya?

I enter the house and follow the sound of voices to the dining room. From the doorway, I watch a nurse stretch white bandages across Everly's eye while Security Forces interrogate her. Saphronia stands nearby. The other Supernovas must be sleeping.

"Wren." Everly's voice sounds hoarse and hollow, as if the pigs stole her voice in addition to her sense of sight and self-respect.

Saphronia spins around and crosses the room. She lifts my chin and tilts my face left, then right. Two Security Force members approach.

"I'm Commander Katherine Arden and this is my colleague, Sergeant Nolan Smith," the tall redheaded woman says.

Sergeant Smith places a passport scanner against my neck. "Please confirm your identity."

"Wren Weiss," I croak. My throat is dry and my mouth tastes like ashes.

"Thank you, Wren. Please have a seat." The Commander motions to the dining room table as she and the Sergeant pull out chairs and sit.

Commander Arden says, "It's my understanding that you and Everly were abducted last night. Can you tell me the approximate time the abduction took place?"

I sit and attempt to piece together the timeline and events. "It was around two or three a.m."

"How many people were involved in the abduction? Male or female? Did you see their faces?" Commander Arden asks.

"Two females pulled me out of bed and covered my face so I couldn't see them. There was a third female in the hallway they referred to as Hamlet."

"Were there any identifiable characteristics? Did you recognize their voices? A familiar smell? Anything else you can tell us?"

Clover's voice rattles around in my head. *Hide your eyes.* I shake my head. "I didn't recognize any of them."

The nurse approaches. "Do you mind if I interrupt to examine that head injury?"

The Commander nods her consent.

The nurse prods the knot on my head. "Have you experienced dizziness or shortness of breath? Any other symptoms or injuries?"

"Just a headache," I respond.

She lifts my chin. "Pupil dilation is normal. That's a good sign. Take this for the headache." She hands me two pills and a glass of water.

I swallow the pills and return the empty glass.

"Ice your injury for twenty minutes every three to four hours." The nurse hands me an ice pack and walks away.

"Please take us through the events in the order they happened," Commander Arden says.

I hold the ice pack against my temple and relay the events while Sergeant Smith diligently takes notes.

When I finish telling them what happened, Commander Arden stands and addresses Sergeant Smith. "Comb through every house and medical facility in Ovation looking for evidence of third-degree burns."

Commander Arden says, "If additional details come to mind later, please ask Golgi to summon me."

Saphronia approaches the table, speaks briefly with the Commander, and then turns to me and Everly. "Girls, you may rest in your rooms. You are excused from Supernova activities until further notice."

I head to my bedroom without waiting for Everly. My head throbs and my hair smells like smoke. Every cell in my body cries out for sleep but I have to shower off the dust, grime, and cobwebs first.

In the bathroom, I consider dropping my flannel and jeans in the laundry chute, but I don't want to lose the only items I have from home. I'll launder them myself later. I take a quick shower and fall asleep as soon as my head hits the pillow.

Twenty-nine

A knock on the bedroom door wakes me. I bolt upright. How long have I been sleeping? I shiver at the thought of how I last woke in this bed. My room glows pink from the setting sun. I sit up as Saphronia enters.

"I hope you're well-rested?" She hands me a fresh ice pack.

"Yes, thanks."

"Good. The security and well-being of Supernovas is of utmost importance in Ovation. Although security measures have been strengthened across the neighborhood to ensure Supernova safety, this will be your last night here.

"Dr. Hahn has summoned you to Nuclei Headquarters. A Helix will transport you in the morning. Please pack all of your belongings tonight."

Summoned to Nuclei Headquarters? Why? Maybe they want to interrogate us about the attack. "Is Everly going, too?"

"Everly will remain here. Get some rest."

After Saphronia leaves, I place the ice pack against my bruised cheek. The headache has subsided, but I'm still exhausted. I trace the raised scab on my side where the knife penetrated. It's only a scratch.

I groggily slog to the closet and empty dresser contents into my suitcase. I yank jumpsuits off their hangers and drop them on top. My jeans and flannel smell like smoke. I remove the contact case from my jeans pocket, hide it in the bottom of the suitcase, and head downstairs with my dirty clothes.

Sneaking into the laundry room, I feel like I'm trespassing in Nadir quarters. Built-in cabinets surround a washer and dryer. I drop my clothes into the washer.

The instructions show where to pour detergent, but where is the detergent? I squat and open the cupboard next to the dryer. Inside, a bottle of detergent peeks out from behind a pile of brown fabric. I tug on the fabric. Two pig masks clatter to the floor.

I flinch, drop the fabric, and scoot away from the eyeless masks. How did the robes and masks get here? Are Berkeley and Harlowe involved? That would explain how the attackers gained access to the house and why Berkeley looked nervous the morning Security Forces informed us of Freya's fate.

The fabric reeks of smoke. I hear the pigs banging their canes. I feel the flames leeching moisture from my skin. I smell burning, roasting, melting flesh. Everly's screams echo in my ears. My heart starts pounding.

I visualize a brick wall being built between me and the sights, sounds, and smells from last night. Brick by brick, I shut them out. Grabbing the detergent bottle and keeping an eye on the door, I start the washer. Water floods the bin and saturates my clothing. I scoop up the robes with trembling hands.

Should I give the evidence to Saphronia? Should I contact Commander Arden? No. I know exactly what to do. I tiptoe to Supernova quarters with the robes rolled up in my arms and knock on Everly's bedroom door. When she doesn't answer, I let myself in. Everly lies in bed with her back to the door.

"Everly?"

"Go away," a muffled voice responds.

I walk around the bed. "I have something to show you."

She cracks her eye open.

I hold up the pig masks and robes.

"Where did you get those?" She sits up.

"I found them in the laundry room."

"Why were you in the laundry room?" She eyes me suspiciously.

I can't stop staring at the bandage covering her missing eye. "Washing my clothes."

"Let me see those." She snatches the robes out of my hands and brings them to her nose. Her facial muscles tighten and twitch. "Berkeley and Harlowe. I should have known."

She jumps out of bed and starts pacing. Rage radiates from her pores as her heels strike the cold floor. The coward I witnessed last night has been replaced by the version of Everly I'm more familiar with.

"I swear to Galileo, I will butcher them," she says through clenched teeth. "But first, I will torture them." Fury sets her lone eye ablaze.

I back away and turn toward the bedroom door.

Everly says, "Wren?"

It's the first time she's called me by my name.

"Thanks. For last night. They were going to kill me."

I fidget with the doorknob. "You would have done the same for me."

Her silence confirms what we both know. I head to my bedroom and try not to worry about why I'm being transported to Nuclei Headquarters, but concerns continue to nettle the folds of my cortex.

I press my forehead against the glass wall in my bedroom and enjoy the morning sunlight's warmth on my face. Ovation has been my home for only a couple of months, yet my family and Hillcrest seem as far away as the barely visible moon.

My door swings open and Berkeley enters. "Your suitcase?" Her blank eyes meet mine.

"Wait." I cross the room, heave the suitcase onto the bed, and rummage through it until my hand grazes the rough edges of the contact case. I hide it in my palm and close the suitcase.

Berkeley approaches and reaches for the suitcase, revealing a red welt across her inner wrist. My neck hair prickles. Could it be an injury from last night? She sees me studying the welt and abruptly turns, leaving the room.

"Please report to the foyer," Golgi says.

Instead of obeying Golgi, I carry the contacts to the bathroom. I remove one of the floating disks, open my left eye wide, and press the disk against it. My eyes water. I blink and resist the urge to remove the disk.

After a minute, it molds to my eye and feels more comfortable. I pop the other disk into my right eye. My irises are a brighter shade of blue. My tapeta are no longer visible.

"Please report to the foyer," Golgi repeats.

I slide the case into my jumpsuit pocket and step into the hallway. I wait for Golgi to remind me to take the pills on my nightstand, but Golgi remains silent.

Blaise, Prisha, Maris, and Saphronia are gathered in the foyer waiting for me.

"Say your goodbyes, ladies," Saphronia says.

Blaise rushes toward me, throws her arms around me, and pulls me into a big hug. "This isn't goodbye. You'll be safe at Nuclei Headquarters and we'll see you at the Winter Harvest."

"Why is Wren being moved to Headquarters?" Maris asks.

Saphronia responds, "We don't ask questions of the Nuclei. Let's get moving. The Nuclei is expecting you."

Maris winks and hugs me. "Don't do anything I wouldn't do."

If Maris accomplishes her plan to return to Clairemont, this may be the last time I see her. I squeeze her hand. "Happy sailing, Maris."

"Best wishes, Wren," Prisha says.

"It has been a pleasure hosting you, Wren." Saphronia's gold sandals trigger the glass doors to slide open. "Berkeley has loaded your belongings into the Helix. You are always welcome to visit."

"Thanks, Saphronia."

As I descend the steps toward the Helix parked at the curb, excitement and trepidation course through my body. I'm excited at the prospect of living closer to Fritz and seeing him more often, but I'm nervous about what will be expected of me once I'm there.

If I no longer live at House of Saphronia, does that mean I'm no longer a Supernova? Will I still be expected to participate in egg harvests? What if they assign me to a worse position?

I slide into the front seat of the Helix and check the center console for snacks. Withdrawing a pack of almonds, I rip open the wrapper and chomp on the nuts as the Helix navigates the streets.

I still feel traumatized from last night. They were calling us transgenics. Half-breeds. Dr. Hart said animal genes were used to give us night vision. I flashback to the cats caged underground at Guantanamo and shudder at the thought of being part-animal, part-human.

House of Juliette members walk to the spa, their red jumpsuits loud against the muted stucco buildings. Other residents mill around shop entrances.

The Helix travels only a few miles before entering the circular driveway of Nuclei Headquarters. Two-story arched windows sit atop a covered colonnade that extends the entire length of the colossal building. The Helix parks under the porte-cochere.

I never thought I would get this close to the Nuclei. I'm excited and terrified—mostly terrified.

Thirty

Shouldn't Nuclei Headquarters be surrounded by Security Forces? The premises are empty. I grip my suitcase handle tighter, press my free hand against the door, and step across the threshold.

"State your business." A young guard sitting next to a bifurcated staircase jumps to his feet, draws his weapon, and aims for my chest.

My passport sends a warning shock down my spine. I inhale sharply. I know I should run away, but I panic and lock up and freeze.

"Intruder alert, intruder alert," a robotic voice blares from the intercom system.

White lights start flashing. Heavy footsteps thunder overhead. Combat boots race down the stairs from both sides. Armed guards descend the stairs lining up their rifle sights on their target: me.

Another shock burns my spine and sends heat coursing to my fingertips. My hand instinctively flies to the back of my neck. I consider digging my fingernails into the soft flesh and ripping out the passport to make the pain stop. The sound of a bullet being loaded into a rifle chamber echoes throughout the grand lobby.

"Don't move! Keep your hands where we can see them!" a guard yells.

My body trembles. My mouth dries out. I let my hand fall to my side.

"Drop the contraband and get on your knees!"

What contraband? I want to obey, but my body refuses to budge. All I can focus on is counting to ten between shocks. A female guard rushes toward me. Her fingers grip my clavicle and shove me down. My knees buckle and slam into the floor. The passport emits another shock.

"Take the contraband outside and neutralize it." She digs her fingers into my shoulder.

A guard rips my suitcase out of my hand and swings open the door. Sunlight floods the lobby. If I could run outside, the passport would stop setting my nerves on fire. As the door closes, the sunlight retreats along with my hopes of escaping.

The remaining guards form a tight circle around me. Stainless steel barrels close in on my face. The barrels smell like metal polish. Heat rises from the collar of my jumpsuit. Sweat rolls down my back.

The female guard releases my shoulder and shoves the barrel of her gun against my bruised cheek. I wince. I'm reminded of being blindfolded and punched in the face. Did they summon me here to finish the job? Is the Nuclei behind Freya's murder and Operation Pig?

"What is your business at Nuclei Headquarters?" a gruff voice growls from my right side while the female guard continues to jam the barrel of her gun into my swollen cheek.

I stare into the darkness of a barrel that hovers over my eyelashes. One trigger pull is all it would take to send a bullet flying down the barrel to pierce my skull and end my life.

I lick my lips and try to speak. My taste buds recoil from the taste of fear. "I… I was…"

"Scan her passport."

A passport scanner is pressed against my neck. Sweat trickles down the side of my face.

"Stand down," an authoritative voice bellows.

The guards snap to attention and form lines on each side of me. Their swift withdrawal creates a gust of air that ruffles my hair and causes strands to stick to my sweaty face. They grip the butts of their rifles in one hand and redirect the barrels from my face to the ceiling.

My view of the stairs had been obstructed by the guards, but now I clearly see who issued the order. A man in a crisp white uniform with salt-and-pepper hair ambles down the stairs. I recognize him and my heart skips.

I keep my eyes locked on him, silently pleading for him to intervene. I flinch as another shock courses through my body.

"At ease," he says.

The guards relax, but remain where they are.

"Treble," he says.

A chubby guard with ginger hair steps forward. "Yes, sir?"

"You will remove all limitations from her passport."

"All? But, sir—"

"Now."

"Yes, sir." The boy called Treble hastens toward me.

I study his freckled babyface as he presses the scanner against my passport. The flush across his ruddy cheeks extends to the tip of his ears. He enters information into the scanner. It beeps and he returns to his place next to the other guards. The lights stop flashing. The intruder alert stops blaring.

Five… four… three… two… one. I flinch in anticipation, but nothing happens. Ten more seconds pass. My nerves throb as if they had been shredded against a cheese grater.

The man in white offers me his hand. "Stand, please." His gentle tone is opposite the tone he used with the guards.

My arm trembles. I accept his extended hand. He pulls me to my feet. My legs feel weak. He keeps a grip on my arm, allowing me to steady myself. His strength surprises me for his age. He must be in his fifties or sixties.

Standing face-to-face with him, I avert my eyes out of habit, but then I remember I'm wearing contacts. His wavy hair is gray, but his eyebrows and eyelashes are dark. He studies my face the same way he did the night of the Science Gala. I couldn't place him then and I can't place him now, but I know his voice somehow. Who is he?

"Welcome to Headquarters. Pardon the guards. We must take certain precautions to assure the safety of those who live and work at Headquarters. I'm sure you understand." His smile deepens the lines around his eyes, making him look older.

I nod but wonder if precautions that include frightening an unarmed girl are really necessary.

He turns to the guards. "You are dismissed. Return to your stations."

All guards but one shuffle past us and climb the stairs. The one with the ruddy complexion gawks at me. The remaining guard takes his seat.

The authoritative man says, "I am Dr. Augustus Hahn. We have been expecting you."

The Dr. Hahn? As in the Head of the Nuclei? How did a girl from Hillcrest end up at Nuclei Headquarters with *the* Dr. Hahn? The Nuclei broadcast: that's how I know his voice. I realize I know his face from photos in the *Nuclei Newsletter*. I try to maintain a neutral expression and swallow the ball of disbelief lodged in my throat.

I step back, happy to find the strength has returned to my legs. The burning sensation in my fingers has subsided. Dr. Hahn told the guard to remove limitations from my passport.

Does that mean I can travel anywhere? I would love nothing more than to return to Hillcrest and confront my parents.

Dr. Hahn walks toward the stairs. "This afternoon, you will meet the other Nuclei members, but now, please join me in my office. I'm sure you have many questions and I may have the answers."

He offers me his elbow. I tentatively link my arm through his and we climb the stairs together. My fear has dissipated. My heart rate has slowed.

I gauge my feelings. Shouldn't I fear the Head of the Nuclei or mistrust him at a minimum? Instead, I feel comfortable and at ease. I never felt like I belonged in Hillcrest or at House of Saphronia. Do I belong here?

Above the second floor, sunlight floods through the tall dome that makes Nuclei Headquarters easy to spot from any location in Ovation. Royal blue and gold tiles surround a circular window in the cupola center.

"Magnificent, isn't it?" Dr. Hahn says. "In the 1920s, this building was one of the tallest on the island. For decades, it served as the Presidential Palace. We spent years renovating it to its former glory.

"The walls hold many stories. If you look closely, you will see bullet holes from an assassination attempt that took place over a century ago. Fifty men barged into the palace in broad daylight and attempted to assassinate the President. They failed. You can imagine their fate."

"How was Genova Island not impacted during World War III when every other land mass was decimated?" I ask, matching Dr. Hahn's slow pace.

Scientists in lab coats pass us and nod to acknowledge Dr. Hahn.

"For decades, a dictator presided over the island. He warned other world leaders of a nuclear holocaust that would wipe out Earth as we know it. While his populace starved, he used resources to develop an anti-nuclear defense system.

"World leaders laughed at his paranoia. They banned him from participating in the world economy by enforcing sanctions and trade embargoes. He died before World War III, but the defense system he developed protected designated parts of the island."

Dr. Hahn leads me to another staircase.

"If there were survivors here, how did the Nuclei come to power?" I ask as we climb the stairs.

"Love leads rational people to do irrational things," he says.

"What do you mean?" I glance at his profile.

"Survivors left protected areas in search of loved ones. Many died of radiation poisoning or by ingesting contaminated water sources. There was no functioning government. We rebuilt from the ground up. Many would have been overwhelmed by the task, but we approached it as an opportunity to start over, to build a world where we could eradicate the darkest corners of humanity."

The third floor opens to a grand ballroom with sleek floors and cream walls framed by gold molding. I admire the arched windows crowning massive doors that lead to outdoor balconies.

"The ballroom was modeled after the Hall of Mirrors at Versailles." Dr. Hahn clasps his hands behind his back and surveys the ballroom with an expression of pride on his face.

"I learned about France in school. Did you ever visit?" I ask.

"Why yes, I worked in Paris as a young man. There was no finer city in the world."

Dr. Hahn crosses the ballroom toward a double door. He waves his hand over a microchip scanner. We enter an office decorated in rich hues of brown, red, and gold. Red velvet curtains with gold accents hang from tall windows.

Dr. Hahn sits behind a dark mahogany desk. Antique wooden chairs face the desk. On the other side of the room, a brown leather couch and matching chairs are arranged over a sun-bleached oriental rug. I study the award plaques hanging on the wall behind Dr. Hahn.

"Please, have a seat." Dr. Hahn motions to the antique chairs. "What questions do you have for me?"

I sit and attempt to get comfortable. Antiques were obviously built for looks, not comfort. If I could get the answer to a single question today, what would it be?

Every day since the Science Gala, I have replayed Dr. Hart's words: *Specimen 33 was born November thirtieth, 2056 at the Northeast Coastal Research Center.*

I clear my throat and make eye contact. "Did you know my biological parents?"

Dr. Hahn leans forward, props his elbows on the desk, and intertwines his fingers. He peers at me over steepled hands. "Doctors Claire and Corbin Beckham."

I scoot to the edge of my seat. My tongue is tangled in question marks. My eyes widen and my mouth cracks open to make room for all the questions lining up behind my lips. Hope swells within me.

"Are they still alive?" I lean forward.

Dr. Hahn unclasps his hands and rests his arms against the desk. "They perished during the war. They were fine people."

"Oh." I slump back. I should have known. I stare at my feet and move the toes of my shoes across alternating lines of sun and shadow from the shutters to my left.

Dr. Hahn breaks the long silence. "I presume you would like to know more?"

I stop fidgeting and meet his eyes. "What more is there to know? I'm a science experiment that nobody cares about other than the scientists winning trophies for their contributions." I hate how sulky my voice sounds.

A look of sympathy softens his serious features. He stands and approaches a self-portrait hanging on the wall near the door. He raises his arm and a portion of the wall opens revealing a hidden corridor.

Dr. Hahn says, "Only two people know about this passage. Me, and now you. I trust you can keep a secret?"

"Of course." Why does he trust me? He barely knows me.

Curiosity drives me to follow Dr. Hahn into the corridor. Lights flicker on as the wall swivels shut behind us.

He knocks on the corridor wall and says, "Soundproof."

I'm not sure if I'm supposed to be impressed or freaked out. I'm leaning toward being freaked out. Why would there be a secret soundproof room attached to his office?

The short corridor opens to a stark white room devoid of the decorative columns, arched windows, and art frescoes that lend a majestic air to the rest of the building. In the middle of the room sits a metal table with four chairs. A worn leather recliner is positioned next to cabinets and an end table stacked with books. A counter on the back wall contains lab equipment.

Dr. Hahn slides a chair back from the table and gestures for me to sit. "I have been preparing for our reunification for over twenty years."

I take a seat and frown. "Reunification?"

He sits across from me and untangles the cords piled on top of the machine centered on the table. It looks like a vintage record player. "You will have the answers you seek momentarily." Dr. Hahn adjusts the dials on the machine and hums a tune I don't recognize.

I look around the windowless room. Where could the lone

black door behind me lead? If the former President was so paranoid of a nuclear holocaust, maybe it leads to an underground bunker. Or maybe it's an escape route for assassination attempts.

Dr. Hahn presses disks against each of his temples. Wires run from the disks to the machine. He hands two disks to me. One side is smooth and slightly concave. The outer side is convex with red wires emerging from the center.

"What are these?" I ask, holding up the disks.

"Emtrodes. This machine enables episodic memory transfer. If you grant me permission, I would like to share my memories with you. Memories of who you used to be."

Who I used to be? I scan his face for a sign that he's joking, but his serious eyes communicate nothing more than a gentle sense of urgency. Could he be senile or is it really possible to transfer memories?

I place the emtrodes against my temples. Dr. Hahn flips a switch. Five circles of varying sizes start spinning on the machine's surface. Dr. Hahn reaches across the table with his palm up. I place my hand in his.

"Now, close your eyes. Once the process begins, do not open your eyes." Dr. Hahn closes his eyes.

Minutes pass. I crack an eye open. Dr. Hahn's brows furrow as if he's summoning all of his brain power. I close my eyes. A vibration begins in my inner ear. The whir of the machine becomes a blur of voices.

A kaleidoscope of colors and patterns moves across the back of my eyelids. Green and blue and yellow fragments gel into a coherent image. It's like watching a jigsaw puzzle put itself together.

I'm walking across a lush lawn where students are chatting, reading, studying. I pause in the shade of an oak tree and scan the faces of lounging university students, but I don't see her.

Who is Dr. Hahn looking for?

There she is: yellow shirt, white shorts, brown hair. She sits on the grass, face half hidden by the book she reads. My heart leaps. I step into the sun and let it warm my skin.

It feels so real. Who is she? I can't see her face.

I sneak up behind her, wrap my hands around her eyes, and whisper in her ear, "Guess who?"

She jumps up, throws her arms around me. "August!"

I swoop her off her feet, we spin around and around, she throws her head back, peals of laughter ring out across the lawn.

I still haven't seen her face.

We stumble to the ground still laughing. I reach over to brush the hair from her eyes—

I stiffen. The girl in his memories is me! I jerk my eyes open. Dr. Hahn's eyes are still closed. He squeezes my hand reassuringly. I want to yank my hand out of his, but I need to see more. I take a deep breath and close my eyes.

I'm at an outdoor wedding. My wedding. Seated guests smile. I look at the man in the tuxedo next to me. My best man. My father.

Dr. Hahn's father, that is.

I inhale the jasmine breeze and try to commit every detail to memory. Sunshine and flowers. Love and promises. My future wife walks down the aisle escorted by her father, Dr. Beckham.

I gape at the vision of myself in a wedding dress.

Pride consumes me as Delilah takes my hands. Her eyes mirror the love within my own. My heart swells.

The image dissolves. I'm floating, but I feel heavy. Indistinct voices buzz in my ears. Fuzzy, white objects float against a brown background. The blurry picture gradually comes into focus.

Astronauts kneel on the barren surface of Mars collecting samples. The sound of my breath fills my spacesuit helmet. Delilah floats toward me. She smiles and holds up a vial filled with surface particles. I float to her, pull her close, and let my visor rest against hers.

Dr. Hahn's reflection appears in Delilah's visor. Only, it isn't Dr. Hahn at all. The man in the spacesuit is an older version of Fritz. Goosebumps rush up my neck and scalp. What is Dr. Hahn trying to show me?

A hospital room. Faceless doctors hover over Delilah. A baby cries. "It's a boy." They place the baby in her arms. She looks lovingly at the swaddled newborn. "My Gregor."

A piercing beep rings in my ears.

"Code blue!"

A nurse rips the baby away and tries to pull me from the bed, but I won't leave her side. They try to resuscitate her.

Please hold on. I can't do this without you.

"I'm sorry, sir, I need you to step away from the bed."

Her warm hand in mine. I don't want to let go. I release her hand and stumble back. Hospital staff rushes in and surrounds the bed. I feel helpless as the minutes tick by, every tick reducing her chances for survival. Grief wells up in my chest. The birth of our son was supposed to be a joyous day. How did she go into cardiac arrest so abruptly? There were no complications. She was in perfect health.

"We've lost her."

Sobs rack my body as the hospital staff, defeated, backs away from the bed.

I open my eyes, yank off the emtrodes, and toss them on the table. Warm tears burn my eyes. I'm disoriented by the emotions Dr. Hahn conveyed to me. I push the chair back. It screeches against the floor. My legs sway and my body shakes. I stand and hold the table for support.

Dr. Hahn powers down the memory machine. "You are one of us. You are one of the original members of the Nuclei."

Thirty-one

*D*r. Hahn walks around the table, places his hands on my shoulders, and leans in so closely I can make out a few gray hairs in his dark eyebrows. There's a familiarity between us I can't explain. I felt it at the Science Gala and again when he intervened downstairs today.

"You, my dear, are a DNA replica of my beloved Delilah."

"A replica? You mean a clone?" My tone relays my confusion.

"Dr. Akimoto used the somatic cell nuclear transfer method which introduces a small percentage of mitochondrial DNA from the egg donor. You are a replica. Not an exact clone, but close."

My thoughts are muddled with the grief I still feel from experiencing Dr. Hahn's memory of his wife's death. Through the haze of loss, I try to focus on the questions I need to ask.

"The clones, I mean, replicas of Delilah, am I the only one or are there others?"

Dr. Hahn removes his hands from my shoulders, takes a step back, and keeps his intense gaze locked on mine. "We celebrated many genetic engineering accomplishments prior to the year you were born, but we also experienced many setbacks in the early years of cloning attempts.

"There were more failures than successes. Every time we created a viable embryo with Delilah's DNA, my excitement kept me awake at all hours. I visited the lab overnight to check on the embryos.

"In the early years, none of the embryos survived the gestational period. Not a single one. Until you. Your DNA was modified to improve health and vision, among other things. When Dr. Akimoto presented the prototype, we all doubted its viability, but she proved us wrong.

"To answer your question: yes, there are other replicas of Delilah but they were born years later. The failure rate of the cloning method we were using was too high. We put the cloning program on hold to refine the process."

I recall the memory of Fritz's reflection in Delilah's spacesuit visor. "You cloned yourself the same year I was born?"

Dr. Hahn lifts his chin and tilts his head. I can see the gears turning as he tries to figure out how I could know. "Correct. The twins, Fritz and Franz, were born a few months before you."

"At the Northeast Coastal Research Center?" I ask.

"You were all born," he taps the table for emphasis, "right here."

"Here?" My voice rises, revealing my shock.

"Accompany me to the observation room." Dr. Hahn opens the black door I had earlier imagined leading to an escape route or underground bunker.

He hums as we descend the dimly lit stairwell. At the bottom of the stairs, Dr. Hahn moves his hand across a scanner. I follow him into a small room with opaque windows. A counter with buttons and levers runs along the wall under the windows.

"It's freezing in here." I rub my hands up and down my arms.

Dr. Hahn says, "The mainframe computer is in the adjoining room. We keep it cold to prevent overheating."

Dr. Hahn slides a lever and the windows gradually become transparent. I cross my arms over my chest to preserve body heat and step closer. Hundreds of glowing blue orbs look like eyeballs staring from the basement below. Something floats in a hazy liquid in each orb.

Dr. Hahn turns a dial until a faint light illuminates the basement. I have no idea what I'm looking at. I look to Dr. Hahn for answers.

"The Northeast Coastal Research Center," he says.

My eyebrows pop up. "This is where I was born?"

"This is where you were born," Dr. Hahn confirms. "We stream classical music through the sound system to create a soothing atmosphere for the fetuses."

"I sat next to your gynopod daily and read to you during the eight-month incubation period."

"Gynopod?"

"Artificial wombs. We have five hundred units with a ninety-eight percent success rate. We produce hundreds of genetically perfect humans every single year. We're moving toward total elimination of natural childbirth."

"You're talking about total government control of reproduction? What if women want to have their own children? Shouldn't they be able to make their own decisions?" I lean into the window and focus on the floating fetuses.

"Millions of women died from pregnancy-related complications in the Old World. Forcing women to endure childbirth is barbaric when fetuses can be grown in labs with no risks to women's lives.

"Giving women the choice to have children naturally not only puts their health at risk, but it also puts society at risk by introducing imperfect offspring."

"But, Dr. Hahn, how do you prevent natural childbirth?"

"Why, mass sterilization, of course."

Mass sterilization? Does that mean I'm sterile? I open my mouth to ask but decide to keep my mouth shut and listen.

"Don't look so startled, dear. Those in power have always manipulated the masses to assert control over the means of reproduction. My own grandfather, Friedrich Hahn, was a Nazi eugenicist. He worked under the guidance of the German leader inspired by eugenics programs in the United States where over 70,000 Americans were forcibly sterilized.

"During World War II, Germany awarded motherhood medals to women considered genetically fit to encourage them to have more children while those deemed unfit were sterilized.

"China implemented a one-child policy to address overpopulation. Decades later, the policy proved disastrous for the aging population. There weren't enough caregivers or taxpayers to support them.

"In the 21st century, Americans once again led the way with population control efforts. American lawmakers criminalized abortion, required doctors to lie to pregnant women, and framed it as a religious issue to gain public support for forced births.

"Hungary's anti-immigration Prime Minister offered income tax waivers to women who birthed at least four Hungarian children. The Japanese Health Minister referred to women as baby-making machines and pushed them to have more children as their civic duty.

"In the Old World, reproductive control was rooted in racism and xenophobia. Men in power feared losing their status to minorities whose high fertility rates would eventually displace them as the dominant group.

"The more highly educated and financially independent women became, the fewer children they provided as future taxpayers, caregivers, and soldiers. Governments acted in their best interests and limited women's opportunities, along with their bodily autonomy.

"My approach is much more humane. Growing fetuses in gynopods doesn't require us to lie or manipulate to hijack control of women's bodies and it doesn't put women's lives at risk."

I move my eyes from the orbs to Dr. Hahn's forlorn expression. "Your approach saves women's lives, but is eliminating natural childbirth and taking away a woman's choice that much different than methods used by other leaders to control reproduction?"

"If this technology had existed before Delilah had become pregnant, she would still be here." The sadness in Dr. Hahn's eyes cranks up my empathy.

I replay the memory of his wife dying and a sorrow pang stabs me in the chest. I feel affection for him in the same way I feel affection for my dad. I place my hand over his.

Tears form in his eyes. "Shall we go?"

I maintain his fast pace up the stairs. "Did the baby survive?"

Dr. Hahn pauses. "You will meet my son, Gregor, this afternoon."

We return to his office. He sits at his desk and shuffles through papers.

"An attendant will escort you to your room. You will report back to my office this afternoon at four o'clock sharp to attend the weekly Nuclei meeting. I was briefed on your abduction from House of Saphronia. That assignment was a mistake and those responsible have been dealt with. You will be safe here."

He skims notifications on his transceptor. His body language says the meeting is over. I rest my hands on the back of one of the antique chairs while working up the nerve to ask my last question. "What was Delilah like?"

Dr. Hahn puts down the transceptor and looks out the window. "Delilah was the most brilliant woman I ever had the pleasure of knowing. Brilliant not only in mind but also in heart.

"We met in college while working on our doctoral dissertations. She was studying stem cell applications, microbiology, and regenerative medicine. Her father's diagnosis of early onset Alzheimer's disease was the catalyst that stoked her desire to find a cure."

"Did she find a cure?"

Dr. Hahn twirls a stylus between his fingers. "Yes and no. The research she left behind allowed us to ensure future generations would not be subjected to debilitating diseases in old age. Unfortunately, she didn't live long enough to see the fruits of her labor."

Dr. Hahn opens his desk drawer, withdraws a photograph and a folded piece of paper, and passes both to me. In the photo, a woman sits on a park bench next to a stack of books. She looks like me, but older. She grins at the camera while holding an envelope and making the thumbs up sign.

"I took that picture after we graduated from our doctoral programs. We had just received letters informing us that NASA had accepted our applications to join their Recent Graduate program."

I place the photo on his desk and unfold the paper. The edges are worn thin and tiny holes run along the crease. It's a sketch of an animal with the signature *Lilah* on the bottom right-hand corner.

I examine the fuzzy-tailed creature. "What is this supposed to be?"

The corners of Dr. Hahn's mouth turn up in a wistful smile. "Delilah was an animal lover. She volunteered with the humane society and was especially fond of cats. She enjoyed teasing me about my interest in genetics. She would sketch hybrid crosses of animals. I can still hear her laughter as she mused about all the possibilities. She jokingly referred to that one as a raccox. A cross of a raccoon and fox."

"I saw cabbits and cogs the first week I arrived in Ovation. It was a little…," I search for the right word, "weird."

"Ah yes, the cabbit." Dr. Hahn's face breaks into a double-wide smile. "In Delilah's sketches, she drew the cabbit with rabbit ears and a cat tail. Little did she know, the rabbit's tail would be dominant. Every time I see a hybrid, it brings me back to the old days. I derive joy from keeping her memory alive even in the smallest ways."

I hand the photograph and sketch back to Dr. Hahn.

"Keep them if you like. I have others." He stands, walks to the window, and asks Golgi to summon an attendant.

Someone knocks on the door.

Dr. Hahn briskly crosses the office and opens the door. "Carmela, allow me to introduce you to a new member of the Nuclei. Please show Wren to her room."

"My pleasure, Dr. Hahn." A Lucinda enters wearing a black dress just like the Lucindas at the spa. She teeters toward me on spiked heels and extends her hand. "I'm honored to make your acquaintance, Wren." She smiles showing off a mouthful of perfect teeth that look like a string of pearls against ruby red lipstick.

Carmela struts down the hallway. I follow, tuning out the click of her high heels and her chirpy high-pitched voice. On the second floor, she pauses to show me the cafeteria and library.

On the first floor, the same guard sits next to the stairs facing the entrance. My heart leaps when Fritz turns the corner and walks straight toward us. I keep my eyes on him and smile. I wait for him to notice me, but his face remains neutral. He passes without acknowledging us.

My smile fades. "Who was that?"

"Who was who?" She stops abruptly.

"That boy who passed us in the white uniform."

"Oh, Franz. That's Dr. Hahn's son." She dismissively waves her hand and continues walking.

His clone, that is. "Does Dr. Hahn have other children?"

"You will meet Gregor and Franz in due time." Carmela turns right at the end of the hall.

"What about Fritz?" I ask.

She pauses at the third door on the left and raises a perfectly waxed eyebrow. "Oh yes, Fritz. Well, Fritz is not one of us. I heard," she looks around the corridor and lowers her voice, "he grew up in the Valley." Her face scrunches as if the words taste sour.

She pauses dramatically waiting for my reaction. When I don't react, she removes an access card from her dress pocket and scans it across the door.

"This," she steps into a large living room and sweeps her arm across the suite, "is where you will be staying."

"Who else has access?" I enter, letting the door slam.

"Oh, don't worry, darling. I heard about what happened to you. Actually, *everybody* heard. It created quite a stir at Headquarters. People lost their heads, literally, if you know what I mean." Carmela slices her hand across her throat, rolls her eyes, hangs her head to the side, and lets her tongue loll.

I frown at her theatrics. "No, I don't know what you mean."

She straightens up and bounces back into a cheerful smile. "Rest assured, you are safe here. My access card was programmed for a single entry. Only you are authorized to enter your suite. Well, except for cleaning staff and Nuclei members. Nuclei members have unrestricted access across the island, so of course, they *could* enter your room, but why would they?"

I picture Franz's icy expression as we passed him in the hallway and recall his snide tone at the Fall Harvest. Is he a Nuclei member? I hope not. My gut tells me not to trust him.

Carmela saunters toward the door. "Make yourself at home. If you get hungry, you'll find drinks and snacks in the mini-fridge. Toodle-oo." She flits out the door.

I drop the mementos Dr. Hahn gave me onto the coffee table and take in my new surroundings. The rooms at House of Saphronia were fancy in a modern way. This place is fancy, but in a century-old palace way.

Thick crown molding borders the high ceiling. White couches back up to gold wallpaper. Gold-threaded drapes glister where the sun peeks through the shutter slats of two skinny windows framing an antique desk. A kitchenette is tucked into the front left corner.

In the bedroom, a burgundy and gold comforter covers the four-poster bed. My eyes dart to the nightstands devoid of water pitchers and pills. I touch my abdomen where the fertility shots were administered. No more shots. No more pills. Maybe things will be better here.

Near the bed, a door leads to a small bathroom wrapped in burgundy wallpaper. I leave the bedroom and walk toward the kitchenette.

Is that what I think it is? I rush to the appliance, remove the glass carafe, and hold it up to the light. My own coffeepot? Could it get any better than this?

I rummage through a nearby basket full of coffee, filters, and creamer. Can I brew a pot now? Dad didn't allow me to drink coffee in the afternoon. But Dad isn't here and how would anyone know? Supernovas aren't allowed to have coffee, but I'm no longer a Supernova.

I set up the coffee and fiddle with the coffeemaker settings until a red light comes on and it hisses to life. Anticipating the first cup of coffee I've had in months, I step back and listen to the coffeemaker gurgle and steam while the first drops pitter-patter into the pot.

Juices and bottled water line the top shelf of the mini-fridge. The second shelf has pre-wrapped items. The bottom drawer overflows with fruit. I grab a chocolate bar and mentally will the coffeemaker to hurry as the final drops drip.

The comforting aroma takes me back to having breakfast with Mom, Dad, Abe, and Addie. I miss them and wonder if they miss me. I sigh and pour a cup of coffee. I stir in a swirl of creamer, hug the warm mug between my palms, and bring it to my lips. Savoring the smooth dark roast, I walk to the window, curious to see how the view here compares to the one at House of Saphronia.

Outside my window, a narrow lawn meets a wide street where towering stone buildings in a uniform shade of business-district gray throw giant shadows on the asphalt. Rippling water from the nearby canal reflects off one building, but the water isn't visible from here.

I close the shutters and move to the couch, careful to avoid spilling coffee on the white upholstery. I study the photograph of Delilah. Dr. Hahn's life continues to revolve around her decades after her death. It's all related to her: the creation of flurtles and cabbits, the cure for degenerative diseases, the genetic engineering of me, and Dr. Hahn's obsession with eliminating natural childbirth.

It's surreal to hold a photo of the woman responsible for putting me on this path. But where does it lead?

A loud knock startles me. I jump to my feet, set the photo and my nearly empty mug on the coffee table, and tiptoe to the door. I rub the tender rope burns on my wrists. Could the people who kidnapped me know I'm here?

Thirty-two

White fabric drapes over a hanger attached to the outer door handle. I remove the hanger and close the door. The material is stiff and starched, unlike the stretchy material of the Supernova jumpsuit. A piece of paper threaded through the hanger reads: *Nuclei uniform custom tailored for Wren Weiss.*

At least they no longer refer to me as prototype or specimen. Am I supposed to wear this to the Nuclei meeting later today? What else would I wear? I would look stupid if I walked in dressed like a Supernova.

I pull the fabric free from the hanger and walk to the bedroom to try it on. The uniform is a perfect fit. The jacket cinches at the waist and flares at the hips.

Gold thread encircles the high collar. Gold buttons start at my right collarbone and form a diagonal line to my left hip. A vertical gold stripe runs down the outside of the pants. I look older, more professional, more mature.

"Golgi, what time is it?" My question is met with silence.

Gold earrings sparkle against the burgundy comforter. The gold studs have four petals in the shape of the government logo. I push the studs through my ears. In the closet, I find shiny gold flats in my size. I'm thankful I won't be required to wear stilettos like the Lucindas.

I move to the kitchen, pour a second cup of coffee, and tear into the chocolate creme bar. As the chocolate melts in my mouth, I feel genuinely happy and hopeful. Coffee and chocolate: two of my favorite things.

A clock on the desk reads 3:50 p.m. The Nuclei meeting starts in ten minutes. A little jolt of panic runs through me. I jerk my mug to my lips and guzzle the last of it. Warm coffee streams down the side of my mouth and soaks my white jacket.

Horrified at the stain spreading across my uniform, I grab a hand towel and dab my face and shirt. Why do I have to be so clumsy? I'm going to look like an idiot when I meet the Nuclei members for the first time. As if I'm not already nervous enough. I drop the dirty towel in the sink, weave my fingers through my hair, and pull it into a braid. I have to be upstairs in four minutes.

I rush into the empty hallway. After I turn the first corner, the guard sitting at the stairs jerks to attention. I move closer to the wall and inch toward the stairs. Halfway up the stairs, I glance down and see the guard has taken his seat.

I sprint across the second floor. Everyone I pass stares at me, their eyes lingering on the coffee stain. The heat in my cheeks isn't from the coffee I spilled down my face. My camisole, damp from coffee soaking through my shirt, sticks to my stomach. I pull my shirt away, but the camisole still clings uncomfortably to my skin. By the time I climb the last flight of stairs, cross the ballroom, and knock on Dr. Hahn's office door, I'm sweaty and my heart is racing.

Dr. Hahn opens the door and smiles. "No need to knock. You may let yourself in."

"But I—"

"Ah, yes, that's right. We will take care of your microchip during the meeting. Let's join the others in the conference room."

I'm relieved he didn't acknowledge the mess on my shirt. He leads me to a door near the couch. I imagine a den of hungry lions waiting to tear me apart. What if they don't think I'm good enough or smart enough or accomplished enough? Maybe it won't be so bad. Maybe they will be nice. But they can't be that nice. These are the same people who orchestrated egg harvests and family planning laws.

I step into the conference room behind Dr. Hahn. Seven people sit around a rectangular table. They wear white uniforms identical to the one I'm wearing. Conversations stop. All I can think about is the coffee stain. I fold my arms across my chest and feel my heart pounding.

"Fellow Nuclei members, please welcome Wren Weiss as the final member of the Nuclei. After Wren is sworn in, we will get to the first order of business."

Dr. Hahn's introduction is met with inquisitive stares. I glance around the room. My heart flutters at the sight of Fritz. He smiles. Franz sits across from him scowling. It's easy to tell them apart by their demeanor.

I recognize Dr. Hahn's son, Gregor. He congratulated me at the Fall Harvest. Dr. Akimoto from the Science Gala sits next to the doctor who administered my Assessment. Dr. Sorrell is a member of the Nuclei. No wonder she refused to answer my questions the day of my Assessment.

The two I don't recognize introduce themselves as Dr. Andrew Toussaint and Dr. Gloria Honeysett. Dr. Honeysett's hair is the color of honey and her eyes, bumblebee brown; the surname is fitting.

Dr. Hahn looks at me. "You will pledge allegiance to the Nuclei and swear to honor our values and keep our discussions confidential. Raise your right hand and repeat after me. I, Wren Weiss, do solemnly swear…"

I raise my hand and repeat the oath.

Dr. Hahn says, "As a junior Nuclei member, your vote carries half the weight of senior members. On your eighteenth birthday, you will be granted full voting power. The same rules apply to Franz and Fritz."

Dr. Hahn sits at the head of the table. He turns to Franz

and says, "Franz, you will sit next to Gregor. Wren will take your seat next to me."

"But, Dad—"

"Now."

Franz shoves his seat back and stomps to the other side of the table.

"Have a seat, Wren," Dr. Hahn says.

I'm seated next to Dr. Sorrell, directly across from Gregor.

Dr. Sorrell stands. "Wren, place your right hand flat against the table. I'm going to implant a microchip that will grant Nuclei access privileges."

She rubs a wet cotton ball across the thin skin between my thumb and index finger. Next, she stabs the sterilized skin with a device that looks like a pen.

"Ouch." I'm embarrassed when I realize I yelped out loud.

I glance across the table at Fritz and Franz. Fritz looks sympathetic. Franz catches my eye and mouths, *baby*. I want to launch myself over the table and punch him in the face, but I look away instead.

A bead of blood bubbles up on my hand. Dr. Sorrell applies a bandage.

Dr. Hahn says, "Let's get down to business. I'm happy to announce we now have sufficient organ supplies to ensure every man, woman, and child in Clairemont and Ovation will have replacement organs if the need arises. The trials conducted by Dr. Sun to implant 3D printed hearts and kidneys were successful. Printed organs will supplement the organ farm and reduce the need to expand storage sites for comatose organ donors."

I squeeze my throbbing hand between my knees. "What about organs for residents in Hillcrest and the Valley?"

"That brings us to the next order of business. Gregor, you found a more efficient way to implement Project Proboscis?" Dr. Hahn asks.

Gregor stands and dims the lights. My mom would be impressed with his perfectly rigid posture. "That's correct, Father."

The table lights up with a 3D map of Genova Island.

Gregor stands behind Fritz and Franz and points a laser beam at the table. "Instead of physically planting infected mosquitoes at sites in the Valley and Hillcrest, we will deliver mosquitoes via GPS-enabled drones."

The laser beam hovers over a grid of homogeneous buildings. It's Hillcrest. I smile when I find Fidelity Forest and the Community Center.

Gregor withdraws a device from his pocket. "When the drones are in designated locations, I will use this remote control to activate the release of the DBH virus. We expect the targeted population to be dead within seventy-two hours of the first infection."

Did he say they plan to infect people with a virus? To *kill* them? Fritz looks as concerned as I am. I glance around the table. Nobody else seems disturbed.

Dr. Hahn says, "In the event of malfunctioning drones, is there a backup plan?"

"Yes, Father," Gregor's voice drips with exasperation. "Our loyal Enforcers have agreed to plant mosquito eggs during home visits in the Valley."

"Why would Enforcers do that?" I ask.

Gregor's dark eyes settle on my face. His aloof disposition reminds me of Franz. "Enforcers who prove their loyalty to the Nuclei will be vaccinated."

I want to ask more questions, but Fritz locks eyes with me and shakes his head. I sit back and swallow my questions while studying the faces of Fritz, Franz, Gregor, and Dr. Hahn. They all resemble each other.

"And the backup plan also applies to Hillcrest?" Dr. Hahn asks.

Dr. Sorrell says, "We thought it best to keep Enforcers in the dark about the virus release in Hillcrest. It's unethical to ask Enforcers to plant mosquitoes in their own neighborhoods anyway. We will rely on drones."

"I see." Dr. Hahn steeples his fingers and stares into the 3D image.

While discussing a plan to kill innocent people, did Dr. Sorrell really express a concern about *ethics*? "What about my parents? My family?"

Franz laughs. "Your parents don't love you. How do you think your mother got that promotion?"

His words slice through my core and stoke a fire of hatred. I glare at him.

"Enough!" Dr. Hahn says. "Your parents are loyal. They will be spared."

I visualize my neighbors, friends, family, and classmates. What about Abe and Addie? What about Opal? What about those Valley boys playing chicken off the cliff? What about the woman who raised Fritz?

Gregor continues, "Now keep your eyes on the red dots over the Valley and Hillcrest. They represent the spread of the virus in eight-hour increments."

A light sprinkle of red dots gradually becomes more dense until a blood-red blanket covers the Valley and Hillcrest.

"What if the virus spreads to Clairemont and Ovation?" I feel Fritz's eyes but I ignore him.

Dr. Akimoto says, "The genetically-engineered population is immune."

That means I'm immune and Fritz is immune. It also means the virus was created decades ago before we were born. This was their plan all along. For a teeny-tiny moment, I selfishly feel relieved to be immune.

"Last year, mass burial sites were created here and here." Gregor points to two sites between Hillcrest and the Valley.

New awareness is accompanied by a sinking feeling of helplessness. There must be a way I can change their minds. "Aren't workers needed to harvest the fields?"

Pride crosses Dr. Toussaint's face. "That won't be necessary. My team has developed robots to complete all tasks related to the food supply. The Valley workers no longer serve any purpose. If we allow them to live, they will deplete resources and continue to breed genetically inferior humans without contributing anything of value to society."

The Nuclei is going to kill workers and replace them with machines? Dr. Hahn doesn't seem like a monster, but only a monster would come up with this plan.

"Is there an update on Project Aphrodite?" Dr. Hahn asks.

Gregor turns on the lights and takes his seat.

My ears perk up. Dr. Hart mentioned Project Aphrodite at the Gala.

Dr. Honeysett stands and rests her hands on the back of her chair. "Since increasing production of female embryos and eliminating production of male embryos two decades ago, we can ensure that within three generations, males outside of the chosen few, will cease to exist."

I sit stunned, not believing what I'm hearing. The goal of Project Aphrodite is to eliminate males entirely? I can't imagine a world without fathers or sons or brothers.

Dr. Hahn nods. "Good. No men. No violence. No war."

Gregor slams his fist on the table. I jump. Others exchange nervous looks.

"Father, this is preposterous! Project Aphrodite should have been shut down years ago as I recommended."

"Gregor, might I remind you that when we took a vote on Project Aphrodite twenty-five years ago, it was unanimous," Dr. Hahn says in a here-we-go-again tone.

Gregor stands and throws his hands in the air. "I was a twenty-year-old boy seeking his father's approval. I didn't have the capacity to understand the long-term consequences of my vote. I can guarantee you, if there are survivors in other parts of the world with access to the same technology, they are engineering powerful armies. Armies that will crush your pacifist paradise."

Gregor runs his hand across his slicked-back hair and paces like a wild animal. "Your vision is narrow. It's short-sighted. It puts everyone at risk. Instead of ordering the disposal of genetically-enhanced male embryos decades ago, you should have created an army of super-soldiers with advanced capabilities. How else can you protect our people?"

Dr. Akimoto presses her lips together and frowns. "I don't know why you're so worried, Gregor," she says in a condescending tone. "Our recon missions have provided ample evidence that there are no survivors beyond this island. The only way to secure a nonviolent future is to eliminate males. Our attempts to remove genes associated with aggression in males failed to reign in their aggression. Violence is etched into the very fabric of male DNA."

Dr. Akimoto continues, "In nature, there are too many examples of male brutality. Female dragonflies play dead to avoid male dragonfly aggression. Groups of male dolphins abduct female dolphins and beat them into submission for mating purposes. Male baboons and chimpanzees maul females, kill their infants, and engage in forced copulation. Where males exist, violence exists."

Dr. Honeysett adds, "Peace flourishes in female-dominated societies. We have few examples in nature, but the polyamorous bonobos are a perfect example of a peaceful social order led by female matriarchs. Resources and mates are shared in a collaborative manner."

"Thank you for the history lesson," Gregor says in a sarcastic tone. "We are all aware of the virtues of females and the faults of males, but there are many ways to solve this problem that do not include eliminating the entire male population for Galileo's sake!"

Gregor plunks into his chair and massages his brow. The tension in the room is palpable.

Dr. Hahn reaches over and squeezes Gregor's shoulder. "As men, we have an interest in propagating our kind, but it's important we prevent our egos from guiding our decisions."

Fritz and I lock eyes. To the casual bystander, his expression is blank and unemotional, but I sense that beneath his controlled expression, he's as alarmed as I am.

I clear my throat. "Aren't males required for procreation?" I'm not exactly on Gregor's side, but eliminating males seems a little extreme.

Dr. Akimoto raises an eyebrow. Her narrow lips form a smug smile. "Sperm has not been required for procreation in decades. Even before the war, it was general knowledge that a female somatic cell, a skin cell for example, could be merged with an egg to create a female embryo. The male function in procreation has become obsolete."

The intercom crackles. Carmela's voice interrupts the meeting. "Dr. Hahn, Commander Arden is here to see you. She says it's urgent."

"Send her to my office." Dr. Hahn rises and leaves the conference room. He returns with Commander Arden.

"I apologize for interrupting your meeting." Commander Arden wrings her hat in her hands. "There has been an additional development in the case of the murdered Supernova."

Gregor lifts his head and sits up straight. "Did you find the parties responsible?"

"I'm afraid not, sir. Two Nadirs were reported missing this morning. Their bodies were discovered an hour ago washed up against the cliffs behind House of Saphronia."

Thirty-three

I picture the Nadirs at the Fall Harvest and wonder who it could be. The dead Nadirs can't be from House of Saphronia. Berkeley loaded my suitcase into the Helix this morning.

Commander Arden says, "The murderer could be the same one who killed the Supernova at House of Lillith or it could be a copycat. The coroner noted something peculiar in her report. Instead of taking both eyes this time, the killer removed only the right eye from his victims. Their ovaries were also removed through a rudimentary cut on the lower abdomen."

An icy chill runs down my spine. I shiver, put both hands in my lap, and pick at the tape on my throbbing thumb. I recall Everly's words the day Cambria taunted her on the way home from the spa: *If she taunts me again, I will cut out her ovaries, fry them in a skillet, and eat them for dinner.*

"Estimated time of death?" Franz's weaselly eyes land on me.

My eyes widen. He suspects *me*?

"Eleven o'clock this morning," Commander Arden answers.

That was hours after I left for Headquarters. I exhale my pent-up breath. Franz sneers at me. The spark of hatred he kindled earlier thaws my spine and grows from a flame to a raging inferno. I narrow my eyes at him and refuse to look away. If I could shoot flames from my eyes and burn him to ashes, I would.

"Have the bodies been identified?" Dr. Toussaint asks.

Commander Arden's face remains stoic, but her voice hitches. "Nadirs Berkeley and Harlowe from House of Saphronia."

A burst of joy threatens to put a smile on my face. I divert my eyes from Franz and stare at an imaginary point on the table, hoping my face didn't betray my satisfaction. I knew exactly what I was doing when I gave the robes and masks to Everly. I might as well have killed them myself. Guilt quickly extinguishes my joy.

Am I as ruthless as the others at this table? Is that why I'm here? Is it in my DNA? The only one I share DNA with is Gregor. He catches me looking at him and returns my gaze from across the table. Is he wondering if his mom would be like me? Being the cause of his mother's death must weigh on him.

If Fritz and I had a son, would he be like Gregor? My face flushes at the thought. I glance at Fritz, relieved he can't read my mind.

Dr. Hahn says, "Thank you, Commander Arden. Today's meeting is adjourned."

"Wait, Father. I have one more thing to discuss." Gregor stands and faces Commander Arden. "You are dismissed. Please keep us apprised of any updates."

"Yes, sir." Commander Arden nods and leaves the room.

"What is so important that it can't wait until next week?" Dr. Hahn asks.

"I want to take a vote on the date of the virus release."

"A vote?" Dr. Hahn looks weary, as though he's been locked in battle with Gregor for years.

"You promised we would release the virus as soon as three conditions were met. We met the first condition two years ago when we automated all working-class jobs held by those in the Valley.

"We met the second condition when we proved we could grow fetuses into adults and store them indefinitely for our blood plasma and organ supply. We no longer need to confiscate blood plasma or organs from the working-class. We no longer need to conduct experiments on children we seize from them. We no longer need them at all.

"Your third condition was met when your precious specimens were transported to Ovation from the Valley and Hillcrest in August.

"It's October and we *still* do not have a firm date for the virus release. I, along with other Nuclei members, am running out of patience. What are we waiting for? I propose we set the plan into motion this weekend."

Gregor doesn't have to say our names. I know exactly who he is referring to when he says *precious specimens*.

"This weekend? We will do no such thing," Dr. Hahn says in an indignant tone.

Dr. Sorrell pushes her chair back and stands. "If not this weekend, when? We are wasting resources on people who no longer serve any purpose. The sooner we eliminate them, the better."

"I have to agree," Dr. Toussaint says.

"We will implement the plan in January, not one day sooner." Dr. Hahn walks toward the door. "This meeting is adjourned."

Gregor puts his hand up. "Not so fast. We will take a vote. All in favor of moving forward this weekend, raise your right hand and say aye."

Only Fritz and I remain seated. I scan the room as hands shoot into the air. Gregor, Franz, Dr. Sorrell, and Dr. Toussaint have their hands raised. Gregor approaches the opposite end of the table and stands between Dr. Akimoto and Dr. Honeysett.

"Doctors Akimoto and Honeysett, the mosquitoes are prepped and ready to go. We have no valid reason to delay. We get it over with and continue to build on our successes."

Dr. Akimoto looks at Dr. Hahn. I sense her fierce loyalty to him. "I agree with August. We must execute carefully and ensure every scenario has been accounted for. Pushing forward this weekend would be impulsive and premature."

Gregor sighs and looks to Dr. Honeysett.

"Sorry, Gregor. I agree with Shiko. I'm fine with accelerating the timeline, but this weekend is too soon. Our first priority should be finding the person responsible for murdering Supernovas and Nadirs and bringing him to justice."

Gregor walks back to the front of the room. "Let Security Forces do their job while we do ours."

Dr. Hahn raises his right hand. "Those in favor of implementing Project Proboscis in January, raise your right hand and say aye."

Dr. Akimoto, Dr. Honeysett, and Fritz raise their hands. Fritz catches my eye and quirks his eyebrows, silently urging me to raise my hand.

"Wren?" Dr. Hahn prompts.

I reluctantly lift my bandaged hand with full awareness that whether I vote for implementation this weekend or in January, it's still a vote for murder.

"Majority rules. We move forward in January. This meeting is adjourned." Dr. Hahn leaves the conference room with Franz and Gregor following closely.

After everyone filters out of the room, Fritz and I get up from the table.

"Do you want to stop by the cafeteria for dinner?" Fritz asks.

"Sure," I say as we walk through Dr. Hahn's office. Franz, Gregor, and Dr. Hahn huddle around the desk, engaged in a heated conversation.

"What happened to your uniform?" Fritz asks as we descend the stairs.

I look down at the dried stain and cringe. "I spilled coffee on it."

"Why didn't you change clothes before the meeting to make a better first impression?"

I want to crawl under a rock. "It's the only uniform I have."

"Oh." Fritz chuckles good-heartedly. He smiles at me through his dark lashes. I blush and smile back.

As we approach the cafeteria, a member of Security Forces walks toward us, comes to an abrupt stop, and freezes. We pass him and enter the cafeteria.

"What was that all about?" I ask.

"They stand at attention to show respect to Nuclei members in uniform. I only wear the uniform when I have to."

In the cafeteria, people nudge and whisper and stare. I feel self-conscious like I'm on display again. A table full of Security Force members becomes quiet as we walk by. I'm glad they don't jump to attention while eating.

The buffet includes steaming piles of fresh seafood, rice, vegetables, and fruit. I didn't think I was hungry, but my mouth waters and my stomach twists in anticipation. I load my plate with a taste of everything.

My eyes wander to a table filled with cakes and pies. "Are we allowed to have dessert?"

"Why wouldn't we be allowed to have dessert?" Fritz looks puzzled.

"Supernovas aren't allowed to have dessert or caffeine."

"Why not?" He scoops rice onto his plate.

"I don't know. Something about egg quality."

Fritz lowers his voice. "That whole egg ceremony at the church was really bizarre."

"You were there?" I want to shrink into a ball and roll away. Heat rises up my collar and flushes my cheeks.

"You have to try those." A hand points to a stack of fried vegetables. It's the baby-faced guard.

Fritz smiles at the guard. "Hey, Treb, how's it going?"

"Staying busy." The guard piles potatoes on his plate.

"Wren, this is Treb." Fritz introduces us.

"We met this morning," Treb says in an apologetic tone.

"Treb's one of the good guys." Fritz grins at Treb and then leads me to an empty table.

I sit across from him. "Did you hear what they were talking about after the meeting?"

Fritz cuts a piece of chicken and chews slowly. "Gregor and Franz were pressuring Dr. Hahn to release the DBH virus within the next month. They were talking about how long it would take to infect the entire non-GMO population given that female mosquitoes can lay hundreds of eggs within days."

"What if the mosquitoes can't be contained and Nuclei members get infected?" I dab my mouth with a napkin.

"Nuclei members have been vaccinated." Fritz's eyes settle on my bruised cheek. "I heard about what happened to you Saturday night after we met on your rooftop. Are you okay?"

My fingers involuntarily move to my cheek. "It doesn't hurt."

He places his knife and fork across his plate. "I wouldn't have left you there if I had known you weren't safe."

I take a bite of shrimp. "You couldn't have known."

"What do you think is going on at House of Saphronia? First, you're kidnapped. Then, two Nadirs from the *same* House end up dead? Why is House of Saphronia being targeted?"

An image of Bacon plucking Everly's eyeball and throwing it into the bonfire crosses my mind. The shrimp I'm chewing suddenly tastes rubbery and slimy like an eyeball. I want to spit it into my napkin. Instead, I take a big drink of water to force it down my throat.

I picture Everly's face when I gave her the robes and pig masks. I know exactly what is going on at House of Saphronia. I glance over my shoulder at the people eating at nearby tables.

Fritz notices my discomfort. "We can talk about it later."

Franz slams his plate on the table like a brute and sits next to me. I raise my eyebrows at Fritz. Franz shovels food into his mouth without acknowledging either of us. He eats without restraint, like the boys in Hillcrest.

I can't hide how annoyed I am. "Did you really have to sit right next to me when there are dozens of empty seats at other tables?"

Looking at the stain on my shirt, Franz glowers and says, "Maybe you should wear a bib next time."

"Let's go." Fritz's voice has a hard edge as he stands and levels an intimidating stare at Franz.

I start to clear my dishes.

"The staff will take care of the dishes," Fritz says.

In the hallway, I lean into Fritz. "Why did he sit with us?"

"That table is reserved for the Nuclei, but Franz and I are the only ones who eat in the cafeteria."

"Do the others live here?" I ask.

"Dr. Hahn lives in the Presidential suite connected to his office. Franz has an apartment near mine on the first floor. I'm not sure where other Nuclei members live."

On the first floor, the seated guard stands at attention.

"At ease." Fritz nods at the guard.

At the end of the hallway, Fritz pauses. "Which way is your room?"

I point to the right. "Third door on the left."

"Mine is that way." He points in the opposite direction.

Would it be too forward to invite him to my room? I want to talk without prying eyes and ears.

Fritz says, "I'll see you tomorrow at breakfast?"

"If you don't have plans tonight, maybe you could hang out

in my room for a little while?" I peer up at him through my lashes.

A slight smile warms his features. "I don't have plans. Give me five minutes."

I play with my braid and smile while watching him walk away. When I'm with Fritz, the stress and concerns that usually plague me fade away. I peel the tape and cotton ball off my hand and stroll to my new room.

At the door, I wave my hand. The lock disengages. I enter the suite and hold my hand up to the light. It looks like someone stabbed me in the hand with an antique pencil that left behind the lead tip.

I tidy up the kitchen and head to my bedroom to change out of the stiff Nuclei uniform. I grab jeans and a t-shirt out of my suitcase and drop the coffee-stained uniform on the closet floor. I release my hair from the tight braid and pull loose curls forward.

After brushing my teeth, I turn my suitcase inside out looking for my lip balm. I glide it across my lips. There's a light knock at the door. I quickly tie my flannel around my waist, jump to my feet, and bang my knee against the nightstand. Ouch! I double over to massage my knee and half-hop to the door.

I open the door and forget about the pain in my knee. Fritz stands before me in a black t-shirt and jeans with his backpack slung over his shoulder and a paper bag in one hand.

I move to allow him entry. "What's in the bag?"

He places the bag on the counter and removes glass bottles and a packet of lavender. "I brought milk, cherry juice, and lavender."

"What for?" I pick up the lavender and hold it under my nose, inhaling the fresh scent.

He reaches into the cupboard and withdraws a pot, a strainer, and two mugs. "I'm going to make moon milk."

"*Moon* milk? Never heard of it."

"Trust me, you'll like it," he says in that flirty, self-assured way I find so attractive.

"Please tell me you didn't get that milk from the Milkmaids?" I wrinkle my nose.

We look at each other for a moment and then burst into laughter.

"I can assure you it is *not* breast milk." An amused half-smile sticks to his face. "It's coconut milk." He takes the lavender from me.

I reflect his smile. It's sweet that he decided to introduce me to something new. I absentmindedly play with my hair as he fills the pot with ingredients, places it on the stovetop, and lights the burner. I let my eyes wander over his muscular shoulders and arms.

Turning to face me, he says, "You look pretty with your hair down."

"Thanks." I feel my smile stretch miles wide.

My parents are the only ones who ever complimented my appearance. It doesn't count when it comes from them. Hearing it from Fritz makes my insides light up like a star-studded sky.

I drop my hand from my hair and slide it into my front pocket. "What you asked me about in the cafeteria, about the House of Saphronia…"

"Wait." Fritz puts his index finger against his lips.

He retrieves a silver cylinder from his backpack, holds it up, and moves around the living room before disappearing into the bedroom.

A minute later, he joins me in the kitchen and drops the cylinder in his backpack. "I was checking for bugs. It's all clear."

"Are you always this suspicious?" I ask, raising an eyebrow.

"When I told you not to trust anyone, I meant it." There's a gravity and weight to his words. He seems much older when he's serious.

Fritz turns off the stovetop and rummages through the cabinets. He places a glass pitcher in the sink, balances a strainer over it, and strains lavender particles from the cherry-tinged milk. Then, he divides the frothy drink between two mugs and passes one to me.

"Moon milk cheers." He smiles and clinks his mug against mine.

I take a sip, rolling the warm milk over my tongue. Tart, slightly sweet, and oddly floral. It tastes the way shampoo smells.

"It's really, um, interesting. I mean, it's good. Thank you."

I carry the mug to the couch and settle into the cushy corner. Fritz sits at the opposite end.

I blurt out, "I know what happened at House of Saphronia. I know who did it."

He sets his drink on the coffee table. "Who? The same people who killed the Supernova and hurt you?"

Staring into my mug, I watch lavender flakes float across the foamy pink milk. "No, it wasn't the same people."

"What happened after I left Saturday night?" Fritz leans closer.

I close my eyes and feel the knife piercing my skin, the fist slamming my face, the heat of the fire. The smell of burning flesh. I shudder and open my eyes.

"We don't have to talk about it if you don't want to," he says, lightly touching my knee.

His touch sends a little thrill through me and leaves me feeling distracted. I glance at his hand, still resting on my knee, and then shift my focus to his face. "No, it's okay. I'll tell you what happened and how I think it's related to the murders."

I describe being forced out of bed at knifepoint and being led to the abandoned slaughterhouse where girls in masks taunted me and Everly before ripping her eye out.

I tell him how we got away and hid in the cemetery until sunrise. And reluctantly, I admit that I gave Everly the robes with full awareness of how she would react.

"You knew she would kill them?" His eyebrows shoot up and the whites of his eyes get bigger. A flicker of emotion skates over his face. Disbelief? Disappointment in me?

After swallowing the last of the moon milk, I twine my fingers through my hair. "Yes. I mean, no. I knew she would take matters into her own hands. I didn't know how far she would go, but after what they did to us, I didn't care." I set my jaw and maintain eye contact, daring him to judge me.

"You have to tell Dr. Hahn the Nadirs formed a hate group and abducted you and Everly. You have to tell him Everly killed the Nadirs for revenge."

"I don't *have* to tell Dr. Hahn anything. I'm not getting involved and I'm definitely not implicating Everly." My rigid tone leaves no room for negotiation.

Fritz leans forward, frowning. "Dr. Hahn plans to completely eradicate males because of his flawed belief that violence is innate to men. He needs to know women are the ones waging war against transgenics. He needs to know women are violent in their own ways."

I place my empty mug on the coffee table, lean back, and cross my arms. "He can eliminate men and women and engineer a world full of perfect little piggies for all I care. The only thing I care about is saving my family."

My defenses soften when I think of Abe and Addie playing with other kids in our tight-knit community. "Do you think we can talk him out of releasing the virus?"

Fritz drapes his arm across the back of the couch and tugs his earlobe while staring into space. "The Nuclei isn't going to change their mind about the virus. They've been waiting decades for the right time. Our arrival in Ovation set everything into motion."

"What about the vaccine? Do you know where it is? Maybe we could distribute it to Hillcrest and the Valley before the Nuclei releases the virus." I can't contain my optimism. There has to be something we can do.

"The vaccine is in a secret location they refer to as the Sanctuary. Even if we could find it, people in the Valley aren't going to trust Nuclei vaccines." Fritz jumps to his feet. "Do you hear that?"

"Hear what?" I stand, feeling a sudden hollowness in my stomach.

Fritz strides to the window and looks through the shutters. His serious expression sounds an alarm within me.

"What is it?" I try to conceal my concern, but my voice cracks.

He steps back to make room for me. Sandwiched between the desk and Fritz, I peer through the open shutter slat.

A sea of black closes in on Headquarters like ants closing in on a crumb. Armed soldiers march in formation. Green utility vehicles like the ones at Guantanamo roll in behind them.

Thirty-four

*F*ootsteps pound down the hallway accompanied by panicked voices.

"I have a gun and ammo in my room. I'll be right back." Fritz charges toward the door.

I flashback to the last time we were separated at the facility. Overcome with terror, I hurry to him, grab his arm, and pull him away from the door. "I don't want to be separated again."

Fritz looks caught off guard. He hugs my waist and pulls me close. He brushes my hair away from my face and tenderly strokes my bruised cheek.

"We were separated at Guantanamo but we found our way back to each other, didn't we?" He leans his forehead against mine. I close my eyes and let my hands rest near his collar while he runs his hands up and down my back reassuringly.

He steps away and says, "Stay here and keep the door locked until I return."

The stubborn streak I always thought I had inherited from Dad provokes me to refuse. I stand tall and put my hands on my hips. "I'm going with you."

At first, Fritz looks inclined to argue, but then he smiles, picks me up, and seats me on the kitchen countertop. "You're pretty cute when you're stubborn," he says, skimming his nose against mine. His breath tickles my cheek and the unusual closeness makes me feel like a live wire is humming and buzzing beneath my skin.

I lift a hand in the air, working up the courage to touch his face. Fritz takes my hand and rests it against his cheek. I run my fingertips over the tiny scar in his eyebrow and trace the outline of his cheek down to his jawline before skating my thumb across the cleft in his chin. His skin feels smooth despite the five o'clock shadow.

As I gaze into his eyes, I feel like I've found something—someone—I didn't know I was looking for. His fingernails graze the back of my neck, sending chill bumps down my arms and legs. He twists my hair around his fist, tilts my head back, and locks me in a kiss. I close my eyes, inhaling his earthy scent, tasting the cherry from the drink still on his lips.

As his warm lips linger on mine, shooting stars burst in my chest and a cascade of sparks blasts down my spine. I loop my arms around his neck and thread my fingers through his hair. My heart booms like a bass drum, drowning out my thoughts. At the sound of commotion in the hallway, Fritz pulls away.

Grabbing his backpack, he moves toward the door. "Let's go."

I hop off the counter. Fritz takes my hand, opens the door, and leads me into the hallway. We creep toward the sound of unfamiliar voices in the main corridor.

A soldier cuts the corner, barges toward us, and draws his weapon. "Freeze!" Muscular biceps and quadriceps bulge against black and gray camouflage. One of his legs is as thick as my torso.

Fritz and I step back. My heart starts pounding like crazy.

"Not another step." The soldier peers into the sights of his gun and moves forward carefully, as if two unarmed teenagers present an imminent threat. A red laser beam bounces over me and Fritz.

I imagine the massive soldier wrapping his strong hands around each of our necks, lifting us off the ground, and squeezing us like lemons until the last drop of life drips out of our flailing bodies.

The soldier presses the barrel of his gun against Fritz's chest and leans so close I can see the pores on his face, the razor-burn on his neck, and the glowing gold tapeta beneath his brown eyes. Stitched on the chest of his uniform is the number 0281.

Fritz grabs the gun barrel and forces it toward the wall. "Who authorized you to harass Nuclei members?"

A look of surprise flits over the soldier's face. He quickly shutters his features. "The Nuclei has been dismantled. All Ovation inhabitants must report to the auditorium immediately."

Fritz and I exchange sideways glances.

"Move." The soldier waves his gun and motions for us to walk ahead of him.

He forces us into the main corridor. The setting sun throws a burnt orange glow on Supernovas streaming through the double doors. Gargantuan soldiers guard the entryway and scan passports. The soldiers nod at the man holding us hostage and clear a path for us.

From the doorway, I get a glimpse of Blaise and Everly. Their black jumpsuits look solemn in the long line of Supernovas winding around the building.

"Move." The soldier's gun strikes my spine. I lurch forward and stumble.

Fritz grabs my arm. I pull away. "I'm fine."

We're guided into an auditorium full of people. Soldiers assemble around a map unrolled on a table near the door.

"Boss, these two say they are Nuclei members. Should we imprison them with the others?"

A man dressed in white enters my peripheral vision. Is it Dr. Hahn? I turn toward the approaching figure. Tired eyes settle on me and Fritz.

"Harmless kids. Keep them here with everyone else," Gregor says and retreats.

Who is he calling kids? I glare at Gregor's back. My anger wanes as the soldier's words and the severity of the situation sink in.

He said Nuclei members were imprisoned. Is Gregor behind all of this? Is Franz involved?

The soldier's wide frame blocks my view of the room. "You will not leave this area without permission," he says as he steps aside to allow us to pass.

Milkmaids stand along the back wall with little girls playing at their feet. House of Juliette Supernovas huddle in the center of the room.

"Over there." Fritz points to Treb and takes my hand.

I search for familiar faces as we step over Ovation residents and make our way toward Treb. Residents sit around chatting as if being herded into an auditorium by an army of supersized mutants is nothing out of the ordinary.

"Hey, Treb. What's going on? Have you heard anything?" Fritz asks as we sit.

"I heard people talking about a wedding ceremony," Treb says.

I raise an eyebrow. "Seriously?" I coat the word in skepticism. "Nuclei members have been imprisoned and we're all gathered here for a wedding ceremony?"

Fritz asks, "Who's getting married?"

"I don't know." Treb shrugs.

"Which Nuclei members were imprisoned?" Fritz asks.

"Hahn, Akimoto, and Honeysett are the only ones missing." Treb names the doctors who voted with Dr. Hahn to delay the virus release.

I spot Toussaint and Gregor conversing near the entrance. At the front of the auditorium next to the stage, familiar black uniforms gather around Dr. Sorrell.

Fritz says, "Enforcers."

I bite my lip, rest my elbows on my raised knees, and massage my tense shoulders. I have to hold myself back from approaching the Enforcers to ask about my parents. Dr. Hahn said my parents are loyal Enforcers. Does that mean they're here? Or did they stay home to plant mosquitos in the Valley? Are they capable of murder? They may be overzealous in their loyalty, but that doesn't mean they would kill for the Nuclei.

Enforcers converse quietly as they roll up their uniform sleeves. Dr. Sorrell raises a syringe and administers a shot to the Enforcer nearest her. There could only be one reason for administering vaccines: Gregor plans to release the virus soon.

"So, it's true." Fritz looks at me.

"What's true?" Treb asks.

"Wren?" Clover's voice cuts him off. "Is it really you?"

I tip my head back and lift an eyebrow. "Who else would it be?"

She looks relieved and plops down beside me. "I approached a girl who looked like you, but it wasn't you."

Could there be other clones of Delilah right here, right now? The thought of multiple copies of me in one room freaks me out. After I introduce Clover to Fritz and Treb, I turn away from the guys to talk to Clover.

"Why didn't you help Everly the night we were abducted? You could have freed her hands."

Clover looks away and twirls her blond ponytail between her fingers. "She didn't deserve my help." Her unapologetic eyes meet mine. "The morning of the Harvest, I found out she was tampering with my fertility pills, but it was too late for me to do anything about it."

The memory of Everly leaving Clover's room crosses my mind. "How did you find out?"

"I told her I was going downstairs for breakfast. Then, I hid behind my bathroom door and watched her switch the pills."

I recall how sick Clover was the night I met her. "That's really messed up."

"We had been friends since elementary school. I never expected her to betray me."

"I don't think it's possible to ever really know someone." I consider my parents' betrayal and my chest tightens. "How did you get mixed up with that hate group, with Bacon?"

Clover unravels threads from holes in the knees of her jeans and stares at her shoes. "Bacon's real name is Bianca. She's a Nadir who disappeared from House of Viola years ago and started an underground movement called the Sisterhood. She recruits Nadirs and weaponizes their resentment."

"But you're too smart to be manipulated by a rogue leader."

Clover stops tugging on the threads of her jeans and looks me in the eye. "It doesn't matter how smart someone is. Everyone has fears and a desire to belong. Tyrants prey on those universal fears and desires. After I was demoted, I was angry and hurt. I contemplated suicide. I hated myself. I hated Everly. I hated everything and everybody."

Clover wrinkles her nose and fights back tears. "I've never been so humiliated in my life. The day I moved to House of Khadija, the other Nadir assigned to the House, Paulina, invited me to attend the Nadir Sisterhood's weekly midnight meeting.

"Everyone was so welcoming. They were the only ones in Ovation who understood exactly what I experienced during the Nadir ceremony. They hugged me, listened to me, and cried with me. It felt like I had instantly gained best friends bonded by our shared experience.

"I gained hope for a situation that initially felt hopeless. The next day while the House of Khadija Supernovas were at the spa, Pauline and I used our free time to meet the Sisterhood in an abandoned warehouse.

"They were planning an event the night of the Science Gala, but I didn't catch all the details. I soon realized Bianca was the leader. Warm and charismatic, she was several years older than the rest of us. When she spoke about her disdain for transgenics, I nodded and went along. I wore contacts and didn't tell anyone I was transgenic. I didn't want to lose my new friends."

I'm uneasy with Clover's ties to the group that tried to kill me and Everly. "Were you one of the girls who abducted me and Everly from House of Saphronia?"

Clover looks taken aback. "I swear if I had known what they were planning, I wouldn't have been there at all. Pauline and Harmony, code names Pork Chop and Hamlet, were the ones who coordinated with Berkeley to gain access to House of Saphronia that night."

She places her hand on my forearm. "I *promise*," she says emphatically, "I never would have been there if I had known they were planning to hurt anybody."

I can tell from her earnest expression that she's being honest. "I'm glad you were there. Can you imagine what would have happened to us if you weren't?" A tremor runs through me.

Everly and Prisha hurry toward us. Blaise joins a group of Supernovas I recognize from the Fall Harvest. They were all raised by Milkmaids in Ovation. I return Blaise's wave from across the room.

Prisha sits between Fritz and Treb while Everly takes a seat next to Clover. As Prisha babbles in Fritz's ear, jealousy wraps its poisonous claws around me.

"What's up, ladies?" One-eyed Everly grins at us.

She looks deliriously happy for someone who recently lost an eye. Clover ignores her while I try not to fixate on her eye patch. My eyes are drawn to her fingernails. If she killed Berkeley and Harlowe this morning, wouldn't her hands be blood-stained? I look closely but find no evidence on her hands or jumpsuit.

"Where is Maris?" I ask.

Everly shrugs and seems disinterested. "I haven't seen her since breakfast."

Maris' absence puzzles me. I turn to Clover. "Do you think Bacon—"

"No. Definitely not. Maris isn't transgenic."

Eavesdropping, Prisha chimes in using a gossipy tone. "Isn't it strange that Maris disappeared only hours before those beasts barged in and ordered us to Headquarters? Could she be involved in what they're planning?"

Clover shakes her head. "I don't think so."

Treb nods toward the stage as Gregor, flanked by two soldiers, climbs the steps. He taps the microphone at center stage. Conversations dwindle. One hand remains in his pocket. Is the drone remote control in that pocket?

Gregor says, "You may wonder why you are here. As of this morning, my father, Dr. Hahn, is no longer with us." Gregor's voice is not the voice of a man grieving his father.

Gasps spatter over the crowd followed by silence.

Did Gregor kill Dr. Hahn? If Dr. Hahn is dead, what happens to me and Fritz? Feelings of hopelessness and panic start building inside me. I glance at Fritz. He reaches over and squeezes my hand.

Gregor continues, "I will be taking my father's place as the Head of the Nuclei. My father became senile in old age and began making reckless decisions. He recently inducted into the Nuclei people who were unqualified to lead."

Gregor's eyes move across the auditorium and settle on me and Fritz. A flick of anger inflames my cheeks. It's not like I asked to be a Nuclei member. Or a stupid Supernova for that matter.

"As an eighty-year-old non-genetically-modified man, it was time for my father to retire. Doctors Toussaint and Sorrell will continue to serve as Nuclei members. Franz Hahn will succeed me when the time comes.

"Until the situation stabilizes, your comfort and safety are our top priority. Pillows, blankets, and food will be distributed shortly. I ask that you exercise patience and place your trust in us. We will release you as soon as possible." Gregor leaves the stage with two soldiers serving as bodyguards.

"So, we're hostages now?" Everly asks as her reduction in status registers.

"Do you guys think Dr. Hahn is dead?" I ask.

Fritz responds, "Franz and Gregor have been ganging up on him since I arrived at Headquarters. The power struggle between Gregor and Hahn has probably been going on for years. It wouldn't surprise me if Gregor killed his own father. He seems ruthless enough and Franz isn't much better."

"I agree." I picture Dr. Hahn's youthful gait and appearance. "Do you think he was really eighty?"

"Anti-aging therapy does wonders," Clover says.

Could Dr. Hahn still be alive and in need of our help? The soldier who forced us into the auditorium said other Nuclei members are imprisoned.

If they were being held at Headquarters, where would they be? Dr. Hahn's Presidential Suite is secure and only accessible by Nuclei members.

"Treb, is there any way to leave without being caught?" I ask.

Prisha's eyes dart around the room. "Keep your voice down. If anyone hears you…"

A half-smile crosses Treb's face. "I might know a way." He pauses as if he wants us to put more effort into prying the secret from him.

"We don't have time for games. Tell us," Everly demands.

Prisha stands and says, "I don't want any part of this. I don't know anything if anybody asks. Leave me out of it." She walks toward Blaise's group and sits with them.

Treb leans in and motions for us to do the same. He lowers his voice and says, "The men's bathroom."

"What about it?" Everly, unable to hide her impatience, prods Treb.

"In the last stall," he pauses dramatically, "there's a hidden panel."

Clover leans back, crosses her arms over her chest, and narrows her eyes. "Are you messing with us?"

"I swear it's true." Treb raises his voice. "My dad used to work at Headquarters. One time, I was playing basketball right here in this auditorium. I took a break to use the bathroom and the electricity went out. The wall next to the toilet started glowing. I thought it was aliens. I ran out of the bathroom. Later, I worked up the courage to check it out."

"What did you find?" Everly's voice brims with excitement.

"I slid the hidden panel aside and climbed through the opening. I saw dead people floating in blue eggs in the basement. I ran away and never went back."

"You didn't need a microchip to open the door?" Fritz asks.

"Nope." Treb holds up his hands to show they aren't microchipped.

"Is the door still there?" Clover leans forward and glances toward the bathrooms.

"I don't know. I haven't thought about it in years." Treb pulls a pack of gum from his pocket and offers everyone a piece.

Everly takes a piece and says, "Go to the bathroom and check."

"But I don't need to use the bathroom," Treb protests.

"Just go," Everly says, popping the gum into her mouth.

Treb reluctantly stands and eyes the soldiers stationed around the room.

"Stop looking guilty or you're going to attract attention." Everly scowls at him.

"Okay, okay, I'm going." Treb wipes his palms on the front of his pants and heads to the bathroom hallway in the back of the room.

Fritz reaches for my hand. "If Treb finds a way to the basement, then what?"

I hesitate and consider how much I should say. I trust Clover, but can I trust Everly? I saved Everly's life so she is kind of indebted to me, but I doubt she sees it that way.

"Can you guys knock off the PDA?" Everly looks at our clasped hands and puckers her face.

Fritz grins and surprises me by leaning in for a quick kiss that warms me from the inside out. I lean into him, smiling.

"You guys are a thing now?" Clover asks. "That happened fast."

"Not really." I bristle at the commentary on our budding relationship. I don't want anything to ruin it or make it weird. "We met before we were assigned to Ovation."

I release Fritz's hand. "Anyway, if we can get to the basement, we may be able to reach Dr. Hahn's office. What if he's being held captive there? If he's alive, he can stop Gregor and tell us where the vaccine is."

"Bad idea," Fritz says. "If Dr. Hahn is alive, he will be under surveillance. There's no way we can help him. Plus, Dr. Hahn has no way to stop Gregor. Gregor has one hell of an army."

I switch to a different tactic. "The mainframe is in a room above the basement. It stores recordings transmitted from Golgi from various locations. We might find recorded conversations or the blueprint for whatever they are planning."

From Fritz's expression, he obviously sees the value in accessing the mainframe. "The mainframe will be protected by passwords and firewalls," he says.

Everly puts her arm around Clover's shoulders and says, "My girl has never met a computer she couldn't break into."

Clover recoils from Everly's touch.

"You hack?" Fritz asks Clover.

She smiles. "A little."

"Don't be so modest," Everly says in a congenial tone, as if she and Clover are middle school BFFs again. She must think they're even—a betrayal for an eye.

Treb approaches the group with a guilty look on his face. His eyes wander around the room as if at any moment someone could arrest him.

"Is it still there?" Everly asks before blowing an obnoxiously big bubble.

Treb nods. "I opened it and listened for voices, but all I heard was music."

I lean in and keep my voice low. "After everyone is asleep tonight, Fritz, Clover, and I will go to the bathroom separately. Fritz, you go first and keep the stall occupied and locked. Clover and I will tap twice on the stall door. We'll enter the hidden passage together."

"What about me and Treb?" Everly asks.

"You guys stay here and cover for us."

"Bo-ring," Everly says.

"Just cooperate this one time." Clover sounds irritated.

"Fine," Everly says.

Thirty-five

Heart racing, I dart into the men's bathroom, race to the last stall, and tap twice. The stall door creaks open. I squeeze into the tiny space, accidentally bump into Clover, and send her crashing into the toilet. She grabs onto me, and for a second, I imagine both of us falling head first into the toilet bowl. I brace an arm against the stall wall until we gain our balance.

"Sorry," I whisper as I lock the stall.

Fritz reaches for Clover's hand from inside the hidden passage. She ducks through the cutout and joins him. Next, I take his hand, step through, and slide the panel closed.

Blue light spills into the passage from a wide opening about twenty feet ahead. The concrete walls, floor, and ceiling appear bruised. Muffled music surrounds us.

Fritz takes my hand and we follow Clover. The warmth of his hand in mine is comforting. I no longer feel alone or like I'm on my own.

"What?" Fritz catches me staring at him.

"Nothing." I blush.

At the end of the passage, we step onto a small balcony that looks down on the gynopods.

Clover leans against the railing. "It smells like mint and something I can't pinpoint."

"Lemons," says Fritz.

I open my mouth and inhale deeply. The lemony-mint scent feels icy in my nose and throat. I imagine the snow-covered mountains and snowflakes my grandparents used to talk about. "I bet winter smells like this in other parts of the world."

"Maybe we'll get out of here someday and find out." Fritz wraps his arm around my shoulders and pulls me closer.

"Maybe." I smile up at him even though I can't imagine living anywhere but the island.

Clover points at a flight of metal stairs attached to the balcony. "There's only one way to go. Straight up."

Above us, a platform connects to a truss bridge concealed within a network of pipes and steel beams. The bridge hangs high over the basement. From here, I can't tell where it leads.

Fritz says, "I'll go first in case we encounter something unexpected."

Clover motions for me to go next. I grip the handrail and instead of focusing on the open rise between steps and obsessing over the two-story drop to the basement below, I focus on Fritz's muscular back. He looks back a couple of times to check on us.

Speakers blare piano notes and cello chords that comingle in a heart-wrenching harmony. I recognize the song as one Opal used to play on the piano.

At the top, Fritz says, "It looks like a road to nowhere."

The bridge ends at a doorless wall with a row of windows overlooking the basement.

"It's the observation room," I say. "There must be a way in."

Halfway across the bridge, I look down at the rows of gynopods. Naked bodies, big and small, bob and sway in blue fluid. Fetuses float in various stages of development. How do they decide which ones will be released and which ones will float for decades as organ donors?

I imagine Dr. Hahn pulling up a chair and reading to my gynopod day after day, hour after hour. A pang of grief hits me when I recall Gregor's words: *My father, Dr. Hahn, is no longer with us.*

I catch up to Clover and Fritz.

"It's a dead end," Fritz says. "We have to go back."

"Let me see." I trade places with Fritz and wave my hand over the wall.

"What are you doing?" Clover asks.

"I want to see if this works." The wall moves under my hand revealing a hidden door.

Clover steps forward and gapes at the opening. "How did you do that?"

"Microchip." Fritz winks at me.

He looks cute when he winks. I try to wink back, but I'm not much of a winker. As half my face crinkles, I consider that I probably look more constipated than cute. Hopefully, he doesn't notice. I smooth my expression and step into the observation room.

"Where's the mainframe computer?" Clover asks.

"Dr. Hahn said it was in that room." I point to the door across from where we entered.

Fritz rests his hand on the door and looks surprised when it pops open under his hand. "They're making this too easy. The first thing they should have done was disable microchips and passport privileges."

"We're just harmless kids, remember?" I say.

We bust out laughing and pile through the doorway to the mainframe. Computer equipment stacked on wire racks gives the room a cluttered appearance. A soft whir coming from the racks makes it seem as though the equipment is alive and breathing.

Clover and Fritz approach a desk that has two monitors and a keyboard. Fritz sits at the desk. A monitor snaps on and displays a blue screen with a password prompt. Fritz strikes the keyboard and gets past the password screen. A black screen pops up where Fritz enters a bevy of letters, numbers, and symbols. The computer responds: ACCESS DENIED.

Clover and I watch from over his shoulder. What if we're just wasting our time? It was stupid to think we would be able to break into the Nuclei mainframe. If we can't access the mainframe, we may never find out what Gregor is planning until it's too late. I let out an exasperated sigh.

"We're in," Fritz says.

"Really?" I lean closer to get a better view.

"What are we looking for?" he asks.

I skim the folders on the desktop. "Open the one that says 'Artificial Intelligence Recordings.'"

Fritz clicks open the contents of the folder. A map of Ovation appears. "Now what?"

"Find House of Saphronia."

Fritz zooms into the map and taps the stylus on House of Saphronia. A window opens and prompts him to enter a date.

"Date?" he asks.

"The night of the Gala when I was abducted, I heard a man in Saphronia's quarters. It was around midnight. October eighth."

Fritz enters the date and pulls up a list of recordings. He randomly selects one. The speakers fill with the voices of Maris and Everly discussing what they're wearing to the Gala.

"Weird," Clover says. "Why is Golgi recording random conversations?"

Fritz glances at me. "I told you this place is full of bugs."

"You think they record every conversation that takes place in Ovation? Like total surveillance?" I ask.

Fritz shrugs. "Looks like it." He hovers the stylus over the list of recordings. "That's strange."

"What's strange?" Clover asks.

"Audio files are missing from that date and location."

"Can you recover them?" I ask.

Fritz opens a new window and enters lines of code. "I'm hitting a wall when I try to access the deleted files. An extra layer of security prevents them from being recovered."

"Let me try," Clover says.

Fritz stands and Clover takes his place.

"I'm going to check Dr. Hahn's office." I back toward the door.

"I'll go with you." Fritz steps closer.

I rest my hand on his chest. "Stay here and see what you can find on the mainframe. There must be a reason they have every resident of Ovation trapped in this building overnight, right?"

I hesitate to voice the concern that has been plaguing me since we saw the army roll into Headquarters. "Do you think they plan to kill everyone? They could poison the food or water or air supply to the auditorium."

Fritz brushes hair out of my eyes. "They aren't going to kill anyone. Most Ovation residents were genetically engineered by the Nuclei. People have too much pride and attachment to their creations to destroy them."

Clover spins around in the chair, beaming at us. "I recovered the deleted files. There have been a *massive* number of deletions over the past two months."

"You got past all the security measures?" Fritz looks impressed.

"Sure did." She blows on her fingernails and buffs them on her shirt.

Why would the Nuclei allow Clover's talent to go to waste? She could have been a computer programmer or a trailblazing scientist. Instead, they assigned her to egg production and when that didn't work out, she was assigned to domestic servitude. What a complete and total waste.

"You guys sift through the deleted files. I'll be right back," I say.

Fritz crosses his arms over his chest. "I'm not comfortable with you going alone."

I offer a compromise. "If I'm not back in fifteen minutes, come find me. The other door in the observation room leads to Dr. Hahn's office."

"You're pretty stubborn, you know that?" Fritz says.

I stick out my tongue and back away feigning confidence. I enter the stairwell and then the soundproof room. It looks exactly as it did during the memory transfer. Nothing seems out of place. No dead bodies. No hostages.

I press my ear against the wall to Dr. Hahn's office, keeping my microchipped hand behind my back to avoid triggering the scanner. If Nuclei members were being held hostage in the Presidential Suite, wouldn't I hear voices in addition to my thundering heartbeat?

Stepping away from the door, I pace back and forth. Back and forth. Maybe I should have asked Fritz to come with me. Why did I think I could do this alone? I'm the girl who is scared of everything. Scared of heights. Scared of tight spaces. Scared of taking risks. And most of all, scared of failing.

I picture Abe and Addie, Mom and Dad. Then, I picture Gregor's hand wrapped around the remote control that has the power to kill them all. I see the hateful spark in Franz's eyes when he looks at me. I can't let Gregor and Franz win. I can't let them kill my family and other innocent people. I can't let them kill Dr. Hahn, either. If Dr. Hahn is still alive, that is.

I see myself shoving the Sisterhood leader into the bonfire and helping Everly escape. I was brave that night and Everly and I survived. If I don't allow my fears to hold me back, people in Hillcrest and the Valley might survive.

Fear loosens its grip on me. In its place, rock-hard resolve spurs me forward. I hold my microchip up to the scanner and step into Dr. Hahn's office. In the absence of daylight, the office looks grim and foreboding. The pep talk I gave myself quickly loses its power. As my eyes adjust to the darkness, I scout for somewhere to hide.

To the right, an open door reveals an empty bedroom. To the left, a super-soldier sits on the couch. My heart thwacks and my calves twitch. I prepare to flee. Does he see me? His breath whistles through parted lips. He's asleep. Of course, he's asleep. It's one in the morning. His hand rests on the semiautomatic rifle in his lap. It would take mere seconds for him to snap awake and point that thing at me.

A Nuclei member must have given him access to the Presidential Suite. And if a Nuclei member gave him access, it's because he's guarding something important.

I take three giant steps and crouch behind the desk. The floorboard creaks. I cringe. Ten. Nine. Eight. Breathe. Did he hear anything? Are other soldiers here? Seven. Six. Five. I peek around the desk. It's just the two of us.

Next to the couch, the conference room door is slightly ajar. A soft glow flows from the edges of the door. Who could be in there? More soldiers? Hostages? Dr. Hahn?

Four. Three. Two. One. I crawl from behind the desk and take cover under the chair I sat in earlier today. I keep my eyes on the soldier, lie down on my stomach, and pull myself across the floor with my elbows. My heart drums the cold floor. When my face is parallel with his feet, I'm convinced that if he were awake, he would feel my heavy heartbeat through the soles of his combat boots.

I keep my chest pressed against the floor and inch forward, aligning my eye with the door crack. Three brightly glowing figures slump around the table, including one in Dr. Hahn's seat. Is it him? All I can see from my position are hands bound behind his chair.

Fritz will be looking for me soon. I have to hurry. I slither into the conference room and rise to my knees next to Dr. Hahn's chair. It's him! A surge of hope rushes through me. A woman at the far end of the table groans. I squint against the brightness of her face. Dr. Honeysett. Next to her is Dr. Akimoto. Their heads fall forward. Their mouths are gagged and their arms are tied behind their backs.

What if this is my last opportunity to talk to Dr. Hahn? I shake his shoulder. "Dr. Hahn? Wake up."

He doesn't stir. I shake him more vigorously. Black liquid spreads across his white shirt. I touch his chest. Wet, warm, and sticky. I bring my hand to my nose. There's a metallic odor, like wet coins—my stomach dips—blood. His wrist is cold, but a faint pulse ticks under my thumb.

Footsteps stride around the adjacent room. Light from Dr. Hahn's office streams through the doorway. I release Dr. Hahn's wrist, shove an empty chair over, and hurry under the table. I grab the legs of the displaced chair, return it to its position, and lie down. My heart is pounding so hard, it feels like it's going to bust right out of my chest.

The door swings open. The light comes on. Combat boots approach the table and pause in the pool of blood next to Dr. Hahn. Minutes pass. The soldier slowly circles the table leaving a trail of bloody footsteps. He squats near my face and tugs on the rope binding Dr. Hahn's hands. If he crouches any lower, he will see me. Just when I think crushing anxiety is going to cause my organs to spontaneously explode, the soldier stands, turns off the light, and leaves the room, closing the door behind him.

I release my held breath, slip out of my hiding place, and approach Dr. Hahn's side. I untie his hands, place them in his lap, and remove his gag. Wisps of breath flutter across my hand. I gently rest his head against the chair back.

Why do I feel like crying? "Dr. Hahn?" I cradle his face and will him to wake.

His eyes open and focus on me. "Delilah?" The name wheezes from his lips.

"It's Wren," I whisper.

"Wren." His eyes fall closed.

"Dr. Hahn, where is the vaccine?" I glance nervously at the closed door, hoping the soldier can't hear me.

Dr. Hahn's eyes remain closed. His breathing becomes more labored. Is he taking his last breaths? Did Gregor and Franz do this? I repeat my question.

"Wren," Dr. Hahn whispers.

I lean closer.

"The answer…"

"Yes?"

"… is… in… your DNA." Dr. Hahn draws a dry, ragged breath.

"The answer is in my DNA? What do you mean?"

Dr. Hahn's head droops. He loses consciousness again. He can't walk in his condition, and I can't carry his weight. Even if I could move him, none of us have medical training. Feeling helpless, I remove my hands from his face and back away.

After unbinding the hands of Dr. Honeysett and Dr. Akimoto, I scrutinize their clothing for blood. Their clothes are clean. Neither is conscious. Maybe they were drugged.

I stay in a crouched position and move toward the door. I carefully rotate the doorknob as if it were a grenade missing its firing pin. The office is dark and empty. Where did he go?

Trembling, I fall to my hands and knees and scurry to the antique chairs. Did the guard really leave Nuclei hostages unattended? I stare at the empty room in disbelief.

I pivot to face the hidden door and start to rise. A rumble from the bedroom startles me. I take cover against the desk and desperately look around for a weapon.

There's a glass vase on the coffee table, a hefty lamp on the end table. A vase and a lamp against a semiautomatic weapon: who am I kidding? The thought of fighting a super-soldier catapults my pulse to dizzying heights. I press my fingers against the frenzied pulse in my neck.

The resonant rumble tears through the office again. This time, it's followed by a snort and a gasp. I exhale and cautiously move to my feet. The super-soldier is splayed out on Dr. Hahn's bed snoring, completely oblivious to the security breach.

I fix my eyes on the soldier until I'm safely inside the secret corridor. I take the stairs to the observation room, puzzling over Dr. Hahn's words. What was he trying to tell me?

As soon as I enter the observation room, Fritz rushes toward me. "I was about to go after you." A look of concern crosses his face. He tips my chin up and runs his thumb across my cheek. "Have you been crying?"

Normally, his touch makes me feel light and happy, but now, my limbs feel as heavy as lead pipes filled with cement. "It's Dr. Hahn. I think he's dying." I sniffle, tired of holding back my emotions.

Boom, boom, boom!

Someone bangs on the door to the bridge. I flinch and step away from Fritz. Did someone follow us? Clover appears in the doorway between the rooms and looks alarmed.

Fritz points to the mainframe room. "You and Clover go in there and lock the door."

Boom, boom, boom!

"Now!" Fritz moves toward the sound.

I'm too shaken to argue this time.

Thirty-six

"Let me in!" A familiar voice yells.

Fritz yanks open the door.

Everly bursts in, pulling Treb behind her.

Clover rushes over, grabs Everly by the shoulders, and shakes her. "Are you crazy? You could get us killed making noise like that."

"I was bored and couldn't sleep." Everly twists out of Clover's grip, loses her balance, and plows into me.

I grab at the wall, the bookshelf, anything to steady myself but the rug slips from under us and we crash to the floor. I land on my hip with Everly crumpled on top of me. I shove her to the side and give her a dirty look.

"Sorry," she says.

Fritz extends his hands and hauls us to our feet.

Clover sits on a stool, props her elbows on her knees, and buries her face in her hands. "Please tell me you slid the bathroom panel back in place?"

"I might not be as smart as you, but I'm not an idiot," Everly huffs.

"I tried to talk her out of it..." Treb says.

Fritz approaches the area where Everly and I fell. The rug is askew, revealing the edges of a trapdoor. Memories of the underground dungeon flood my mind. I back away.

"What are you waiting for? Open it." Everly peels back the rug, throws it across the room, and grabs the circular brass handle on the trapdoor.

Clover leaps from the stool and stands on the door. She puts her hands on her hips and scowls at Everly. "Could you stop being so impulsive for once? What if those mutant killing machines are down there?"

Fritz says, "Treb, any idea where the door could lead?"

Treb rubs his forehead. "Maybe to the tunnels that run under the city."

"Like the catacombs under Paris?" Everly asks.

"Minus the skeletons," Treb says.

My curiosity overrules my cautious side. "If there's a way out of Headquarters, maybe there's a way for us to warn others or to get help. We have to see what's under there."

Clover reluctantly steps off the trapdoor. Everly straddles the door and grips the handle with both hands. She strains to lift it. Treb and Clover wedge their fingers into the opening and help Everly prop open the door, perpendicular to the floor.

I step closer to the gaping void.

Fritz peers into the darkness. "A ladder leads from the trapdoor to an empty tunnel."

"Do you hear anything?" I ask.

Fritz listens for a minute and then shakes his head.

"Me first." Everly steps around Fritz and descends the ladder before anyone can object.

"You guys go ahead," Treb says. "I'll stay here."

"What's wrong? Scared of the dark, Trebby-poo?" Everly flashes a mischievous grin at Treb and disappears into the tunnel.

Fritz, Clover, and I descend the ladder behind Everly. When we gather on the dirt floor, Everly is missing. The three of us cautiously survey the surrounding tunnels that branch out north, south, east, and west. Metal signs denoting street names hang at the mouth of each tunnel.

Fritz points to the one leading south. "Belgica Avenue. The train station is that way."

"Everly?" Clover's voice is shaky. She blinks rapidly, as if she's frightened.

Everly pops out from a recess in the wall. "You guys will not believe what I found!"

"Shh!" Clover shushes her.

I'm on edge. "What if we are walking into a trap? Why aren't soldiers patrolling the tunnels to prevent people from escaping?"

"Maybe Gregor doesn't know about the tunnels," Clover says.

Fritz says, "Even if Gregor knew about the tunnels and his plan had as many holes as a slice of swiss cheese, he would be oblivious. He thinks he's smarter than everyone."

Everly pokes her head into the tunnel. "You guys, c'mon."

Clover repeatedly looks over her shoulder. From the look of concentration on Fritz's face, I can tell he's listening to make sure we're alone. I'm not the only one on edge. We all are.

Except Everly.

When we join her, she sweeps her arm around the room as if she's a hostess offering us a feast of delicacies. Tables are piled high with every weapon imaginable: machetes and rifles, crossbows and axes.

Everly's eye glitters maniacally as she presents her discoveries. "Ninja stars, knives, ropes, and guns." She leans over, pulls the leg of her jumpsuit up, and buckles a leather holster to her calf. She slides a knife into the holster.

Clover and I make brief eye contact. Did Everly use a knife like that on Berkeley and Harlowe? I shudder at the image of Everly kneeling over Berkeley, slashing her abdomen, and plucking her ovaries. She probably took their eyes last to force them to watch.

Why would the Nadirs target someone as crazy as Everly and think they could get away with it? If Berkeley and Harlowe had targeted any other Supernova, they might still be alive.

"Well, don't just stand there staring at me," Everly says. "Get what you need."

I approach the weapon-covered tables and pick up a small revolver. The weight and size are a good fit. It's solid in my hands.

Fritz seems surprised by my choice. "Do you know how to use that thing?"

"Pretty sure I can figure it out." I pop open the cylinder and spin it. It rotates smoothly, as if brand new. I open a box of bullets and fill the empty chambers with ammunition. After snapping the cylinder back in place, I raise the gun to read the engraving on the side.

"Who is Smith and Wesson?" I ask.

"An ancient gun manufacturer. You'll be lucky if it still works," Fritz says.

I drop extra bullets into my jeans pocket and hope I don't find myself in a situation that requires me to use them.

Clover picks up two pieces of rope and slides them into her pockets.

Everly looks at her like she's stupid and hands her a knife. "Take this. What are you planning to do with rope? Lasso cows?"

Clover waves the knife away. "I don't like knives or guns. I was thinking rope would be useful if we need to tie someone up."

Everly looks at Clover as if Clover has earned her respect. "Now you're talking." She scoops a length of rope into her own pocket.

Fritz deposits a pocketknife in his back pocket and hands me a switchblade. "Take this in case the gun doesn't work. When this is over, we can use the corkscrew on my pocketknife to open a bottle of wine and celebrate."

I laugh. "You're silly." I appreciate that Fritz knows how to make me laugh when I feel as tightly wound as a bug spun in spider-silk. I grab an extra pocketknife for Treb. Everly continues to fill her pockets.

Fritz says, "Clover and I found some interesting info on the mainframe and you have to tell us what you found in Dr. Hahn's office."

"There's a soundproof room upstairs. Let's talk there." I head back to the ladder with Clover, Fritz, and Everly close behind. At the top of the ladder, Treb grabs my arm and helps me up. I hand him a pocketknife.

"Cool, thanks." Treb takes the knife. "What was down there?"

"You were right about the tunnels." I offer my hand to Everly and then Clover.

Fritz and Clover close the trapdoor and rearrange the rug over it.

Everly digs into her pockets and shows Treb a sparkling assortment of knives, bullets, and ninja stars. "You missed out. I found a stockpile of weapons. It was awesome."

I open the door to the stairwell and we climb the stairs to the soundproof room. Everly immediately starts prowling through cabinets and drawers. The rest of us take seats around the table.

"Jackpot," Everly says. "Granola bars, anybody? Bottled water?" She drops food and water on the table and plops into the leather recliner.

I reach for a bottle of water.

Fritz grabs my wrist. "You're bleeding. Are you hurt?"

I follow his eyes to the bloodstains caked around my fingernails. "Dr. Hahn was losing a lot of blood when I found him."

Everly perks up. "Dr. Hahn is alive?"

"Hahn, Akimoto, and Honeysett are tied up in the Nuclei conference room." I take a drink of water. "Dr. Hahn is hurt. I couldn't tell what type of wound, but his chest was covered in blood."

"And the others?" Fritz asks.

"Alive, but unconscious. I think they were drugged." I lock eyes with Fritz. "Is there any way to get Dr. Hahn medical help?"

He shakes his head, reaches across the table, and holds my hand.

I stare at our interlocked hands. "Dr. Hahn gained consciousness long enough for me to ask about the vaccine."

"Where is it?" Clover leans in.

"He was delirious. He called me Delilah and said the vaccine is in my DNA." Their faces are blank. They don't recognize Delilah's name.

"But that doesn't make sense." Everly rips into a second granola bar and takes a bite. Her teeth grind the granola and my nerves with it. I try to ignore the smacking, mashing, chomping.

"What did you find on the mainframe?" I ask.

"They plan to release a virus Wednesday night via drones," Clover says.

With a mouth full of granola, Everly asks, "What virus?"

Fritz answers, "The one that will kill everyone in Hillcrest and the Valley."

Everly chokes on her food and starts coughing.

"Shh!" Clover says.

"It's okay. The room is soundproof." I remind Clover.

"What about Clairemont?" Everly asks.

Fritz says, "Everyone in Clairemont is immune. Nuclei members and select residents have been vaccinated. Gregor will release the virus after the drones are in place."

The gears of my mind start spinning out of control. I prop my elbows on the table and lean my forehead against my palms.

We have two days. Two days to stop the virus. Two days to save my family. I picture Gregor in the Nuclei meeting holding up the remote control. Two days to find the remote control.

I lift my head. "For all we know, the drones could already be in Hillcrest and the Valley. We need the remote control. We need the vaccine. And, if there's a cure, we need that, too."

"We also found out why Ovation residents were corralled into the auditorium," Fritz says in a grim tone.

"Why?" Treb asks.

Clover responds, "The night of the Gala, it was Gregor in Saphronia's quarters."

"Why would Gregor be there after midnight?" I dig through my memories. I see Gregor standing in the foyer speaking with Saphronia. I see him standing with a group of Zeniths at the Harvest.

"They were discussing a top-secret wedding ceremony," Clover says.

"So, I was right." Treb leans back in his chair.

"Well, not exactly," Fritz says. "Wren, you heard them mention Project Aphrodite during the Nuclei meeting?"

"Yeah," I nod.

Fritz continues, "We were able to piece things together from the audio files and documents on the mainframe. Twenty-five years ago, the Nuclei agreed to create a genetically-modified population in Clairemont that would eventually consist of only females. Dr. Hahn ordered the destruction of genetically-modified male embryos."

"That's why there are no boys our age in Clairemont." Everly's mouth falls open.

Clover picks up where Fritz left off. "Instead of destroying the male embryos, Gregor initiated Project Ares. He moved the male embryos to a location outside of his father's purview."

I recall the soldiers marching in formation at the creepy facility and the comatose pregnant women. "Guantanamo?"

Fritz nods. "At puberty, kidnapped female orphans and confiscated female children were used as surrogates for the male embryos. Gregor kept the girls in a comatose state of constant pregnancy. He implanted them with two to three embryos at a time. Milkmaids raised the boys at Guantanamo. They all have night vision, ultrasonic hearing, and immunity to the DBH virus."

I think of the poor girls hooked up to machines, trapped and pregnant. Celeste was pregnant with a super-soldier. She was targeted because she was an orphan.

"Wow," Treb says. "Night vision and ultrasonic hearing sounds like something straight out of the future."

"It's not *that* impressive," Everly says. "Most of us have night vision. What's your superpower?"

Treb's face turns red.

"Well?" Everly persists.

Treb stammers, "I... I've never told anyone."

"It can't be that bad." Everly looks Treb up and down. "You definitely aren't a runner."

"Just don't tell anybody." Treb stares at his hands. "I'm non-GMO."

Everly gawks at him. "You're *not* genetically-modified? How is that possible? Everyone in Clairemont is GMO. I thought everyone in Ovation was, too?"

Treb says, "They didn't sterilize the first generation of survivors. I mean, they did sterilize indigenous survivors, but NASA employees and their children were granted waivers. Most in Ovation are GMO, but there are exceptions like me."

The room gets quiet and everyone stares at Treb as if he has two heads. He squirms and tugs the collar of his shirt away from his flushed skin.

I change the subject to take the spotlight off Treb. "What else did you guys find? Are Gregor and Saphronia getting married?"

Clover cracks her knuckles and rolls her head from side to side. She has dark circles under her eyes. "Fertile women of Ovation and Clairemont will be wed to super-soldiers at noon, Wednesday," she says in a flat tone.

Everly slaps her hands against her thighs and springs out of the recliner. Her words come out in an excited rush: "*We're* the ones getting married? Do we get to pick who we marry? I didn't see any cute soldiers in the auditorium, but I wasn't really looking."

I stand and squeeze past Everly. She stares into space with a silly smile on her face like she's already picking out a dress and planning her wedding. At least one of us is happy. Everyone else looks solemn. I lean against the counter containing lab equipment.

"Gregor promised wives to the super-soldiers, but what's in it for Zeniths like Saphronia?" I ask.

Fritz says, "The Zeniths will have their freedom instead of babysitting Supernovas. Gregor said Dr. Hahn was wasting perfectly good resources by not allowing the genetically fit to have their own children."

I roll my eyes. "And by 'perfectly good resources,' " I curl my fingers into air quotes, "he means women's wombs. He wants to use women as cheap baby-makers and morale-boosters for his army. Sounds ideal." I inject as much sarcasm as possible into my tone.

Everly crinkles her nose. "Well, that's gross. What if we don't want to give birth?"

I turn and touch the ridged knobs, smooth dials, and raised buttons on the lab equipment. The news of a wedding ceremony seems insignificant compared to Gregor's plan to murder all non-genetically-modified people.

We have to find a way to vaccinate everyone or destroy the infected mosquitoes. But where is the vaccine? Where are the mosquitoes?

I jerk my hand away from the machine it had been resting on. How do I know this machine? I lean down to examine it. My heart leaps and high-fives my brain. I've found a missing piece to the puzzle. Did Dr. Hahn put this here intentionally?

"You guys, I think I know how to find the vaccine."

Thirty-seven

"These machines," I point to the lab equipment, "are used for DNA sequencing and decoding. Books, pictures, and videos can be stored in DNA and retrieved later."

"So?" Everly sticks out her lower lip and blows her bangs off her face.

"When I asked Dr. Hahn about the vaccine, he said the answer is in my DNA. What if there's a code or message or location coordinates?"

Fritz eyes the equipment. "Do you know how to decode DNA?"

"I think so." I close my eyes and picture the article I read my first day in Ovation: "DNA Data Storage." I scan the labeled diagrams in my memories. I open my eyes, grab a swab, scrape my inner cheek, and insert the swab into the machine capable of detecting encoding.

"Nothing's happening," Everly says.

"Just be patient," Clover responds.

A helix fragment appears on a miniature computer screen. We all huddle around watching and waiting as the 3D image slowly increases in size.

"Look. It's spitting out a scrap of paper." Everly swipes at the paper.

Clover blocks her hand. "It isn't done yet." Her tone is that of a parent scolding a child.

Paper shoots out of the machine and flutters to the countertop. I pick it up and read aloud:

My face is asymmetrical,
my song ecclesiastical
My lies, embalmed with gold,
for centuries were told
People once loved me,
but those were days of old
Abandoned and forgotten,
voices of the past now haunt my soul

"It's a riddle," Treb says. "Read it one more time."

I read it again. The words feel foreign and unfamiliar on my tongue. How could they have been a part of me, inside me, all of this time? Who inserted the riddle in my DNA? Dr. Hahn? Dr. Akimoto?

Everly drums her fingernails against the counter. "I don't get it. It's a riddle about gold and songs and being forgotten.

Is it a famous singer? Like that guy we learned about in music classes—Elvis?"

Clover rolls her eyes at Everly. "The asymmetrical bell towers."

Fritz takes the slip of paper and flips it through his fingers. "We had the answer all along."

"The vaccine is at the Cathedral of the Virgin Mary," I say.

Fritz passes the paper back to me. His fingers linger on mine. I feel as though warm caramel is flowing through my veins, delivering a sugar rush straight to my heart.

"I always thought Sanctuary was a codename. Nice work, Detective." He smiles.

I blush and return his smile. How can a single touch from Fritz make my insides feel coated in powdered sugar and my mind feel like it's wrapped in a cotton-candy haze?

"Now what?" Everly's voice draws me back. I tuck the riddle in my pocket.

Fritz says, "Even if we find the vaccine, we have no way to transport thousands of units to the people who need it."

"So, bring the people to Ovation," Clover says.

Fritz lifts his head and rubs his chin. "You might be on to something."

Fritz reminds me of my dad when he rubs his chin like that. I push aside the prickle of pain that pokes me when I think of my family and return to my seat. The others follow. Everly sinks back into the recliner and yawns.

I picture the Enforcers being vaccinated in the auditorium. "We can't trust people in Hillcrest. And it sounds like Gregor has alliances with some Enforcers, Zeniths, and Milkmaids. What about Valley residents, Fritz? Could you recruit them to help us? You could update their passports and they could stow away on the cargo trains."

"I don't have much credibility in the Valley. I was someone who, if you ask them, thought he was smarter than everyone else. Even if I could organize an army, how would they win against genetically-modified soldiers who have state-of-the-art equipment?"

"I have an idea," Everly says. "When all the super-soldiers are gathered in the auditorium for the wedding ceremony, we lock them in and blow the place up. Set it on fire or something." She claps her fists together and then dramatically flares her fingers to indicate an explosion. "Boom! Mission accomplished. No more Gregor. No more super-soldiers. No more virus."

Clover looks taken aback. "So, we're going to blow everybody up, including innocent residents and children? You should keep your sociopathic thoughts to yourself."

"Wait," I say. "Everly has a good point."

Everly leans back in the recliner, clasps her hands behind her head, and aims a smug smile at Clover.

"We could use it to our advantage that the soldiers will be in the same place at the same time during the ceremony." Thoughts are running through my mind faster than I can catch them.

"Treb, do you know where the Headquarters intercom system is located?"

"The communications room is on the second floor, near the cafeteria."

"Fritz, you said certain frequencies give you headaches?"

Fritz looks confused by my question. "That's right."

"We could broadcast those frequencies across the intercom system. You said all super-soldiers have ultrasonic hearing, right?"

Fritz snaps his fingers and jumps out of his seat. "Genius!" He starts pacing. "Not only do certain frequencies cause migraines, but certain frequencies incapacitate people and animals with ultrasonic hearing. They cause nausea, memory loss, disorientation."

He rifles through his backpack and holds up a device that looks like a miniature speaker. "I can program this to transmit head-splitting, nausea-inducing frequencies."

I turn to Treb. "If you can get to the communications room during the wedding ceremony, you could blast the frequency over the intercom."

"Fritz, you have to persuade people in the Valley to join us," I plead. "Tell them Gregor is going to kill them. All of them. Men, women, and children. Tell them we have the vaccine. Tell them whatever it takes to get them to fight with us. If they rush the auditorium while the super-soldiers are incapacitated, we could capture Gregor. We could neutralize the drone remote control and force Gregor to call off the virus release."

Fritz shakes his head. "I can't get them to trust me, but I know someone who can." He hesitates and then says, "Prisha's family has been in the Valley for generations. If her dad knew what was going on, he could galvanize people to fight Gregor."

I picture Fritz and Prisha going to the Valley together. I see her flirting with him at the Harvest and again in the auditorium. If I was feeling a sugar-high before, I must be feeling a sugar-low now because instead of feeling warm and airy, I feel cold and heavy. I lean back and cross my arms.

"It's worth a shot," Clover says.

I direct my tired gaze at Fritz. "If you take the train, you could be back in time, but what if Prisha doesn't go along with the plan?"

"I can talk her into going." Fritz smiles sheepishly.

I stare at the table and avoid eye contact with the others. If anyone looks into my eyes, they might see the jealousy I feel when I envision Fritz sweet-talking Prisha. I peek at Fritz through my eyelashes and realize it's more than jealousy. It's fear. Fear of losing him. Fear that he might like her more than he likes me.

Treb says, "Traveling by Helix to the Valley would be a lot faster than going by train."

"How would Fritz and Prisha access a Helix?" I ask.

"You're Nuclei members, aren't you?" Treb shuffles in his seat. "Just have Golgi summon a Helix to a specific location."

Fritz and I trade surprised looks.

"You need to find a Golgi-enabled room," Treb says.

The energy in the room shifts from hopelessness to excitement. I stand and reiterate the plan. "Fritz and Prisha will head to the Valley before sunrise. When they return, they will hideout in the cathedral until the wedding ceremony. If the vaccine is at the cathedral, everyone who comes here from the Valley will be vaccinated."

"If the vaccine is at the cathedral, it will be guarded," Fritz says.

"Maybe." I twirl my hair through my fingers. "Or maybe, not. Gregor believes all Ovation residents have been moved to Headquarters. You said he underestimates people."

"They will need food," Treb says. "Next to the cathedral, there's a supermarket and a pizza place where the locals eat."

"Good point," I say. "Treb, you will broadcast the frequency during the wedding ceremony. Fritz, assuming you and Prisha are successful, you will return to the auditorium during the ceremony with people from the Valley who will help us stop Gregor."

Fritz rolls his broad shoulders. "Sounds like a plan."

I move toward the door. "We should head back so Fritz can talk to Prisha before everyone wakes up."

"I wish we could just stay here overnight," Everly says as she stuffs granola bars into her bulging pockets. "The auditorium is going to start reeking if they don't let people shower soon."

Fritz holds open the door. I step aside to let everyone else pass. As their footsteps pound down the stairs and their voices echo around us, I glance once more toward Dr. Hahn's office.

"There's nothing we can do," Fritz says gently.

"I know." I brush by Fritz and descend the stairs overcome with guilt for leaving Dr. Hahn behind.

At the bathroom panel, Fritz and I hang back to allow Treb, Clover, and Everly to enter the bathroom ahead of us.

Fritz says, "There was something else on the mainframe you should know about. After the Assessment, you were supposed to be transported directly to Nuclei Headquarters. You were never supposed to be a Supernova. Someone changed your assignment in the system."

"Who would do that? And why?" I hold my palms up.

"I compared the timestamp on the falsified record to users logged in at that time. Franz was the only one logged into the system that day. He tagged the record with someone else's user id."

I place my fingertips against my chest. "Why would Franz care where I was assigned?"

"Maybe Franz felt threatened by you, especially if Dr. Hahn expressed interest in having you succeed him as the Head of the Nuclei. I can't think of any other reason Franz would care."

I mull over the possibility. "It was strange that Dr. Hahn trusted me immediately. He showed me the secret passage shortly after I arrived to Headquarters. He said nobody else knew about it."

"Why would he trust you when he doesn't even know you?" Fritz asks.

I realize from Fritz's confused expression that he doesn't know who I am. Or rather, *what* I am. I look away. I cuff and uncuff the sleeves of my flannel shirt.

"What is it?" Fritz wraps his fingers around my wrist.

I stop playing with my cuffs and meet his eyes. "Do you remember the night of the Science Gala? When I was on stage, Dr. Hart mentioned someone named Delilah?"

"I remember, but I'm not following."

"Delilah was Dr. Hahn's wife." I hesitate to say more. To label myself as a clone or replica makes me feel less than human. Like I'm a fragment of someone else. Someone I'll never compare to.

"You used past tense. She's no longer alive?" Fritz tries to follow.

"She died during childbirth. After Gregor was born."

Fritz says, "So, that's why Dr. Hahn is obsessed with eliminating natural childbirth."

I stare at his chest. I don't want to see the look in his eyes when I tell him. "They used Delilah's DNA…" I take a deep breath and work up the courage to finish the sentence. "To create me." The confession scalds my cheeks. I don't dare lift my eyes to his face.

"You're a clone of Dr. Hahn's wife?" Fritz asks incredulously.

His words buzz around inside my head like a dozen bees stinging me simultaneously. *You're a clone? A clone. A clone of Dr. Hahn's wife?*

"Replica." The word tumbles from my lips, and immediately, I want to take it back, to crush it in my fist, to squeeze the life out of it, and shove it back into the darkness where embarrassing secrets belong.

Blood rushes to my cheeks and heat rises under my collar. I feel Fritz watching me, waiting for me to say more, but I have nothing more to say. I spin on my heel and turn toward the bathroom panel.

Fritz moves in front of the panel, blocking my path. He tilts my chin up and forces me to look into his eyes. "It doesn't matter what DNA they used to create us. We are who we are, not who they want us to be."

He isn't judging me or looking at me like I'm a freak. I exhale and feel the tension melt away. "Do you think it was a coincidence that you and I met in the woods that night? Or did the Nuclei plan for the replicas of Dr. Hahn and Delilah to meet and fall in—" I bite back the word before it slips from my lips. *Love.*

"The night we met wasn't the first night I saw you." Fritz looks down and kicks the toe of his shoe against the concrete.

"What do you mean?" I step back as the foundation of our relationship buckles and cracks under my feet.

Fritz rakes his fingers through his hair and avoids eye contact. "I had been watching you for about six weeks."

"Watching me? Like a stalker?" I fold my arms, creating a barrier between us, and search his face for answers.

Fritz's eyes snap onto mine. A flicker of anger hardens his face for the millisecond it takes him to hide it. I've offended him.

"Stalker? Hardly." His tone is sharp and cutting like a knife. "The first time I saw you jogging toward me, I darted off the path and hid. I thought you were part of the night patrol."

"Me? Night patrol?" I elongate the words to make the notion sound as ridiculous as it is.

"You ran past me and crossed the Valley boundary. I wanted to know how you had access to both cells. Either you were with the night patrol or you hacked your passport like I did. I was intrigued."

I touch the back of my neck. "But my passport didn't vibrate."

Fritz moves his backpack to his other shoulder. "You always crossed the boundary around midnight. I started timing my runs so I could cool down and wait for you on the Valley side. It wasn't safe for you to be there alone."

"Why didn't you say something when you saw me?" The thought of being watched during what I thought was my alone-time annoys me. I glare at him and consider our past interactions through a filter of distrust.

Fritz clenches his jaw and looks flustered. "What was I supposed to say? I didn't want to be some creepy guy ambushing you in the woods in the middle of the night to introduce myself."

"Well, you kind of were that creepy guy who ambushed me in the woods the night we met. Are there any other secrets you're keeping from me?" I can't help the hostility in my voice, the anger in my eyes. I want more than anything to trust him, but he keeps planting red flags.

Fritz pulls me into a hug and starts massaging my shoulders. "Relax. I know you're worried about the virus, worried about your family, but you can trust me. We're in this together. I won't keep anything else from you. I promise."

I let my arms hang at my sides and close my eyes as he kneads my shoulders and upper back. I inhale his familiar scent and take comfort in it. My anger, fear, and suspicion drain away.

I open my eyes and step back. "How long will it take you to return from the Valley?"

"If Prisha and I leave soon, we could arrive in the Valley before workers are transported to the fields. We should be back by Tuesday evening."

"If you tell them about Gregor's plan, they won't have any choice but to join us, right?"

"I hope so." Fritz's voice lacks confidence.

"I wish I could go with you instead of Prisha." I turn my face away so he can't see my pouty expression. I cut my eyes back, peering up at him through a fringe of lashes.

His eyes twinkle and his lips curl into a smile, as if he's amused by my jealousy. He wraps his arms around my waist. "You have nothing to worry about." He sweeps his lips across mine. I wrap my arms around his neck and welcome the promise in his kiss.

Thirty-eight

The morning sun hammers the windows along the back wall, covering residents in a patchwork of golden light. Lucindas enter the auditorium and roll food carts between rows of stirring people. They distribute coffee, water, and breakfast items. My back is stiff from lying on the floor all night. I sit up and twist from side to side.

I nudge Everly, Clover, and Treb. "Wake up. Breakfast time."

"What time is it?" Clover props herself up on an elbow and yawns.

I consider how long the sun has been up. "Around seven a.m."

I accept coffee and a muffin from a Lucinda. Despite the unpleasant circumstances, I'm looking forward to the hot drink.

Everly surveys the room. "Did Prisha and Fritz leave?"

"A few hours ago," I reply.

"When will they be back?" Everly peels a banana.

I sip my coffee and bite into the blueberry muffin. "Fritz thinks they will be back tonight."

"Good." Everly stops chewing and stares at the door.

Gregor and Dr. Toussaint enter and walk toward the stage with a steady stream of super-soldiers following close behind. Four soldiers join them on stage. The remaining soldiers line up in formation.

Gregor flips on the microphone and taps it twice. "Good morning, Ovation residents."

"Good morning," the half-asleep crowd murmurs.

"Thank you for your patience as we transition and progress toward our new goals. I am here today to share those goals with you. It isn't fair to continue to keep you in the dark about why you are here.

"As you all know, my father believed the only way to evolve properly was to control every aspect of reproduction. He worried that even if only the fittest reproduced naturally, undesirable gene mutations would still be introduced into the population, resulting in mental and physical health issues that would be passed down for generations.

"I do not agree with my father, nor do I share his goal to eliminate natural childbirth. A byproduct of controlling reproduction in a lab was the creation of a loveless society. A society where women spend the best years of their lives meeting egg quotas instead of falling in love and raising children of their own.

"As of today, the positions of Supernova, Zenith, and Nadir will cease to exist. Thanks to plentiful harvests, we have an abundance of eggs for future use.

"Under my orders, DNA-compatible couples of child-bearing age will join in marriage and have children of their own. Meaningless lives of public service will be transformed into meaningful lives where people will know what it means to be loved."

As Gregor drones on about his gift of love and fulfillment, I wish I had a rotten tomato to chunk at his lying face. He doesn't care about love. All he cares about is feeding residents a sweet story to justify his use of women as baby-making machines for the government.

I glance at the other Supernovas. They giggle and elbow each other while checking out the soldiers soon to be their husbands. How can they be so blind to Gregor's motives? How can they support a power structure that treats women like objects instead of human beings? Why do highly-educated, powerful women like Dr. Sorrell go along? Frustration and helplessness take root inside me. I itch to go for a run to escape it all.

"…I share my father's belief that some aspects of reproduction require proper oversight. Dr. Sorrell has created a program to analyze DNA profiles of all residents and determine the best genetic match for reproduction.

"Tomorrow evening at five o'clock, fertile women from Ovation and Clairemont will be wed to DNA-compatible super-soldiers. The Nuclei expects at least three children to be produced from each union."

Treb whispers to Clover, "I thought you said the weddings were scheduled for noon?"

"That's what they said on the recording," Clover says.

I angle toward Treb. "We have to go to the cathedral tonight to tell Fritz the ceremony time changed. We can use the underground tunnels."

Treb shifts his weight to his other hip and doesn't respond.

I tune back into Gregor.

"You will be released after the wedding ceremonies take place. Upon release, you will return to your homes in Ovation. If you do not have a residence in Ovation, you will be assigned one.

"Married couples are expected to engage in procreation immediately. Every woman of child-bearing age will be assigned a Reproduction Enforcer. Again, thank you for your patience. I assure you, we will return to some semblance of normalcy very soon." Gregor concludes his speech and walks off stage.

Thirty-nine

*R*esidents play cards and engage in idle chatter as if they have no concerns. Of course, they have no concerns. It's not like Gregor announced his plan to kill over half the population. But even if they knew about the virus, would they care? Everyone in this auditorium is probably immune. With a few exceptions like Treb.

"Hey, Clover." A pair of red tennis shoes squeak to an abrupt stop in front of our seated group. The shoes belong to a girl with a pixie haircut and mismatched earrings. "What are you doing sitting with these losers? Why don't you come sit with us?" Her eyes land on Everly and her face twists into a smirk.

"No, thanks. I'm good, Harmony," Clover says.

"If you change your mind, the Sisterhood is over there." The girl points to stage left. She leans down and whispers in Clover's ear, loud enough for the rest of us to hear, "Nothing good happens to transgenic-lovers."

Everly rises to confront the girl. I grab her arm and hold her back. From a safe distance, Harmony turns and blows a kiss.

"Who was that?" Everly hisses through gritted teeth.

"Harmony," Clover says.

Hamlet.

"Is she the one who disfigured me?" Everly asks without taking her eyes off Harmony.

Clover shakes her head. "She was there that night, but she isn't the one who hurt you."

Everly strokes her calf. The knife strapped to her leg is likely the object of her affection. "What do you know about that night?" Everly narrows her lone eye at Clover.

"It's a long story. Some Nadirs formed a hate group. They're responsible for what happened to you and Freya. The leader of the group, the one who hurt you, isn't here."

The desire for revenge prickles my spine. "Clover, where does Bacon live?"

"The abandoned meat processing plant near the slaughterhouse."

Everly and I lock eyes. For once, we may be thinking the same thing. The Sisterhood will regret they ever targeted us.

"And you found out about this group after you were demoted to Nadir?" Everly pries.

"Yes, Everly." Clover spits the name from her mouth. Fury festers behind her eyes. "I found out about the Sisterhood after *you* sabotaged my fertility pills."

Confessing nothing and asking no additional questions, Everly stretches her legs out, leans back on her hands, and directs a smoldering look at the Sisterhood.

I can only imagine the frenzied thoughts consuming her. It wouldn't surprise me if we woke tomorrow to the news of another massacre.

"Maris!" Everly stands and waves as Maris enters the auditorium. Residents from Clairemont have been streaming in all day packing the auditorium to maximum capacity.

"Who is Maris?" Treb asks.

"She was a Supernova at House of Saphronia," I say. "She disappeared yesterday."

After a soldier scans Maris' passport, she moves toward us without smiling. Her hair, normally in a neat braid or ponytail, is wild and tangled. Smudged eyeliner borders her puffy eyes. She's wearing jeans and a pink sweatshirt that matches her hair.

"Where have you been?" Everly asks.

Maris sits, pulls her knees to her chest, and wraps her arms around them. "I went home."

"Home?" Everly repeats. "How did you go home?"

"I hid on the train." She sounds tired and emotionally drained.

Clover asks, "How did you know Gregor was going to overthrow Dr. Hahn?"

"I didn't know anything about anything. I just missed," Maris makes eye contact with me before she lies, "my family."

Maris barely spent a day in Clairemont before super-soldiers escorted her back to Headquarters. I hope she was able to reunite with her boyfriend, if only temporarily.

"You're back just in time," Everly says. "We're getting married tomorrow!" She enthusiastically announces the news as if we've all won a prize.

Maris looks confused. She sits up straight and scans the auditorium. "Who's getting married?"

Clover grimaces. "Genetically-modified women from Ovation and Clairemont will be wed to super-soldiers tomorrow. Couples will be matched based on DNA profiles."

"Like arranged marriages?" Maris asks. "What if the person I want to marry isn't here?" Tears well up in her eyes.

A surge of sympathy threatens to wet my eyes. I look away as Maris, overcome with emotion, hides her face in her hands. What will become of us? We're supposed to marry these mutants, have three babies for the government, and live happily ever after? Are we supposed to be appreciative that we no longer have to participate in egg harvests?

What if Maris is right and there is inhabitable land beyond this island? Could Fritz and I sail away and start a new life somewhere else? Somewhere women are free to make their own decisions about their own lives. Has a place like that ever existed? A place where the government doesn't police women's bodies?

I glance toward the bathrooms. How many hours have Fritz and Prisha been gone? I examine the light pouring through the windows to gauge the time. The soft peach glow of sunset confirms they should be at the cathedral by now. Hopefully, their recruitment mission was successful. I don't want to consider the alternative.

"Maris?" I tap her shoulder.

"What?" Her tone is glum. She stares at a delicate gold band on her ring finger and continuously spins it with her thumb.

I lower my voice. "When you returned to Ovation, did you see suspicious-looking people on the trains or around the train station? People who looked like they don't belong here?"

Maris shakes her head. "The soldiers rounded up girls from Clairemont and forced them onto trains heading to Ovation. There was nobody else. Why?"

I sigh. "I'll tell you later."

Treb is falling asleep sitting up.

I nudge him. "Treb?"

"Hmm?" His voice is groggy.

"You know the streets of Ovation better than anyone. You have to go to the cathedral with me tonight."

His drowsy eyes jerk open. He studies the swarm of super-soldiers who have tripled in number in recent hours. "I'm not sure if that's a good idea."

Everly pipes in, "I'll go. Actually, we should all go and never come back."

"We have to be back before the ceremony," I say. "They'll have our DNA profiles in the system. If they call for us and we aren't here, they'll know something is wrong. Plus, Treb has to be here to broadcast the frequencies."

Everly slumps. "Fine, but if you leave, I'm going with you."

"Treb? Are you in?" I ask.

"The tunnels are pitch-black," he says.

Is he afraid of the dark? In my most reassuring voice, I say, "I can guide us through the dark, but I can't find the cathedral without you."

Treb runs his hands through his hair, fidgets with his boots, and nervously looks around the room. "We're all going to die, aren't we?"

Clover looks as though his words slapped her in the face. Maris looks up from her ring and assesses Treb. The thought hadn't crossed my mind.

"Why would you say that? No, we aren't going to die." My voice doesn't sound as certain as I would like.

Sulking, Treb says, "I don't know which would be worse. To die at the hands of a super-soldier or to be bitten by a mosquito carrying a death sentence."

"Stop being a baby." Everly curls her lip as if Treb's cowardice disgusts her.

I rest my hand on Treb's shoulder. "If we go to the cathedral, you'll be vaccinated. Personally, I would prefer a quick death verses contracting a virus that incinerates victims from the inside out."

Treb closes his eyes and rubs his temples. "I'll go with you."

I turn to Clover and Maris. "You guys stay here tonight. Everly, Treb, and I will leave after midnight and be back before dawn."

"Fine with me," Clover says.

Maris says, "Is someone going to fill me in on what's going on?"

"I'll fill you in later," Clover says.

Satisfied, Maris twists her hair into two braids. She wets her finger and rubs it under her eyes to remove evidence that she had been crying. "I'm going to say hi to Blaise."

Clover grabs Maris' elbow. "You can't tell Blaise anything. You can't tell *anybody* anything."

"I won't say anything." Maris yanks her elbow out of Clover's grip. She and I make eye contact. We haven't known each other long, but we trust each other.

I accept a bowl of soup from a passing Lucinda and try not to allow doubts to chip away my resolve.

Forty

I'm last to descend the ladder under the trapdoor. It seems too good to be true that no soldiers are patrolling the tunnels. The bulging gun in my front pocket reassures me of the protection I have if I need it.

I yawn. A few hours of sleep after dinner wasn't enough to make up for staying awake overnight. "Where did Everly go?"

Treb points to the room filled with weapons.

I roll my eyes and charge over to the room. "Everly!"

She cocks an eyebrow and loads a clip into a handgun.

"Don't point that thing at us," I say.

"Take it." She waves the gun at Treb. "You're going to need more than a pocketknife if we run into danger." She plucks items off the shelves and pockets them. "We should take weapons to the Valley army."

Part of me fears the cathedral will be empty. What if Fritz and Prisha couldn't convince anyone from the Valley to return with them to Ovation? Valley residents don't even know Ovation exists.

Instead of voicing my fears to Everly and Treb, I act certain that an army awaits us. "The Valley army will have to come this way. They can get their own weapons."

Everly looks at me as though I'm a child. "That's assuming they won't need weapons before they reach Headquarters." She hands me a piece of rope. "Put this in your pocket."

I oblige, cramming the rope into my back pocket. "Okay, okay. Now, let's go."

We stand at an intersection of four tunnels. "Which way, Treb?"

Treb squints and points at a tunnel to our right. "We need to travel east for about a half mile. We'll go down Chacon Street until we see the San Ignacio intersection. Then, we'll go south on San Ignacio until we reach the cathedral."

"How about English?" Everly scoffs at him. "At San Ignacio, do we go left or right?"

"Right," Treb says.

Everly bounds in the direction of the Chacon Street tunnel. She surreptitiously moves deeper into the tunnel, her stealthy footsteps as silent as the blink of an eye. The list of things I don't like about Everly is long, but I wish I possessed half her boldness. She peers into side tunnels as if ready for anything, as if built for battle. Could a scientist have engineered her to be a ruthless killer? A female super-soldier?

Treb stays glued to my side. Despite the cool underground temperature, his forehead glistens and his breathing quickens. He holds the gun out in front of him. The barrel wobbles.

"It's really dark down here." His voice, fractured with fear, is barely audible.

I wrap my fingers around his upper arm. "Stay close. You'll be fine." My eyes move to the gun in his shaky hand. "Do you have experience with guns?"

"I learned how to shoot during Security Forces initiation." He lowers the gun to his side.

Ahead of us, Everly crouches. Unease creeps up my spine. My hair follicles pucker and swell with goosebumps. Is someone watching us? I look behind me. The tunnel is empty. Treb and I cautiously approach Everly.

I touch her shoulder. "What are you doing? Are you okay?"

"Tightening my shoelaces." She tugs on the laces of her shoe. "Go ahead. I'll catch up."

Treb and I move past her at a leisurely pace.

"We're halfway there," he says.

My heart skips a tick at the thought of Fritz waiting for us at the cathedral.

"Nooooo!"

The stomach-curdling scream slices through my spinal cord, hot-wires my nerves, and jump-starts my heart. This is the second time I've heard that scream. I spin around searching the darkness for Everly.

She launches herself at a super-soldier as he aims a rifle at me and Treb. I flinch and yank Treb against the wall. A spray of bullets streaks past us, tiny sparks of death intent on forcing us to an early grave.

But I'm not ready to die.

Treb fiddles with his gun. The click of the disengaged safety does nothing to reduce my anxiety.

"Treb, shoot him." My voice sounds choppy and weak through my chattering teeth.

Treb points his gun at the soldier. "I can't see. What if I hit Everly?"

Everly shrieks and climbs the super-soldier's giant frame like a deranged monkey. A mass of thrashing angles, she elbows, knees, whacks, and wallops the soldier.

I cover my mouth in horror and stare wide-eyed as she wraps her legs around the soldier's waist and headbutts him. The loud smack echoes around us.

"Treb, now!" It takes all my effort to squeeze the two words out of my mouth.

Treb is huffing and puffing and sweating like he's hyperventilating. His arm is extended, handgun bobbling.

Everly pulls the knife from the sheath on her leg. She rears back her arm and drives the serrated blade into the soldier's eye socket. The soldier stumbles backward. He maintains his hold on her despite the knife jammed into his skull.

Her wild eye meets mine. "Run!"

Her scream ricochets off the walls, penetrates my skin, and sends shockwaves up and down my spine. I can't leave her. Hands trembling, I pull the revolver out of my pocket and aim for the super-soldier's head. Everly shifts and ducks to give me a clear shot. I squeeze the trigger. A spark erupts from the barrel. My arm jerks from the recoil and my eardrums split. The smell of gunpowder fills my mouth and peppers my lungs.

The soldier yelps and grabs his thigh. He throws Everly as if she weighs no more than a ragdoll. The back of her head cracks against the wall like an egg cracks against a skillet. In slow motion, her body slides down the wall and crumples to the ground. Blood oozes from her nose. She doesn't get up.

The soldier grips the handle of the knife protruding from his eye and jerks it out in one smooth motion. It clanks to the ground. He points his rifle at Everly. Bullets strike. Her body convulses.

Shock and grief batter my gut. My stomach rolls and judders. My entire body trembles. I can't think straight. Can't move. Can't breathe. My lungs are shrinking, shriveling, rolling in on themselves. The soldier's good eye focuses on us. I suck in a shallow breath and grab Treb.

"Run!" I scream.

We take off full throttle, barreling down the corridor. I run with no idea of where I am or where I'm going. Treb said to turn where? Which way is the cathedral? The sound of the soldier's uneven gait rattles my core and jangles my nerves.

He's chasing us, hard and fast, as if he didn't just experience a knife through the brain and a bullet through the leg. Clover was right when she called them *mutant killing machines.*

A blast of bullets booms behind us. I wait for the bullets to knock us down. Nothing happens. I sideways glance at Treb. He wasn't hit either, but he's slowing down. I dig my fingers into his forearm.

"Faster!" My yell comes out as a desperate whisper.

I look ahead just in time to avoid slamming into a dead end. The only direction we can go is left. I pull Treb left. After less than fifty yards, he dodges into a side corridor.

"I can't. Go. Any farther." His words hitch on heavy breaths.

Stepping into the side corridor, I rest my hands on my knees and try to catch my breath. "If we stop here, he'll kill us."

"This corridor circles back to Headquarters. I'll wait for you and Fritz there."

I open my mouth to protest. Treb's crossed arms and clenched lips tell me that no matter what I say, he isn't going to budge. "Okay, fine. Where does this one lead?" I point the revolver at the tunnel we just came from.

"It's the underwater passage to the abandoned fortress. Morro Castle. You'll be safe there until you can go to the cathedral."

"What street is the cathedral on again?"

"Go back the way we came. Take Chacon to San Ignacio."

The thump of the approaching soldier spurs us into motion. Treb backs away. I peek into the tunnel. The soldier hasn't turned the corner yet. I spring into the tunnel and sprint in the opposite direction of the soldier.

If the soldier turns the corner before I reach safety, I'll spin around and unload every remaining bullet into the darkness behind me. If I make it to the next tunnel, I'll wait there until he's closer and then I'll jump out and distract him before he reaches Treb's corridor.

At the tunnel's end, I dart to the right into a connecting tunnel where a sign reads: *Tunel de La Habana*. I poke a fraction of my head out until I see the soldier turn the corner and lumber down the tunnel. Fluid drips from his empty eye socket, creating the appearance of black tears running down one side of his face.

I dip back into the tunnel and lean against the wall calculating how long it will take him to reach Treb's corridor. Fifty yards. Forty yards. *Not yet. Not yet.* I shift the gun from my right hand to my left and wipe my sweaty brow.

Twenty yards.

Ten yards.

I move the gun back to my dominant hand and rest my finger against the trigger. My pulse pounds. My blood pressure spikes. I take a deep breath and jump into the tunnel.

"Over here!" I wave my arms and yell like a maniac.

The soldier stops and stares at me.

I press my elbows into my ribs, aim the gun, and squeeze the trigger. The gun sucks my jittery heart through its barrel, leaving me breathless and light-headed. The bullet takes with it a piece of my innocence. A piece of my humanity. I never wanted to hurt anyone. I never wanted to kill anyone. But now, more than anything, I want the soldier to die, die, die.

I dash into the adjacent tunnel, the warm gun hanging heavy in my hand. The soldier lets loose eight or ten rounds of bullets. As if he were firing a marathon starting gun, I take off determined to make it to the finish line of Morro Castle. Breathless, ears ringing, legs burning, I run deeper into the underwater passage. The ground slants downward and the air becomes frigid. Running downhill stresses my knees, but I don't dare slow down.

Did my bullet hit the soldier? Is he still chasing me? All I hear is the blood rushing in my ears and the pounding of my own feet. I replay the image of Everly stabbing him in the eye and shiver. I shut out images of Everly lying motionless on the tunnel floor.

I should have gone to the cathedral alone. I shouldn't have let Everly or Treb join me. What if Treb encounters other soldiers on his way back to Headquarters? He has a gun, but he can't see in the dark or run long distances without getting winded. Maybe I should have returned to Headquarters with him.

The ground starts sloping uphill. A gust of wind lifts my hair and cools my neck. The breeze feels good against my sweat-soaked skin. A patch of trees and a shimmering night sky beckon me. Anxious to leave behind the tunnel system and everything that happened inside it, I run for the exit. Grains of sand crunch and roll under my sneakers.

I keep moving full speed, clear the exit, and take cover in a thick cluster of palm trees. I pocket the revolver and shake out my aching hands. I fill my lungs with big gulps of ocean air that smells of salt and seaweed. The wind violently whips the palm trees along with my hair. I pull my hair into a ponytail and survey my surroundings.

To my right is the abandoned fortress Treb mentioned. From here, I see the top half of a lighthouse rising from the water's edge. It emits a bright flash that illuminates an open platform encircling the lantern room at the top.

From that platform, I could see the entire city. I could look for movement around the cathedral. A heavy thud comes from deep within the tunnel. I yank the revolver from one pocket and a handful of bullets from the other. My hands shake as I jam bullets into the empty chambers. After the gun is reloaded, I speed toward the lighthouse.

A dim glow draws my eyes back to the tunnel. Someone is approaching the exit. My heart lurches. My anxiety hits the sky. I grip the gun so tightly, I expect it to melt in my hand and puddle at my feet, leaving me weaponless.

I jet toward the fortress center. Its stone walls will obstruct the soldier's view and block the brutal wind. I run between the fortress walls, keeping my eyes peeled for movement in the nooks and crannies of its stone façade.

At the lighthouse, I tilt my head back and let my eyes travel to the tiptop. My stomach fills with dread at the thought of climbing eight to ten stories, but I don't have a choice. It's probably the safest place to be right now.

I inch around to the entrance. The doorless arch faces the water. I back into the doorway and grip the door frame. It crumbles in my hands. Debris falls around my feet. I smack the sand from my hands and observe the water.

The calm waves I'm used to seeing outside my bedroom window have become giant fists rearing back and slamming against the concrete foundation surrounding the lighthouse. The ocean furiously batters the concrete slab as if attempting to rip the lighthouse from its foundation and devour it whole. Dark clouds gather overhead like vultures waiting to ravage nature's spoils.

I start climbing the spiral staircase. The wind whistles through deep fissures in the stone wall. I place my palm over one of the cracks. Moist air licks my hand. What if the structure can't withstand a bad storm? It probably hasn't been maintained in decades. Yet, it's still standing so it should be safe enough, right?

I keep a hand on the gritty wall and force myself to climb the stairs. The walls and winding concrete steps squeeze inward like quicksand sucking and slurping at my feet, surrounding my legs, wetting my chest, filling my lungs, suffocating me. I push forward, visualizing a wide-open lantern room awaiting me.

As I hike up the stairs, images of Everly screaming and fighting and bleeding strike me like shrapnel: tiny slivers of pain that burrow so deeply into my psyche, I know I'll never be able to purge the sights, the sounds, the trauma.

I suppress the tears wetting my eyes and shudder at the image of Everly's body convulsing on the tunnel floor. Death is so finite, so irreversible.

The flash of the mariner's beacon brightens the stairwell, beckoning my weary legs to climb the final steps. My legs quiver, my breath is short. I need a break. On the last platform, I sit against the wall, stretch out my legs, and place the gun next to me. The muscles in my left thigh twist, pinch, contract. I massage the cramp and lick my chapped lips.

What happened to the soldier? Did he follow me into the lighthouse? If he had, I would hear him stumping up the steep stairs, wouldn't I? As the silent minutes tick by, my confidence grows and my heart rate slows.

I cautiously peek around the curved wall into the lantern room. The prisms of a rotating Fresnel lens capture light and force it into a single beam. The golden light warms the room, creating an inviting ambiance. I feel safe. Nobody knows I'm here.

I rest my head against the wall, close my eyes, and take deep breaths while thinking through my next steps. From the lighthouse platform, I'll be able to see where super-soldiers are stationed. I'll look around the fortress to make sure nobody followed me.

After I confirm it's clear, I'll leave and make a quick stop at the cathedral to tell Fritz about the wedding ceremony time change. I'll return to Headquarters before sunrise. I open my eyes and feel more energized.

With renewed purpose, I pick up the revolver and stand. I stoop under the low door to the lantern room. The lens blocks my view of half the room. The lens hums and the floor vibrates. The roof is partially missing as if a giant hand peeled it back.

Storm clouds undulate overhead like a rhumba of rattlesnakes preparing to strike. The wind carries a sharp electrical smell: the smell of rain. I need to get back to the tunnel system before the sky opens. My eyes catch on a door on the opposite wall. It must lead to the outdoor platform.

I march straight to the door and grab the doorknob. As soon as I touch it, the hair on the back of my neck bristles. A small movement pulls my eyes to the right. An Enforcer with his back to me arranges a pile of black drones on a countertop.

My blood freezes. My heart turns to ice. I lift the revolver and aim for his head: gray hair, neatly trimmed. His thick neck leads to even thicker shoulders. The light catches on his wedding ring. A lump the size of an iceberg rises in my throat. I lower the gun.

"Dad?"

Forty-one

The Enforcer's shoulders stiffen. He slowly pivots to face me holding a drone against his abdomen. Shock, confusion, and disbelief take turns on his face. Dad was never good at hiding his emotions.

"Dad? What are you doing here?" My voice trembles uncontrollably like my hands.

His silence sends a tiny shred of doubt coursing through me. What if he isn't my dad? What if he's a clone? Every fifteen seconds when the light beam hits his face, I look for something familiar.

"Wren?" His eyes move to the gun in my hands.

It *is* him! I want to throw my arms around him, to tell him I miss him, to ask him about mom, Abe, and Addie, but something holds me back. Something deep and primitive in my gut tells me to keep a safe distance.

"What are you doing with the drones?" My eyes flick to the drone he holds.

Dad sighs and rubs his thumb and forefinger across his eyebrows. His eyes are red, as if he hasn't slept in days. "I'm doing my job."

"Since when does your job include killing innocent people?" My voice rises with the accusation. My hands start sweating and the gun feels slick against my skin. I release the doorknob and shift the gun to my left hand.

Dad glances at his watch. His chest muscles ripple and his biceps bulge against his black t-shirt. "Valley dwellers are far from innocent. Eliminating them is in everyone's best interest. I need you to trust me. I've been working closely with Gregor for twenty years. Gregor is an honorable man."

My lips curl in disgust as the man I thought I knew morphs into someone I don't recognize, someone beholden to Gregor and to some cynical worldview that requires most of the population to die to allow the elite to flourish.

"Is Mom involved with Gregor, too? Is that why she was promoted?" *Please don't let Mom be involved.*

There's a long pause and then Dad responds, "I thought it best that your mother didn't know about my alliance with Gregor. I wanted Jackie to believe her promotion was based on merit alone. She worked hard and she deserved it."

"How did you end up raising me? Did you know they were going to take me away someday?" The questions that have been swimming laps in my mind for months pour out in an unrestrained stream.

"When Gregor asked me to raise you, I was honored that he placed his trust in me. Your mother was pleased when I told her the Nuclei selected us to be a Golden Ova family. All Golden Ova families take an oath and are aware of the sacrifices they may be required to make."

I can barely contain my rage. "So, you knew about Ovation all along? You *knew* they were going to take me away and keep me caged like an animal while they harvested my eggs?"

I feel like my chest has been ripped open and rubbed raw. My heart is burning, breaking; I can't stop shaking. I want to shake Dad and force him to tell me why, why did he do this to me?

I shout over the howling wind and tumbling thunder. "You *knew* all the hours I spent preparing for the Assessment didn't matter? You knew all along *this*," I wave the gun over my head, "was going to be my life, my destiny and you didn't try to stop them from taking me?"

Fire burns in Dad's eyes. "Do you think I didn't try to keep our family together? That I didn't plead with Gregor to keep you in Hillcrest?" His voice is a low growl and I can tell he's a hair-trigger away from losing control, but I don't care.

"Did you even love me?" The words, heavy with longing, sputter from my mouth. I need to know he truly loved me. I need to know my entire life wasn't a lie.

"I've loved you since the first time I held you in my arms." He holds the drone up to the light and clicks a switch. The propellers begin to spin.

The side of me screaming for answers is appeased by his admission of love, but the side of me intent on stopping the virus shudders at the sight of the readied drone.

"If you love me, you have to trust me. Gregor isn't who you think he is." I search for words to dissuade him, to make him believe me.

"I'm following orders," he says in his Father-knows-best tone.

"If you follow orders, our friends and family in Hillcrest will die!" I'm screaming, yelling, pleading. My vocal cords are frazzling, unraveling. "The drones aren't programmed for the Valley. The drones are going to Hillcrest. You have to believe me! You have to help me destroy them."

"Nonsense! Gregor assured me the virus would only affect Valley dwellers." His voice sounds harsh and grating and full of grit, as if his throat is raw from swallowing Gregor's lies.

"How can you believe Gregor over your own daughter! Gregor lied! He lied! He's using you! How can you be so naïve? How can you not see that you're just a puppet, a pawn? Gregor doesn't care about you! All he cares about is power. Don't you care about mom? About Abe and Addie? About me?" My words are shrill and tinged with the desperation I feel.

Dad holds the drone over his head where it has a clear path through the damaged roof.

I raise the revolver and aim at his chest.

"Turn off the drone or I'll shoot!" My voice quakes and my

stomach quivers. I don't know if I have what it takes to pull the trigger.

Hesitation flickers over Dad's face as he looks at the gun, but then his eyes meet mine. "You won't shoot me." His tone is steady, fearless, confident.

Dad releases the drone as if it's a harmless balloon instead of a biological weapon.

The drone wobbles, then straightens, then soars into the night sky.

In a panic, I pull back the hammer on the gun.

"Drop the gun!" Dad barges toward me.

I squeeze the trigger.

The drone explodes. Debris rains down on us. Dad ducks. A smoking-hot piece of plastic lands on my forearm. I brush it off and fire two more rounds at the stack of drones.

A swirl of white flurries engulfs us: mosquitoes and their eggs. Wings buzz by my ear like screaming sirens. Tiny winged bodies poke holes in the light beam. The air smells like charred plastic.

Dad stands upright. The vein on his neck is throbbing. He gives me the same intimidating look he gave the men in front of Charlie's Bar. He doesn't trust me. He trusts Gregor. Nothing I say will change his mind.

I turn the doorknob behind me.

Dad's face is tight and twisted like a clenched fist holding back a knockout punch. His large size never intimidated me.

Until now. The certainty I felt that Dad would never hurt me fades. The long spindly fingers of fear take hold of me: unbuckling my spinal cord, draining my spinal fluid, making me feel like nothing more than a hollow, brittle, spineless girl.

I hold fast to the gun and step backward onto the outdoor platform. The wind lashes my hair and thrashes my shirt. I back up until the platform railing bites into my lower back.

Dad's frame fills the doorway. I sidestep to the left. If I don't stop him, thousands of people in Hillcrest could die. I wrestle with indecision.

"Give me the gun." Dad raises his voice over the roaring ocean. His voice is threatening, his eyes menacing. He extends his hand within inches of me.

I shrink back. The metal railing digs deeper into my skin. I raise the gun. He rushes me and grabs my wrist. I yowl. Pain shoots up my arm. My fingers involuntarily open, nearly releasing the gun. He shakes my arm, banging my wrist against the railing, trying to knock the gun from my grasp.

I grit my teeth and close my fist over the revolver. With my other arm, I shove him hard. He lifts me off my feet and pins me against his chest. My nose presses into his neck. He smells like home. I stifle sobs. Dreams of being reunited with my family dissolve. There is no going back. I struggle and flail and strike at him.

He clutches me tighter and yells, "Stop struggling! I don't want to hurt you."

I plant both hands against his chest and push away.

A gunshot rings out.

Dad stumbles forward. My back crashes against the railing.

The railing creaks and snaps under our combined weight.

I lose my balance and tumble backward off the platform.

Dad falls into me.

Did I shoot him?

As I plummet toward the concrete slab, my body twitches as if trying to wake up from a dream of falling. I'm reminded of a recurring dream I had as a child.

Dad is driving. Mom is in the front seat. We drive over a rickety, one-lane bridge with no guardrails. The car veers off the side of the bridge. It plunges down, down, down and I know we're going to die.

We keep falling and falling. Finally, the falling sensation stops. From the car window, I see blue skies, a carousel, a Ferris wheel, balloons, fried foods. Mom opens my car door and says: *Conquer your fears and the world will be all you want it to be.*

Falling from the lighthouse, my senses sharpen. My heart beats as loudly as thunder. The salty, stormy air feels textured against my skin. The wind carries the smell of churning seas, budding trees, fear and death, hope and rebirth.

This is it. I'm going to die.

Something clamps down on my bicep and stops my fall. Dad dangles above me, his left hand digging into my arm, the fingers of his other hand clinging to the platform's edge.

Blood spills from his thigh. Our eyes meet. He swings to the side and heaves me toward the broken piece of railing hanging over my head. I reach high, high, higher and curl my fingers around the horizontal bar. Dad's grip on me and the platform slips.

I close my eyes and clutch the railing as he falls.

"Daddy…" The word clogs my throat, blocks my lungs, smothers me.

I'm too scared to open my eyes. I'm too scared to move. The broken railing moans as the wind pummels it. It swings outward.

"Wren!" A voice from above yells.

I keep my eyes squeezed shut. I'm hallucinating, hearing things. I feel the railing being jerked closer to the platform. I open my eyes. Treb is on his knees, straining, pulling the railing toward him. It screeches and resists and drops two more inches. I hold my breath. Red-faced, Treb pulls harder until the rail swings forward bringing me eye-level with the ledge.

"Give me your hand!" Treb yells.

I feel depleted, tiny, weak. My arms tremble from the weight of my suspended body. I can't move. I can't reach. I'm not sure how much longer I can hold on.

Treb digs his hands into my armpits and lugs me onto the platform. The railing breaks away and plunges to the ground. Lying on my gut, I elbow forward until not even my toes hang over the platform's edge. I rest my face and palms against the damp platform. Metal clatters against concrete below: it could have been me.

"Thank Galileo, I found you," Treb says.

A low-pitched wail fills my ears: the sound of a cub caught in a trap. I take a breath and realize the wail is coming from my own throat. I can't suppress the sobs that well up in my chest. I still see Dad's frightened eyes and feel the warmth of his hand gripping my arm.

Heartache and grief rack my body. I shake from head to toe. I want to cry. I feel the tears building like a volcano about to explode. But I can't cry. I won't cry. Not now. Not when I need to be strong.

"Wren?" Treb gently touches my shoulder.

I flinch from his touch. I won't feel safe until I'm off the platform. I force myself to crawl through the doorway and pull myself to an upright position.

Sitting against the open door, I draw my legs to my chest and rest my cheek against my knees. The missing chunk of railing confirms the reality of what just happened. I try to replay the sequence of events, but everything happened so fast. My recall is disjointed.

Treb kneels, sets his gun on the floor, and takes my hand in his. "You're okay now."

My eyes settle on Treb's gun. "Did you shoot him?" My voice is barely a whisper.

"He was going to kill you." Treb's face is pinched with regret. The burden of taking a life must weigh more than the relief of saving one.

I rise to my feet, unsure if my legs will hold or crumble beneath my sorrow. I anchor myself against the door for support and bend in half trying to breathe. Tightness stretches across my chest, constricting my lungs.

I swallow hard, straighten up, and look across the canal. Smears of light blur together at the base of Nuclei Headquarters. The streets surrounding the train station and cathedral are empty.

If Fritz were at the cathedral with an army, wouldn't I be able to see them from here? My eyes sweep past the fortress toward the underwater tunnel. No sign of the soldier.

"Let's go." Treb moves toward the stairs.

The spinning lens bathes him in light, then darkness. The jarring contrast reminds me of the flashing lights at Guantanamo, the flashing lights at Headquarters.

I grip the doorframe. "Why didn't you go back to the auditorium?"

"After you killed the super-soldier, I couldn't let you go to the castle alone."

"I killed him?" My tone reflects my shock.

"He fell after you shot him." Treb swats at his neck.

The light catches on the mosquito's translucent wings. My gut twists into tangled knots. I stare at Treb's neck where the mosquito landed and grab his arm. "We have to go. Now."

"It's just a mosquito." As soon as the words leave his lips, a look of alarm crosses his face. He briskly brushes his hands over his face and neck and backs toward the stairwell.

"Am I going to die?"

"No." I'm disappointed with the meekness in my voice. I follow him into the stairwell. "No, you aren't going to die," I say with as much confidence as I can muster. "We'll head to the church and get you vaccinated."

Treb sprints down the stairs ahead of me. I don't have the courage to tell him the vaccine may not work. If he's infected, we will need the cure. But what if there isn't a cure? If there isn't a cure, Treb will be dead by Friday. He saved my life. I have to save his.

We exit the lighthouse and Treb hastens in the direction of the tunnels.

"Treb, wait!"

He faces me while stepping backward toward the tunnels.

"You go ahead." I use energy I don't have to project my voice over the wind. "I need a minute."

Treb begins to protest.

I cut him off. "Please. I'll be right behind you. Wait for me outside the tunnel."

Treb reluctantly takes off and when he's out of sight, I approach the body at the bottom of the lighthouse. After a fall from that height, Dad can't be alive. Can he? I have to know for sure.

Dad lies on his stomach facing away from me. I slide my thumb under his watch and press against his cold wrist.

Please.

I wait for his pulse to answer my plea, but it's silent. Withdrawing my hand, I watch the light fade from his body. My eyes are drawn back to his wrist. The watch was a Father's Day gift. I unbuckle it and run my thumb over the engraving on the back: *With Love.*

I clasp the watch around my wrist next to the tracker. The ocean snaps and snarls and slams twenty-foot waves against the concrete foundation. A layer of frothy water rushes toward me, wetting the concrete, foaming at my feet. The wind shoves me, challenging me to release my bottled-up anger.

As I look at my dad's dead body, a primal scream begs for release, but I bite down and trap my screams inside with my tears. Instead of screaming and crying, I'll purge myself of all the things I didn't get to say.

I take a deep breath and yell as if my lungs were on fire. "How could you do this to us? How could you be so stupid? Trusting Gregor cost you your life! It cost me and Abe and Addie our dad! It cost Mom her husband.

"Why didn't you believe me! Why didn't you love me enough to fight for me? Why didn't you love *them* enough to listen to me?

"What were your last words to me? *I don't want to hurt you,* you said. Well, you did hurt me, Dad. You hurt me more than you'll ever know." My voice starts strong and trails off, ragged and frayed like my heart.

I rip the tracker off my wrist and slam it on the ground.

I drive my heel into it. Once. Twice. Three times. Over and over, I smash it with all my might, with all my rage, with all my heartache.

My heel throbs as the tracker crunches and crumbles underfoot. I snatch the shattered tracker from the ground and hurl it over the water. The tracker breaks the surface with a splash. It sinks, taking the pieces of my broken heart to the ocean floor with it.

A mosquito lands on my arm. I squash it and wipe away its sticky residue. What if I was too late? What if I reached the lighthouse after Dad had already released drones headed for Hillcrest? I picture Abe and Addie sleeping soundly. Spinning toward the fortress, I race to the tunnel.

Forty-two

My heartache and pain have been sucked into a vacuum. My heart is numb. My mind is numb. My body is numb. I felt nothing when I retrieved the rifle from the super-soldier I killed. No guilt. No regret. No sympathy.

I rap my knuckles against the cathedral's back door. The sound barely penetrates the heavy wood. Stained-glass windows peer down at us like soulless eyes, dark and devoid of color in the pale moonlight.

Please let Fritz be here unharmed. The stillness of the night stirs doubts within me.

"Do it again," Treb says.

I tap, tap, tap and step back, adjusting the rifle strap so it isn't digging into my neck. "Is she still breathing?" I motion to Everly's lifeless body in his arms. Her hair is wet with blood, her face bruised and battered.

Treb studies her face. "Barely."

Red splotches cover his cheeks and neck. I wonder if his complexion is mottled from overexertion or from the virus.

I rest my hand on his shoulder. "I know you're exhausted from carrying Everly for miles, but we can rest soon."

The door cracks open. A male eye peers at us. "Who are you? What do you want?"

"Wren and Treb," I say. "We're here to see Fritz."

The door opens wider revealing a balding, middle-aged man. He nods at the rifle. "I'll take that," he says, as if used to giving orders.

I lift the strap over my head and pass him the gun.

"I'm Ray." He slings the rifle over his shoulder and focuses on Everly. "Is she dead?"

I shake my head. "She needs medical help."

He holds the door open and gestures for us to step inside. The room contains dust-covered boxes, books, hymnals, candelabras, and candles. Ray slams the deadbolt into place and props a chair against the door.

"The nurse is this way." He brightens his lantern. The flame licks the stone walls of the pitch-black corridor. Macabre shadows twist and turn and lurch at us. I shiver and pull my flannel tighter.

Every time we pass an empty hall, I tense up and hold my breath. I can't relax. Look at what happened last time I relaxed. I glance over my shoulder at Everly. When Treb and I reached the place where we last saw her, I half-expected her to have walked away, but instead she was lying in a pool of blood, the flutter of her pulse as delicate as an eggshell.

Ray leads us through a door with a window in the shape of a cross. I hear the voices before I see the mostly male faces filling the pews. My heart soars with hope. My eyes search for Fritz. I push away memories of the last time I was here during the Harvest.

"Ms. Klein?" Ray calls.

A woman in a black pantsuit turns to face us. Two cowlicks converge at her widow's peak, splitting charcoal bangs into a sweeping shoulder-length mane. Her alert eyes quickly assess the situation. She grabs a black medical bag from a pew and moves toward us.

That name: *Ms. Klein*. How do I know it? I dig through the pockets of my mind and empty each one until I find what I'm looking for. The day I went ziplining with Fritz, he mentioned Ms. Klein, his adoptive mother. My eyes drift to the space she left behind. Fritz!

Ms. Klein steps in front of me, obstructing my view of Fritz. She places her fingers against Everly's neck. Then, she lowers futuristic-looking glasses from the top of her head to the bridge of her nose.

The lenses produce a soft light that travels down Everly's limp body. "Gunshot wounds… internal bleeding… spinal fracture." Maybe the glasses give her x-ray vision or the ability to assess injuries somehow.

Ms. Klein props the glasses on her head. "Place her on the altar. Very gently. Ray, assist please."

Treb lowers Everly on the altar while Ray cradles her head. Treb's gray uniform is smudged with blood. Prisha rushes to him and asks what happened.

Ms. Klein catches her breath when her eyes meet mine. "Oh my."

She looks familiar. I glance at the weathered, sunbeaten faces of the men and women sprawled across the back of the pews with their feet propped on the seats. It's apparent from Ms. Klein's pale skin that, unlike the others, she hasn't worked a single day in the fields.

"Have we met?" I ask.

"I believe we have. A long, long time ago." Her voice sounds warm and refined. It lacks the undercurrent of suspicion that sharpens the voices of people from the Valley.

Ms. Klein backs away and hurries to the altar. She unzips her medical bag, retrieves supplies, and inserts an IV into Everly's hand. Ray fetches a music stand.

Ms. Klein hangs a bag of fluid from the stand and sits on the stool used by Dr. Jensen during the egg extraction ceremony. Memories of the procedure and the resulting hallucination flitter across my mind. I quickly look away from the altar and statue of Mary and find Fritz at my side.

"What are you doing here?" Fritz's voice is laced with anger.

"Gregor changed the time of tomorrow's wedding ceremony to five o'clock."

"You should have stayed at Headquarters. It's too dangerous to be roaming the streets while the entire city is on lockdown." He nods toward Everly. "That could have been you."

I bite my lip and look at my feet. The emotions I thought I had suppressed rise to the surface. Grief and guilt. Guilt and grief.

Fritz wraps his arms around me and pulls me close. I press my cheek against his chest and close my eyes. I feel safe in his arms.

"You're shaking," he says.

"I'm okay," I lie. I want to tell him everything. The tunnels. Everly. The soldier. The drones. Dad. The mosquitoes. Treb.

My spine stiffens.

I pull out of the embrace and look into his eyes. "Did you find the vaccine?"

Fritz nods.

"Is there a cure?" I beat back tears at the thought of Treb succumbing to the virus. It would be my fault. Just like what happened to Everly was my fault.

"What's wrong?" Fritz looks worried as he scans my face.

"A mosquito bit Treb." I swipe at my eyes, preventing tears from falling.

Fritz exhales and his features soften as if the news wasn't as bad as expected. Using his thumb, he brushes away the remaining wetness under my lower lashes. "They would never release infected mosquitoes in Ovation."

"They were infected, Fritz." I say in my best trust-me-I-know tone. I'm too exhausted to explain how I know.

"Are you sure?" He examines Treb from afar.

Treb stands at Everly's side talking to Prisha. He looks tired but far from death. Ms. Klein withdraws metal tongs from one of Everly's wounds. The bloodied bullet gleams and pings when dropped in a nearby bin.

Ms. Klein closes the gash and stops the bleeding. How does a nurse from the Valley know how to treat bullet wounds? What if she could help Treb and Dr. Hahn?

I take Fritz by the hand and approach the altar. We unlock hands and stand silently as Ms. Klein removes another bullet. "Ms. Klein?"

"Hmm?" She keeps her eyes on Everly's wounds.

"Someone else is hurt. At Headquarters. Maybe you could help?"

"What type of injury?" She sterilizes a patch of skin.

"I don't know. Blood was seeping from Dr. Hahn's chest. He was slipping in and out of consciousness."

The gloved hand maneuvering stitches freezes in midair. Ms. Klein stares blankly for a moment before pushing her glasses to the top of her head and swiveling her stool to face me. "August?"

"Yes," I say softly.

"Where is he?" she asks, peeling off her gloves.

I look at Fritz. He trusts her so I can trust her, right? His nod gives me the assurance I seek.

"He was tied up in the Nuclei conference room."

Ms. Klein frowns and stands. "You will take me to him."

Fritz says, "I don't think that's a good idea. Look at the damage a single super-soldier inflicted on Everly. Headquarters is swarming with hundreds of soldiers."

Unperturbed, Ms. Klein insists. "I am Dr. Lenore Klein. Dr. Hahn is my colleague and friend."

Fritz looks stunned, as if her words hit him over the head. Empathy moves me to reach for his hand. Today, we both learned our lives were built on lies.

"I will take you to Dr. Hahn," I say, "but first, Treb needs our help. He was bitten by a mosquito infected with the DBH virus." I nervously slide my eyes toward Treb. "He isn't immune."

Dr. Klein sucks in a breath. Her hand flits to her throat. She looks closely at Treb. "Where were you bitten?"

Treb points to his neck. All the color has drained from his face, as though the mosquito took a pint of blood instead of just a pinch.

Dr. Klein rummages through her bag and withdraws a pen light. She puts on her glasses and aims the narrow beam at Treb's neck. She examines the mosquito bite and then tosses the light in her bag. "To the lab immediately. He must be quarantined away from the others."

"Haven't they already been vaccinated?" I ask, looking at the men and women scattered around the room, most of them wearing work uniforms.

"They have," Dr. Klein lowers her voice, "but it can take days or weeks for a vaccine to be effective." She turns to Ray. "Sit with the girl and alert me if she wakes."

I'm relieved someone other than me has taken charge. My heart is broken. My nerves are frazzled. My mind reels with images of what tomorrow could bring.

Dr. Klein advances toward a door behind the sanctuary. She flattens her fingers against the door and the lock disengages. Microchip. Fritz and I exchange looks. How did she hide her identity for decades in the Valley?

I shield my eyes from the bright overhead lights as Fritz, Treb, Prisha, and I follow Dr. Klein into an expansive underground lab. She turns a corner and motions for Treb to sit at a quartz island while she approaches a transparent refrigerator.

She removes a vial and turns it upside-down to force a drop of liquid into the slide attached to the top of the vial. Holding the vial up to the light, she rotates a dial on her glasses and examines the slide. She picks different vials and repeats the process.

Prisha says, "Wren, I'm not going back to Headquarters. I feel safer here, and besides, I can't bear the thought of marrying one of those Neanderthals." Her eyes dart around the room and land everywhere but on my face.

"That's okay, Prisha. Thanks for convincing Valley residents to come to Ovation."

"I didn't really do anything. My dad did all the talking." Prisha chews on her fingernails and avoids eye contact.

"We couldn't have done it without you," Fritz says.

Prisha keeps a safe distance from Treb and asks, "Do you have any symptoms? Fever? Nausea?"

"I don't think so." Treb hunches over, intently watching Dr. Klein.

"This one." Dr. Klein holds up a vial and walks toward Treb. She unwraps a syringe. "Roll up your sleeve."

Treb wipes his palms against his pants and then cuffs his sleeve. "Am I going to die?"

"You are not going to die," says Dr. Klein.

"There's a cure?" I ask.

Dr. Klein injects the liquid into Treb's arm. "If Delilah had her way after she created the virus, there would be no cure. Thankfully, Shiko and I had the foresight to develop one, but quantities are limited."

"Delilah created the virus?" My eyes widen. "But she couldn't have known it would be used to kill innocent people?"

Dr. Klein bandages Treb's arm. "It was her idea to cleanse society of the genetically inferior. She created the virus for that very purpose." She shakes her head in disapproval. "I never thought August would go along with the plan after she passed."

I splay my hands across the quartz countertop. The DBH virus. Delilah Beckham Hahn. I study my hands. Delilah's hands. If I could cleanse my cells of her noxious DNA, I would scrub every bit of it away. My blood pressure starts rising.

Fritz places his hand over mine and leads me to a quiet corner. Dr. Klein's eyes follow. She must experience déjà vu when she sees a young version of Delilah and August together.

Fritz encloses my hands in his. "You're still shaking. Your eyes are red. Are you okay?"

I hesitate and nod. His sweet demeanor and soft touch make me want to melt into him and admit I'm not okay. But I don't want to talk about it. Not here, not now.

"Come with me." Fritz leads me to the stairs where we can be alone. He sits on the bottom step and motions for me to sit next to him. Still holding both of my hands, he leans in close. "You don't have to maintain the tough façade with me."

I bury my face in his chest, soaking up the warmth of his skin against my cheek, listening to the steady rhythm of his heartbeat. He strokes my hair and holds me tightly. Time slips by. No words are exchanged; no words are needed.

As I fight to keep my head above an ocean of emotions, to avoid succumbing to a powerful undertow of guilt and sorrow—his energy is steady and soothing: a rock to which I can cling. Calmness washes over me.

I sit up and look into Fritz's eyes. I tell him how Everly risked her life for me and Treb. I tell him about the drones and my dad's betrayal and death. He listens without interrupting and lovingly caresses me as I share my pain, telling him everything.

"I'm going to marry you, Wren Weiss. We'll build a house over a waterfall and grow old together. We'll have our own family. A boy and a girl." He kneels on the floor and plants kisses on my belly.

"Stop, that tickles!" I shriek with laughter and clutch his unruly curls, pulling his face away from my stomach.

He rises to his knees and rests his forehead against mine. My heart twitters into a tizzy. The anticipation is unbearable. I want him to kiss me. He kisses my cheek and playfully rubs his stubble against my face before leaving a whisper of kisses down my neck.

I wrap his hair around my fingers and gently move his head until his eyes and lips are within an inch of mine. "Stop teasing me."

As if given permission, he kisses me so softly and sweetly. I part my lips, inviting more. He accepts my invitation, kissing me more deeply. He slides a hand under the edge of my shirt and strokes my lower back. A wave of ecstasy rushes through me sending chill bumps up my spine.

I pull away from our kiss and study his face. I feel like I'm free-falling, plummeting toward something that's simultaneously wonderful and scary and exciting. From the tender look in his eyes, I think he feels the same.

"Have you ever been with a girl?" I ask sheepishly.

"I've never met a girl I wanted to be with until you." He cups my face and runs his thumb over my chin.

The stirring of unfamiliar feelings warms me. The sadness I've been carrying is swept away by dreams of the life together he described. I cradle his face and pull him in for another kiss.

"This is for you." He places a necklace over my head.

I examine the gold disk hanging from it.

"Press the back of the pendant," he says.

I squeeze the pendant. It projects Fritz's voice: *"I'm going to marry you, Wren Weiss. We'll build a house over a waterfall and grow old together. We'll have our own family. A boy and a girl."*

"You were recording us?" I'm surprised and overjoyed at the sentiment.

"I wanted to give you something special, just in case." He kisses me softly.

I don't want to think about the *just in case* he mentioned. I tuck the necklace into my shirt, grateful for the thoughtful gift and grateful for Fritz.

"Break it up, you two." Treb rounds the corner ahead of Prisha and Dr. Klein.

I redden and jump to my feet. Fritz stands and possessively wraps an arm around my waist. The warmth of his hand and the certainty in his embrace makes me feel like we can face anything together.

He winks at me. "If we get separated tomorrow, we meet back here, okay?"

I nod. Everything will be okay with Fritz at my side. I just know it.

Dr. Klein climbs the stairs. "I'll check on the girl and get Treble a change of clothes. Then, we will go to Headquarters."

"Mom, I wish you would stay here," Fritz protests. "You can tend to Dr. Hahn tomorrow."

"Tomorrow may be too late." Dr. Klein pushes the door open. "Don't worry, Fritz. Ray will accompany me."

I squeeze Fritz's hand as we enter the sanctuary.

Forty-three

*P*reparation for the wedding ceremony has been underway for hours. Blooming flower arrangements color the auditorium in festive reds, oranges, greens, and yellows. Lucindas weave tropical orchids through the solandra vine covering the wooden arbor erected on stage. A narrow carpet unfurled from the stage divides the room between super-soldiers and their brides.

After Ovation residents were escorted out of the auditorium to create space for the soldiers, Lucindas distributed white Harvest dresses and heels to the brides-to-be. I declined the heels, kept my tennis shoes on, and advised Clover and Maris to do the same. Thankfully, the dress has pockets, so I was able to transfer weapons from my jeans.

Super-soldiers filed in after we changed clothes. I stopped counting heads at two hundred. Lucindas pinned boutonnieres on their chests after they stacked their rifles on racks near the door. In disbelief, I watched them exchange guns for flowers.

I glance at Dad's watch for the tenth time, ignoring the needle of loss that pricks my heart full of tiny holes every time I look at his watch or feel its weight against my wrist.

It's four-thirty, but the lack of natural light makes it seem later. Overnight, nature's teeth ripped the sky apart, unleashing a torrential downpour. Blustering rain drums against the windowpanes, creating background music for my anxiety.

I bite my lip and look toward the bathrooms. The ceremony will begin soon. Everything that could go wrong runs laps around my mind.

Treb was escorted out of the room with Ovation residents, but what if he's unable to break away to the communications room? What if the frequency broadcast doesn't affect the soldiers and they slaughter the Valley fighters? What if the virus kills Treb?

On the way back to Headquarters, when we were gathering weapons from the underground stockpile, Dr. Klein assured us the cure would work. If it doesn't work, I'll feel guilty for the rest of my life.

Clover nudges me. "They're kind of cute."

Two super-soldiers rush through the double doors vigorously shaking their wet heads like dogs coming in from a storm. They stroll across the room laughing and fist pumping each other. Their jovial mood irritates me.

Gregor, Dr. Toussaint, Dr. Sorrell, and Franz climb the stage with two armed super-soldiers. Gregor and Dr. Toussaint exchange words. Gregor throws back his head and laughs. I clench my jaw and ball my fists in the folds of my skirt.

How long has Gregor been planning this? Genocide with a side of patricide isn't planned last minute like a dinner reservation. Anger sets ablaze every fiber of my being.

Gregor is the reason my dad is dead. Gregor is the reason Dr. Hahn is bleeding to death. Gregor is the one who wants to kill my mom, Abe, and Addie.

Gregor is the one who deserves to die.

Stopping the virus release isn't enough.

We have to stop Gregor.

Despite sharing DNA with Delilah and Gregor, I swear to the sun and moon and stars and to every planet in the sky, to everything good in the world, I will never be anything like them. I will never be a monster.

Dr. Sorrell adjusts the microphone for her height. "We are gathered here today to unite genetically superior women and men in matrimony. Although, each of us may have many genetic matches that would result in healthy offspring, there exists a single superior genetic match for all of us. The program I developed pinpoints that match.

"Super-soldiers, when I call your number, you will form a line on the right side of the carpet. Ladies, when your name is called, line up facing your future husband. After all genetic matches have been announced, each couple will be summoned to the stage where the union will be validated."

I chew on my cuticles and listen for the intercom to crackle. My eyes are drawn to the stage. Gregor pulls the remote out of his pocket, flips it through his fingers, and puts it back in his pocket.

My heart wallops my chest. I lift my eyes from Gregor's pocket. They snag on Franz's face. His eyes lock onto mine like a missile launcher locks onto its target.

I return his hostile stare, imagining my red-hot anger as a tangible weapon capable of melting his bones, reducing him to a pile of blubber.

His eyes travel down my dress. Does he suspect I have a gun? Did he see me looking at the remote control? I tear my eyes away.

Dr. Sorrell removes a stylus from her suit pocket and scrolls through her transceptor. After a moment, she looks up and leans into the microphone. "Soldier 0121."

A grinning soldier steps forward. His comrades clap him on the back. He takes his position at the foot of the stage. Most seem genuinely happy about the arranged marriages.

"Maven van Alsteen," Dr. Sorrell says.

As Maven of House of Lillith takes her place across from Soldier 0121, I catch a glimpse of Blaise and Eugenia. Blaise is on the verge of tears. Eugenia has a sympathetic look on her face as she runs her hands up and down Blaise's arms. I would be upset too if I thought these marriages were binding, but I know the Valley soldiers will be here any minute.

I impatiently tap my foot. Is the intercom broadcasting yet? Is Fritz near? I put my hands in my pockets. What if the knife or gun falls out when I'm taking my place in line? I remove my hands from my pockets to prevent suspicion.

Maris touches my forearm. "Stop fidgeting. You're going to attract attention."

"I can't relax. What if Treb can't get to the communications room? What if everything goes wrong?"

Maris places her hands on my shoulders. "Just be cool and go with the flow."

Clover says, "Treb will have no problem sweet talking the guards with his baby face. They'll never suspect him of anything. He won't let us down."

I lower my voice. "Remember what we discussed. The two of you will lead the girls to the Cathedral and hide out there."

"Clover Kirkpatrick," Dr. Sorrell says.

Clover pulls me into a conspiratorial hug. "Don't worry. We've got this." She pivots on her tennis shoes and walks away.

When my name is called, I nearly miss it. Dr. Sorrell repeats my name and the words cut through the fog of my thoughts. Hundreds of couples have lined up facing one another. The soldier at the end of the line excitedly scans the room. It's one of the wet dog soldiers who came in late.

A pit of dread in my stomach weighs down my feet. The handgun in my pocket thumps my upper leg with each step.

When the soldier sees me approaching, his chest puffs up and his lips spring into a smile that quickly spreads to his cheeks and crinkles the corners of his eyes.

I take my place across from him, next to a Supernova from House of Juliette. He beams at me, reaches across the carpet, and grabs my hands. He flips my arms over and kisses my inner wrists.

"Don't." I snatch my arms back and glare at him.

"You're beautiful. Your name is Wren?"

I ignore him as he continues to grin at me. He folds his arms against his wide chest to make sure I see the size of his biceps. He must be at least six foot five. Do these mutants even have names? The nametag on his uniform reads 0010.

He catches me looking at his nametag. "They call me Deca. Like the metric system."

"I know the metric prefix for ten," I snap.

He chuckles and flashes his perfect teeth. "Beautiful and smart. Looks like I hit the jackpot."

I roll my eyes and let them linger briefly on his tan face: square jaw, full lips, bright green eyes. Clover was right. Under different circumstances, he would be cute. As if he can read my mind, he flirtatiously waggles his eyebrows. I blush and focus on the streaks of rain striking the windows.

"Soldier 0379 and Everly Lockhart." The name reaches through the speakers, grabs me by the throat, and shakes me to my core.

"Everly Lockhart," Dr. Sorrell repeats the name that gives me so much anxiety.

I take a deep breath and will my heart to stop racing, my hands to stop shaking. Whispers scatter through the crowd as heads turn in search of the missing Supernova.

Dr. Sorrell steps away from the microphone and speaks to Gregor and Dr. Toussaint. Gregor nods and motions to a super-soldier. After a short exchange, the soldier leaves. Was he sent to look for Everly? Soon, they will realize Prisha is missing, too.

Dr. Sorrell returns to the microphone. "Soldier 0254 and Amelie Sperling, please join me on stage."

The couple nearest the stage moves forward. We must be lined up in the order we'll be married. I'm glad Deca and I are nearly last in line. The line moves gradually as Dr. Sorrell calls couples to the stage one at a time. Men approach the stage from one side and women approach from the other; they meet in the middle.

Dr. Sorrell stands under the arbor and says a few words to each couple. After the couple is pronounced husband and wife, they leave the stage separately and take their places at the end of the line.

Crackle. Hiss. Pop.

Was that the intercom? Did anyone else hear it? I try to make eye contact with Maris and Clover, but their eyes are glued to the couple on stage. The line of soldiers and brides tip toward each other: flirting, preening, touching—absolutely enamored. If eyes could drool, the auditorium would be flooded. They seem spellbound by the magic of marital dreams, the fulfillment of some ancient need—to possess and be possessed, to belong.

I want to shake them, to wake them. Gregor isn't doing this for us. He's doing it for himself. As we inch forward, Deca makes small talk. I provide short, meaningless responses.

I don't want to get to know him. I want to get this over with so I can stop the virus and start my life with Fritz. I can't wait to go home to introduce Fritz to my family. Addie will be smitten. The thought makes me smile.

"That gorgeous smile is more like it. It's almost our turn." Deca's face seems to be stuck in a permanent smile.

I wipe the smile off my face and frown at him. I wish I could tell him I already have a boyfriend so he would leave me alone. I'm definitely not having three kids with him even if he is my perfect match.

"Soldier 0010 and Wren Weiss." Hearing my name over the loudspeaker fills me with dread.

Deca and I climb the stage from opposite sides. He looks excited as he strides toward me. A miniscule part of me feels sorry for him. If he had been matched with any other girl, he may have experienced the happily-ever-after he seems to want so badly.

Deca's wide smile and easy manner make it easy to forget the sole purpose for his existence. Super-soldiers protect Gregor's interests, kill his enemies, and as of today, breed his vision of the future.

"Please join hands," Dr. Sorrell says.

Under the flower-covered arbor, it smells more like a funeral than a wedding. Deca eagerly clasps my hands in his own. He doesn't look like someone trained to kill. He looks like a lovesick boy. I grit my teeth and scan the room for Fritz. I hope he isn't watching. I zone out until Dr. Sorrell grabs my arm.

"What?" I ask.

"I said to hold out your arm." She holds a device over my inner wrist.

What is this? Another microchip? I flinch when the device zaps my arm. Wisps of smoke rise from the white digits tattooed on my wrist. I scowl at the number: *0010.* Am I supposed to be his property now?

"You may kiss your bride," Dr. Sorrell says.

Deca grabs my waist, lifts me off the ground, and kisses me deeply. I wedge my forearms between us. To my dismay, my body responds. My lips part. My heart rate jumps. I'm no longer resisting. I abruptly break our lip lock.

He lowers me, dramatically raking my torso over his muscular chest and hard abs. My feet touch the floor and I feel off balance. I stumble away from him.

I liked the kiss. My cheeks burn with the acknowledgment. What makes him think he can kiss me like that? I glower at him and wipe my mouth across the back of my hand.

Deca licks his lips and flaunts an I-know-you-liked-it grin.

Dr. Sorrell pronounces us married and dismisses us. I hurry to the back of the line. Deca takes his place across from me. I ignore him even harder than before.

I notice Fritz casually leaning against the bathroom hall. My stomach swoops and my heart dives. He's wearing ear plugs to block the frequency broadcast.

Our eyes meet and the intensity in his eyes burns a hole right through me. Did he see me kiss Deca? Embarrassment stings my cheeks. I look at my feet.

Forty-four

The final couple is validated. They kiss and head off stage. At the stairs, the soldier leans over, hands on his knees, and vomits. Dr. Sorrell rushes to his side.

A soldier halfway up the line pukes on his bride's shoes. She jumps back.

It's happening.

Soldiers start retching, dry heaving, gagging. Confused murmurs ripple through the room. On stage, doctors surround the vomiting soldier.

"I need to sit down," one soldier says as he backs away holding his stomach.

"I'm not feeling well," Deca says.

"Symptoms?" My voice is shaky.

"Dizzy. Disoriented." He wipes away the perspiration forming at his temples.

"Maybe it was something you ate." I look away.

I hate lying. Lies are like acid: they eat away at you, bit by bit, lie by lie, until your integrity is completely compromised.

I cram my hands in my dress pockets. My tattooed wrist burns as it slides against fabric. I wrap my fingers around the reassuring hunk of steel in my pocket. I hope I don't have to use it.

An ear-splitting blast sends shattered glass skidding across the floor. I cringe and cower and nearly shoot my toe off. My heart slams against my chest. I swing around. A giant palm tree rammed through the back wall of windows, threshes against the wall as if it's a living, breathing thing.

The wind caterwauls and rages through the broken window, tearing at my hair, slashing at my dress. Thunder builds and explodes in an earth-quaking crescendo. Lightning pops and cracks and zags down the walls.

Light bulbs burst overhead raining down splinters of glass on the newlyweds. It feels like a black cloud has rushed into the room, sucking up all the light and good vibes.

Deca doubles over and pukes. At the sight and smell of vomit, my stomach convulses. My throat squeezes. I step back and cover my nose and mouth.

It's working.

Soldiers are reeling, kneeling, sweating, puking.

A burst of bullets ricochets around the room and just like that—as if a neon sign were flashing: *YOU'RE UNDER ATTACK*—the soldiers snap into action like a pack of wolves tracking, hunting, strategizing.

One word blazes down the line of soldiers like a lit fuse rushing toward a stick of dynamite: *ambush, ambush, ambush.*

Men from the Valley rush into the auditorium yelling, shooting, attacking. People scatter.

"Run!" I yell at the girls next to me.

Clover and Maris step out of line.

"Move! Move! Move!" They herd brides toward the hallway.

Brides scramble and scream and smash into each other: a stampede of stilettos and chiffon and lace. Maris grabs two rifles at the door. Smart Maris. She throws one to Clover. Clover catches it and leads the girls into the hall. The girls nearly trample one another as they jab, jostle, jam themselves through the door.

"Faster!" Maris shouts.

A bewildered Toussaint and Sorrell run off stage and vanish into the smear of skirts and camouflage. Valley fighters rush the stage. The armed bodyguards on stage spray the Valley men with bullets. They fall.

Blood splatters and pools in puddles on the floor. Blood, blood, so much blood. My pulse pounds in my ears. Guilt and terror immobilize me.

A flash of white darts across the stage: Gregor. He slinks to the back of the stage, hits a button on the wall, and disappears into an elevator. I can't let him get away.

Men are grunting and grabbing, clobbering and kicking. A Valley man pulls his fist back and lands decades of pent-up anger into a super-soldier's nose. Blood spurts from his face. I dodge two men rolling around exchanging punches. A soldier picks up a Valley man by the neck squeezing and shaking him until his face turns purple. *Keep moving!*

The last of the Supernovas, Ada from House of Rosalind, catapults through the air, her body arching, twisting, convulsing. Blood buds across the back of her white dress: a scarlet bouquet. She crumples to the ground. A super-soldier lifts her in his arms and sprints toward the hallway. All of the girls are gone now.

Except me.

I stay low and run for the stage as bullets obliterate everything around me. My foot slips in blood. I gain my balance and run up the stage steps. My hair is grabbed from behind. I'm yanked off the steps. My hips land on the floor. Air is knocked out of my lungs and my heart feels like it took a punch.

"Where do you think you're going?" Franz growls in my ears. He yanks my head back, keeping his fists buried in my hair, forcing me to look up at him.

I glare at him.

Franz leans down until we are cheek to cheek. "We should have tied you up with the rest of them, but Gregor wouldn't listen."

His nostrils flare. His breath, hot against my neck, smells of whiskey. His hands, heavy in my hair, snap my neck back harder. I squirm and try to stand. He shoves me down.

"Stop! You're hurting me!" I say.

"You haven't seen anything yet, precious." He drags me by the hair toward the exit.

I blindly feel for my gun and dig my heels into the floor. What if Gregor already activated the drones? What if all of this was for nothing? I search the room for Fritz. He won't let Franz get away with this.

"Let her go." Deca steps in front of me, hunched over, hands on his knees. His stomach convulses and his lips purse as if he's fighting off nausea.

"Stand down, soldier," Franz orders.

"I said. Let. Her. Go." Deca stands up straight, rolls his shoulders back, and steps closer, towering over Franz.

A streak of hope runs through me. The grip on my hair tightens. Men yelling. Bullets. I cover my ears. Franz draws a hand back. A hot slap lands on my cheek. My head reels. Tears sting my eyes. I look up at Deca.

He clenches his jaw. Narrows his eyes. Raises his fist. Bones snap. Blood drips on my dress. Cupping his mouth, Franz staggers and releases me.

I scoot backwards and scramble to my feet. Blood pours from Franz's mouth. Shock pours from his face. He wide-eyed stares at Deca.

"You're going to pay for this, soldier!" Bloody, broken teeth fall from Franz's mouth. He spits blood and lunges at Deca.

With one hand, Deca catches Franz by the collar, throws him into the air like a volleyball, rears his fist back, and slams it into his jaw. Franz falls to his knees. Deca picks him up, throws him across the room, and charges after him.

The charming super-soldier has transformed into something fierce, scary, unstoppable. Like the soldier who killed Everly, Deca was trained to be a killer. It frightens me to see this side of him.

I run to the stage, dodging fallen bodies and fistfights on the way. *Almost to the stage. Keep going. Don't look back.* A hand shoots up and grabs my ankle, tripping me, knocking me down. My chin collides with the floor. My teeth snap together. I taste blood.

"Help," a man from the Valley croaks. Blood bubbles from a hole in his neck. He keeps a strong grip on my ankle.

I snake forward on my stomach and kick my leg free. I did this to him. I did this to all of them. If people die today, it's my fault. Everything is my fault.

Choking back a sob, I lift my head. The sonic attack slowed the soldiers, but it didn't incapacitate them. Tears burn my eyes as I survey the bloodshed.

I won't cry. I can't cry.

I have to move. I have to stop Gregor.

I push up and crawl to the stage. At the bottom of the stairs, I put my hands over my ears to block the screams of rage, the howls of pain.

Behind me, soldiers reclaim their weapons. If I don't do something soon, the Valley men will be slaughtered.

The stage is empty except for the floral arbor and the microphone. The microphone. I dash up the stairs and grab the microphone. "Retreat! It's over!"

Gregor is gone. The remote is gone. Fighting is pointless.

"Retreat!" I scream into the microphone.

A super-soldier wheels around and points his weapon at me. I raise my hands and back away. *Please don't shoot.* Sweat rolls down my face. Panic lights up my spine.

Just when I think the soldier is going to shoot me, a Valley man tackles him, landing blow after blow to his skull.

I rush toward the wall where Gregor disappeared. My eyes sweep the room for any sign of Fritz. I don't see him. The smell of vomit and flowers and blood makes my stomach lurch. I press my hands against my stomach.

"Wren," Deca's voice strains over the wind, rain, bullets, shouting. He stands over Franz's unconscious body.

I give him my best thank-you look and move toward the elevator. Deca climbs the stage. Blood trickles from one of his ears. His complexion is gray, sickly, slick with sweat.

I maintain eye contact with Deca as I back into the wall, blindly feeling for the elevator. My fingers catch on buttons. A chime rings and the doors slide open. I step into the elevator. Deca just wants to protect me, but what if he's loyal to Gregor?

"I'm okay." I reassure him.

We lock eyes until the doors close. The elevator drops and so does my stomach. I squeeze into the back corner, close my eyes, and massage my head where Franz ripped out clumps of hair. Sweeping my fingers across the necklace Fritz gave me, I picture the last time I saw him safely tucked into the bathroom hallway.

Warm liquid drips down my shin. I open my eyes and dislodge a glass shard protruding from my leg. I toss the glass to the floor and swipe at the blood. With all the adrenaline pumping through my body, I don't even feel it.

The elevator opens and a blast of lemony-mint air hits me. The mint tingles my nose and throat where the stench of vomit still clings. Tension burrows into my neck and shoulders. The classical music doesn't soothe me. Instead, the screeching violin claws at my nerves like fingernails against metal.

Gregor couldn't have gotten far. The truss bridge overhead is empty. The observation room is dark. I peer down aisle after aisle of twelve-foot tall gynopods. It's like an orchard of human beings: hundreds of men, women, children, babies, and fetuses.

Cradling the gun in both hands, I tiptoe into the nearest aisle of gynopods. Long hair swirls and curls around the faces of children floating in the fetal position. Their catatonic eyes stare blankly ahead. I swear they are looking at me, through me. I shudder. So creepy.

Moving into the center of the room, I feel exposed: too easily seen from the observation room. Heart pounding, palms sweating, I hear a *swish-click* beyond the last row of gynopods: a door closing.

Forty-five

I zigzag down the aisles of gynopods, speeding toward the sound of the closing door. Drumming under the classical music is an irregular beat—bullets or thunder or rain.

Or maybe it's just my heart ticking like a bomb.

Beyond the last row of gynopods is a door: no sign, no microchip scanner. I wipe the sweat from my palms and dry the gun between the folds of my dress. I tug at the scratchy lace around my neck and wrists to release body heat.

Touching the cool metal of the door sends a jolt of anxiety through me. I don't want to open it. I feel like the biggest chicken. My heart is beating so fast, I imagine it detonating and feathers flying everywhere.

I take a deep breath, crack open the door, and slip through. I'm in an underground parking garage containing rows of dark green military vehicles, modern sedans, and Helixes. A musty miasmic odor permeates the place. It's dark, but not too dark.

Fluorescent tubes spotlight water damage: rusty pipes mounted to fractured walls, clumps of green and black speckled mold clinging to corners, streaks of mildew fanning across the concrete floor. It's as quiet as the backseat of a hearse.

A flash of white moves between vehicles. A shoe scuffs concrete. My heartbeat accelerates. I lie down next to the closest vehicle and look under it.

I see white uniform pants with gold threading. I have to get closer. I inch around the back of the cars, gripping the gun tightly. I'm covered in a sheen of sweat. I feel the dampness on my back, my stomach, my calves.

I squat and peek over the hood of a utility vehicle. Gregor looks deep in thought as he chews the end of an unlit cigar. I see a little of Fritz in the angle of his jaw and the shape of his eyes.

Relief and fear well up inside me: relief because he thinks he's alone; fear because soon he will know he's not. He withdraws the remote control from his front pocket.

I jump into the aisle, pointing the gun at him. "Put the remote on the ground." My voice is strong, calm, steady. For a split second, I'm proud of myself.

Gregor snaps his head in my direction. An expression of shock flickers across his face. He looks me up and down and then lets loose a roar of laughter that bounces off the concrete and metal surfaces.

"I said drop it." I use my best I-mean-business tone. I'm feeling somewhat confident: I have a gun; he doesn't.

Gregor places the remote on the car behind him, withdraws a match from his pocket, and lights the cigar. He puffs and then jabs at the air with his cigar. "What is this? You're going to be a hero? Save the world from the villainous Gregor Hahn?" His tone is smooth, unrattled by my presence or the loaded gun aimed at his chest.

I hold the gun against my stomach to still my shaking arms. "Why can't you do things your way without hurting people? You can have it all without releasing the virus."

Gregor holds the cigar smoke in his mouth for a beat too long, as if we're in a cigar lounge and people aren't dying above us. "If past societies had the technology to cleanse their gene pools, there would have been no Hitlers, no Stalins."

I frown as I try to follow his thought process. "We'll never know what might have been."

He leans against the car and crosses his ankles, completely at ease. "Those with enhanced DNA will never sink to the levels of depravity seen throughout history. I can't say the same for people in the Valley and Hillcrest."

The faces of Everly and Bacon and Berkeley and Harlowe flash through my mind. All genetically-modified, all violent.

"Why did you hurt Dr. Hahn?" I ask. The lace collar on the dress is making my neck itch, but I don't dare move to scratch it.

He clicks his tongue and inhales. "You have a soft spot for the old man, but you wouldn't know what it's like to grow up without a mother and with a father obsessed with bringing her back. He coddled clusters of cells and neglected his only son."

He's trying to make me feel sorry for him, to manipulate me the way he manipulated Dad. This smooth-talking man is the reason my dad is dead and my family is in danger.

Gregor stubs his cigar on the hood of a car, picks up the remote control, and starts entering a code. "Someday, every child in Ovation will have a father *and* a mother. Now, if you'll excuse me. I'm growing bored with this conversation and I have work to do."

I extend my arms and aim the gun at his chest. "Put the remote down or I'll shoot."

"This remote?" Gregor casually flips the remote into the air and catches it. He backs between two cars, smiling from ear to ear, and moves out of my view.

"If you want it, come and get it." His voice comes from behind a row of cars.

I swing the gun in the direction of his voice. A wave of panic crests over me. I've lost control. I should have shot him when I had the chance. He starts whistling a tune and wandering around the garage like a psycho.

I spin around, tracking the sound. He was across from me. Now, he's behind me. I move across the aisle. The blink of a shadow on my left. A smear of movement on my right. He's circling me, hunting me, taunting me.

The whistling stops.

Every cell in my body is on high alert: listening, watching, waiting. My entire body is quaking. I step back and hide between sedans.

Hot breath on the back of my neck.

A whistle in my ear.

Terror, sheer terror guts me.

I spin around, gun raised, heart racing. Gregor hooks me under the ribs and body slams me against the hood of a car. My back spasms, my head cracks against metal. The gun skitters into the aisle.

The gravity is sucked out of the room and for a moment, I'm hovering, looking down at Gregor pinning me against the car, binding my wrists together over my head, the gun six feet to my left.

The gun.

"Silly girl. Did you really think the remote was the only way I could activate the drones?" His face is inches from my own. His breath is cigar-sweet.

"Let me go," I gasp. "You're hurting me." I twist and kick and buck, but his body is like a concrete slab pressing down on me, crushing me.

He shakes with laughter, but his eyes aren't laughing. His eyes are dark empty pits devoid of humanity, devoid of empathy. He analyzes my face with the detached eyes of a scientist analyzing a specimen or a serial killer studying his next victim.

I push and shove, but he doesn't budge. "Please," I whimper and I'm instantly embarrassed by my cowardice.

Gregor strokes my cheek. "The damsel in distress routine is so passé, wouldn't you agree?"

His touch sends a shiver down my spine, draining my courage, filling me with fear. I flinch away from his hand and go limp. Maybe he'll think I've given up, maybe he'll let his guard down if I stop fighting. I feel his warm breath against my lips and I want to sink into the hood of the car.

In my periphery, the gun is a black smudge screaming for my attention, consuming my thoughts. I don't dare twitch an eyeball toward the gun. I can't let him know what I'm thinking.

His fist tightens around my wrists. He continues stroking my face. "It would be too easy to kill you. Instead, I will break you and make you a good little lap dog like your dad, Joe."

And just like that.

Something dark and wild and primal explodes inside me. I jerk my head to the side and sink my teeth into the flesh of his wrist, deeper, harder, gnawing, hacksawing his arteries like a rabid animal, tasting blood on my tongue, feeling warm blood gush down my chin.

"Bitch!" Gregor yelps and releases my hands.

I spit out his wrist, roll off the car, fall to my knees, and scrabble for the gun. My fingers reach for it, so close, almost touching. Every part of me is on fire with one desire: survival.

I wrap my fingers over the butt of the gun. Sweet relief rolls through me. The heel of Gregor's shoe slams down on my hand like a hammer, crushing my fingers.

I scream and try to pull my hand away, but he pivots his heel, grinding it against my fingers, burning my skin, trapping my hand.

Finally, he steps back, picks up the gun and points it at my head. Blood drips from his wrist staining his pants in streaks of red. I did that. I made him bleed. I feel a swell of satisfaction.

I sit back on my haunches and hold my throbbing hand against my abdomen. I won't beg. I won't be a coward. I'll look him in the eye as he circles me, daring him to shoot me.

"It didn't have to be this way." His voice is quiet and I detect the slightest hint of regret.

Cold metal slides against my sweaty temple. It was all for nothing. A hysterical wail starts rising in my chest, but I cage it and padlock it and hold it down. I won't let him see me cry.

Gregor cocks the hammer. My heart slams my chest.

I close my eyes and cycle through the faces of the people I love: Fritz kissing me on the rooftop; Abe and Addie and Mom and Dad on a hike—picking blueberries, the twins pelting each other, inky-blue stained clothing.

Click.

My mind goes blank.

The images go black.

I open my eyes.

The gun jammed.

The will to live rushes through me and I feel manic, desperate. I jam my hand into my pocket, pop open the forgotten switchblade, and slam the razor-sharp edge into Gregor's foot.

"Son of a bitch!" He stumbles back.

I crawl forward, grab the grill of a truck, and pull myself to my feet. Then, I do what I do best: I run. Twenty feet to the exit. I'll run through the basement, climb to the control room, and escape to the underground tunnels. I'll run back to the cathedral and—

Something twists my hair, snags me, lifts me off my feet. My head is slammed into a windshield. A snapping crack: my neck or the glass? I think of coffee cherries bouncing off glass. My legs crumble. My vision glitches. Cars melt into glossy puddles. A flurry of dark and bright spots—red, black, white—barb my vision.

Something warm and wet on my head. Gregor's face. Gregor's hands—the smell of blood and cigars. I'm lifted, thrown over a shoulder. My hair drags on the floor. Moving away from the exit, deeper into the garage.

Bobbing and swaying. Blood dripping onto the concrete. My blood or his blood? Blackness attacks my eyes. Numbness attacks my limbs.

A door slams. Pitch-black hallway. The smell of urine and bleach. Blood rushing to my head. Blinking eyeshine everywhere.

Prickly fur against my arm. I scream. It screams. They all scream. Terror stabs me in the chest, taking my breath away.

Where are you taking me? The words roll around my mouth, roll around my mind. I try to speak, but my tongue is thick; my thoughts are slurred.

Focus. Remember how to get out. Metal scrapes concrete. I turn. A hairy leg chained to the wall. Hairy human things. Hunch-backed things. A woman: four eyes sunken into a twisted face. An ape with a man face.

Teeth. Sharp, gleaming teeth.

Feet padding up and down walls. Little girl giggles. I'm hallucinating. They said there was no Hell, but I think this is Hell. Flames of darkness engulf me. I'm falling, spiraling into the dark bottomless pit of those two brown eyes.

"Welcome to the Menagerie, Wren. You're going to wish you had never crossed me."

The last thing I hear before the world melts away: laughter.

Forty-six

The sweltering sun beats down on my face. My mouth is desert dry. Thirsty. Headache. I open my eyes. A dazzling double sun looms over me. I blink once, twice, three times; two suns merge into one.

Where am I?

Disjointed memories flare up and then dissolve: the last time I saw Fritz; Deca's kiss; Deca's fist; my dad's eyes; screeching violins and floating faces; the parking garage, the gun, the knife, the windshield, the creatures.

Gregor.

Terror shatters my disorientation. Where is Gregor?

I try to sit up, but I can't move. A guttural sound claws up my throat. I try to cry out, but my mouth won't open.

I raise my head. Tools tacked to one wall—scissors, pliers, saws, scalpels. Medical tray next to me. Makeshift operating room.

I look down. Straitjacket. Legs strapped to an operating table. Crushing weight on my chest. Pins and needles in my hands. Can't open my mouth, can't suck in a deep breath.

Cool air blows across my legs. Then, it's gone.

My heart pounds. My head pounds. My blood pounds. Everything pulsing, pounding, thrumming.

"Well, well, well." Gregor materializes at my side. "Sleeping Beauty has awoken."

Let me go comes out as a gurgle: "Mm-gg…" My mouth is tender, my lips hurt.

Gregor presses his finger against his lips. "Shh. Save your energy. You'll need it later." He pulls down the surgical light and angles it close to my face. His wrist is bandaged where I bit him. "The stitches look good," he says as the light glides away from me.

Stitches? I slide my tongue between my teeth. Threads crisscross the back of my lips in an X-shape. While I was knocked out, he mutilated me.

My heart slams. A bottleneck of screams builds in my chest.

Gregor selects a pair of pliers from the wall and smacks them against his open palm.

Smack.

Smack.

Smack.

"You didn't think you could sink your teeth into me and get away with it, now did you?" He sets the pliers at my feet and runs his fingers up my inner calf.

I cringe and jerk my leg away. Restraint straps bite into my ankles. My whole body is shaking, sweating. I can't take my eyes off the pliers.

"Do you know how to ensure a dog never bites you twice?" He pulls my dress down over my knees. His touch makes me want to scream.

"Pry the dog's teeth out, one by one, with a good set of pliers. Or, sew the dog's mouth shut."

He raises his hands in the air. "What can I say? I'm a nice guy. I decided to let you keep your teeth." He drops his hands. "For now." The last two words are loaded with malice.

If I could pull my feet free, if I could reach the pliers, or go for the scissors. Terrified, I writhe and roll and fight against the straitjacket.

"Allow me to show you what you missed while you slept for two hours." Gregor turns off the lights. "Golgi, roll live drone footage of the Valley."

Dread is a boulder tethered to my ankle, dragging me to tenebrous depths where every breath is one step closer to death. The walls, ceiling, and floor light up; I'm trapped in a cube of color and action and sound. Chaos: Valley dwellers in the streets running, screaming, tripping over decaying bodies, frantically beating on doors.

"Beautifully effective, isn't it?" Gregor surveys the carnage on every wall. "Some die instantly of heart attacks, strokes. Others hold on for days as their organs shut down."

Brittle sounds collide in my chest and rupture in my throat. A low-pitched moan rattles my vocal cords. I want to close my eyes, to block out the images, but I'm too scared to take my eyes off Gregor.

Gregor seems transfixed by the images of suffering. "They say Mother was inspired by the Marburg virus, the flu, and coronaviruses. But what she created was more deadly, more brilliant than anything the world has ever known." His tone is boastful, as if he's proud of her lethal legacy.

His eyes settle on mine. I squirm but maintain eye contact. If I look him in the eye, maybe he'll see his mother in me, maybe he'll let me go. Maybe I can uncover a shred of humanity.

"Golgi, connect to the camera at the intersection of Honor Street and Acacia Lane," Gregor says.

I scream *no*, but it comes out as a raspy groan.

The pixels flicker and rearrange themselves. My hometown. My neighborhood. My street. It's too late. I couldn't stop the virus. I couldn't save them.

The tears building in my chest feel like shrapnel lacerating my heart and lungs. Every breath burns with the need for release. I fight to suppress the tears, the pain, the guilt.

"Golgi, zoom in on 923 Acacia Lane."

Please, no. I moan.

The footage is dark. It's late. The house is lit. Abe's bike leans against the tree in the front yard. It looks so normal, so peaceful. So quiet.

Where is the chaos? The screaming people? The dead bodies?

I jerk my eyes away from the images and look at Gregor.

"The drones haven't reached Hillcrest yet, but they are on the way. Soon, the entire island will be cleansed. It's too bad you won't live to see it."

The drones haven't reached Hillcrest.

There's time.

Hope swells within me and for a minute, I don't feel the pain on the side of my head, the tenderness of my bruised lips, or the pressure of the straitjacket.

Gregor turns on the light. His fingers graze my ankles as he unbuckles the leg straps. He walks out of my view and reappears with a wheelchair. He motions for me to sit.

I strain to sit up. He grabs my shoulders and moves me to the wheelchair. Our eyes meet and the dead emptiness in his eyes is more frightening than any emotion his eyes could convey. If my arms were free, I would claw out his eyeballs, I would make him feel something—*anything* more than nothing—when he looks at me.

"Don't try anything stupid," he says as he shackles my ankles together.

He wheels me into the hallway. I hear the limp in his gait from the knife wound in his foot and my lips curl into a tiny, scabbed smile.

Forty-seven

Gregor parks me near a door marked *Authorized Personnel Only*. He positions his eye against a retina scanner on the wall. "You blacked out before I had a chance to give you the official tour. I think you'll be very impressed with my pet project."

The door opens to a dimly lit passage that tunnels through an aquarium. The arched walls and ceiling pulse with floating tentacles and zagging fins. The floor appears to be rimpling and cockling—a sea of blue. I wriggle against the straitjacket and ankle shackles.

"I've sequenced the genome of everything here: the sting rays, the octopi, the jellyfish and sea urchins. If we take the best genes of every species and combine them into new life forms, the possibilities are endless." His tone is full of wonder.

I'm tired and thirsty. My body aches. I would give anything for a glass of water and aspirin instead of a dose of gloating. I go to lick my dry lips; my tongue catches on stitches.

My fear and fatigue turn into blistering-hot molten rage—the kind of rage that lies dormant in all of us until one day, something snaps and a primeval instinct erupts like wildfire, incinerating everyone and everything in its path. Gregor has unleashed my rage and I have no doubt that Gregor will pay.

"My crowning achievement is this way." Gregor rolls me toward the door at the end of the tunnel. Inhuman sounds come from the other side.

Flashbacks of the creatures I saw hours ago flood my mind and I feel like I'm being pushed toward an edge to look down on something I don't want to see.

The door swings open and I'm struck with the stench of urine and bleach and animals—live animals and dead, rotting carcasses; the sound of shrieking voices and clamoring feet, a dull repeating thud running under it all. I want to shrink back, to slam a brake, to get up and run away.

Gregor pushes me into a dark, gloomy corridor. Dust motes float in dingy streaks of light cast from strips on the floor. The door slams behind us like the lid of a coffin.

The feeling of being trapped makes my heart beat fast. The voices and pattering feet become louder as if our presence has agitated the prisoners the way kicking a beehive agitates bees.

We pass a row of jail cells on the left. Something darts between the iron bars and grabs my hair. My heart clenches. I jerk my head away; the grip tightens. I blink rapidly trying to make out the figure behind bars: a hunchbacked woman with gray floor-dragging hair, gnarled hands.

"Pretty, pretty," she whispers in a singsong voice.

Gregor bangs a baton against the bars. "Back off!"

She releases my hair and scurries into a corner. The throbbing in my head intensifies. The noise in other cells dies down. In the next cell, a little boy sitting on the floor bangs his head against the wall, over and over and over.

"Regeneration is the gift I bestowed upon Timmy." Gregor sounds pleased by his generosity. "If you cut out his tongue; it grows back. Slice his arm; the wound closes immediately. Damage his organs, they repair themselves."

What kind of psycho experiments on a little boy and keeps him locked in a cage?

"Did you know non-human primates share up to 99% of their DNA with humans? Imagine harnessing the strength and aggression of gorillas and chimpanzees in human hybrids.

"In the next cell, we have chimpanzee-human conjoined twins. I've seen them tear apart super-soldiers with their bare hands.

"Then, we have the King of the Jungle. A four-hundred-pound gorilla-human hybrid. He isn't capable of human speech, but someday it will be achieved."

I turn my face away and stare at the gray wall as the wheelchair glides down the hall. I tune out as Gregor boasts about his science experiments.

Despite his attempts to quiet them, they keep squawking and shrieking and banging. The farther we go, the riper the smell. I take shallow breaths and try to suppress the urge to vomit.

Finally, Gregor cuts left and punches a code into a keypad. We enter a room the size of a basketball court. A sheet of glass shields bleachers to my right. In front of the bleachers is a five-foot drop to the floor.

"This is where your journey ends." Gregor walks around the wheelchair and unbolts three deadlocks on a steel door.

My stomach fills with dread as he pushes me through the door. My eyes widen. What I see bludgeons my hope of getting out of here alive.

Scattered across the blood-stained floor, piled in heaps, sitting atop drains: bones, bones, and more bones. Femurs and skulls and spinal columns.

Gregor steps forward. "I've been very busy this week. The hybrids haven't eaten in days." He kneels and unshackles my legs. "Stand."

I glare at him and hope he can feel the hatred emanating from me. I stand and feel light-headed. Dehydrated. He loosens the straitjacket and it falls away. I expand my chest and flex my fingers. A couple of fingers on my right hand feel swollen. Maybe broken.

Gregor tosses the straitjacket and shackles into the wheelchair. Balling my hand into a fist, I imagine punching him in the face. He lifts his shirt, revealing a gun tucked into his waistband.

"Don't even think about it." His voice is cold and hard like his eyes.

Something silver in his hand. He shoots his fingers toward my mouth, snips the stitches, and rips them out. I cry out. My lips burn as if I've kissed a hot skillet.

Blood fills my mouth, drips down my dress, and splatters the floor. I grab the hem of my dress and press it against my bloody lips.

Gregor rolls the chair away and pauses at the door. "They said you would be like my mother. They were wrong. You're nothing like my mother."

He slams the door and deadbolts it. Taking a seat on the bleachers behind the glass, he lights a cigar.

Suddenly, I'm free to speak and I can't think of what to say. My heart is beating so fast, I feel like I might have a heart attack.

"Golgi, open door number one and activate the cameras." Gregor draws on the cigar.

I drop the hem of my dress and spin to face a wall of doors at the far end of the room. The first door starts sliding up, revealing the dark cavity of a jail cell. An indistinct figure moves inside.

Gregor stands and looks out over the glass. "Please welcome Lucy." His voice takes on the tone of a sports broadcaster.

"Lucy hails from the Southeast Research Center. She was born with progeria, a rare disease that ages children at ten times the normal rate. Lucy is twelve-years-old, but she has the body of a fifty-year-old. Thanks to Lucy and those like her, we have refined anti-aging techniques."

From behind a curtain of cigar smoke, Gregor says, "Consider this your warm up."

I suck on my bleeding lips and wait.

Gregor leans forward and says, "Don't be shy, Lucy. I know you're hungry."

A fragile girl with sunken eyes and translucent skin steps into the light. Pale blue scrubs swallow her tiny barefoot frame. Even from far away, I can see the needle marks on her arms. She clings to the wall and stares at me as she moves closer.

I glance at the bones licked-clean around me and have a feeling I know what comes next, but I don't want to hurt her. The girl lowers her chin and the animal look in her eyes sends a shiver down my spine.

She squeals and launches herself at me. The top of her head cracks against my sternum, throwing me off balance. My heart rate skyrockets. I stagger backwards, grab her hair, and fling her off me.

She lands on her knees, bounces to her feet, and comes at me. I see a fleck of blue and then feel a block of steel against my chest, knocking me to the floor. She's on top of me, head bowed, teeth shredding my dress, piercing my flesh.

A sharp pain in my shoulder. I spin over, slamming her head against the floor: once, twice. She releases me and scampers away, sending bones clattering in her path. Warm blood dribbles down my arm. I stand and face Gregor.

"Is this what you wanted?" I scream, spitting blood from my mouth. Rage and hatred, glittering and razor-sharp, ravish every ounce of my humanity. Maybe I am like Gregor. Maybe I am like Delilah. All I want is to kill and slash and burn.

Gregor yawns and props his feet up. "Actually, I find you immensely boring." He drags the words out as if he has better things to do. "Golgi, open doors two through ten."

The grind of all the doors rising simultaneously ratchets up my anxiety. I back away from the doors. The muscle-bound chimpanzee hybrid is first to duck under the rising doors.

Conjoined heads circle two wide-open mouths showing off yellow teeth and dagger-like canines. It walks upright with human-length limbs.

My heart is beating a million miles per second. There has to be something I can use for a weapon. I dart quick glances to my left and right. More hybrids emerge. I lick the blood off my lips and push my hair off my sweaty brow.

"Hungry, hungry, hungry, mine, mine, mine." The hunchback woman moves forward with a hand outstretched, staying behind the chimpanzee twins.

The twins screech and run at me. I feel like my heart is going to implode. I have to fight back. I bolt toward them like a crazy person shaking my arms in the air, making myself bigger and bolder than I feel.

All around us: stamping feet, clapping hands, animal snorts and shrieks.

I slam into the twins; we smash into the bone-covered floor, spinning over each other, wrestling for an upper-hand. I clutch clumps of hair, poke at eyes, pinch and scratch and claw.

Something in my pocket digs into my thigh. The smell of dirty, filthy animals smothers me. A tongue licks my bloody shin. My head cracks against the floor and my body hits a wall.

I look up. Not a wall. Ape-man rears back and roars at the chimpanzees. His breath is rancid like he has a mouth full of cavities. The chimpanzees bare their teeth and scream at him while simultaneously releasing me and retreating.

I feel desperate, stressed, close to death. Shuffling away, I stand and trip over a butterfly-shaped hip. From the floor, I grab a femur—the longest, strongest bone in the body—and shake it at ape-man.

Gregor laughs. "Well, this is a first. I've never seen anyone use a femur as a weapon."

His laughter revives my hatred, my focus.

Ape-man lifts his nose in the air, inhaling my scent. Staring at me, he circles to the left. Then to the right. I keep the femur extended between us. The others stay behind him. He's the alpha: the one who eats first and leaves scraps for the others.

Ape-man is so close; he could rip out my throat in seconds. I pull the rope out of my pocket and start running for the deadlocked door. Ape-man's heavy footsteps follow; he moves sloth-slow, as if he isn't worried about dinner escaping. The others chirp and chatter and scream, their padded feet patter behind me.

I draw back the femur as if it were a crowbar, leap toward the wall shielding Gregor, and drive the femur into the glass. The glass shatters into a zillion pieces. The fear in Gregor's eyes feeds my fury.

I vault across the wall, loop the rope around Gregor's neck like a noose, and yank him toward me while throwing myself backward.

We crash onto the floor ten feet away from the approaching hybrids. I shift out from under Gregor, thrusting him off me. He scrambles to his knees.

But it's too late.

Ape-man drives a foot into Gregor's back, pinning him to the floor the way a cat pins a rat. I spring over the wall to safety. Slivers of glass slice into my hands and knees like glass teeth.

The uncaged hybrids descend on Gregor like ravenous hyenas, ripping and tearing and shredding his flesh. He flails and yells something incoherent. He looks at me, eyes wide with shock.

"You were right, Gregor," I yell. "I'm nothing like your mother."

As I'm backing toward the hall, the chimpanzees nearly rip Gregor's arm out of socket and gnaw on it like a cob of corn. Blood spurts all over the white floor. A part of me feels satisfied, but overall I feel sickened.

I dart my eyes from Gregor to the ape-man. Ape-man's stare is unwavering. I can't tell if he's looking at me as if I'm a steak or if he's going to let me escape. I move slowly to avoid attracting the attention of the others. The cold metal door presses against my spine. Ape-man places his hand over his heart. He's going to let me leave.

Trembling and covered in blood, I back into the hall and close the door, thankful for the barrier between me and the savage feast. I lean forward trying to catch my breath while I figure out what to do next.

I'll summon a Helix to the cathedral.

And then, I'm going home.

Forty-eight

I run up the cathedral steps and push through the double doors, surprised to find them unlocked. The nave is brimming with Supernovas and Valley dwellers, bloodied and battered but alive.

At the sight of two super-soldiers, I stiffen. They sit with their brides: they aren't a threat. I relax and sprint up the aisle, spinning around, looking for Prisha or Maris or Treb. The church smells like old books, furniture polish, and dirty, sweaty people.

"Wren!"

I turn in the direction of Prisha's voice.

"Oh my Galileo, what happened to you?" Prisha gushes. "You're bleeding everywhere." Her eyes move from my swollen face to my blood-stained dress.

"I'm okay. Is Fritz here?" I scan the hundreds of faces seated in the pews.

Prisha shakes her head. "Haven't seen him. It looks like a shark attacked your shoulder. It needs to be cleaned and bandaged." Prisha grabs my good arm and pulls me toward the sanctuary.

I resist. "There are twenty Helixes parked outside. We have to load vaccines and cures and take them to Hillcrest and the Valley. Now!" A tinge of hysteria colors my voice. I picture people in the Valley ravaged by the virus. Prisha's people.

Prisha's eyes fill with concern. "You're scaring me."

"The virus was released in the Valley. It's headed to Hillcrest."

Prisha sucks in a breath and looks away. When she looks back, her eyes are filled with tears. "Are you sure? My family… " She nervously rubs her throat.

"I'm so sorry. I tried to stop him." I reach out and put a hand on Prisha's shoulder.

She pulls away. "I'll be right back."

She returns with four men and women from the Valley. "While I bandage your wounds, they will load the Helixes."

Downstairs, Prisha directs the men and women to cover the vials in ice wraps to keep them cold during transport. I'm surprised by her take-charge attitude.

She grabs supplies from a cabinet and holds up a pair of scissors. "Sit. I'm going to cut off your sleeve."

She removes the sleeve and applies antiseptic with cotton balls. It burns, burns, burns. I clench my fists and my teeth.

Think good thoughts: Gregor is dead; I'm going home; all of this will be over soon.

"Did Everly gain consciousness?" I ask.

"She's still out." Prisha unrolls medical tape and stretches it across bandages on my shoulder. "We moved her to a quiet room and have someone monitoring her." Prisha hands me antiseptic-soaked cotton balls. "For your legs."

I run the cotton balls down my bloody shins. The cotton catches on glass splinters. Prisha opens and closes drawers on the hunt for something.

I press a clean swab against the two holes on my upper and lower lips. My eyes sting with tears from the pain.

Prisha gives me aspirin and a cup of water. "What happened to your lips?"

Washing down the aspirin, I say, "Gregor."

"You found him?" Prisha's voice rises in disbelief. "They said he got away."

"He's dead." I swish water around my mouth and spit bloody water into the cup.

"How do you know?" Prisha sounds skeptical. Her eyes skim my injuries. "Wait, did *you* kill him?"

"Shh." I glance at the people carrying vaccines upstairs. "Did Dr. Klein and Ray make it to Dr. Hahn's office?"

"They moved Dr. Hahn and the others to the soundproof room attached to Hahn's office."

"Is Dr. Hahn going to live?" I ask.

"Nobody knows." Prisha shrugs. "Your turn. How did you end up with a shredded shoulder and busted lips?"

I step down from the stool. I can't talk about it. I won't talk about it. I head to the stairs, wishing the aspirin was kicking in already.

"Wait," Prisha says. "You can't let your family see you like that. You're covered in blood." She digs through a cabinet and withdraws a lab coat. "Take this."

"Thanks." I put the lab coat on over my dress. "Find out if anybody wants to return to the Valley with you. You'll need help administering the vaccines. And, brace yourself. It's worse than you could ever imagine."

We enter the sanctuary and Treb rushes toward us. A flutter of joy fills my chest. Treb is alive. Fritz may be with him.

"You look like crap." Treb eyes my bloody shins and lips.

"Thanks." I wrap the lab coat tighter to hide my bloodied, ripped dress. "Have you seen Fritz?" My voice is riddled with anxiety.

Treb shakes his head. "I thought he would be with you."

Dread opens inside me like a faulty parachute. *Please don't let Fritz be dead.* "I haven't seen him since the Valley people stormed the auditorium. That was hours ago." I check Dad's watch. "It's almost midnight."

"I'm sure he's fine," Treb says, but he doesn't sound convinced. "I heard the frequency blast worked. Soldiers got smashed." Treb holds up a hand to high-five.

Prisha smacks his hand. I'm not ready to celebrate. Not until I know Fritz and my family are okay.

"Were there a lot of Valley casualties?" I eye Prisha and feel the heavy weight of guilt.

"There were casualties on both sides but it could have been worse. The Valley volunteers said they started retreating after you got on the microphone."

"I didn't think they heard me," I say, surprised at the news. "Are you feeling okay, Treb? Any symptoms?"

"All good," Treb says.

"I'm glad you're feeling better," Prisha says to Treb. She gently squeezes my elbow. "We have to get going." Urgency runs under her tone; concern clouds her eyes. She heads toward the cathedral doors.

I turn to Treb. "I'm worried about Fritz. What if he was hurt or captured? Why else would he be missing for hours?"

I want Treb to reassure me, to tell me Fritz is okay. I can't voice my other concern out loud. I have to believe he's alive and we'll be together someday.

"I'm worried, too." Treb rubs the side of his face and exhales heavily. "I'll return to the auditorium to look for him when things calm down."

"Thanks, Treb." I rest my hand on his arm. "Tell Fritz I went home to 923 Acacia Lane."

Forty-nine

The Helix rolls to a stop. I jerk my eyes open and unfold from my sleeping position. The sight of my house takes my breath away.

I step out of the car and stand at the curb. No signs of drones or death or destruction in the streets of Hillcrest. The houses look like untouched porcelain slabs beneath a smoky quartz sky in the gloaming hour before sunrise.

It feels as though the world changed—I changed—while everything here remained the same: a hummingbird feeder hangs from a tree; white flowers grow in heaps; the air smells like butterfly jasmine and cut grass; birds chitter and cheep and hopscotch from tree to tree.

Conflicting emotions swell inside of me: sadness and happiness, fear and hope. I try to quell my emotions and work up the nerve to approach the house. I touch the watch on my wrist and the pendant around my neck: tokens from people I love.

As I walk up the sidewalk, a white owl hoots from the rooftop. Helixes loaded with vaccines parallel park down the street.

I can't shake my lingering unease, my concerns that Fritz could be dead and Gregor could be alive. I recall the gun in Gregor's waistband. I should have stayed to watch him die.

On the way home from Ovation, I obsessively checked the rearview to make sure nobody followed me. Just before the Helix was sucked into the Hypertran tunnel, I looked back one last time. The top of the lighthouse was burning like a roman candle setting fire to the oily black sky.

Knocking on the front door, I listen for movement. Nothing. I kneel next to a flowerpot and dig until my fingers catch on the spare key. I dust the soil off the key and insert it into the lock.

Please let them be okay.

I step inside and it feels like I'm stepping into a past life: a life where things were much simpler. The living room is tidy. In the dining room, canned food, jugs of water, and bags of soil are stacked against the wall; the table is covered with flashlights, first aid kits, hospital masks, seed packs.

At first, I feel confused but then I understand: Dad knew the virus might reach Hillcrest. I touch the bruise Dad's fingers left behind when he grabbed my arm and saved my life. I swallow the lump in my throat and hold back the tears in my eyes.

"Mom?" My voice is tattered and frayed.

The silence is nuclear: sucking the oxygen from the room, pressing down on me like the heat of a hundred suns. Every silent second that passes feels like another neutron aimed at the nucleus of my heart.

Just when I think I can't take the pressure, that my heart is going to break in two—Mom steps into the hallway with Abe and Addie. For a moment, we stare at each other.

And then the most beautiful thing happens.

The silence is broken.

They run toward me: arms outstretched, squealing, crying. I drop to my knees pulling them into an embrace. My chest cracks open like an eggshell, shattering my protective walls, exposing my vulnerabilities.

Tears flood my face. I cry for my dad. I cry for all the lives lost, for humanity's desire to destroy itself, for the naïve girl I used to be. I cry tears of sadness and tears of joy. My family is alive. I'm alive.

And for the first time, I understand that being vulnerable isn't a sign of weakness. The weak allow fear and insecurity to rule their lives: they build walls, amass armies, and assert control over women and nature. They use fear and hatred to manipulate and divide.

Only the strongest shed their protective façades, speak their truths, and risk being hurt. They tear down walls, bring people together, and treat everyone with dignity and respect. The way forward is through unity, vulnerability, and love.

Thank you

Thank you for reading *The Scarlet Harvest*. If you would like to be notified when the second book in the Ovation Duology becomes available, please submit your email address at the following link:

https://kateashbrook.com/contact/

Please consider writing a brief review for *The Scarlet Harvest* on your preferred platform. Reviews are very helpful for new authors and always appreciated.

Acknowledgments

Thank you to friends who enthusiastically supported me on the long journey to writing my first novel: Pallavi, Lara, Ananya, and Tom. To Kam, I was delighted to discover we were simultaneously working on our debut novels; it was great to compare notes over coffee.

Beta readers Mel, Maddy, and Sarah: thank you for helping me pinpoint areas for improvement. Special thanks to Sarah for her in-depth review and ability to make me laugh.

Big thanks to Margie Lawson. I learned more about the craft of writing from Margie than from all other resources combined. Thanks to authors Vanessa Riley, Denny Bryce, June Converse, Jacki Kelly, Piper Huguley, and Sally Kilpatrick–workshopping together was very insightful.

Thanks to my mom for reading my work and cheering me on. Thanks to my husband for his patience, encouragement, and unwavering love and support. Thanks to my favorite lap cat, Olive, for keeping me company during many late nights of plotting, editing, and more editing.

And last, but not least, I'm grateful to the readers who took a chance on my debut novel.

Thank you all.

About the Author

Kate Ashbrook started her career as an Air Force linguist at the National Security Agency and went on to become a technical writer. When she's not writing, you can find her learning a new language, volunteering in the community, or planning her next getaway to Pacific Grove where she enjoys feeding her coffee and speculative fiction addiction at Bookworks Cafe. She lives in Boise with her husband, two senior labs, and four rambunctious cats.

CPSIA information can be obtained
at www.ICGtesting.com
Printed in the USA
LVHW011243190821
695611LV00001B/163